A MAN OF GOOD FORTUNE

ALI SCOTT

Quills & Quartos
PUBLISHING

Edited by Jo Abbott and Mary McLaughlin

Cover by Hoja Design

ISBN 978-1-956613-47-6 (ebook) and 978-1-956613-48-3 (paperback)

For Stuart, Isla and Emilia

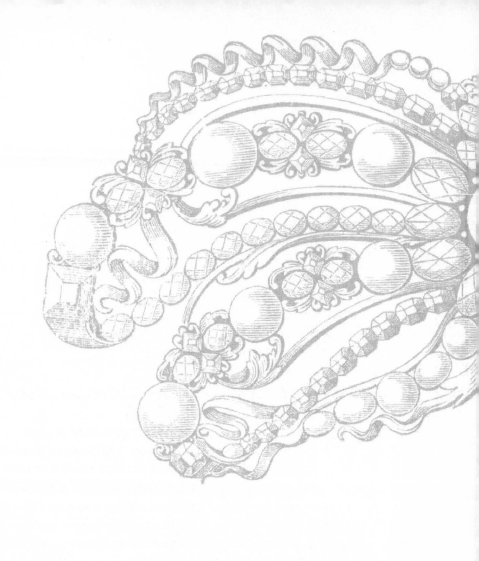

CHAPTER ONE

*O*nly a fool would ride in this kind of weather, Fitzwilliam Darcy thought grimly.

It was not a day for riding. Tempestuous August clouds hung low over the valley that morning, and the air was heavy with unshed rain. Everything signalled an oncoming storm. Darcy knew that he should return to the safety and warmth of Pemberley, but still he rode on. *You should return to your wife,* he lectured himself. *You should never have left Elizabeth in such a manner.* Behind him, ripples of water whipped across the ornamental lake, softly at first but with gathering speed. Shivering leaves trembled in the blustery wind; treetops swayed dangerously; the long grasses curved like sabres; and the landscape quivered with anticipation.

Above, a crack of lightning snapped through the air. Droplets of icy water began as a patter, swelled to a downpour, and ended as a torrent. Every path was dangerously waterlogged. Darcy had scarcely a moment to wonder whether his horse would keep his footing before lightning cracked again and the sky tore in two. A fresh wave of rain pelted down. Thunder ripped the heavens asunder.

And somewhere, amid the dark chaos, a riderless horse

screamed, and Darcy heard the echo of thundering hoofs. Panic and pain assailed him in equal measures as he realised it was *his* horse and that he was no longer upon it.

Darcy moaned softly. His leg throbbed. He reached down to touch it, and a searing pain shot down his left side. What had happened? Overwhelming fear flooded him. The lightning and the horse. He could not move. He tried touching his leg again. Stretching trembling fingers over his body, he was horrified by the dark red stain oozing from them. Were his fingers bleeding? Or was it his leg? *It could be both*, a little voice inside him croaked. *You are alone, bleeding to death.*

All around him, waves of piercing rain pelted down. Rivulets of water rushed past his ears as he turned his head one way and then the other. Continuous streams of ice-cold liquid coursed past his skin. Where was he? It was not a river, yet he was surrounded by dark eddies of suffocating water. A sudden gush filled his nostrils and, spluttering, he twisted his head away in panic. Unable to breathe, he was paralysed by fear. Everything was growing darker and colder. Coarse, wet grass stuck to the side of his face. Was this to be his grave? With every ounce of strength he had left, he lifted his head and cried for help. His voice sounded so faint. Who was this man, lost at the bottom of a steep, lonely valley? Was it him? Sharp, blinding pain shot through his forehead. *You are dying.* That voice again. *You are alone and you are dying.*

"No." Darcy heard his voice aloud. "I am not alone and I am not dying. I have Elizabeth." He spluttered as the water caught at his throat. The throbbing worsened. Unable to move, he could feel his life's blood seeping from his leg. "I have Elizabeth and I will not die." He repeated his vow. "I have Elizabeth and I will not die."

Exhausted, he heard his voice, weakened by the loss of blood. "I have Elizabeth and..." A stabbing sensation shot through him, and his fingers scrabbled at the waterlogged ground, wanting to allay the agony. His last thought was of her. He could only whisper her name. "Please," he begged. "I cannot leave her. I cannot leave Elizabeth."

Another wave of pain tore through him, and then there was only darkness.

Some time later, shadowy hands pulled at him. His body no longer hurt him; he was beyond that now.

"You there, Simmonds. Watch his leg. If you still want to be employed this evening, then you damn well need to stem that bleeding." It was his cousin Fitzwilliam. Blessed, obstinate Fitzwilliam. Darcy tried to move his head towards his cousin's voice. "Have a care how you move him, John. He has lost a lot of blood, and he will lose a damn sight more if you do not take care."

Darcy heard his cousin's voice break with anger. Or perhaps it was fear? "Fitzwilliam." His voice emerged as a whisper.

"All is well, old man. Save your energy for your lovely wife. Heaven knows how you will explain this away."

His cousin's voice was forced calm with an edge of suppressed panic. Darcy recognised the tone all too well. It had been the same when his father had died. A vision of himself, as a younger man, clutching his beloved parent's cold hand appeared before him: he had masked his fear with empty assurances as his father writhed about, his ashen face struggling to breathe. Darcy relived the anguish that had contorted his sister's countenance as he told her of their father's passing. *She cannot suffer another loss. I cannot die.* Suffocating fear filled his lungs, and ragged breath caught in his throat.

"Help me, I beg you. Do not let me go. Protect my family. Spare them...this agony."

The gasping plea faded to nothing. His voice was lost in the disordered clamour of male voices swarming around him. Fitzwilliam barked an order somewhere in the space above Darcy; his cousin's pretensions of calm were rapidly vanishing. Someone gave an urgent call for a doctor, and then Darcy heard no more.

More time passed; how long, he knew not. He found himself indoors, in a room that was filled with a sweet, sickly scent. *Blood,* thought Darcy dully, *I can smell blood.* He was too tired to keep his eyes open, but he could hear a woman sobbing. Something warm and soft squeezed his hand tightly, and he knew he was not going to die alone. Hardly knowing what he was about, his hand tightened over whatever was in it, the warm little object that anchored him to this world.

"Stay with me, my love, stay with me. Be strong. You must not leave us."

Such a tender tone! Such loving strength! Who could resist such a plea? With every resource left, Darcy opened his eyes. Turning in the direction of the voice, he said weakly, "Do not let me die."

"You most certainly will not die." The soft hand resting in his tightened. A pair of beautiful eyes, so fine in their brilliance, gazed into his face. For a moment, Darcy was transfixed. Long, dark lashes encircled deep shades of oak-brown interwoven with flecks of green; their effect was of a silent lake nestled in a sun-lit forest. Identical circles of gold encased pupils, alive with determination. The eyes blinked. A veil of unshed tears rippled across their surface. "You are forbidden to die. I will not permit it."

Darcy nodded and his throat burned. "I am not allowed to die."

Closing his eyes, he dreamt of a forest, with shafts of light breaking through green-brown shadows and a beautiful voice calling him to safety. *Could this be Heaven?* Darcy could resist no longer and surrendered himself to the enveloping darkness.

CHAPTER TWO

Fragments of candlelight flickered across the sickroom. An oppressive silence filled the cavernous space; not a sound could be heard save the crackling fire in the grate and his own rasping respirations.

A clang from the water basin roused him from his stupor. Soothing water trickled down his chest, a cooling balm to the feverish sweat bubbling like molten wax on his skin. Whoever was tending to him paused, allowing Darcy to raise his head slightly. He cast his eyes over his body. Heavily bound, his left leg was immobile, but thankfully there was no longer an effusion of blood coming forth from it. His torso was an unrecognisable labyrinth of scratches and cuts. He tried to run his fingers across the bloody etchings on his chest, but all he could feel were the rough edges of his bandaged hand against the sensitive surface of his skin.

A movement in the room caught his notice. Beside his bed, a small figure took shape. A woman, with a slender frame and serene countenance, tended his bedside. Her face was not pretty, nor was it plain. Darcy was drawn to the quiet expression of her eyes. Her clothes were dark and of good quality, yet she lacked any ostentatious sign of wealth. This woman was timeless and had an aura of divinity about her. She could be Epione, goddess of soothing, answering prayers for the sick and dying in ancient Greece; or she might have been Saint Agnes, princess and nurse, shrouded in heavenly dignity. Perhaps she was a nun, come to anoint him before laying him out? Darcy could not be sure.

The undulating edges of the room wielded a dreamlike power over him. His notion of reality was weakened continuously by the trembling shadows. His throat was paper-dry; the desire to quench his thirst unbearable.

"Drink some water," the woman insisted softly. "I shall help you." Plunging a cloth into a basin of clean water, she drained it and let him suck the droplets from it. Darcy had a sensation that he had seen this tableau before. *The sickbed*. The dutiful woman tending the dying: a chiaroscuro vignette of light and shadows, hope and despair, of suffering and relief.

From behind the woman, a man spoke. With immense relief, Darcy recognised his cousin's voice, its usual volume tempered by the quietness of the room. The relief was short-lived as the man came into view; he had Fitzwilliam's voice and manner but he looked older—much older. Had Fitzwilliam been away? There was a scar running across his face that Darcy had not seen before. How could it be when only hours earlier—or was it days? Weeks?—he had been by Darcy's side, helping him in the muddy field.

Fitzwilliam spoke gently to the woman, his voice inaudible, and she nodded in agreement. She gave Darcy a reassuring smile and exited the room.

"Well, old man, you certainly scared us. What the devil were you doing, riding out in that infernal storm?" Fitzwilliam adopted a jovial tone, but his true feelings were betrayed by the expression of infinite sympathy in his eyes.

"What happened to me?" Darcy's voice was hoarse.

His cousin settled himself gingerly on the bed. "Nobody quite knows. It appears you had a riding accident. Perhaps the lightning worried your horse and you were thrown? From the look of your leg, I would wager that your foot became caught in the stirrup as you fell. The muscles are quite damaged, and we suspect a fracture. There was no obvious break, mercifully." Fitzwilliam paused and his voice became gentle. "Your hand was also badly crushed."

"I see." Darcy held up his arm in front of himself. He could not make out his hand, covered as it was in bandages. A wave of nausea consumed him as he imagined the damage underneath the binding. He tried to move his fingers and groaned softly at the agony his movements produced. His head began to throb.

"What says the doctor about this? Will it heal?" he gestured towards his leg.

"We know not. It has been impossible to look too far ahead. You were bleeding profusely. Our prayers were answered when you survived the first night. We can surely hope you will walk again, albeit with a cane." Seeing the stricken look on Darcy's face, Fitzwilliam added, "I am sure you will make it look dashing."

"How long have I been here?"

"It has been six days, but in truth it has felt like a lifetime."

"And where am I?"

Concern flashed across Fitzwilliam's face. "Do you not know? This is Pemberley, of course."

"Of course I know my own home. I mean to say, I do not recognise the room."

Fitzwilliam blew a sigh of relief. "This is one of the little-used guest rooms on the first floor of the east wing. It was not as far to place you here, and it prevented you from bleeding all over your expensive carpets." Darcy managed a weak smile at his cousin's flippant tone.

"Why was I riding in a storm?"

"Perhaps you could be so kind as to answer that. What do you recall?"

Darcy closed his eyes and turned his vision inwards as he attempted to order the swirling, disconnected mass of images which had beset his mind over the last six days. The first image that came to him was of his parents; he knew they were dead, but he could not say how. He could only picture them as he remembered them from his childhood, laughing and picnicking in the walled gardens at Pemberley. A gnawing ache filled him. What had happened to them? They had all been so happy, all four of them, his parents each holding Georgiana's hands, swinging her so high her giggles filled the air.

"Georgiana." Darcy opened his eyes abruptly. Alarmed, he turned to Fitzwilliam. "Where is Georgiana?"

If Fitzwilliam was confused by Darcy's change of questioning, he did not show it. "She is in London, beside herself with worry. As soon as she heard of your accident, her first wish was naturally to be at your side. Elizabeth has been sending her daily news with reassurances of your improvements."

"Why is she not here?" Pain was clouding Darcy's mind, and each piece of information doubled the throbbing ache.

"It would not be wise for her to travel in her condition."

"Her condition! What can you mean? You cannot mean that she is to be a mother!" Darcy began to shake his head. "She is but fifteen! It cannot be true." Horror flooded his body. "Do not tell me it was that damned scoundrel Wickham."

"Heavens no!" Fitzwilliam spoke with reassurance, although he peered at his cousin questioningly. "Fifteen? Georgiana is no longer a child. She has been married for nearly two years to Robert Ashcombe, Viscount Luxford."

Darcy's mind was racing. How could he not remember his beloved sister's wedding? His heart began to beat erratically, thudding sharply against his chest. "What year is this? What has happened to me? And what in God's name has happened to my sister?"

Fitzwilliam regarded Darcy with concern. "It is the year 1817. Dearest Georgiana is safe and well. Her husband cherishes her. You do approve, although it took Elizabeth a great deal of cajoling to get you to consider his suit. I do believe we should refrain from talking of it until you are better. You are unwell, and this agitation cannot help you."

Darcy looked at him in shock. How could it be that years had gone past and he could remember nothing?

"When did Georgiana marry?"

"You do not recall?"

Darcy shook his head at his cousin's question. Closing his eyes, he searched the fragments of his memory. Georgiana's face, swollen with tears, appeared before him. He opened his eyes. "I remember Ramsgate. It is the last recollection that I have of her."

Fitzwilliam looked at him in sympathy. "That miserable affair was years ago. We no longer speak of it, so happy is Georgiana in her present situation."

"But how is she married? She can only have been nineteen at most when she wed. That is far too young. I would never have consented to such an arrangement." A dull throb began to beat a rhythm at his temples.

At this, Fitzwilliam again spoke very gently to Darcy. "You have indeed lost your memory, Cousin. We have had many heated discussions over this very matter. Would you believe that my heart was the more romantic out of the two of us? Dearest Georgiana has blossomed since her terrible entanglement with Wickham, thanks largely to that lovely husband of hers." He glanced at Darcy. "You were reluctant to be parted from Georgiana, but thankfully Elizabeth helped you to see sense."

Darcy's eyes narrowed. "And who is this Elizabeth that she should have a say in our family's affairs?"

Fitzwilliam fell silent, his eyes unconsciously looking to the shadows on the opposite side of the bed. Darcy's eyes followed Fitzwilliam's gaze. Unseen by Darcy, the woman had returned. Her eyes were brimming with unshed tears. She reached for Darcy's hand and spoke softly.

"I am Elizabeth. I am your wife." Silence filled the room.

Darcy snatched his hand away. "Madam, you are a liar." He stared at Fitzwilliam with a wild look in his eyes. "I am unmarried. This is surely an ill-conceived joke."

He looked again at this usurper who would claim his heart as her own. This plain, quiet little slip of a thing—his wife? Georgiana married and about to be a mother; he wed to a stranger; Fitzwilliam covered in scars—every part of this conversation was inconceivable in its absurdity.

Darcy was consumed by the conviction there was something amiss. There had to be. "Where the devil is my sister? What do you keep from me? What do you not tell me?"

Elizabeth and Fitzwilliam exchanged a look, which inflamed Darcy's temper all the more. "Do not look at her, Fitzwilliam. It is me that you answer to."

Elizabeth turned to look at him, her gaze unreadable. "No, my love, you and I only answer to each other. Your cousin speaks the truth, but I fear you are not well enough to hear it." She addressed Fitzwilliam, "We should leave. I do not wish him to be further distressed. His injuries have left him confused."

Darcy retorted, "I, confused! I think I should remember if I were married!" His whole manner became agitated as he struggled against the bed covers, attempting to move his strapped leg. Breathing erratically, Darcy's chest began to tighten as he fought against waves of panic, heightened by the fact that he was so restrained.

Elizabeth drew closer to the bed, but Fitzwilliam put out his hand to prevent her approach. Darcy could see her face; her expression was one of horror and great sadness. He did not care. Every part of his body wished to flee, to escape from this all-embracing sensation of helplessness and confusion, of being inserted into a life he did not recognise. Thrashing his unbound arm, he was insensible to all but the fear that consumed him.

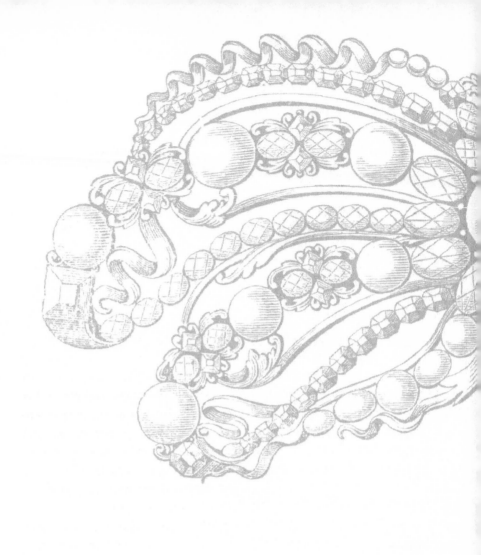

CHAPTER THREE

D arcy knew not how he spent the days following his conversation with Fitzwilliam. Fitful bouts of sleep were interspersed with the comings and goings of various people. Darcy was unsure whether they were strangers or not. Sometimes, he could tell the person was a servant by his or her dress, as well as the duties they performed for him: changing his sweat-soaked sheets, cleaning his chamber, and the like.

One man attended him more than any other; his face was familiar but Darcy could not place him. Quiet and serious, this stranger had an assistant who had run his hands along Darcy's leg, causing a sensation so violent that Darcy nearly fainted. The pain had subsided eventually, but it was now unbearable for anything to touch his injured limb. Even the brush of his cotton sheets against it was enough to make him wince. The man must have been a doctor, pronouncing as he did that Darcy's injuries were severe but improving. Instructions were left as to his care and recovery, but no answer could be given as to his future prospects.

As for his supposed wife, Darcy did not know whether she was by his bed or not. Sometimes, he fancied he saw her, sitting on the chair opposite him; at other times, he was convinced that the shadows about the room had teased themselves into her form.

There had been one moment of lucidity when he knew she was near. It had been a long, restless night. He had slept fitfully and awkwardly, and his bandages had somehow worked themselves loose. The agony of losing his bindings had been acute and brought about greater restiveness.

She had come to him; only half-conscious and half-mad with agony, his arms had flailed about and he had made contact with her. There had been no malice nor intent to his movement; indeed, he had only become aware of her presence when his hand had touched her, but it had been enough to break him from his internal prison. The feel of her smooth skin under his touch was so powerful, it tethered him to the tangible world beyond the feverish confines of his injuries.

Breathing heavily, Darcy had watched her face, so still and silent in the darkened room. She had stroked his arm gently until he had closed his eyes. The soothing motion had, for the most blissful of moments, replaced the sharp stabs of pain darting up his leg. She had continued her caresses until he had regained control of his breathing.

After some time, Mrs Reynolds and Robertson, his valet, had arrived to help Elizabeth move him back into a more comfortable position. He could hear them speak as they attended him and realised they thought him unconscious. His wound was weeping and oozing, and Robertson had discouraged both ladies from looking at it.

"Why must men persist in their belief that women are to be shielded from the sight of blood?" Elizabeth's voice had a clear, bell-like quality, and she spoke quietly to Mrs Reynolds. It had been shocking to hear her speak so frankly to his housekeeper. What kind of woman was she, this so-called wife of his? His astonishment was compounded further when he heard the demure Mrs Reynolds's uncharacteristically dry response.

"It is because men are not present during childbirth, and thus they can cling to their illusion that we are the weaker sex."

As she spoke, an image passed through Darcy's mind of a tiny baby, its newborn face puffy and red. Was it Georgiana? Had he ever held her when she was so small? Like a stone skimming on the surface of a lake, the image rippled and vanished, its true origin lost to the murky depths of Darcy's shattered memory. So lost was he in his own thoughts that he did not hear what Elizabeth might have said in reply.

Some time later—days or hours, he hardly knew—he overheard her again, this time speaking to his cousin. "How does Darcy?" Fitzwilliam's voice sounded low and anxious.

"Dr Amstel says he has much improved physically. It is the unseen injuries that worry me," Elizabeth said. She sounded fatigued.

"How so?"

"He remembers so very little of his recent life. His natural sense of purpose seems greatly diminished."

"I am sure much will return to him when his strength is restored. Dr Amstel has prescribed laudanum, and he has been living on scraps of porridge. I have seen first-hand the effects of hunger and pain on a body. You must allow him time to heal."

"But what if he does not? You were present when I told him of our marriage. His response has haunted me. He was so vehement in his denial."

"Elizabeth." Fitzwilliam's tone was gentle. "I have known Darcy his entire life, and I have never known him to be happier than he has been since his marriage to you."

Darcy could hear Elizabeth sigh. "He does not seem to remember that. How am I to tell him all that he seems to have forgotten? You saw his reaction. I do not wish to further impede any improvements to his health. What if the shock is too great? What do I reveal? How much should I conceal? I do not wish to hurt him or cause a shock to him." Her words sent a chill through Darcy's body. What information could she possibly wish to keep from him? He stilled his breathing as he tried to catch their conversation.

"Your superior knowledge of him will guide you. I am sure of it." Fitzwilliam paused. "Pray know that what I am about to say next is meant with only the sincerest affection and concern for your well-being."

"I would expect nothing less."

"Shortly before Darcy's accident, I received a letter from him. Its tone was most unlike him. He spoke of a matter of the greatest sensitivity that he was not able to name. He asked for help to overcome a great sense of betrayal. Do you know anything about it? I ask only to offer my discretion and assistance." Darcy could hardly breathe. What could he have meant by writing such a letter? Did Elizabeth know of it? He strained his ears to listen for her reply.

Elizabeth was silent for several moments. When she spoke, her tone was sombre. "I am unaware of any letter sent to you. My husband must have wished for your assistance to be kept secret."

"Do you know what it refers to, this sense of betrayal?"

There was another silence. Darcy longed to open his eyes and see her, to see her expression, but he did not wish to give himself away. "There are a great many matters between a husband and wife that are private. I cannot name them all in the hope we can guess his thoughts. I am unaware of any pressing betrayal that needed urgent remedy. I shall, of course, depend upon you if this changes."

"You have my word."

"Thank you, sir." Darcy heard Elizabeth pause. "I know you are his cousin, but I wish you to know that we both love you as a brother. I shall never forget your unexampled kindness through all of this."

There was another silence, and for a moment Darcy thought they had embraced. Or might they have simply shaken hands? In any case, Darcy heard no more. Breathing deeply, he shifted uncomfortably on his pillow, trying to shake off the growing unease at his cousin's words. What could he have meant by writing Fitzwilliam that letter? He gazed down at his bruised body. What if he had written to Fitzwilliam fearing for his own safety? A stab of panic tightened in his chest. He exhaled again, willing the pain to leave his body. Did Elizabeth truly not know what the letter was about? His head ached as doubt clouded his mind. *You must rest,* he told himself. *Rest and gather your strength.* He stretched out his body, trying and failing to find a comfortable position. *You will need your strength to regain all you have lost.* It was Darcy's last cogent thought as his eyes grew heavy and he fell into a fitful sleep.

CHAPTER FOUR

A rich, floral smell woke Darcy. He could not make out its source. From his bed, he could see a woman quietly moving about the room. Her back was to him, but he could tell it was not Elizabeth. This woman was thickset, and her shoulders were stooped over, indicating her advancing years. He frowned as he focused on her movements. She moved silently, or at least so quietly that Darcy could not discern what she was doing. He tried to shift his weight, and the pain seared through him. Biting his lip in agony, he moaned softly, causing the woman to turn. In her hand was a dark vial. Darcy's vision blurred as she approached the bed. The heady aroma grew more potent as the woman drew nearer. The heat from the room was so oppressive it clouded his mind. His head began to swim. The woman dropped a little of the liquid onto a spoon. Wordlessly, she motioned her hand towards Darcy. Panic seized him. Who was this grim-looking stranger? Instinctively, he moved his face away. He did not trust her. As he tried to resist, the pain in his leg intensified, and he struggled to focus. What was happening to him? The woman's unsmiling face was so severe. Darcy's heart pounded in his chest. How to escape this horror? He wished to speak out, to protest, but to do so would allow her to pour whatever she wanted down his throat. He braced himself, ready to fight as best he could against this unknown assailant.

A soft knock called the woman's attention away. She left his bedside and attended the door. Darcy heard Elizabeth's voice, and some of the tension left his body. Turning his head, he watched as Elizabeth's grave face bent low towards the older woman. They were deep in discussion. He frowned. The older woman was obviously known to Elizabeth. Eventually, Elizabeth came to his side. She placed her hand tenderly on his shoulder. He did not know why but her simple touch soothed him greatly. Closing his eyes, he allowed his body to relax; the pain subsided with every steadying breath.

"Be still, my love," he heard her voice so clearly. "You do not need to take the laudanum if you do not wish it." He felt her fingers stroke his neck, the sensation of which was so delightfully gentle that he turned his face towards her hand. She lightly brushed her fingers over his forehead, and for the briefest instant his pain disappeared. Darcy opened his eyes.

"Laudanum?" he repeated dully. His voice sounded entirely disconnected from his body.

"Yes," Elizabeth nodded. "For the pain. But it confuses you." She turned her head briefly to the doorway. "You should not fear Mrs Taylor. She is here under strict instructions."

"Instructions?" He searched for the older woman's silhouette in the darkened corners of the room. "Whose?"

"The doctor has given us a tincture to administer if the suffering becomes too great." Her large, deep eyes met his. "But the choice is yours. I will not have it forced down your throat."

He nodded weakly. "I do not desire to take it now. I feel so unwell."

Elizabeth reached out and clasped his hand. "Very well. It pains me to hear you feel ill, yet I am glad you do not wish to take another dose of laudanum presently. I have heard stories of those who can never be free of its potency." The line of her mouth grew firm. "I do not want you to lose your mind to its influence."

Darcy nodded again. "I wish to sleep."

"Then close your eyes and rest, my love. As you can see, I am not far away." He watched as she nodded a polite but firm dismissal to Mrs Taylor and drew a chair next to his bed. She reached over and motioned to pull up the coverlet.

"No." Darcy reached out to still her hand, doing his best to ignore the pain his action caused. Her delicate fingers felt cool against his hot palm. Elizabeth quickly moved her hand away; the suddenness of his action had startled her.

"Forgive me, my love. Does it hurt you to move the covers?" Her eyes wandered down his body towards his injured leg.

Feeling unexpectedly exposed, Darcy's vision blurred as he attempted to articulate his meaning. "It is not just the pain. I feel as though I am burning. I cannot stand to be covered."

Gently, Elizabeth placed her hand on Darcy's forehead; her soft, cool fingers were a balm to his feverish brow. His cheeks burned as he relished the relief her touch yielded. When had he ever permitted a woman to touch him so? Elizabeth stood quietly. She disappeared briefly from view as she moved gracefully behind a pretty screen at the far end of the room. A moment later, Darcy felt a cool breeze fill the space, the exquisite freshness clearing away the confusion from his mind. Elizabeth moved back into view, and Darcy watched as she opened another window nearer to his bed.

"The doctor has said to keep you warm," she spoke softly, almost to herself. "But it cannot harm to have a little clean air about the place." She turned and gave him a conspiratorial grin. "I shall shut the windows before Mrs Taylor's return."

Darcy smiled weakly. "I thank you."

In the distance, beyond the confines of his room, Darcy could hear leaves rustling in the trees. Adjusting his head, he caught sight of the oak trees from the open window. From his position, he noted the golden hues glittering in the sunlight as their delicate leaves danced in the wind.

Returning his attention to Elizabeth, he asked, "How long have I been here?"

"It has been six weeks since your accident." Elizabeth sounded weary. "The laudanum has kept you sedated. The doctor said you should not be moved until you can tolerate the pain of such an action."

"Where is my cousin? And what of Georgiana?"

Elizabeth's tone was gentle. "Fitzwilliam has been dividing his time between here and his family's own estate. He will return tonight. I have been corresponding daily with Georgiana. She writes to assure me she is doing well."

"And what is the month?"

At this, Elizabeth's expression changed to one of intense sadness, and Darcy felt a fool for asking the question.

"We are in late September. The trees have delayed changing their colour this year. Perhaps they are waiting for you to be well enough to enjoy their splendour."

"They will be left waiting a long time." Darcy soberly cast his eyes over his injured hand, bound up in freshly-changed bandages.

"You seem better now than you were before." Elizabeth's tone was soothing.

"Your optimism surprises me. I cannot recall a time when I have felt worse." He had not meant to speak so sharply, but the pain had become too great. He winced again, attempting to regain equanimity.

Rather than taking umbrage at his tone, Elizabeth smiled mischievously at him. "You are right, of course. Indeed, I cannot recall a time when you have looked worse either." Before he could reply, she reached out suddenly, running her fingers across the uneven stubble on his chin. "I have never seen you with such an impressive beard."

Her movement was so unexpected, and spoke of such familiarity, that Darcy instinctively flinched away. Her eyes full of sorrow, Elizabeth removed her hand, the moment between them broken.

"I believe I shall close the windows now. I shall be scolded if you become cold." She very carefully pulled the coverlet over him, its weight providing a comforting warmth now he had experienced some fresh air. Standing, she moved away from his bedside and did not look back as she busied herself about the darkened room. She still kept her face hidden as she left him and bid Mrs Taylor to return. Was she crying? Darcy could not fathom her change in mood. What had upset her so? Darcy had never been one to catch the tone of another's conversation, but Elizabeth was another matter entirely. She was impossible to read. Mrs Taylor returned to his bedside, her dour face as formidable as before. He glanced at the older woman's chapped, work-worn hands. Mrs Taylor appeared to be a capable nurse, yet he doubted her ministrations would cause quite the same effect as Elizabeth's tender, loving touch.

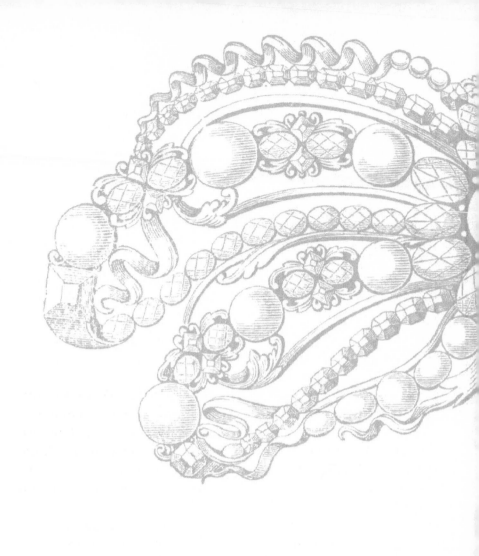

CHAPTER FIVE

Almost seven weeks after his accident, Darcy left his sickroom for the first time. He was to be moved from the guest chamber where he had been ensconced to his private chambers in the west wing of the house. It had been Fitzwilliam's suggestion to move him, prompted, no doubt, by his concern for Darcy's memory loss. "Perhaps you might feel better in your own rooms," his cousin had said.

Darcy had not known how to reply. His own rooms did not contain his memory, nor would being therein be sufficient to teach him to walk unassisted. Furthermore, his bedchamber was adjacent to the room belonging to the mistress of Pemberley. In his remembrances, it had been empty ever since his mother died; he did not know how to feel now that it was occupied by Elizabeth.

"I do not know how comfortable I should be there."

"Familiar surroundings should do you good. You and Elizabeth might even wish to take your dinner up there."

"Why should I wish to dine alone with her?"

"Because she is your wife and you love her dearly."

"Perhaps *you* should tell me all you know of Elizabeth."

"You do not remember her at all?" Fitzwilliam raised his eyebrows in shock.

Darcy shook his head.

"I should think myself a man of tremendous good fortune to have such a wife."

Purposely misunderstanding him, Darcy asked, "Ah! So she had a good fortune? What of her family?"

"Darcy, you must be gentle with her. Your present affliction grieves her deeply."

"I do not know her in the slightest," said Darcy, his panic, always held just at bay, rising. "She could be Napoleon's sister for all I know, so little is she recognisable to me."

"I am no relative to Bonaparte—I am afraid my French is rather lacking." Both men turned as Elizabeth entered the room hiding a wry smile. "My Italian is not much better. I am also much younger than thirty-five, which is the age of Napoleon's youngest sister."

She does look young, that much is true, Darcy thought. *And she looks immensely tired.*

Fitzwilliam was correct; he might not remember her, but, by the pallor of her face, this woman who was his unremembered wife had clearly been suffering from worry for him. He started to apologise, but Elizabeth simply waved her hand, her eyes beginning to twinkle in her pale face. "There is no need. It is certainly not the first time you have insulted me. Indeed, I take it as a rather auspicious sign."

"How so?"

"That the infamous Darcy charm has remained unscathed by your ordeal." She was undoubtedly laughing at him now. "Your awkwardness in social situations has forever been a great source of amusement to me."

Inwardly chafing, Darcy began his retort, but he was stopped by the expression of her eyes. When she smiled, her whole face became alive with vibrant merriment. For a moment, he was completely mesmerised. As he struggled to find the words to make a reply, Elizabeth continued, "Fitzwilliam, I should like to speak to my husband if you please."

With a short bow, Fitzwilliam swiftly complied, and Darcy found himself alone with his wife. For the first time since his accident, he allowed himself to look at her. Although she was not the sort of notable beauty he had always imagined he would marry, her figure was slim and pleasing, and her dark, glossy hair was very pretty, swept up high with a few unruly curls trailing down her slender neck. It was, however, her eyes that truly caught him. In the shadows, they looked simply dark, but when the light caught them, they shone with unbridled intelligence. Darcy had never seen anything like them. *I wonder what first attracted me to her. Was it her eyes?* The thought passed through Darcy's head as he waited for her to speak.

Elizabeth cleared her throat and drew a chair closer to the bed, her hand shaking a little as she smoothed out creases in the bedclothes. In her other hand, she held a small bundle of papers. "How are you feeling today?" Her voice was so gentle and full of concern.

"Excessively tired and in a great deal of pain."

"I am sorry to hear that. Have you been able to eat at all?"

"A little." Good Lord, it was so hard to converse with her. Darcy did not know what to talk about.

Elizabeth appeared to sense this and continued speaking in her soft tone. "I have heard from Georgiana. She reassures me as to her health, although she is anxious to hear from you. I have been writing to her every day, but I am sure a note from you would assuage her concerns."

"Yes, of course." Another silence followed. Clearly, Elizabeth could bear the awkwardness no more. She leant a little closer and opened her lips to speak. Sunlight flooded into the room from the nearby window, illuminating her profile as she leant forwards.

"Forgive me but is there nothing you remember?"

Darcy stared at her for a moment. "I remember my parents," he said at last. "And Georgiana." He inhaled sharply at the recollection. "But I cannot find a clear sequence to my thoughts. In one instance, I see them all together here at Pemberley, and in the next moment, it is only Georgiana and I."

He glanced up at her face; her eyes had filled with tears. Uncomfortably, he continued, "I know that both my parents are deceased, but I can no longer recall the exact moment either of them died. It is as though the book containing all my memories has become unbound, and a great monstrous hand has pulled all the sheets from it. I can recall some aspects with clarity, other instances have a transient sensation akin to the feeling when first waking from a dream. Nothing seems clear. Indeed, the harder I try to remember, the more uncertain the images become."

Unshed tears rippled on the surface of Elizabeth's eyes. Darcy felt an unwelcome stab of guilt at the anguish he had unwittingly bestowed upon her. "Forgive me. I do not wish to cause you pain."

Elizabeth wiped a tear from her face. "We have a great deal of happy memories together. It hurts me to think that you have lost them."

Darcy knew not what to say.

"Our happiest memory—nay our greatest pride—you must have surely forgotten," Elizabeth continued. "You have not breathed a word of it since you regained consciousness."

"And what is our happiest memory?" Darcy could hardly breathe, so arresting was her face bathed in the gentle light.

Elizabeth took a deep breath and gave him a trembling smile. "The birth of our daughter, your darling Molly."

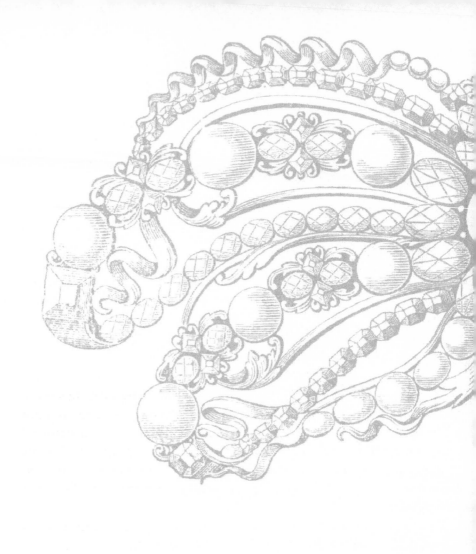

CHAPTER SIX

ime stood still. Or in Darcy's case, it was the illusion of time that stood still, for he knew not how many minutes passed before he could find his voice. *"Our* daughter?" The question quivered from deep inside his throat. He felt his heartbeat quicken in his chest. How could he not remember an event of such importance? He swallowed, his mouth suddenly dry. "Tell me of her," he said at last.

Elizabeth's smile lit up her whole face. "She is but three years old. We called her Marianne to honour your mother. When she was born, she became your little Molly. You insisted that it should only be a pet name, but it suited her so well that everyone calls her by it."

"Where is she?"

Elizabeth's happy expression faded, and she cast her eyes down. "She stays with her beloved aunt Georgiana—hopefully not causing too much trouble."

"Why is she not with us?"

"We were called back to Pemberley at the very last minute. We did not intend to stay for long, and so we left darling Molly with my sister Jane." Elizabeth's mouth curved into a grin. "My beloved sister has a son who is rather a handful. After your accident, I wrote to Jane, and it was agreed that Molly should stay with Georgiana, as we shall be here for longer than anticipated." Her smile widened further. "It was for the peace of mind of all concerned." Leaning forwards, she motioned to the parcel in her hand, "I have brought something that I wish to show you. I hope it brings you happiness, not any undue distress."

With the trembling of her fingers renewed, Elizabeth unwrapped the bundle to reveal several well-read letters and a handful of sketching paper. "These are letters of congratulation upon Molly's birth. They are a most precious keepsake are they not? I thought reading them may perhaps help you in your recovery."

She seemed to have recovered her composure, but Darcy was not insensible to the emotional importance of her gift. "There are letters congratulating us on our marriage as well as some drawings of Molly. She is too small, naturally, to sit for a portrait, but I wanted her likeness captured nevertheless."

Darcy took the sketches with his uninjured hand and gazed over them in wonder. Pencil drawings, light and loving, depicted a round cherub face with a halo of dark curls. He could not say whether they were a true likeness, but the care with which they were drawn revealed to him their artist.

"Did you draw these? They are exquisite." He grinned softly at her, and Elizabeth smiled back, her expression both bashful and proud under his praise.

"It is much easier to draw when one is familiar with the subject."

As she spoke, Darcy turned over the final sheet of paper and words failed him. It was a picture of him, in such a relaxed and unguarded pose that he almost did not recognise himself. He was not unaware of his appearance; indeed, in a vainer moment, he would not disagree if anyone should call him handsome—but in this picture of him, in his shirtsleeves, reclined on a chair cradling his baby daughter, he saw himself through Elizabeth's eyes: beautiful, content, fulfilled. He blushed deeply. It was profoundly moving and all the more painful that he could not recollect such an intimate moment. He fought to keep his emotions in check. "She looks very young in these," he said at last.

"She was indeed. I believe she was no older than a year in the sketches."

"What is she like now?"

If ever there were a question to unlock a mother's tongue, Darcy had discovered it. Elizabeth's love for her daughter was as abundant as her words in describing it. "I do not know whether you should care to hear it, but she looks nothing like you." Her manner was teasing. "She is like me in every way, except her eyes are rather more like your family's than mine. The only time she resembles you is when she scowls, which is when you bid her goodbye. She assuredly has your intellect, for she is the most inquisitive creature. Between us both, we have managed to give her a head of curls that are impossible to brush, and she has the sweetest, most irrepressible spirit you should ever have the good fortune to encounter. All of the older servants insist she has your father's smile, but you always said she had an air not unlike your mother."

Darcy smiled at her description and sincerely wished he could picture its subject. "Where did you draw this?"

"In our private sitting room here at Pemberley. She had been unsettled and wanted nobody but you. She has not changed one bit since. I am her very best friend until you walk into the room, then I become no more important than one of her dolls or her nurse-maid." Elizabeth's body relaxed as she recollected her daughter. "She cannot bear to be parted from you, and I dare say you are not much better. She is the shadow to your sun, constantly following your brilliant path."

Yet she is not here. The thought struck Darcy. Both her parents came to Pemberley without her, leaving her in London. *Why was that?* Darcy could not claim to be an expert in these matters, but he could not imagine a small child, bereft of her parents, would be a welcome addition to a household.

Fitzwilliam had chosen not to answer any of his questions regarding Elizabeth's past. He looked up at Elizabeth's face. She had every appearance of sincerity, but she was still a stranger to him. The pictures had inspired a strong emotion within him, but now was not the time to be guided by sentiment. They were only drawings after all. He looked again at the sheets of paper, but he could recall nothing. Molly was no more a memory to him than Elizabeth was. What did he really know about this wife of his? He would read the letters when he was alone—he would be able to decide for himself then.

Elizabeth sensed his hesitation and filled the pause with an application of support for Fitzwilliam's plan to move Darcy out of the guest room. Despite all his reservations, the suggestion was a great deal more appealing when uttered from Elizabeth's soft, full lips. Darcy wordlessly nodded his agreement and earned another smile.

Gathering up her precious sheets, Elizabeth placed them carefully on the table next to Darcy's bedside. Neither knew how to proceed.

"Thank you for these." Darcy gestured to the bundle.

"I pray that it helps you," she replied. After a short pause, she added, "You seem excessively fatigued. I should leave you to rest. I shall speak to Mrs Reynolds about preparing your room for tomorrow."

She rose and began to remove from his bedside. He watched her as she softly moved across the room. Who truly was Elizabeth? A contradiction to be sure. She had been both shy and bold with him. How was it between them? What had happened? Questions flooded Darcy's mind. For all that Elizabeth had told him, there was still much he did not know about her.

"Wait!" he called suddenly. Elizabeth turned, her graceful silhouette framed by the heavy oak-panelled door.

"Do I call you Elizabeth?" What a question for a husband to ask of his wife! It was not what he wished to ask her, but the question of who she truly was to him was buried deep in his fragmented memory. He was not brave enough yet to ask it.

She smiled lovingly at him. "You do, as do most of our family save for those who still remember me as Lizzy, as I was when I was young." A look of mischief danced upon her lovely face. "When you *think* we are alone, you call me your dearest love."

Darcy caught something playful in her voice and, before he could stop himself, replied, "And what about when I know we are alone?"

"Oh, that is easy." Elizabeth met his gaze. Darcy had never received such a bold look from a woman before. An impish grin suffused her features.

"When you *know* we are alone, you call me your minx." And with that she closed the door, leaving nothing but a stunned silence broken only by the sound of Darcy's thudding heartbeat.

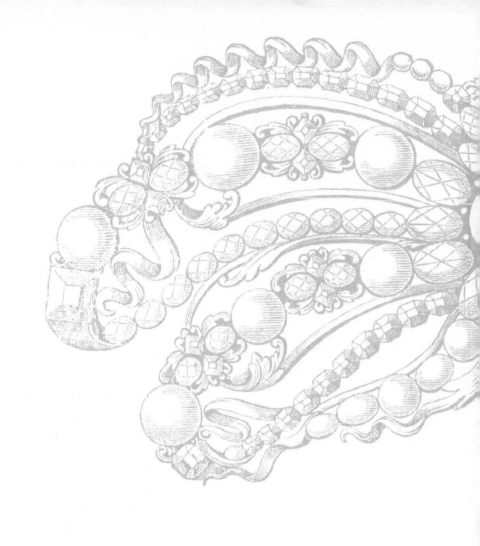

CHAPTER SEVEN

Handed a mirror by his valet, Darcy surveyed his reflection with care. Who had he become? *Robertson has done an admirable job. He has taken a bruised, dishevelled shell and transformed it into something resembling a gentleman.*

As Darcy had sat in the chair, listening to the scrape and wipe of the blade against his chin, he realised that it had been a reassuring sensation to enjoy something familiar, even something so trivial as having a shave. *I wonder how much I pay Robertson?* Darcy mused. He had certainly earned his salary. The man staring back at him in the mirror was a good deal more recognisable at the end of Robertson's care than at the start.

His face looked thinner—caused no doubt by the intermittent meals over the past weeks. Scratches still covered his forehead, but thankfully his mop of curls could hide the worst of it. If he ran his hands through his hair, he could still feel the tender swollen area at the left-hand base of his skull where he had been injured. He looked older than he remembered; a few silver hairs that he did not recognise rested among the curls at his temple. Now was not the time for vanity. There were much more pressing matters that were preoccupying Darcy's mind.

The first such matter was that of the letters entrusted to him by

Elizabeth the night before. Darcy had tried to read them after she left him, but the light had been too poor to read them properly. Darcy had woken at daybreak in anticipation of their perusal. With great difficulty, he had managed to sit upright with his leg bound. He had succeeded in shaking the letters open with one hand still strapped. Pain had coursed through his aching body, but he had managed nonetheless.

However, it was when he tried reading them that the true problems began. The first was from Henry Bellington, a friend from Darcy's student days. Darcy could recall Henry's red face beaming at him from across the quadrant during their first week. Bellington was a first-rate gentleman from a respectable family of consequence. If he had been pleased by Darcy's marriage to Elizabeth, it would be a promising sign. Opening the letter, Darcy's eyes had skimmed over the yellowing pages, struggling to read Henry's spidery writing.

Dear... Dearest... My dearest... The words swam in and out of Darcy's vision. He squinted. *My dearest friend Darcy.* There, that was it. *Congrat... Congratulat... Congratulations...on your...your fort...forthcom...forthcoming...* Darcy could not make out the next word. He could see it but the meaning was elusive. *Congratulations on your forthcoming marriage.* Darcy attempted a guess. He sighed. Perhaps he should try another letter.

The next was from his aunt, and Fitzwilliam's mother, Lady Matlock. She was his mother's sister-in-law and had a rigorous sense of propriety. If she approved of Elizabeth, then all would be well. Unfolding the parchment, Darcy heaved another sigh. It was that word again. *Con... Congrat... Congratu...late... I am write... I am writing to congratu...late... I am writing my congratulations dear... dearest... dearest...* What in Heaven's name was this next word? *Nepnep...* Heavens above, it was impossible! *Neph...neph...nephew.*

With a frustrated growl, Darcy turned to look out of the window—the sunrise had given way to an early morning light. He had been struggling with these letters now for some time and had only deciphered a few unrevealing sentences. Since his childhood, he had known Pemberley's library to be one of the best in the county, and now he could not read more than a few phrases of a simple letter. First his leg and fingers, then his memory—and now this. What else would be taken from him? Bitterness twisted his heart, and he slammed his uninjured hand against the mattress.

The second matter that had troubled Darcy was Georgiana. He could picture her at many different points in her life but never above the age of fifteen. He remembered all too clearly her look when he had told her Wickham had gone, never to return. It was Wickham who had broken her heart, but it had been left to Darcy to lay out the extent of his deception. It was Darcy who had held her as she cried anguished tears, sobbing that she would never love or be loved again.

To hear that Georgiana was married was indeed a shock. Having been so ill used by Wickham had increased her natural shyness. Darcy had privately thought that Georgiana might never marry, such was her anxiety in other people's company. Darcy reminded himself to ask Elizabeth about Georgiana's husband. Fitzwilliam had intimated that Georgiana had made a love match. It was painful to think she was so far away with no news from him directly. How must she be feeling at the news of his accident? It would not do to leave her so neglected. He had been overcome with the urge to write to her and had rung for his valet.

Robertson had arrived promptly and had quickly set up a travelling writing desk so Darcy could work from his bed. Fortunately, he had not hurt his dominant hand and was able to manoeuvre the pen across the page—albeit awkwardly to avoid jostling his injuries. How to begin such a letter? What to say that was truthful but not alarming? Dipping the pen in ink, Darcy's hand had hovered over the paper. *Dearest Georgiana* had seemed a safe starting point. When his pen embraced the parchment, the words were not forthcoming. He attempted the salutation many times but no attempt looked correct.

Tears pooled in his eyes. Unable to write his beloved sister's name was surely the lowest point. It would not do to cry about it, especially within viewing distance of the servants. *Never show weakness.* That had been Father's advice, but Darcy had never felt more vulnerable. How could he ever overcome his injuries when he could not fully comprehend what he had lost? He drew his right hand across both eyes and shook his head in a protest against the aching sadness. How was he to be a brother, a husband, and—God help him—a father in such an emasculated state?

His mind drifted to Marianne. *Darling Molly*—that is what Elizabeth had said. His bond with his own father had been so unshakeable, perhaps meeting her might reawaken something inside him. He cast his eyes over the sketches. Mercifully, they did not contain any words, yet their meaning was clear. He had a family. A family that stretched out far beyond Georgiana and Fitzwilliam, a family that he was responsible for and looked to him for strength.

Thoughts tumbled round Darcy's mind. It had been a welcome relief when Robertson had suggested a shave. There was nothing like a razor blade running across your throat to remind you that life could be a great deal worse. Reclining in his chair, Darcy closed his eyes and, with a cruel twist of irony, tried his hardest to forget.

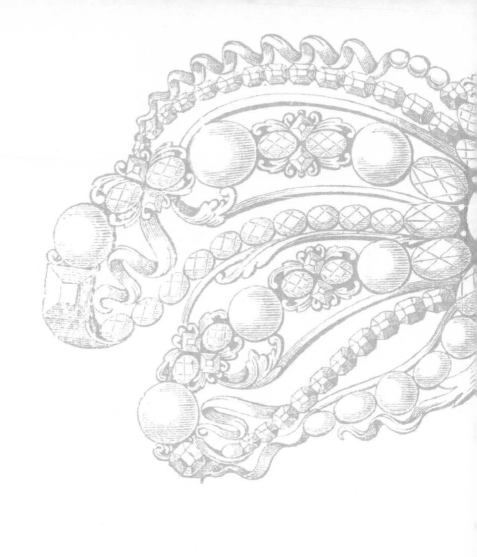

CHAPTER EIGHT

Clean-shaven and properly attired, Darcy made his way to the breakfast room. Or rather, he was assisted by two impeccably turned-out footmen as he was still unable to put any weight on his leg. His unbandaged arm wrapped over one lad's young shoulders had embarrassed him, but nothing could have prepared him for the sight he encountered when he entered the upper hall.

The servants lined the main staircase to greet him. Everyone, from the invaluable Mrs Reynolds to the nameless scullery maids, gazed up at him as he shakily made his way down the stairs. A few faces he recognised, but many he did not. Perkins the gardener had been in charge when his father was alive. It was good to see a friendly face. To his surprise, Darcy could see Perkins's eyes were twinkling with manly tears. Old Mrs Norris openly wept into her cook's apron. Many of the maids were beaming at him through their sniffs. Someone, perhaps one of the grooms, started to clap, and soon the spontaneous applause echoed through the sunlit entrance hall.

Acutely embarrassed, Darcy flushed at such a welcome. He smiled weakly, painfully aware that the tips of his ears were burning crimson. Averting his eyes, he gazed down the staircase to see Elizabeth, a vision of loveliness, smiling up at him with undisguised pride. Her dark curls were bound upwards revealing the elegant line of her neck. Amongst her curls wove an ivory headband interlaced with tiny iridescent beads. The headband was the same ivory shade as her lace-trimmed dress, which was flawless in its simple beauty. *Is this what she looked like on our wedding day?* Darcy could only hope.

"I thought perhaps we could eat breakfast in the orangery today as it is not so far for you to walk. The weather is so pleasant, and I thought we might enjoy the vista together. The table has been set accordingly." Elizabeth spoke gently. Darcy nodded. The footmen also seemed pleased at the news that they would not be required to transport their master farther. Darcy was sure he could smell perspiration from the younger one. "Perhaps we should allow Harry and John a rest."

She dismissed them and called the names of two new footmen to assist Darcy. Turning to face the assembled household, Elizabeth thanked them in such a manner that no one could mistake her for anyone but the mistress of Pemberley. *She certainly is well-liked,* thought Darcy.

The orangery was laid for breakfast, and Darcy took a moment to appreciate the elegance of the setting. Everything was to his fastidious taste, but there was an informality that was most pleasing. Perhaps it was the arrangement of the dusky roses in the chinoiserie vases, or maybe it was the gold thread embroidered into the cushions arranged along the lounging chair, but everything seemed softer, brighter, and more inviting than he remembered it.

"Where is Fitzwilliam?"

"He has gone for an early ride," Elizabeth replied. Darcy fell silent. He had hoped for an opportunity to press his cousin for more information.

Darcy was eased into a chair by the footmen who then gladly departed. He watched as Elizabeth gracefully took her place opposite him. Her every movement was so elegant, and for a moment Darcy found himself quite transfixed. Suddenly, she looked up and smiled at him. Darcy felt himself redden at being caught staring so helplessly at a woman.

In an attempt to hide his awkwardness, he asked, "What news of Georgiana? I cannot believe she is to be a mother."

Elizabeth's cheeks dimpled as her smile deepened. "None yet, I am afraid. I promise you will be the first to hear of it. God willing, her baby should arrive before the end of October." She busied herself with her plate. "Would you like some assistance?" she asked, indicating Darcy's injured hand.

He nodded curtly, chagrined to be reliant on another. "If you would be so kind." Elizabeth reached over and filled his teacup. She did not, he noticed, need to ask him how he took his tea. *I wonder how often we do this?* It was so unsettling that she should know him so well, and he could not recollect a thing about her.

The teacup clinked as Elizabeth placed it beside him. She turned her attention to his plate. "How much should I give you? It has been a long time since you had a decent meal." The warm aroma of fresh bread rolls filled the orangery as she used the tongs to serve him. Everything seemed so familiar, yet he felt so disassociated from it all. Unexpectedly, his stomach lurched, and the thought of eating made Darcy feel unwell.

"Thank you but I only want a little." He fought back the growing nausea as he spoke.

"Of course." Elizabeth looked at him sympathetically. She, too, had taken very little food, and Darcy wondered how much she had slept and eaten since his accident.

Gingerly, he sipped his tea and attempted to draw the conversation away from breakfast. "What can you tell me of Georgiana? Fitzwilliam tells me she is happily married."

"You do not recall?" Elizabeth's voice was full of concern.

"Sadly, no. It has been worrying me gravely that I remember nothing of her husband. Perhaps you could tell me a little of her marriage."

"Of course." Elizabeth wrinkled her nose in a decidedly fetching manner as she contemplated her words.

Darcy looked upon her in amusement; for the briefest instant, this morning's ill-temper was almost forgotten.

"Dear Robert is quite the loveliest man. His father is Lord Sidmouth, perhaps you recall him?" Elizabeth caught Darcy's expression. "Oh no, you do not? Well, let me tell you that Lord Sidmouth is genial and respectable but rather overbearing. Robert is much gentler. As a child, he had a stammer, and he is incredibly uncomfortable in new company." She glanced slyly at Darcy. "A trait that I have learnt to associate with only the best of men."

Darcy could feel himself redden again and was relieved when Elizabeth continued. "I did not believe in love at first sight until I witnessed Robert meet your sister. He was so flustered he dropped his teacup and spent a great deal of time apologising to the hostess while all the time keeping his eyes firmly only on Georgiana. He was so painfully shy that his stammer came forth every time he approached her."

"How did they come to an understanding?"

"Georgiana knows what it is like to have all eyes on oneself and have no desire to talk." Elizabeth's eyes gleamed a little wickedly. "I appealed to that very kind heart of hers and persuaded her that she was in the unique position of being able to help Robert. Upon their second meeting, it was *Georgiana* who approached *him*. She was the one who helped him overcome his shyness, and I daresay he was excessively grateful." She smiled wistfully. "When two gentle souls such as they fall in love, the world seems to feel a little bit brighter. I miss them greatly, but I thought we could visit them in London once the baby is born."

"Who is with her now?"

"My sister. Mrs Bingley," she added for clarification.

"Bingley—as in Charles Bingley?"

"Of course. He took a lease on an estate neighbouring my father's, and it is through his acquaintance we met. Perhaps you recall."

"Bingley was a very good friend to me at school and at university. He has a truly affable nature. I remember he has two sisters, Caroline and Louise...or perhaps Louisa."

"You remember Caroline?" Elizabeth looked aghast.

"I recall that she was an attentive hostess when I sojourned at their father's house one summer."

"I am sure she was *most* attentive," Elizabeth muttered *sotto voce* as she dutifully refrained from rolling her eyes.

"Why did we not stay near Georgiana?" Darcy could see his abrupt question caught Elizabeth off guard. She paused, only for their notice to be drawn to the arrival of Alasdair Patterson, steward of Pemberley.

"It is good to see you on your feet, sir." A perspicacious Scotsman, Patterson's keen eyes appraised Darcy from under bushy, greying brows. Patterson had taken over after the death of the previous steward of Pemberley, Darcy recalled. Save for a few extra wrinkles around his shrewd eyes, Darcy was relieved to see that his current steward had changed very little. Respectable and formal, Patterson had been a welcome contrast to Pemberley's previous steward, the gregarious but indulgent Harold Wickham. During Darcy's father's lifetime, Wickham Sr had cast a watchful eye over Pemberley but a blind one towards his wayward son. Patterson's appointment had been a conscious decision away from the indiscretions of the past. The only memories Darcy had of Patterson were of an austere and stately man; a pleasing blend of dependable and deferential.

It was therefore to Darcy's complete astonishment to see the serious, stiff Patterson utterly unbend, chuckling and blushing like a schoolboy when addressing Elizabeth.

"Of course, Mrs Darcy, it is always a delight to see you."

"Thank you, Patterson. My husband was getting so much attention, I was in danger of becoming jealous. Your words are a balm to my wounded pride." Elizabeth placed a hand on her chest as though in receipt of an injury.

"It is no hardship to praise the mistress of Pemberley, especially one as charming as yourself."

Good God, was Patterson flirting with her? With decades of experience in estate management, Patterson had been the closest Darcy had had to a father figure since his own father's death, and he had never seen him so...giggly. He had no memory of Patterson ever smiling. The joke had been that Darcy had managed to employ the only man in Derbyshire more reserved than he.

"Am I allowed to discuss business with your husband, or shall I ask you a few questions first to appease the mistress's vanity?" In other circumstances, Patterson's words could have been interpreted as patronising or even disrespectful. When received by Elizabeth, whose twinkling humour took them with the affection with which they were intended, Patterson's speech could only ever be light-hearted and playful. Elizabeth was respected by him. That was a relief.

"I have taken the liberty of overseeing the replanting of the south-facing borders. My special instruction to the gardener was to plant bulbs of pink and purple tulips ready for next spring, for I know they are Miss Molly's favourite colours."

To hear his daughter's name on another man's lips, to hear something of her preferences when he himself could not even remember her face, aggravated Darcy deeply. A clawing sense of inferiority took root, and his previous good-humour rapidly disappeared.

"Those borders are commonly daffodils and violas, are they not? They were my mother's favourite," he interrupted. His voice emerged sharper than he had intended.

"The fig tree she planted has grown too large. Nothing will grow in that border due to the shade. We agreed we would experiment with new plants to see what would grow rather than cut down the tree," Elizabeth said gently.

"I see." It was such a small detail, yet it annoyed Darcy that he could not recall it.

To cover the awkward silence which ensued, Patterson coughed gently and pushed a small ledger of accounts towards Darcy. "I am sorry to trouble you, sir, but I have a list here of purchases as we look towards the new year. Perhaps you could read it through and place your signature for approval."

Darcy's heart sank as he saw the quivering sea of incomprehensible words placed before him. It would take him weeks to decipher all of this. Steadying his hand against a growing tremor, he took the pen that Patterson had provided. When had he ever had cause to doubt Patterson's integrity? The account would not need checking. He would sign it and be done with it. It was not unheard of for him to be decisive. With a flourish, he signed off on the account without even opening the ledger. He caught Patterson's look of surprise and Elizabeth's brow knit with confusion. *Let them think what they like,* he thought. *Surely the master of Pemberley still has some authority.*

"Perhaps I should leave to find Fitzwilliam now and give you a chance to look over the rest of your correspondence in peace." Elizabeth rose to take her leave.

"Patterson, you may leave the rest with me. I shall peruse it later. As you can see, I am now a gentleman of leisure." It was difficult for Darcy to keep the resentment from his voice.

"I shall leave it with you, sir, and may I say it is a relief to see you so well recovered."

"Thank you, Patterson. It is indeed good to see a familiar face." Darcy had not intended to hurt Elizabeth, but it was only when he heard her sharp intake of breath that he realised the insensitivity of his words.

"Fitzwilliam must be quite lost this morning." Her voice had lost its sparkling quality as she repeated her previous wish to greet Fitzwilliam from his ride. Both she and Patterson left Darcy alone at the breakfast table. The orangery lost a good deal of its brightness once she had gone. Darcy sat in his chair brooding. It was only after the maids came to clear the plates did Darcy recall that Elizabeth had never answered the question of why it was they were not near Georgiana.

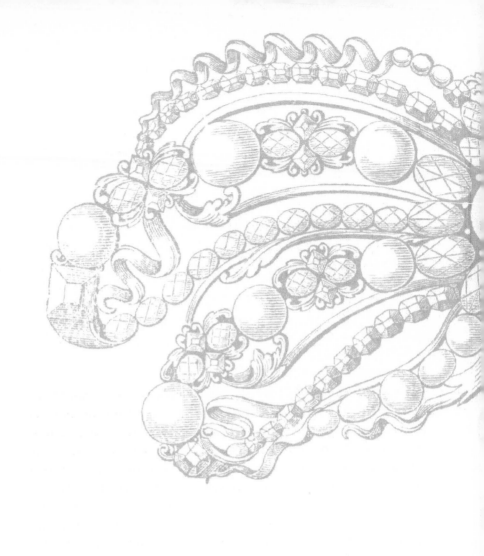

CHAPTER NINE

After Elizabeth had gone, Darcy requested that he be moved to the library. It had long been a sanctuary for him. Never did he envision that it would one day become a place of torment. He had asked for a walking cane to be placed near him and was gratified to discover he could manage a few steps without needing to ask for assistance. At least he was not completely at the mercy of others. He was able to take a short turn about the room as long as he did not put too much weight on his leg. He sat still for half an hour or so, flicking through the pages of a book that looked somewhat familiar but not making much headway through it. Twisting his back to relieve his stiffness, he stood up carefully and took a few steps towards the window that overlooked the terrace and the Italian gardens.

An abrupt movement caught his eye. It was Elizabeth, rushing down the path. Her face was dreadfully pale. And who was that with her? Darcy narrowed his eyes. It was Fitzwilliam. He could not hear the words, but it appeared that they were having an animated conversation. Fitzwilliam was gesturing at her, shaking his head in frustration. After some minutes, Elizabeth buried her face in her hands and began to weep, the picture of utter despair. Darcy could not help feeling moved. Fitzwilliam leant towards her, asking her something. Shaking her head in answer, Elizabeth turned from him. Darcy saw Fitzwilliam fling his hands skyward in apparent disgust and stamp away.

To his shock, Darcy saw Elizabeth crumple to the ground. Fitzwilliam must have heard her sobbing as he turned instantly and knelt before her, gathering her in his arms in a brotherly embrace. Darcy watched unobserved as Fitzwilliam put his arm about Elizabeth's waist and gently guided her to the house. The two figures cast one shadow as they disappeared from Darcy's view. What could have caused that outburst? Darcy could not speak for Elizabeth, but only once before had he ever seen Fitzwilliam so angry. *Wickham.* Only Wickham could cause such a reaction.

Darcy rang for a footman and asked that a note be sent to Fitzwilliam requesting his presence in the library. He decided he would not mention the scene in the garden. Nor would he mention Fitzwilliam's overheard conversation with Elizabeth about the letter. *Trust in God and keep your powder dry, Darcy.* There was a tension that had yet to be explained. Perhaps the betrayal he had written of was directly linked to his accident. Horror flooded his bruised body. What if it had *not* been an accident?

No. He could not countenance it; Fitzwilliam would never wish him harm. Elizabeth on the other hand—she was yet a stranger to him. He could not comprehend her. She did not behave towards him in a manner that he would have expected from his wife. But that did not mean that she wished him ill. There must be another explanation. Distracted by his thoughts, Darcy was brought back to the library by Fitzwilliam's arrival. It would not do to make any sort of accusations until Fitzwilliam had had a chance to explain his conduct.

Remembering he should probably smile, Darcy greeted his cousin with as much cheer as he could muster and attempted a feeble joke. "Please accept my apologies for my poor manners. Be assured I long to stand and receive you properly."

Fitzwilliam returned it with an equally feeble laugh. He was clearly still agitated from whatever had just passed between him and Elizabeth in the garden. Darcy could see Fitzwilliam's nostrils flare as he tried to steady his breath and regain his composure.

"Let me say that in this instance, you are quite forgiven. Next time, I hope you will be able to stand. Your progress thus far has been admirable."

"Thank you. Tell me, are you quite well?"

"Yes, quite." Fitzwilliam was a superb soldier but a terrible liar. He paced round the room several times, turning objects over in an attempt to stay calm.

"Pray, sit and tell me what aggravates you." Darcy's authoritative tone broke his cousin's reverie.

"Whatever do you mean?"

"I cannot recall a time when you have been so unsettled, and I do not think my injury is to blame."

"Nothing is the matter." It was unlike Fitzwilliam to speak so defensively. He caught himself. "Forgive me. I should be offering my assistance to you. Is there anything you need?"

Darcy did not believe him, as every word and action of his cousin belied his denial. He decided he would do best to leave it for now. "I do need your help."

"Name it and it will be done."

Darcy took a deep breath. "Tell me everything you know of Elizabeth."

Silence fell between the cousins. "I am not sure I am the best person to ask," said Fitzwilliam finally. "Why do you not ask her yourself?"

"She evades my questions. I know that I may look to you for a full and complete picture. Tell me what she does not. What of her family, of her standing in life?"

Fitzwilliam rolled his eyes and snorted. "Elizabeth's family—the Bennets—are the scourge of my existence. The mother is a ridiculous woman, prone to fits of hysteria. No, that is unfair—she is silly but she is not unkind. Mr Bennet, you will be pleased to know, is a gentleman. However, his estate is entailed to the next male heir, and as the father of five daughters, he neglected to make any provisions for their future. Certainly, he has not exerted any effort to improve their minds, preferring instead to make wry observations of their deficits."

Darcy's alarm grew at this news. "What is this? Elizabeth told me that her sister is currently with Georgiana."

"Forgive me. I have misspoken. Elizabeth's elder sister Jane is a lovely, genteel woman. She is Aphrodite herself, and Bingley is the happiest of men. It must be said that Elizabeth's sisters decline as you go down the line. Their charms diminish exponentially until you reach the youngest. A charmless and utterly irresponsible chit, that Lydia W—" Here Fitzwilliam stopped himself, the bitterness and anger of his tone surprising them both.

"What you tell me is distressing," said Darcy. "How is it that I married Elizabeth?"

"I do not know everything. You did not tell me much about your courtship. I know that you met before at Hertfordshire and became reacquainted during our annual trip to Rosings Park." Fitzwilliam took a breath and shook out the tension in his shoulders. "Elizabeth's cousin is Lady Catherine's *parson*. A ridiculous man who pays such deference to Lady Catherine's opinions that I am sure he would agree if she pronounced it beneficial to eat cow dung at luncheon."

Shocked, Darcy confirmed, "Lady Catherine's parson is now my relation?"

"I am afraid so."

"How did it come to this?" He shook his head. "Was I entrapped in some way?"

At this, Fitzwilliam laughed. "You were entrapped in the best possible way. You fell in love with a woman who knew her own worth and made you realise it too." He sighed. "I have come to you in a bitter mood, and I have filled your head with all my dark thoughts. The Bennets are not first-rate, but Mr Bennet is a gentleman, and therefore Elizabeth is a gentleman's daughter. Let us leave it there."

He rose quickly to take his leave. His face looked sombre. "You may not remember everything, but Elizabeth does. Be gentle with her. For both your sakes." And just like that, he was gone.

CHAPTER TEN

A knock startled Darcy as he gazed into the fire.

It was Elizabeth. It had been some hours since his interview with Fitzwilliam, and Darcy did not know how to receive her after he had learnt more about his wife's family. His wife was cousin to Lady Catherine's rector. He could almost hear his father turning in his tomb.

Be gentle. Those were Fitzwilliam's words. Being gentle was different from being a gentleman. Darcy knew how to be a gentleman, but he did not think he could be any more civil towards her than he had been already. He had every intention of keeping her at arm's length, but his resolve was sorely tested as she stood before him, her beautiful face glowing in the soft afternoon light.

"Are you hungry? I have ordered us a cold collation. I shall eat what you do not." She sat down in the chair opposite his. "Do you feel better for leaving your bed?"

"Yes, much better."

"I see you have been using a cane."

"I was able to take a few steps about the room." *And was able to witness you crying in the garden.*

"Delightful news!" Elizabeth's face lit up. "We should have

some cake to celebrate. I believe Mrs Norris has made your favourite sponge pudding in honour of your recovery."

"That is rather premature. I am hardly recovered."

Elizabeth's face fell. "Of course. I chose my words poorly."

Darcy noticed that she had red rims around her eyes. *Be gentle.* Whatever she had been prior to their marriage, she was now his wife. "Forgive me. I should not have been sharp. It has been a trying day."

"I understand." Elizabeth looked around the library. "I see you have found your way to the library. We sit in here most evenings when we are not entertaining guests."

"Do we?"

"Certainly. I know you must have forgotten because we do not often sit where you are now."

"How so?"

"These wing-backed chairs are for when my father or my uncle visit us."

"Where do we sit?" Darcy looked around. Tucked away in a corner was a chaise longue. Elizabeth rose from her chair and pushed it closer to them. "We usually sit by the fire. You recline in this corner—come, allow me to show you."

Without warning, she gently helped Darcy from his chair and eased him into the comfortable seat. As she did so, Darcy could feel the soft contours of her body press against him while she bore his weight. Two gentle hands were placed on his forearms, and he found himself lowered down into a much-loved chair. So distracted was he by her beauty that he hardly noticed the pain in his leg. His face was near hers as she helped him. Her skin was like the finest porcelain. Darcy wondered whether she had combed something into her unruly curls. Whenever she turned her head, he could smell sweet, hot lavender. It was intoxicating, like walking through a garden on a summer's evening. Conscious suddenly of his proximity to her, he averted his eyes.

She smiled and asked, "Are you comfortable now?"

Truth be told, Darcy could not remember being more self-conscious. Her simple gesture had completely unmanned him with its unassuming intimacy. He could only nod in response.

Arranging him on the reclining chair with the utmost gentleness, Elizabeth tended to his bandaged leg, ensuring it was supported by soft cushions. Swallowing hard, he shifted about on the chair until he felt more at ease.

Being on the receiving end of Elizabeth's cosseting affection made it difficult to keep his composure. For her, there was nothing amiss in her actions. She was obviously accustomed to putting her hands on his body, and if Darcy were honest, she was skilled at it. She had no awkwardness, or if she did it was in deference to his wounds, not due to lack of familiarity with his person. His last recollection of an embrace was that of a goodbye hug with Georgiana. An embrace between brother and sister was a far cry from the tender ministrations of an affectionate wife.

Taking a deep breath, he willed his body into submission. He was in very great danger of reaching out and caressing a wayward curl that had come loose from her chignon. What would possess him to do such a thing? Darcy clenched his unbound hand in an effort to regain his equanimity.

Elizabeth smiled again, unaware of his turmoil. She had a very expressive face. Every twitch of her eyebrow alluded to an undercurrent of mischief. To capture that expression would be impossible for even one of the great Italian masters. He wondered whether anyone had ever attempted it.

"Once you are settled, I shall entrust myself with the weighty task of choosing a book." Darcy's heart sank; he had, at once, a new concern to overtake his natural responses to his wife's beauty. Of course, she would expect him to read to her. And of course, he could not.

Elizabeth moved about the room silently. She was graceful; she hardly made a sound. Running her dainty fingers over the book spines, she hummed quietly, apparently looking for something.

A maid came in with their refreshments which distracted Elizabeth from her search. Upon drawing closer to Darcy, she seemed to notice that he was cold and asked for a fire to be lit. "The nights are drawing in. One moment the sun is happily shining, the next we are shivering."

And I nearly lost my life riding out in a biblical storm, Darcy thought wryly.

Elizabeth did not seem to notice him grow quiet as she knelt down in front of a carved chest in the opposite corner. Out of it, she pulled a loosely woven blanket and began to arrange it over Darcy's legs. When he started to protest, she disarmed him with a smile. "Do not be stubborn. You are to be kept comfortable. The doctor has advised me. Besides, we have shared this blanket many times before without complaint."

When Darcy looked up in surprise, she added, "I often sit in the spot where your foot is currently resting. We regularly come here to speak of our day to one another." She settled on a footstool beside his chair, her hand resting near Darcy's, their fingertips almost touching.

Taking the hint, Darcy began, "How has your day been today?"

Elizabeth did not answer immediately. "Eventful," she offered at last. She looked at Darcy, her expression unreadable. "It is not every day that one's husband regains his strength."

Darcy cast his eyes down. "I am afraid I am far from recovered," he replied.

"But you are making small steps in the right direction—certainly a far cry from your worst." Her eyes swept towards the cane. Her action reminded Darcy of his walk by the window and his resolve to find out more about her. How to begin his task? Darcy was never one for easy chit-chat with unfamiliar people. *Come man, think. She is your wife after all, wholly unfamiliar as she might be.*

"Perhaps we could talk a little." Elizabeth filled the silence helpfully.

Darcy smiled tightly, thankful that she seemed much better at this than he. Fitzwilliam had always laughed at his lack of ease around strangers. Conversation in most of his circles revolved around blank pleasantries and meaningless compliments. What did he and Elizabeth speak of habitually? She did not strike him as someone who would sit around gossiping, but in all fairness how accurate were first impressions?

Endeavouring to find out more, he said, "That would be pleasant. Perhaps you might tell me more about...us."

"What do you wish to know?"

"Tell me how we met. I am sorry to say I do not recall. You mentioned Bingley."

"Charles took a lease on an estate near my father's property in Hertfordshire—Netherfield Park. He was looking to make an investment after his father died, and it was his first major project since the late Mr Bingley's death. I do not know how well you recall Charles, but he looked to you for advice in all matters, and thus you accompanied him to Netherfield."

"And you and I met there...at Netherfield?"

"No, we met at an assembly in the nearby town of Meryton."

Darcy wrinkled his nose in disbelief. "I went to a public assembly of my own volition?"

Elizabeth laughed merrily. "To be sure, my love, you could not have been less interested if you tried. You walked in with the air of a man condemned to the gallows. Now I understand a little of why you despise such events, but you certainly were not there to find amusement."

"I found you, it would seem." Darcy could not help himself; it was so hard for him to remain aloof around her. She was so inviting to talk to. It was endearing and heart-warming when she called him her love. Keeping his guard up when in her presence would be next to impossible.

"You did indeed find me."

"I suppose you must have caught my eye."

Elizabeth blushed. "Of sorts."

Darcy could not help but smile then, wondering what he had done to make her blush so prettily. Perhaps their eyes had met across the room. Perhaps he had assisted her in some way or had paid her a compliment...and from there an understanding had blossomed. Darcy had no memory of having ever courted a woman. Whatever had happened at that assembly, he hoped it had been romantic.

"Please continue...I am all anticipation."

Elizabeth's eyes flashed playfully. "Do not get too excited...and do not be cross with me when I say that you turned your noble head to me, swept me up and down with your proud eyes, and declared I was tolerable but not handsome enough to tempt you to dance."

"No!" Darcy gasped. Surely he would not have behaved so rudely.

"This story is truly mortifying for both of us! I would not make it up!" Elizabeth laughed.

"I cannot credit it. You are far too lovely to be ignored." Darcy caught himself. He had spoken his thoughts without consideration and flushed at his unguarded admiration of her. Speaking so openly to a woman was a new sensation, but Elizabeth's liveliness made him forget himself.

"As freely as you insult, so do you compliment. For a man who prides himself on his reserve, you are notoriously outspoken." She was teasing him again. "I am relieved to hear you think me pretty now."

"I cannot believe I said such ungentlemanly words to you."

Elizabeth looked at him in bemused affection. "Steady yourself, my love, this tale will get a good deal worse before it improves."

"How so?"

"I shall get to that soon enough. Where was I in our story?"

"I believe I had just been struck with some kind of temporary visual impairment and was not able to see properly. It is the only defence I can offer to my conduct." Good God, was he flirting with her? Had he not just told himself to be on guard?

Elizabeth smiled at his attention. "Perhaps you were indeed suffering from a megrim. It would certainly explain the fearsome scowl written upon your face that night. In any case, we came away from that evening with the following understanding—you thought me inconsequentially plain, and I thought you abominably rude."

"Yet now we are married." Darcy could not keep the confusion from his voice.

"Now we are married," Elizabeth confirmed. "Ours is a story with many twists and turns."

In the most playful of tones, she continued to explain to a mortified Darcy that there had been little of courtship between them, no pretty words of love and flirtation but instead an exchange of verbal sparring that only a fool would understand to be admiration. Darcy's confusion only grew as she spoke. He could not understand how they came to be married. Yes, she was pretty, but he had not thought so when he met her. Their acquaintance was built on a set of clashes from which neither came out satisfied. Fitzwilliam had explained that she was from an ill-mannered family of rapidly reducing means. Everything about this marriage seemed highly unlikely. He had always imagined his wife to be from the same social sphere as he.

Darcy's confusion turned to outright shock when she began to describe his disastrous first proposal—in his aunt's rectory of all places. Here, Elizabeth had blushed again. By now, Darcy realised she was not blushing *because* of him but *for* him.

Elizabeth's expression became more animated as she spoke. "You began by telling me that you loved and admired me most ardently. You then proceeded to tell me it was totally out of character to love one such as I, and it was entirely against your better judgment. You had battled with your decision as my status in life was so beneath you, but, in the end, you must have me despite it all. I told you that you were the last man on Earth that I could be prevailed upon to marry."

"Then why did we marry?" Darcy hoped she was not offended by his surprise. Elizabeth's body softened into one of compassion. If his lack of memory hurt her, it did not show. Her eyes were overflowing with a mixture of sentiments—sympathy, sorrow, and affection.

"Because you showed me that for all our exchanges, good and bad, what really mattered were our actions. It was your deeds, not your words, that proved to me beyond doubt that yours was the noblest heart I had ever met." She stretched out her hand and gave his a small squeeze. "I cannot account for your love for me, but I thank God for it daily. You are the very best of men."

Darcy did not know how to reply to her. Elizabeth caught his embarrassment and continued airily, "If it consoles you, after much reflection I have decided it was not the most awful marriage proposal I have ever received—that award belongs to my cousin, Mr Collins.

You, at least, spoke to me from your heart. He thought only of his position in life. Within a week of my refusal, Collins was engaged to my generally sensible friend, Charlotte Lucas. My cousin's ridiculousness is matched only by his sense of self-importance. I was very surprised that Charlotte chose to align herself with such a man."

"Why did she then?"

"Why does any woman throw herself away into an unequal marriage? What else is there for her if she does not? He offered a chance for Charlotte to have her own home, her own family, to go into society on her own terms. For her, the price of her self-respect was worth the reward." She added quietly, "People marry for many reasons. Love is not always one of them.

"Did you read Patterson's accounts?" Her question caught him by surprise; he had been yet in contemplation of her words.

"No," he replied, a little too quickly.

"Forgive me, I do not mean that you must defend yourself. I only wish to offer you assistance."

"Why should I need assistance?"

"You did not check the account before signing it. It was unlike you. Once you told me that your father always said, 'Measure twice, cut once'. You always read the accounts twice before signing."

Darcy took a breath. Could she be trusted? Fitzwilliam would not be here every day, and she was observant enough to notice something was amiss. He would risk it. "I applaud your perception. It is true. I did not want Patterson to know my memory has been damaged."

"I could send for the previous accounts and tell you what I know of them."

"It would be of no use. It is not just a question of memory." A muscle in his face twitched. He detested admitting he needed help.

"Whatever do you mean?" Elizabeth's lovely face looked up at him. Her eyes were wide and anxious. She waited patiently for Darcy to speak.

Reluctantly, Darcy explained his recent discovery and its implications.

"So you cannot read or write at all?"

"I can," Darcy became defensive. "But I do not find it easy. In truth, I can only manage a little at a time. Even then, it is very laboured."

"How can I help you?" Elizabeth gazed into his eyes. "Perhaps I could read to you. I could help you with your correspondence."

"No." Darcy was overcome with embarrassment. "Do not speak of this to anyone. No one can know."

"Very well. But allow me this. If you find yourself in a position where you need my assistance, you must let me know."

Darcy smiled at her. She may not be what he had imagined for a wife, but she was uniformly charming.

"Speaking of unnecessary suffering, why are you in the library if you cannot read anything?"

"It has long been my sanctuary at Pemberley. I always call it my favourite room, as I am sure you probably know."

Elizabeth's eyes sparkled mischievously. "I do not wish to correct you, but you once told me it was your *second*-favourite room."

Darcy's eyebrows shot up. "And what room would replace this as my favourite?"

Elizabeth bit her lip, looking unexpectedly coy. A most-becoming crimson hue stained her cheeks and neck. Suddenly, Darcy had his answer. A thrill rushed through his body. They were speaking of *her* room. He was caught by an overwhelming desire to picture it, to picture her opening her bedroom door with her exquisite eyes laughing at him. He wondered what it looked like. What might she have changed? He was certain she could read his mind as he could not help blushing. Thankfully, he was saved by the dinner gong.

"Shall I see you at dinner? Let me ring for the footmen to attend to you." Elizabeth busied herself around him until she was satisfied that he was comfortable. Bending down, she placed a chaste kiss on his temple. Every one of Darcy's senses came alive under her touch.

"You have done very well today. Be sure to rest your leg. Send me a note if you are too fatigued to eat in the dining room. I do not mind dining alone."

"Why would you be alone?" Darcy said, surprised.

"Did Fitzwilliam not say? He was called away on urgent business. I thought he might have mentioned it when he spoke to you before." It was Elizabeth's turn to sound surprised.

"No, he spoke not a word of it." Darcy grew quiet. He could have added that Fitzwilliam had not mentioned his earlier altercation with Elizabeth in the garden. Nor had he brought up Darcy's letter and the betrayal of which it spoke. There was only one conclusion that Darcy could draw from all this—whatever they were keeping from him, Fitzwilliam's loyalty belonged to Elizabeth.

His previous warmth turned into heated irascibility. She had charmed him into letting his defences down, and he felt like a fool, an addle-pated gudgeon.

"I believe I shall remain upstairs," he said icily.

Elizabeth looked confused at his change of mood. "As you wish, my love."

Mercifully, the footmen arrived, and Darcy was able to leave his former sanctuary for another one: the master's room. He drew his breath in pain as one of the footmen jostled his leg. For the briefest of interludes, he had entirely forgotten about his injuries, such was the effect of his mysterious wife.

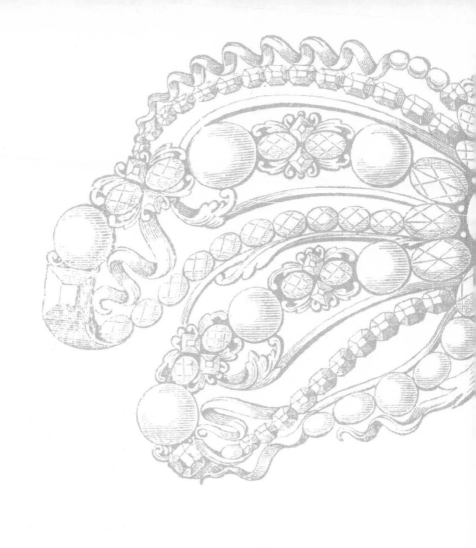

CHAPTER ELEVEN

Patterson's ledger sat untouched on the corner of Darcy's desk. In his desire to reclaim some status as master of Pemberley, he had requested to be removed to his study under the pretext of examining accounts. It had been a gesture of defiance against his bodily ailments, yet he felt more trapped than ever. Two days had passed since Fitzwilliam had quit Pemberley, and a clawing desperation had begun to grip at Darcy since his cousin's abrupt departure. How best to manage his estate? At some point, it would also be noted that he had not corresponded with Georgiana. His hand, although still suffering the ill effects of his accident, did not hurt him as much as before. His leg still troubled him, but there would be a point where he could no longer use his injuries as an excuse. And there was still the question of his cousin and his wife. Elizabeth had still not spoken of whatever had passed between them in the garden. Troubling too was the lack of communication from his cousin. It would have been reassuring to get a letter from Fitzwilliam—however much Darcy would struggle to read it. Sighing, he managed to stand from his chair. Pain struck him intermittently, intermingled with a lingering soreness that he attributed to the purple bruises disfiguring his calf. *At least I did not lose my leg.* He glanced at the writing materials in front of him. *Although perhaps it would be less humiliating to lose a limb than my autonomy as a man.*

From his position next to the window, the wide-open spaces called to him. The weather was bleak but that mattered not. What would he give to be atop a horse, pacing freely across the grassy hillsides? A ride would be just the thing to rid himself of this ill humour. Shutting his eyes, he transported himself back to a time that he could not place. The last occasion he had ridden a horse had ended in disaster, so it could not be that particular memory he was reliving now. No, his mind's eye would torment him by conjuring up an unrecognised place of heavenly freedom. Wind whipping his hair as he pushed through the elements; pounding hoofs trampling the purple heather underfoot; holding his breath in anticipation of a jump; the connexion between himself, his horse and his land—all were lost to him now. Opening his eyes, he leant heavily on his cane and surveyed his sore leg. One day, perhaps, he would be able to ride again. For now, he would settle for walking unassisted.

A respectful knock broke his sombre musing. He called out for whomever it was to enter, fully bracing himself for an awkward meeting with Patterson. Not yet able to admit his memory loss, he had been dreading this encounter. To his surprise, he saw Mrs Reynolds enter. Glancing at the clock, he noted the hour. Did she always call upon him at this time? Judging from the thin, firm purse of her mouth and the way she was anxiously smoothing down the folds of her dress, Darcy surmised that this visit to his office was not a regular one.

"Mr Darcy, sir, it is good to see you up and about at last." Mrs Reynolds's serious face broke into a reserved smile. She gave him a fond look, as a governess might gaze upon a once-naughty but newly reformed pupil. He returned her smile with a careful one of his own, unable to completely agree with her optimistic assessment of his health.

"What brings you to my study?" He beckoned for her to take a seat across the desk from him.

She paused, as though to refuse his offer, then glanced involuntarily at his leg. Clearly, she thought it best if Darcy was seated too, and so she sat down quietly, her hands folded in her lap. Balancing his cane on the side of the chair, he valiantly attempted to sit unaided. Pain coursed through his body unequal to anything he had felt since leaving his bedchamber. Biting back a curse, he glanced at his housekeeper. Her expression was a mixture of amusement and barely-hidden exasperation. *What exactly am I trying to prove?* He gritted his teeth and exclaimed with rather more force than he would have liked, "I have a great deal to attend to. Is your business urgent?"

"Forgive me, sir, it is not urgent but..." Mrs Reynolds stopped, searching for the right phrase, "...I do believe it is important." This held his attention. Colour rose in her cheeks as he looked at her, and she cleared her throat.

"It is about Mrs Darcy."

For the strangest moment, Darcy thought she meant his mother. *No, of course she can only mean Elizabeth,* he chided himself.

"I do not wish to speak out of turn, sir, but I am worried for her health. I am afraid that she is not resting properly. She eats little and has been excessively anxious since..." This time, she glanced at Darcy's hand. "...since recent unfortunate events."

Darcy nodded curtly. "You are asking me to speak to her?"

Mrs Reynolds's eyes widened in alarm. "Oh no, sir, I do not presume to tell you what to do. I am sure my mistress would not like me to interfere."

"Then what precisely are you asking of me?"

Here, Mrs Reynolds looked at him curiously, and Darcy sensed his blunder. *She expects me to be more concerned,* he realised. A man so violently in love as he was supposed to be should surely be more worried at ill tidings of his wife's health. If he were honest with himself, he had been avoiding Elizabeth since his cousin's departure. This would not do. He consciously softened his tone. "What I meant to say was, how may I be of assistance?"

A little more satisfied with his response, Mrs Reynolds replied with authority, "Mrs Darcy should rest. She kept a constant watch over you when you were abed. Her shock at seeing you so ill was great. I worry that her cares will overburden her. Heaven knows she had enough to contend with before your accide—" She caught herself. "Pardon me, sir. I am sure you have no wish to be reminded of such matters."

Darcy's curiosity burned at her words, yet to ask her their meaning would reveal the extent of his injuries. Instead, he asked, "Where could I find Mrs Darcy?"

Mrs Reynolds glanced at her watch. "Her routine has been changed of late, but I believe she will be in her own sitting room." The lines around her eyes deepened as she looked at him with affection. "There are a great many people who wish to know of your recovery. She makes it her business to correspond with them daily."

"Of course." Darcy wondered how long Elizabeth spent writing. Apart from Georgiana, she had not mentioned communicating with anyone else. "Thank you, Mrs Reynolds, for bringing this to my attention."

Nodding, she rose from her chair. "Shall I arrange for you to be taken to her?"

No, I thought I might walk. Darcy bit back his sarcastic reply. It would not do to be rude. He could not remember ever speaking a cross word to Mrs Reynolds; now was not the time to start. Suppressing another sigh, he nodded, then simply watched as she called upon two young footmen to aid him.

ELIZABETH'S SITTING ROOM USED TO BELONG TO HIS mother. He recognised the door as soon as he was inelegantly deposited outside it. When Mrs Reynolds had suggested he call upon Elizabeth, it had seemed prudent to agree. Now he was here, he found himself uncertain of what to do next. If only he had some kind of memory to draw upon. His wife was an utter stranger to him, yet everyone else expected him to be on the most intimate terms with her. It was simply a ludicrous situation. Darcy was glad the footmen had gone and were not witness to his indecision. In the end, it was the door handle that decided it for him. It had not changed since his mother was alive; he recognised the embossed flower motif instantly. He may not remember Elizabeth—or any of his new family—but he had not completely lost everything. Now was not the time to hesitate. Pemberley was *his* estate, and he was still the master of it. Bearing his weight on his cane as best he could, he raised his hand and knocked upon his wife's door.

Elizabeth's voice was faint, but it gave him encouragement enough to enter. She was a picture of elegance, of course. Sitting at her writing desk by a window, the streaming light bathed her graceful frame. Her profile was in silhouette, and Darcy found himself momentarily captivated by the soft feminine curves of her figure. She was truly beautiful; the realisation of it caught him completely off guard. Unbidden, the image of her crying in his cousin's arms returned. Unsure of what to say next, he felt suddenly foolish for disturbing her.

"Are you well?" Elizabeth hastily brushed her hand across her face as she rose to greet him. "Is anything the matter? Do you need assistance in any way?" He noted her eyebrows contract with worry. Glancing at his leg, she exclaimed, "You should be sitting down! I was assured that you would only be resting in your study." She busied herself by drawing up a chair for him to sit on.

"Nothing is amiss," Darcy lied as he carefully lowered himself into the seat opposite hers. She raised an eyebrow at him as he winced. "Nothing new in any case."

"Then why are you here?" Elizabeth's face looked drawn and tired.

"Would you prefer that I left you alone?" Darcy's eyes caught sight of her writing materials. There was a sizable pile of unopened letters next to her elbow. He wondered with whom she was corresponding. He looked again more carefully at her face. Upon her ivory cheeks, he perceived traces of tears reflecting in the light. "Pardon me for disturbing your solitude. I can see you are upset."

Elizabeth smiled weakly at him. "It is nothing really. I was reading a letter from my sister Jane. She spent the afternoon with Molly and Georgiana. My heart longs to be there with them." Her bottom lip began to tremble. "I have never been apart from Molly for so long." She motioned to the letter nearest to her. "Jane writes that Molly asks for you too. Would you like to read what it says?" Upon seeing Darcy's expression, she caught herself. "Forgive me, dearest. I remember now that you cannot."

"I *can* read," Darcy replied a little too quickly to be convincing. "Only it takes longer than before."

Elizabeth drew out the letter and underlined a passage with her pen. "Read this part aloud. It is where Jane mentions you."

"Whatever for?" Perspiration began to form at the back of Darcy's neck.

"So I may know how to help you."

"I do not wish for your assistance," he replied hotly. "That is not why I deigned to visit you." And to think that Mrs Reynolds had counselled him to support her! He put his hands to the armrests in an effort to move from the chair. "I am sorry to have troubled you." Ignoring the wave of nausea that standing caused, he began to turn back towards the door.

It was Elizabeth's voice that stopped him. She had picked up the letter and had begun to read it aloud. *"Dear sister, I hope your husband is recovering well. Convalescence must be difficult for him, given his propensity for melodrama—"*

"I am *not* melodramatic."

"So says the man who cannot properly walk as he attempts to storm out of the room." She gave his leg a pointed look.

"You misrepresent me entirely."

"How so?" Elizabeth bestowed upon Darcy a smile of such sweetness that he momentarily forgot how to speak.

Reluctantly, he returned to his seat and found his voice. "You accuse me of histrionics."

"*I* accuse you of nothing. I am merely relating to you what Jane has written."

Darcy frowned in confusion. "Your sister truly wrote that of me?"

Elizabeth gave him a sly look. "Perhaps I have taken certain liberties with her words. Why do you not read it for yourself? It is just the two of us here. What harm could it do?" Upon sensing Darcy's hesitation, she continued in a gentler voice, "I am sure, at some point, you might wish to read letters from your sister. Practising with me can only help you in that quarter."

Unable to argue against such logic, Darcy reluctantly took the paper and regarded the passage she had underlined. Horribly self-conscious, he studiously ignored Elizabeth as he began to read aloud.

"*Oh, my dear...est Lizzy. I pray for poor Darcy's re...recovery. Little Molly is all smiles until some...one says Papa, then she asks for him persist...*ent—Here Darcy paused, overcome with embarrassment—*persistently. We are com...com...comforting her as best we can, but we all long for your safe return to London. Give my fondest wishes to Darcy and tell him he is...* Screwing up his eyes, Darcy attempted to make out the concluding part of the sentence, but it was no use. Clearing his throat, he tried again. *Give my fondest wishes to Darcy and tell him that he is...he is...* Groaning with frustration, it took every ounce of self-restraint not to rip the letter in two.

Suddenly, he became aware of Elizabeth's presence just over his right shoulder. Leaning over him, she traced along the words with her finger, her hand almost touching his.

"Jane's writing can be so hard to read sometimes. I fear Charles's illegible ways may be rubbing off on her," Elizabeth's voice murmured. Finding the place, she read softly, "*...tell him that he is forever in our thoughts.*" She moved her head slightly; she was so close now that it would not take much for him to turn his head to one side and kiss her on the cheek.

Breaking his gaze from her, Darcy turned back to the page in front of them. "No mention of melodrama then?"

"Maybe I have confused Jane's letter with another of your acquaintances." Elizabeth gave him a saucy smile as she returned to her place opposite Darcy.

"Do you have many people that you correspond with?" Darcy asked, mindful of his original task. "Surely you must take some time to rest yourself."

Elizabeth's smile widened. "That is very thoughtful, but if I neglected my duties then I would have twice as much the next day."

"I am sorry I cannot assist you."

"You can assist me by taking your rest," Elizabeth adopted a mock scolding tone, "or else I must inform your family of you doing far more than you ought." She rolled her eyes. "Think of how many letters I should have to write then."

Laughing, Darcy nodded. "I see now the error of my ways. I shall stay abed, thereby reducing your workload."

Elizabeth laughed in return. "It would be greatly appreciated. I would be spared a great number of lectures."

Darcy gazed at Elizabeth intently. Her spirits seemed brighter than before. He had cheered her up, and he felt a swell of pride at doing so.

"Was there a reason for calling upon me?" Elizabeth's voice broke him from his thoughts. Reluctant to share Mrs Reynolds's concerns with her, he looked about and his eyes fell upon her correspondence.

Thinking quickly, he said, "I wondered whether you had heard from Fitzwilliam?"

A deep blush rose up Elizabeth's neck, and she glanced quickly at her letters. "I have not received anything from him today," she said quietly.

"But you do anticipate hearing from him soon?" Darcy could not understand her change in manner. Surely it was not so strange a question.

"I...I cannot say. He left so abruptly." Elizabeth fell silent. Avoiding his gaze, she reached out and shuffled through the letters. "I am sorry, dearest, but I really must reply to these."

So he was to be dismissed just like that! Darcy chafed inwardly. And still not a word about her dealings with his cousin. Summoning all the dignity he could, Darcy rose from his chair.

"Do not let me take up any more of your time," he said coldly. He saw Elizabeth open her mouth as if to protest, but she closed it again without a word. Turning from her, he rang for assistance. Glancing back, he caught sight of her face. So sorrowful was her expression that his anger temporarily abated. Mrs Reynolds's advice returned to him.

In a cool tone, he addressed her with a grave air of authority, "You must rest. As you can see, I am much improved and therefore do not need to be constantly watched. You should use your time to recover your own strength." Thankful for the footman's prompt arrival, he did not wait for her to answer.

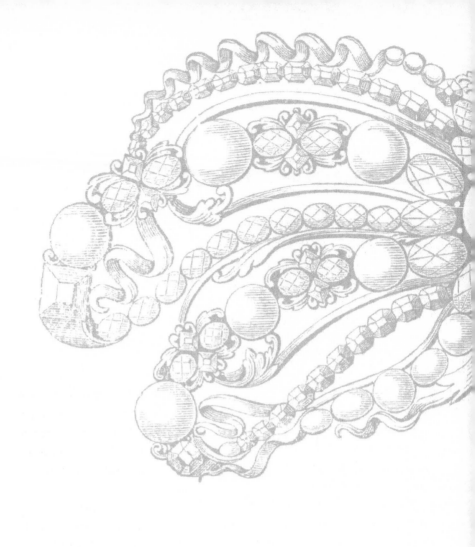

CHAPTER TWELVE

D arcy stepped into the empty church. The aisle stretched out before him, leading to the gloomy altar. It was night-time, or nearly night-time, such were the shadows cast by the ornate windows lining each side of the nave. Footsteps echoed as he made his way down the aisle. He could hear somebody crying, and he was shocked to discover it was him. Where was he? He needed to ask Elizabeth.

Kneeling before the altar, he clutched something small and precious in his hand. Turning it over, he unclenched his fist to see his mother's engagement brooch; its pin had caught his skin, causing it to bleed. Tiny drops of blood pattered quietly onto the cold flagstone floor. The brooch fell too, sliding away into a dark corner. It was lost, just like his mother and just like Elizabeth.

A sob caught in his throat. Where was Elizabeth? What if she was gone forever? He needed her; he could not bear this pain without her. He put his hands together to pray. The church grew colder and menacing in the moonlight. Darcy prayed for safety, for sanctuary, for deliverance. He knew not the words he spoke, but the meaning was the same. Help me. A noise from the chapel drew his attention; it was rain thundering down against the weather-beaten walls. It was deafening. He turned back towards the altar and looked down at his hands. To his horror, they were mutilated, the fingers *shorn off at the knuckles. They were covered in blood. Terror filled him as he screamed into the night.*

Warm arms surrounding him brought Darcy back to his senses. It was Elizabeth, in her nightdress, with her beautiful curls framing her worried face. The church had gone, replaced by Darcy's soft bed, in Darcy's safe room, with his wife's arms holding him in a loving embrace. She was rocking him a little, rubbing a soothing hand along his back. He did not know how long they sat in such a posture. She waited until his breathing returned to a steady rate. His hands were still trembling a little, and he tightened his grip on her for comfort. Her body was soft and welcoming. To his surprise, he felt her flinch slightly at the pressure of his hands. Gently, she put a little distance between them.

"My love, you have had a bad dream. Do not be alarmed. You are quite safe," Elizabeth said soothingly. She disengaged herself from him carefully. Darcy gazed up at her wide-eyed. Was she leaving him again? Losing her touch felt like a bereavement. He did not want her to go. Why had she backed away? Everything hurt and he was so very weary. When would life begin to make sense again?

Elizabeth helped him back under the coverlet. As his head touched the pillow, a worrying thought struck him. For all his suspicions, perhaps Elizabeth was not at fault. Perhaps it was *he* who had betrayed *her*. Closing his eyes, he could just make out her shadowy form sitting patiently by his bedside.

As his own breathing steadied, he could hear Elizabeth's breathing become ragged. Peeping from the slightest crack in his eyelids, he watched as she covered her face, sobbing into her hands.

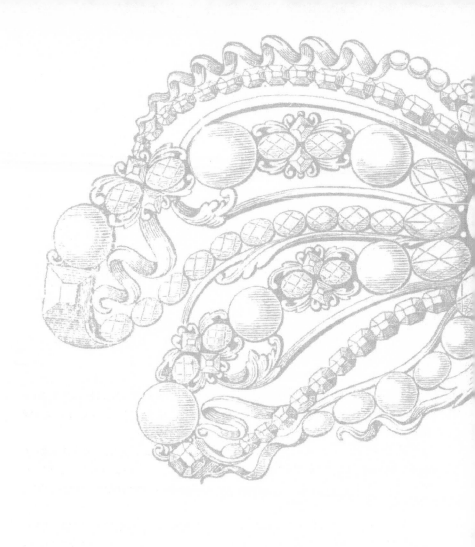

CHAPTER THIRTEEN

A flustered knock woke Darcy from his sleep. He had hardly time to open his eyes when Elizabeth flung the door open, her face beaming.

"I have had word of Georgiana! She has safely delivered a boy. His name is to be Robert Fitzwilliam after her two favourite men, and he is rapidly supplanting you both in her affections!" She rushed to Darcy and threw her arms around his neck.

"Mother and baby are safe and well! Is that not the most joyful news?" Her rapturous embrace was so different from the previous night's actions that Darcy was momentarily stunned.

As the news finally entered his sleep-addled mind, he began to smile. "Both are safe?" he repeated.

"Quite safe. Poor Georgiana is rather tired, but that is only to be expected. Luxford sent me an express. He writes so lovingly of them both." She beamed at him. "I have taken the great liberty of calling for the doctor to attend to you at his earliest convenience. I hoped he might assess your injuries, and we could travel back to London as soon as it was safe. I trust that I do not presume too much. Certainly, I am sure that you would wish to see Georgiana as soon as you could."

"That would please me greatly." Darcy was smiling now. "Perhaps you could read the letter to me."

Elizabeth found a chair near Darcy's bed and read the letter aloud. Although Darcy could not remember Georgiana's husband, each word of praise reassured him that his sister was much loved. He gazed at Elizabeth from his bed. Curls of dark hair tumbled from her plait that wound around her elegant neck. She seemed rather pale, and Darcy wondered how well she had slept last night. An unwelcome pang of guilt ran through him. How long had she stayed by his bedside? He did not like to think of her in distress, yet he did not remember her leaving his room. He stole another glance at her, the sound of her crying haunting him anew. Mercifully, whatever had caused her unhappiness was now gone, so overjoyed was she by Luxford's letter.

Reading with animation, Elizabeth breathed life into the stranger's words as though they were in the room speaking. She was so artless, so charming, so unaffected by any sense of false modesty that she truly was a pleasure to listen to. Even in her dressing gown and slippers, she possessed an elegance that could not be learnt from any deportment lesson. Elizabeth was, Darcy decided, impossible to dislike. As she reached the end of the letter, she paused. "Robert writes that Molly is asking for us every night. Neither of us have ever been away from her for this long. It will soon be two months since your accident. I miss her greatly—I cannot imagine what it must be like for her."

Her face looked so wistful that Darcy could only reply, "Then I shall do all I can to persuade the doctor. I should very much like to speak to Georgiana."

"Very good. Were you able to sleep at all after your dream woke you? I am so very sorry to have disturbed you at this early hour. I thought you would want to know as soon as I did."

Darcy reddened at the mention of his dream. It was bad enough that she should see him so injured; it would not do for her to worry about the weakness of his mind. "No, I am grateful. What time is it?"

"It has just gone six. Dear Mrs Reynolds woke me to deliver the letter herself. She could not sleep any more than I could—she is, even now, in the next room, weeping with joy. I suspect she holds Georgiana in her heart as she would one of her daughters. She has asked whether we could take some little pieces of embroidery that she has made for the baby. I trust that is to your satisfaction?"

"Of course." He still could not comprehend it. His young sister, now a mother.

"I am glad of it. Would you like to rest again, or would you like to breakfast up here? Forgive my impertinence, but I thought it would be best if you do not move about too much before Dr Amstel arrives."

"I cannot promise a clean bill of health, but he cannot stop me from leaving if I so desire it."

"That may be true, but remember I can make your life excessively difficult if you attempt to do more than is medically advised. Our years of marriage have honed my skills in scolding, and I fear they have been perfected to your disadvantage." She arched her eyebrows teasingly.

Darcy could only smile. "Am I to understand that I am to remain in bed and have breakfast brought to me or else suffer the indignity of being carried downstairs like a sack of potatoes? Accept my assurances that you will not need to scold me in this instance."

"You make a rather handsome sack, it must be said." Elizabeth started to laugh. "But you have been justly warned—as hard as it is to be apart from Molly, Georgiana, and her little family, your recovery still takes precedence."

She tentatively placed her hand over his. "You have done very well, but there is still a long journey ahead. You will need to regain all your strength." Squeezing his hand, she stood. "I shall ask Mrs Reynolds about breakfast for you and to prepare our luggage in the hope of our imminent return to London."

Pausing, she smiled broadly. "Do you mind if we allow the servants a small glass of sherry to toast a celebration? We did so for Molly; it is only fitting we do the same for little Robert."

Darcy returned her smile again. "Certainly," he said. The gesture reminded him of his parents. They had loved to finish their evenings with a glass of sherry together, but he suspected that Elizabeth already knew this.

"Then I shall busy myself with our preparations. I shall send for your breakfast to be ready in the next half hour, then Robertson will attend to you thereafter."

Darcy sat up in his bed, trying as best he could to take stock of all that had occurred. He was elated by Georgiana's news and, to be honest, not a little relieved. Fitzwilliam's absence still bothered him, however. He recalled their last conversation over and over. It could not be a coincidence that Fitzwilliam had left so soon after his quarrel, or whatever it had been, with Elizabeth. To leave without saying a word was highly unusual; indeed, even Elizabeth had presumed that Fitzwilliam would have mentioned it to him beforehand.

And then there was Elizabeth. Every rational, reasonable part of Darcy knew that under no circumstances would he have ever considered someone such as Elizabeth to be his wife. Yet, whenever he was near her, he felt an admiration that he simply could not repress. No, admiration was not sufficient to describe Elizabeth. He could think of a great deal of women whose accomplishments he could admire. Elizabeth had never once boasted of any such talents, yet still she attracted him. Indeed, she attracted him more than he could account for.

Whenever he was near her, their conversation would take such a playful, familiar turn that he quite forgot his reserved nature. He could not remember a time when he had felt truly easy in a woman's company. She did not simply agree with him as so many others did, rather she *conversed* with him. She was interested in his opinion because she truly cared for it, and for him, and in turn assumed he would want to know hers. It was only when he was apart from her, in the cold light of day so to speak, that he could not ignore the inconsistencies in her behaviour. Why did she not speak of her exchange with his cousin?

There was indeed a long journey ahead, and he intended to put his admiration aside to discover more about her and about them. She should at least offer an explanation for the conversation she had with Fitzwilliam before he left. She was his wife and

Fitzwilliam was his cousin; he had every right to know whether a disagreement had taken place between them.

Dr Amstel came as soon as he could, which was thankfully after Darcy had eaten. A small, wiry man, the good doctor had tended to the Darcy family for many years, and Darcy trusted his judgment. He always wore a pristinely pressed dark brown suit that contrasted with the shock of white hair crowning his head. Darcy had only ever known him to be immaculate. Everything about him was neat: his thin little lips were framed by a trim beard; the chain of a perfectly positioned watch hung expertly from his pocket; his nimble hands, which were always a touch too cold, were exquisitely manicured. He watched carefully as his assistant examined Darcy. Trying not to wince in pain, Darcy forced a grimace as the doctor's assistant pressed his leg. *Never show weakness.* Father's advice continued to serve him well.

The doctor did not speak a word. When his assistant turned his attention to Darcy's hand, it was altogether too difficult to put on a brave face. Part of him wished to turn away, even as another was compelled to look. As the bandages were unwrapped, Darcy was immediately struck by the desire to gag at the extent of the damage. Angry red lines marked out the worst of the injuries. He doubted the scars would ever fade. Tentatively, Darcy flexed his hand, an unfamiliar tugging sensation pulling at the tendons under the scar tissue. At least he could move it. That was a relief.

"Some of my finest work, Mr Darcy." Dr Amstel seemed pleased with himself. "You will not see neater stitches than these." Privately, Darcy could not conceive of anything more grotesque than the deformed flesh before him, but he thanked Dr Amstel with all the civility he could muster.

"And how is your lovely wife faring?" Dr Amstel queried. "Your injuries must undoubtedly cause a lot of strain."

"She is bearing up very well."

"I can well believe it. She is made of iron. I have seen it first-hand."

Darcy raked his uninjured hand through his hair, attempting to understand the older man's meaning.

Before he had a chance to ask, Dr Amstel continued, "As ill as you have been, you must keep an eye on her. We do not want her to take a bad turn again." Darcy started at this new piece of information.

Dr Amstel could sense Darcy's discomfort and began to apologise, fearing he had caused offence. "Forgive me. I know that you always take prodigiously good care of Mrs Darcy. I do not mean to imply otherwise, only that Mrs Darcy has a tendency to take too much upon herself and not listen to her body when she should rest."

He began to pack away his equipment into his leather bag. "I would not like to see such a lovely young woman unwell if it can be prevented."

"You have my word." Darcy was not sure what he was promising. He placed it on a mental list of questions to put to Elizabeth. "Shall I be able to travel?" he asked, gesturing towards his leg.

"I cannot entirely condone it. In an ideal world, you would stay put until we were certain that it had healed. However, there are no signs of infection, and the skin is beginning to mend itself."

His eyes twinkled as he raised his head from his bag and looked at Darcy. "I do not underestimate the importance of a tranquil mind to one's recovery, and I should hazard a guess that you will not find peace until you are reunited with Miss Molly and Lady Luxford. I therefore propose a compromise. I shall permit you to travel if you promise to convalesce properly in London. If you attempt to move about too much, you risk causing more permanent damage."

"So I may travel?"

"Under the strict instruction that you do so with care, and you travel slowly with plenty of attention given to your injuries."

"We plan to travel in my carriage and stop as often as I need to."

"That would be wise. I shall inform Mrs Darcy of our conversation and my...well, I shall not call it approval, but rather my lack of disapproval."

Elizabeth was summoned and arrived directly. Standing at Darcy's bedside, she looked excessively tired and unable to keep the worry from her eyes. When Amstel saw Elizabeth, he was quick to reassure her of all that was good in Darcy's prognosis. Darcy watched as the tension escaped from her body. Amstel must have sensed it too as he gently encouraged Elizabeth to take a seat. Just as with his steward, Darcy was gratified to see the cordiality with which Amstel greeted her. It also did not escape his notice that she looked very pretty in a deep-blue sprigged-muslin dress.

Moving to the other side of the bed, Dr Amstel reached out to snap the clasp of his bag shut. "One journey taken at a gentle pace followed by copious amounts of bed rest upon arrival in London. It is not ideal, but Mr Darcy does not present any signs of a dangerous fever or infection."

Elizabeth smiled. "That is a relief."

"Now, I hope you take this in the spirit with which it is intended, but it would please me greatly if I did not see either of you in a professional capacity again."

"You will have to come and dine with us in that case."

"There would be no greater pleasure. Why I remember last time—"

Whatever Dr Amstel was about to say was cut off by Elizabeth placing her hand on his arm and declaring, "I shall put marzipan on the menu. The last time you were here, Molly kept finding you flowers in exchange for a nibble."

"You are right, of course. She had just begun to walk more confidently if I recall." Darcy did not hear the rest of the conversation as Dr Amstel and Elizabeth walked away from him, exchanging pleasantries. He rang the bell for Mrs Reynolds. He and Elizabeth would soon depart for London. He would need to be well prepared. It would be a slow and careful journey, and there would be no hiding place for her to evade his questioning.

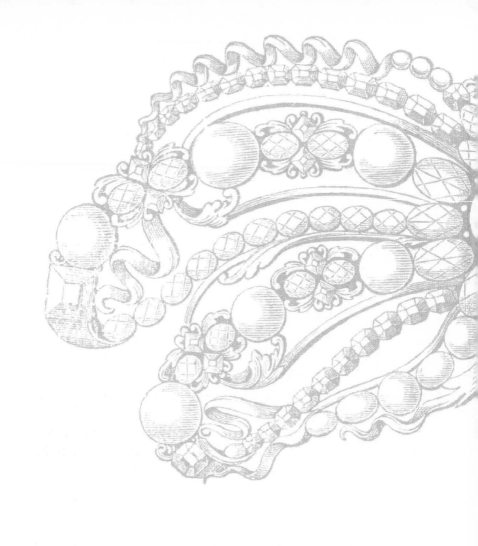

CHAPTER FOURTEEN

B y first light the next day, the Darcy carriage had been readied and its passengers settled inside. A flurry of activity had preceded their departure: a hastening of luggage; a swarming of servants around the carriage; kindly smiles; and offers of assistance to Darcy and Elizabeth as they entered the coach.

"I hope I do not presume too much to ask for news of Lady Luxford," Mrs Reynolds requested.

"We shall write to you as soon as we see her," Elizabeth replied.

Elizabeth will write but I cannot. Darcy attempted to keep the bitterness, which flooded him every time he was re-acquainted with his limitations, from his thoughts.

Ever since Amstel left, his mood had taken a sour turn. He kept returning to the doctor's words about Elizabeth's health. What was it that she had not told him? How best to proceed when he was at the mercy of others? Trapped and useless, he was powerless to move without assistance, unable to correspond without help, and wholly unable to recall information from his past that might help him understand the present.

His entire body ached and they had not yet departed. Even the journey from the house to the carriage had been painful. The footman had seen to it that his leg was propped up and that his walking cane was near his uninjured hand. There had been a brief moment of hesitation from Elizabeth about where she should sit. She started to take the seat next to him, presumably out of habit, but had settled instead in the seat facing him, allowing him to stretch out his good leg.

The deliberate act of distancing herself from him reminded Darcy that she still owed him an explanation for her behaviour. How to broach such a topic? It was a long way to London, and Darcy did not know what was worse: sitting in stifling silence or a confrontation he was unable to escape from.

They were some way into the journey when Elizabeth broke the silence. "Is there anything you wish to know before we arrive in London?" She turned her gaze from the carriage window to Darcy, her expressive eyes large and luminous in her pale face.

"What do you mean?" Darcy's reverie was broken. He had been so long thinking of what he wanted to say he had not noticed Elizabeth's own introspection. In fact, he had been so engaged in his own ill humour that he had not truly looked at her since their departure. He did so now, consciously taking in all that he saw. Her eyes were so arresting, it was all he could do not to stare into them. She had such a distinguished air, the darkness of her hair complementing the deep brown shades of her eyes. Yet, when she turned her head, all he could see were their green hues twinkling most charmingly against her creamy skin. Her face was entirely unforgettable. *Except*, thought Darcy sadly, *I have forgotten her.*

He wondered whether now was the time to ask about Fitzwilliam, but before he could do so, she smiled so gently and continued, "I was thinking of darling Molly. Naturally, it is not your fault that you do not remember her, but she will not understand. I do not wish her to be hurt in any way. It will be enough of a shock to see you so changed. I began to reflect upon all the charming rituals and games that you have with her. My mind turned upon the notion that you may wish to be prepared before meeting her. And Georgiana too, for that matter."

Darcy took a breath. It would be a welcome change to hear of something cheerful rather than stew in his own misery. "Nothing would please me more, in truth. Tell me something about her that only I would know."

A faraway look fell across Elizabeth's face, so lost was she in happier memories. But for all her smiles, Darcy could not help the feeling that she was not entirely at ease. She looked very tired and wan, he noted. He recalled Amstel's counsel about her health and decided that a trip to London was a rather long one to commence with an argument. Far better to pave the way for harmony before making demands. A pleasant conversation about their daughter would lay a much better foundation for the uncomfortable one regarding his cousin. He repositioned himself in his seat so as to hear her better. "I want to learn of Molly. I do not wish for her to be alarmed when we meet. It would not do for my tragic accident to affect her."

"Our wishes are very much aligned," Elizabeth said quietly. She was looking much paler than before. She closed her eyes and smiled softly. "It is impossible to name just one thing that only you would know. The bond you have with her is so precious. You are a very generous and affectionate father. You always kiss her good night, and, before you go away for any length of time, you will kiss her the total of all the nights you will be absent before you go." Her eyes still closed, her smile deepened. "Indeed, never before have I met a more sentimental father than you. I once overheard you request a shelf in your library to be cleared. You turned every shade of crimson before you privately admitted it was for Molly's books once she had outgrown them. You wanted them as a keepsake of all the stories you had read together." She opened her beautiful eyes which sparkled joyfully as she regarded him. "Why, I do believe I recognise the same shade of red upon your face now."

Darcy was indeed blushing most handsomely before her. "It is unfair to tease me about events I do not recall."

"When is it ever fair to tease?" Her grin widened. "You never complained too strenuously before."

Darcy could not resist smiling back. Tired and pale she might have been, but she had an innate ebullience that he found charming. A natural flirt, some might say. His mind could not help wandering back to his aunt. Lady Catherine had a great deal to observe when it came to the deportment of young ladies, especially when he was in earshot. He had always avoided such playful conversations with young women given how easily an arch comment could be misconstrued. Conversing easily with others had never been his forte, and it was often easier to let the women think they were being listened to rather than take the trouble to think of a reply.

But this was different. It was a wholly more enjoyable experience to be teased by one's wife, especially when she had a wit sharper than many of the satirists that he used to enjoy reading. Unconsciously, he leant forwards in his seat, her presence drawing him in. "I am at a disadvantage to counter your point. This is a decidedly one-sided argument!"

Those dark, expressive eyes widened as Elizabeth's eyebrows playfully rose in mock surprise. "Are we arguing? This feels much more pleasant than an argument."

Darcy smiled again. "Do we argue often?"

Elizabeth's smile dimmed a little. "Everyone argues occasionally. Our marriage is like any other in that regard."

Darcy noted the change in her voice and deliberately changed tack. "What of Georgiana? It sounds like she has greatly changed also."

Elizabeth's smile returned. Her demeanour relaxed as she began to describe how Georgiana had blossomed since her engagement and marriage. "In many ways, she is very different from the shy girl that I met years ago, but in essentials she is the same kind-hearted darling she has always been, only now she has the confidence to show it."

Darcy nodded. "I am pleased. That is what I always wished for her."

"I am longing to see her and her family."

"I too am the same. More than I should like to confess."

Darcy felt a familiar tug of guilt as he spoke. He did not wish to offend Elizabeth, but he could not help missing Georgiana. Out of all of his memories, the ones containing her were the most vivid. He sighed deeply. Elizabeth seemed to catch his conflict and offered her reassurances. "Georgiana is impatient to see you too."

"And the rest of my family?" Again, Elizabeth's smile faded. "Lord and Lady Matlock are well. Their oldest son Frederick is married, and his wife is expecting a darling companion for their daughter Grace." She paused, searching for the most tactful phrase for her next description. "Your aunt Lady Catherine has not changed since time immemorial, you will be pleased to hear. Her opinions are as prehistoric as her taste in furnishings."

At this, Darcy tipped his head back and laughed aloud. "I should take offence at your tone, but it is clear to me you are well acquainted with my aunt."

"Forgive me, your aunt is an older woman, and for that reason I should try to pay her due deference." Elizabeth's lips twisted in amused contrition.

"My aunt has been demanding deference since she was an infant. I do not think her advancing years alone should demand respect." Darcy caught her eye and was pleased to see he had made her smile.

"Do not trouble yourself on that front. We have long since healed the breach there."

"And what of our cousin Fitzwilliam?" They had been travelling and chatting for the best part of an hour. Darcy decided now was his moment to press.

"What of him? He is still the same decent man he ever was. I think the last campaign took a good deal out of him. You have seen the scar upon his face. He has never revealed the cause of it to us. My conjecture is that the remembrance is as painful as the injury was."

Darcy nodded his agreement. "I see." He paused, taking a deep breath. He glanced again at her. When she had been speaking, her face had been animated, and her cheeks were flushed. But now that she had stopped, her pallor had returned, and he could see she was fatigued. *Be gentle.* Fitzwilliam's words continually echoed in his mind.

With all the mildness he could summon, Darcy began, "Is there nothing else you wish to say of Fitzwilliam?"

Elizabeth smoothed her dress. "Whatever can you mean?"

Darcy looked at her carefully. "Forgive my blunt words, but I fear you have not told me everything."

Elizabeth's face flushed from white to red, and she asked quickly, "Why do you say that?"

"Call it instinct."

"Instincts are, by definition, the opposite of logic and reason, two attributes you may wish to call upon before you interrogate your wife." Elizabeth's tone sounded defensive, and she shivered a little, wrapping her arms around herself as she spoke.

Darcy felt a touch of guilt, but he continued nonetheless. The truth must out. "I do not wish to interrogate you. Indeed, I do not. But I must tell you—you are undoubtedly unaware of it—I was witness to a conversation between you and Fitzwilliam that appeared anything but cordial. I saw you from the library window. You must explain to me its meaning. He is my cousin, and you are my wife. You should tell me of any dispute between you."

Elizabeth frowned. "I did not know you saw us. I understand now why you may be confused." She paused, her lips trembling a little as she regained her composure. "We were not arguing as such. Fitzwilliam wished to do something that I disagreed with. Eventually, we came to an agreement, and he departed on civil terms."

"With no word of it to me?"

"I cannot justify his actions or lack thereof." Elizabeth spoke quietly.

"Yet you knew of his intentions."

"That point I shall concede. However, I did not know he would leave so soon." She drew a deep sigh. "I see that my actions have troubled you. Forgive me, it was unconsciously done."

"I beg to differ. You have most consciously concealed the truth from me. I cannot view it any other way."

Elizabeth's face fell at his retort. It was as if he had slapped her, such was the impact of his rebuff. Instantly, Darcy regretted his words, but before he could apologise, she spoke, her voice low and even. "I have never lied to you."

"Withholding the full story may not be an outright lie, but it is certainly less than honest."

Elizabeth broke her gaze from his, visibly fighting tears. A multitude of emotions were playing upon her lovely face. "Did it ever occur to you that I might have a weighty reason to keep you from knowing everything?"

"What reason could a man's wife have to conceal the truth from him?" Darcy's anger began to rise. How could it not at such an answer? She turned back to face him, hot angry tears glistening upon her pale skin. Her beautiful eyes held his in a long, hard stare. He had overstepped a mark, but he did not know what it was.

Eyes glinting dangerously, Elizabeth soon put him right. "I told you the truth once before," she retorted. "And look what good it did you."

Had she? He did not know when she meant, but it did not signify, not now as he bore witness to the sorrow in her eyes. She was trembling with emotion—anger or hurt, Darcy was not sure which. Her breathing came through fast and ragged as she fought back the sob threatening to break in her voice. He watched as she struggled to regain equanimity. His own treacherous heart was beating dangerously. He was angry, and he felt justified for it. But he did not wish to be the cause of any pain. Never could he recall making a woman cry. That had been Wickham's lot, and Darcy had vowed never to be like him.

Taking a steadying breath, he leant himself across the carriage as best he could and took her hand in his. "I do not wish to make you unhappy, but I consider myself a liberal man. I do not understand why you cannot trust me." His gentle gesture broke Elizabeth from her unhappiness, and she stared at his hand.

"You are quite right, my love." She drew her thumb lightly over Darcy's hand, the simple gesture leaving a trail of tenderness on his skin. "There is more to say, but I cannot tell you presently."

"You cannot or you will not?" It took every inch of restraint to keep the resentment from his voice.

Elizabeth appeared to appreciate his efforts and responded a touch more calmly. "It is a little of both. I *cannot* tell you all without accusing another. And I *will* not do so until I have more information. Once the accusation is made, it cannot be unsaid. The ramifications of which have lasting implications for our life as a family."

"When will you have the information you require?"

"When Fitzwilliam returns."

"Was this the urgent business that made him depart so soon?"

The carriage lurched as Darcy spoke, and Elizabeth closed her eyes and nodded. "Forgive me, travelling along this road makes me feel quite unwell." With tremendous effort, she opened her eyes and looked into his. "I vow, on all that I hold dear, that I shall tell you all that I can upon Fitzwilliam's return. Could you trust me enough to wait?"

Darcy looked upon her. She was so drawn. Amstel's words came back to him. *She does not always listen to her body when she should rest. She takes too much upon herself.* He had no choice but to place his faith in her.

"I promise to wait if you promise to tell me the minute you need assistance. It would not do for Molly to have two unwell parents." Her shoulders eased.

Darcy had no remembered experience to draw upon, but he sensed that he had said the right thing. Elizabeth dried her eyes and nodded weakly. He wished he knew her well enough to wrap his arms around her. There was something about Elizabeth that ignited every protective instinct in him. "You are unwell, and my leg has begun to hurt. I propose that we stop earlier than anticipated—perhaps you could suggest a place to the coachmen. Once our destination has been decided, I believe you should rest until we get there. There will be time enough for conversation later."

Darcy rapped the side of the coach with his cane, and Elizabeth spoke to Spiggs from the window. The fresh air appeared to do her good, and she seemed a better colour when she settled back down in the seat. "I have settled where we shall stay tonight. It is still a considerable distance, yet it is not as far as we had originally planned. We shall stop in an hour to change the horses. We should both rest until then," she informed him.

Elizabeth drew a blanket over herself and curled up to sleep. It did not take long; she was obviously exhausted. It took Darcy longer to rest. He watched Elizabeth's eyelashes flutter as she slept, wondering what information Fitzwilliam could be seeking. He might not be able to wait until his cousin's return, but he vowed to himself that he would try. He did not think he could bear to be the cause of Elizabeth's tears again. He gazed out of the window, the countryside drifting past him as he reflected on his conversation with his wife. He could not say why, but he knew that he had just passed his first test as a husband. He wondered what his next would be.

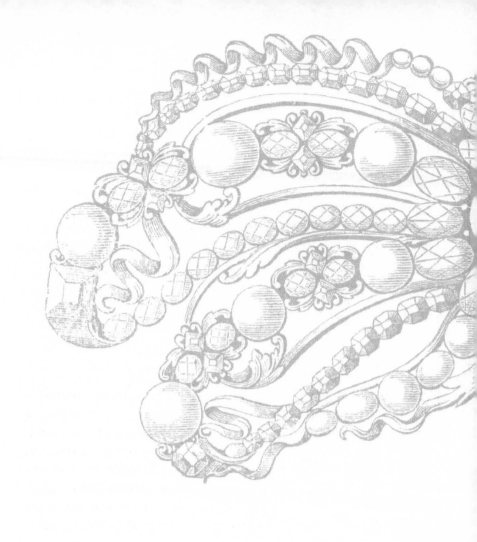

CHAPTER FIFTEEN

The suggestion to stop earlier than planned proved a prudent one. Spiggs had done his very best to provide a smooth journey, but Darcy's body had reached its limit. He had only slept a little as his leg was sore from the constant rocking of the carriage. Shifting in his seat, he attempted to loosen his back, stiff from holding his body still for so long. His injured hand throbbed up through his arm. He had reached the point where nothing but fresh air and proper bed rest would give him relief.

Mercifully, the carriage slowed outside a small, respectable-looking inn. Darcy did not recognise it, but Elizabeth did.

"We have finally arrived at Mr and Mrs Opposite's inn!" She gave a laugh as she peered out of the carriage. She had woken before him, and some of her natural colour had returned to her cheeks. She looked a good deal better for her rest.

"That cannot be their true name!" Darcy raised his eyebrows in surprise.

"No, my love, that is only our little sobriquet for them." She gave a quick smile. "You will see why in an instant."

Spiggs went inside, and the proprietors came out to see the carriage. Darcy immediately understood Elizabeth's joke. The couple before him were the complete opposite of one another. Where the woman was excessively tall, the man was incredibly short. Where he was plump, she was slim. And where he was silent, she filled any and every gap in the conversation with endless silly prattle. Darcy gritted his teeth. He had never been one to converse with the ridiculous, but Elizabeth seemed to thrive upon it. "Bear up, my love. Keep in mind she does a lovely breakfast should you feel your patience flag."

Darcy smiled. "As long as the beds here are well turned out, I shall be happy." She smiled back. It appeared that they had reached an unspoken truce after all that had happened in the carriage.

"Mr and Mrs Darcy! Well, I never! It has been such a long time since we had the honour. Why, I was speaking to Lady Heffron the other day—she is a very dear guest and regularly graces us with her presence—and she informed me that poor Mr Darcy had an unfortunate accident. These young men can be fools when it comes to their horses, and they do insist on riding out in all sorts of weather, I said to her, and it was most gratifying to hear her ladyship to be in agreement."

She paused, suddenly mindful that she might just have insulted possibly the richest man ever to stay at—and indeed return to—her fine establishment. "Goodness, Mr Darcy, I did not mean to imply you were careless in any way, rather that it takes a man of great sporting vigour and fortitude to ride out whenever he so chooses. Indeed, many young men of our acquaintance enjoy a good ride, do they not Mr Mulroney?" She did not wait for her husband to answer as she continued her breathless chitchat.

Sensing that food and a soft bed were fast slipping out of reach, Darcy impatiently put up his hand to interject. "Yes, madam, you are quite correct." Mrs Mulroney did not seem to take offence—or notice—of his curt tone. Elizabeth, however, appeared to sense that Darcy had expended all reserves of civility on the journey and could not be trusted to be in company entirely unsupervised.

"Perhaps, Mrs Mulroney, you have a manservant, or similar, that could help assist my husband from the carriage. I believe he is in dreadful need of some rest, and I have reminded him of your delicious breakfasts."

At this, Mrs Mulroney verily burst with pride and bobbed her head up and down in delight at Elizabeth's compliment. "Of course, of course. It would be a pleasure—nay an honour—to assist you in any way that we are able to." She flapped and clucked as her monosyllabic husband helped Darcy from the carriage.

"We shall put you in our very best apartments—you can be sure of it, sir! Such lovely views along the estuary! It will please me greatly for you to grace them again."

Elizabeth smiled at the woman. "I thank you but there is no need to prepare them. We are unable to accept your generous offer." When Mrs Mulroney started to protest, Elizabeth simply shook her head. "I am afraid a room on the ground floor would be preferable. Mr Darcy is to rest his leg, and therefore we must avoid the stairs. It is the doctor's request rather than our own."

"Oh, but Mrs Darcy! A woman of elevated standing such as yourself must certainly be accustomed to only the very best. You surely must desire to stay in our superior rooms."

"No, indeed." Elizabeth's eye caught Darcy's and she smiled mischievously. "I wish for quite *the opposite*."

Darcy stifled a laugh at the look of pure delight on her face. Thus, it was thanks to Elizabeth's powers of persuasion that Darcy found himself enjoying a first-rate dinner in a second-rate room. How many times had he passed this inn on his way to and from Pemberley and not taken another look? He certainly never would have thought to stop anywhere but the best available. *You would have thought it beneath you to stay here, let alone return,* Darcy mused to himself. *Yet it is surprisingly pleasant,* he thought, looking about at the dark-panelled room with its heavy oak furniture, light, cosy furnishings, and quilted eiderdown. It was small, but the bed was large and seemed comfortable enough.

It appeared as though he and Elizabeth would be sharing it tonight. A wave of nervous energy flowed through him. He had no recollection of what it would be like to spend the night alone in bed with a woman. He had been raised to treat the opposite sex with the utmost respect. For many years, Darcy had studiously kept the majority of his female acquaintances at arm's length. Paying notice to a woman for any length of time raised expectations from them, and Darcy had never found any woman worth his interest. *Elizabeth must have caught your notice. You have a child together, and you only need to talk to her to know she is warm-blooded.* He blushed, inwardly chafing. What was he thinking? She had as good as admitted that she knew the cause of his injuries but would not tell him more. Fitzwilliam had not thought it wise to speak to him either—what did that mean? He sighed, wondering when his wife would return, dreading it and hoping for it in equal measure.

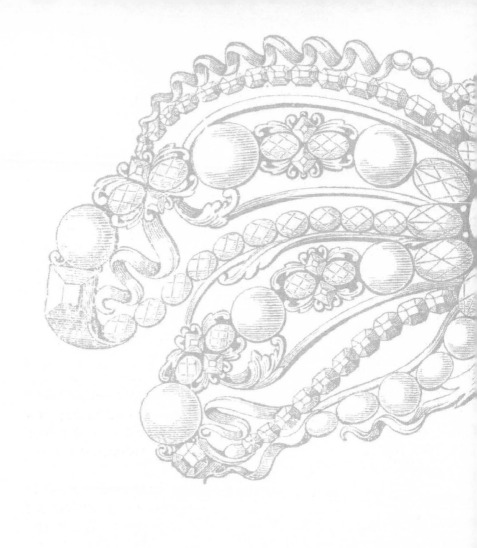

CHAPTER SIXTEEN

Elizabeth had taken a walk to get some fresh air before nightfall, leaving Darcy settled in a wing-backed chair near the fireplace, his leg resting upon a cushioned footstool. She had seen to it that the meal was to his satisfaction but had eaten very little herself.

He looked about the room. Robertson had travelled ahead to their intended stopping point, so he would have to do without his valet for tonight. He could not ask Elizabeth to help him, surely? He would be able to do much of it one-handed, but he did not know whether he could tolerate the pain if he got stuck. It rankled him to be so dependent on another. A knock on the door told him of Elizabeth's return. To Darcy's mind, she had never looked prettier. Her healthy colour had returned, and her eyes sparkled with the vigour brought on by exercise.

"I feel excessively better for some fresh air. How are you faring?" She found a chair and sat opposite him.

"I have not had the luxury of a walk, but I am not as sore as I was previously."

"Forgive me, my words were insensitive. Would you like me to open a window for you?" Her face was at once alight with concern.

"I thank you, no. In truth, it is a little cold."

"You poor thing. It must be dreadful not being able to move about to warm yourself." Elizabeth started to busy herself around Darcy, calling for a maid to light their fire.

Waiting for the maid to return with some kindling, Elizabeth turned to Darcy. "There is a small dressing room attached to this one. I shall ask the girl to attend to me, then I shall see to you." Upon seeing Darcy protest, she laughed. "Do not be stubborn. Would you rather be undressed by a stranger or by your wife?"

You are both to me, thought Darcy, but he did not say anything. Taking his uncertainty for embarrassment, Elizabeth smiled. "You will not offend my sensibilities. We are well beyond that."

Darcy swallowed. He nodded wordlessly and watched as she left the room to speak to the maid. A mouse of a girl came to quietly prepare the fire, and Darcy stared into it, trying his best not to eavesdrop on whatever was happening in the small room next to theirs.

At last, Elizabeth returned, looking lovely in her nightdress. Her hair was loose and fell about her shoulders in cascades of dark, glossy curls. With her dark doe-like eyes contrasting against her pale skin, she had every appearance of a forest nymph. *It is as though some sprite or pixie has ingratiated themselves into my life totally unbeknownst to me,* thought Darcy. She had a dressing gown tied tightly around her, and Darcy could see silken slippers on her slender feet. He swallowed again, his mouth suddenly very dry. This situation was entirely new to him. He did not know what to expect or even how to behave.

Gently, she helped him to his feet and guided him to the edge of the bed. She was so very close to him that he could see her blush extend all the way from her ivory cheeks down the curve of her neck. Leaning him forwards, she pulled his coat from his shoulders. How many times had Robertson performed this simple task? Never before had such an innocent gesture made him feel so utterly exposed.

Elizabeth gently untied his cravat. "Do not ask me to tie it up for you. You have suffered enough indignities without my efforts." Next, she unbuttoned his waistcoat before removing it. With soft fingers, she loosened his shirt and turned from him. "Perhaps you could try to remove your shirt yourself while I find your night clothes."

Darcy managed to pull his shirt past his injured arm and over his head. He sat on the edge of the bed awaiting Elizabeth's return. She came out of the dressing room holding his nightshirt in her hands. She stopped suddenly in front of him, her eyes fixed upon his exposed torso. "My poor love, I cannot believe how strong you have been to endure this." Moving closer to him, she traced her fingertips over the scars criss-crossing his chest. Darcy trembled under her touch.

"You are cold," she murmured.

Darcy felt anything *but* cold, but words failed him; the sensation of her fingers caressing his body was nearly unbearable in its softness. She eased the nightshirt over his head, then bent down to help loosen his boots and trouser buttons. Propriety dictated that Darcy should look away, but he could not. All he could do was to keep his dark eyes fixed upon his wife as she ran her hands along his body. He could not speak. It was too much, too intimate a gesture to know what to do.

Elizabeth was not insensible to the tension flowing between them and graced him with a bashful smile. "Do you think you could finish the rest?" Darcy nodded. He could no longer trust his body in Elizabeth's presence and was almost grateful for the respite in her attentions.

She returned to the small dressing room, presumably to finish getting ready to retire. Darcy somehow managed to divest himself of his remaining clothes until he was only in his nightshirt, thankful it reached somewhere just above his knees. He carefully swung his legs under the warm quilt and waited for her to return.

She re-entered the room softly; he was pleased to see her hair was still loose and free. Darcy wondered what she would do if he ran his fingers through her curls. She caught him looking at her and blushed.

"I had a moment to reflect during my walk," she said as she slipped under the covers. It was such a natural gesture, one that she had undoubtedly performed many times before, yet Darcy could only stare at the sight of her, so slender and light against the hard, imposing headboard. So natural was it to her to be there that she continued, completely unaware of the effect she was having on him.

"I am sorry for the way I spoke to you before. You have suffered greatly, and I do not wish to add to it." Elizabeth inhaled. "I shall not speak to you again of what you saw between Fitzwilliam and I —not until I know more—but I do wish for us to become close again. It pains me to see you at such a loss."

Darcy felt the pressure of her body on the mattress next to him. He turned his eyes towards her, this bewitching imp who seemed to know him so well. The dwindling light from the fire bathed her face, setting it aglow with a comforting warmth. He nodded; at this moment he would like nothing more than for her to speak to him with such gentle intimacy.

"Tell me of our wedding day. I wish to picture it." Darcy's voice came low and urgent. Never before could he recollect such an alluring vision as she was before him. "Help me to understand that I am a married man."

Elizabeth nodded and smiled so beautifully up at him. Eyes twinkling, she teased, "Scholars proclaimed our wedding day as one of historical importance. Rain clouds gathered overhead, and biblical gales blew through the streets of London. All who attended declared it an omen."

"I thought I could trust you to be honest!"

"It is the truth!" She opened her eyes wide in feigned offence, all the while grinning at him. "On the carriage ride to the church, would you like to know what I heard upon the breeze—above the noise of the inevitable bolts of lightning you must understand?"

Darcy returned her grin. "Must I guess? I dare not speculate."

The dimples in Elizabeth's cheeks deepened, and she became more animated with her tale. "Upon my life, I heard the most sorrowful caterwauling echoing across the rooftops. And what, do you imagine, was its cause?"

"Pardon me but I cannot think." Darcy leant closer to her, completely enchanted. Elizabeth, echoing his movement, leant towards him.

"It was the sound of every mama of the *ton* mourning the

wedding day of Fitzwilliam Darcy, the most eligible bachelor in London!" She began to laugh. "You could hear it all the way from Hertfordshire."

He chuckled with her. "You, madam, are incorrigible!"

"How did you know those were the exact words the vicar said to me upon my arrival at the church?" Elizabeth's eyes sparkled as she laughed.

Darcy laughed out loud, his ribs beginning to hurt. Before he knew it, the words tumbled from his mouth, "Stop it, you minx."

Elizabeth stopped instantly. Her face was so close to his. "I have missed you calling me that." Her eyes studied every part of his face. Holding his gaze, she continued softly, "In truth, our wedding day was the happiest day of my life. We were married from our church in Hertfordshire, surrounded by our closest family and friends. We departed for Pemberley not long afterwards. I was an insufferable creature—laughing and smiling far too much to be allowed. You were not much better. I do not think your acquaintance had ever seen you so animated."

Darcy smiled softly and she continued, "You were very handsomely turned out. After being your wife for these past years, I know that the more nervous you are, the more care you take with your appearance." Her full, perfect lips curved into a smile.

"You do know me well." Darcy laughed softly. "And what of you? I wish to picture you."

Elizabeth broke their gaze. She looked past their bed into the smouldering embers of the fireplace. "I wore the most perfect dress. You had it made especially for me. I have never owned a finer one, although I love you so very dearly that I would have married you wearing only rags. I wore your grandmother's Honiton lace for a veil, and you gave me some of your mother's jewellery."

She looked back at him, her eyes misty. "It is not for me to say whether I looked beautiful or not, but after we said our vows, you turned to me and whispered that you would never forget this moment."

Darcy nodded mutely, suddenly overcome by an intense melancholy. He had indeed forgotten it, and he began to suspect it would never be returned to him.

Elizabeth seemed to have thought likewise. "But enough of that. No more sorrow, it is agreed." Darcy nodded.

She asked, "Is there anything else you wish to know?"

The firelight had all but disappeared, and now the only thing keeping Darcy warm was her body pressed against his. Suddenly, he knew there was only one thing he desperately wanted to envision. "Tell me of our wedding night." Darcy held her gaze.

Elizabeth bit her lip. "You are asking me to speak to you openly?"

Darcy tried to ignore the colour rising in his own cheeks. "I have no recollection of any of it. None at all. And I find myself here, alone with you. You know me so well, and I know so little of you—of us. You must help me understand what you expect from me."

Comprehension dawned on Elizabeth's face. "You wish to understand how it was between us?" Darcy nodded wordlessly.

Shutting her eyes, Elizabeth put her hands to her cheeks, laughing a bit awkwardly. "I am sure I shall blush as red as a tomato as I tell you all."

She drew in a deep breath. "After our wedding breakfast, we travelled to your London residence before departing for Pemberley. We spent the day wandering around Hyde Park like hopeless fools doing nothing but laughing, then we returned to dine alone at the house. You could not stop kissing me and touching me. You did not care who was nearby. It made me feel light-headed—I had never known what it was like to be so close to a man, much less be alone with one.

"After dinner, I told you that I would need some time to be ready and you should come to my room in half an hour. In truth, I only needed twenty minutes, but I remember using those additional ten minutes to think about all that was to come. When you arrived, I had never been more nervous, and I believe you were the same. You were so tender, so loving that all my fears disappeared in an instant. You told me how ardently you loved me, and you kissed me so gently that I felt as though I should melt in your arms."

Elizabeth exhaled deeply. "I had never seen a man's body

before, not in the flesh—only statues at the galleries in London. I had always thought you handsome, but I never knew you to be so truly beautiful as you were before me." She sighed. "I had known for a long time that I loved you, but I fell in love with your body that night. By the light of the fire, I could see every curve of muscle ripple as you moved towards me. Every line of your body was strong and masculine."

She reached out, her eyes now open. "There is a line from here" —she touched his neck, just below his ear—"to here"—she traced her finger down his neck to the tip of his shoulder blade—"that I have always adored."

Darcy shivered. Who knew such a feather-light touch could wield such power?

Elizabeth smiled at him. "I always thought our temperaments complemented each other well, but I learnt that, with our bodies, it was our contrasts that so mattered."

Darcy raised his eyebrows, puzzled. Elizabeth closed her eyes again. "Where you were strong, I was yielding. Where I was nervous, you were confident. And...where I was soft, you were hard." She groaned softly. "It is a good thing that it is dark. I am sure I shall burn from shame."

"Do not stop." Darcy could hardly breathe. It was too much to hear such words about his own body from a woman's lips. *This, surely, is why women do not talk openly to men of desire. No man could withstand it.* He reached out and touched her arm, caressing her wrist until he took her hand into his uninjured one.

"You told me I had nothing to fear, that you loved only me and your first thought was of my happiness. You made me promise, just as you did earlier, to tell you if I needed anything from you. I should never be afraid to tell you of my heart. And then..."

She paused. Darcy inhaled sharply, waiting for her words. "And then you were everywhere...your face was above me, your arms were around me...and...and you...and you were *within* me." She stopped, overcome by embarrassment. Darcy looked at her steadily. "I can still remember your eyes. They were so fine and dark. You looked into mine just as you are now, and I had never felt so loved and cherished."

"And what happened then?" Darcy's voice was so low it was almost a whisper.

Elizabeth's face was so close to his now he could feel her breath upon his lips. "You closed your eyes," she whispered back. "And then you lost yourself to me."

At that moment, Darcy had no other thought than to kiss her. She was too intoxicatingly beautiful to resist. *She is your wife in the eyes of the law and God. It does not matter that you do not remember your vows. She has just told you of her love for you. It is not a sin to desire your own wife.*

With the greatest reverence, he leant towards her face and stole the gentlest of kisses from her lips. Then, running his unhurt hand along her body, he pulled her softly towards him. His injured hand moved towards her waist, and Elizabeth broke from their embrace instantly.

"My love, I am sorry." Elizabeth was breathless. "We should stop. The doctor said you should rest."

Darcy nodded, wincing with pain and embarrassment. He turned from her, suddenly ashamed. *She fell in love with your body before the accident. Who would want you as you are now?* It was all he could do not to shout with anger at the thought.

"My love, are you quite well?"

"You are right, we should stop. I am not yet healed." Darcy let the silence between them deepen.

"Good night then," she whispered.

Darcy nodded and said no more. He felt her sigh and turn away.

He lay there for some time in the darkness. He did not remember the first time that Elizabeth had rejected him all those years ago in Kent, and he therefore did not know how much gentler she had been in this refusal. All he knew was that his wife no longer welcomed his touch. A powerful sense of rejection flowed through his body, adding itself to the new aching feeling of acute embarrassment. Every feeling twisted back on itself, leaving him confused and sore. He did not think he could bear another moment of it.

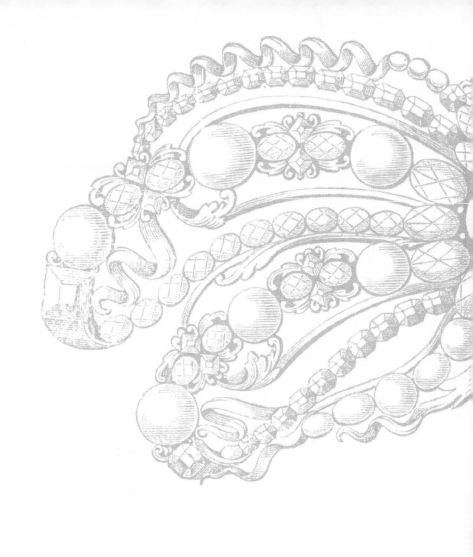

CHAPTER SEVENTEEN

Darcy awoke early the next morning to an empty bed. Sunlight peeped through cracks in the curtains, and he could hear the faint rumblings from the livestock in the fields surrounding the inn. He stretched a little and began a mental inventory of his body. The pain in his head and leg had subsided. There was a fine balance to be struck between the sharp jarring pain of using his leg or the stiff dull ache of sitting still. He pressed his fingers into the muscles in his calf, easing some of the pressure. It was his hand that troubled him the most now. The scar tissue gave his hand a warped appearance and constantly felt tight and uncomfortable. Perhaps it would ease over time. Darcy fervently hoped so.

Relieving the cramp from his legs, he looked down and realised that someone—Elizabeth presumably—had wedged a folded blanket under his injured leg. A dart of pleasure rushed through him at the thought of Elizabeth's hands upon his body in the night, but then the unpleasant memory of her rejection returned. She had not wanted him to touch her.

Darcy sorely regretted asking her of their first night together. It was now impossible for him not to imagine it. As soon as he had kissed her, he knew that he would never want to stop.

Part of him wished he had not slept so long. He wondered what it would have been like to be there as she woke. Would her eyelashes flutter as she opened her eyes? How would she have received his presence? Would she have bestowed upon him a loving smile? Given she was not here when he awoke, she must have wished to avoid a repeat of last night's awkwardness. The sensation of her lips against his set his pulse racing. He winced again and raked his hand through his hair in an attempt to dispel some of the tension coursing through him.

A movement from the other end of the room caught his eye. It was his wife, sitting upon a chair by the empty fire, her legs and feet tucked under a blanket. Her hair wild with tumbling curls, she was bent over a little book. Turning a few pages, she scanned over the words then stood quietly, shivering a little in the early morning air. She took the book into the dressing room. Darcy closed his eyes. Thankfully, she had not seen that he was awake, and he would have a moment alone to compose himself before greeting her.

She returned shortly, wrapping her dressing gown around her for warmth. Darcy could see she still had the little leather-bound book in her hand. Upon seeing him she smiled and drew closer to the bed, sitting down tentatively by his side. "How did you sleep?"

"Not well. I feel rather sore."

Elizabeth looked at him with sympathy. "I heard you moaning in the night. I think perhaps you had struck your leg against something in your sleep."

Her words were so innocent, but Darcy could only blush at the thought of her sleeping so close to him. In an attempt to divert his thoughts, he nodded towards the folded blanket. "I thank you for your concern." His voice was colder than he had intended.

Elizabeth fell quiet for an instant. "I have something for you, if you would care to see it." She spoke softly, but there was an undertone of steel to her voice. She held out the little book and showed it to him.

"What is this?"

"My diary. You gave it to me as a gift before the very first time you departed on business. You said I should write in it whenever I missed you. I was diligent when you were absent." Her mouth gave a wry smile. "When you returned, I was less so. It is a faithful account of our life together whenever I had need to write of it."

"Why do you wish me to have it?"

Elizabeth's expression changed. She seemed older and wearier than last night. "It appears that we cannot speak of the past without it ending in distress for us both. Perhaps this way you will be able to understand our life together at your own pace."

"You understand that I shall struggle." A sense of trepidation filled Darcy. "What if I shall never be able to read as I used to?"

"As I said to you once before, much can be overcome once we take the trouble to practise." She placed the book gently upon the bed beside him. As she did so, her eyes unconsciously swept across his form.

He felt a prickle of embarrassment creep up his neck—he was not yet used to being so informally attired around a woman as he now was. It took a Herculean effort for his eyes not to wander across her lovely person in return. His eyes met hers, and he gazed into their shadowy depths. "Did I follow your advice?"

Her face broke into an irrepressibly impish smile. "Of sorts." The dimples in her cheeks deepened charmingly. "We are married, are we not?"

Darcy could only guess at her meaning. "Then I shall take your advice, and I shall also take your diary."

"Good." Elizabeth paused. "It is for your eyes only, you must understand. There are some passages about certain family members that I would not want repeated." Her eyes flashed merrily. "And there are some passages that I would not want read by anyone but you."

Darcy nodded, his mind racing as he interpreted her words. Blushing, she rose from his bedside. "I promised you a delightful breakfast. Should I arrange it for you?" Darcy nodded again, trusting that she would know what to order. She left him to ready herself for the day.

Breakfast was served not long after Elizabeth left. His instinct had been correct, and Elizabeth had seen to it that everything was prepared to his taste. His brow contracted thinking of it. It unsettled him that she should know him in every intimate detail, yet he could not even say when her birthday was. His eyes flickered over the little diary. He *would* read it, or at least he would try to. Any insight into this new life he had acquired would be very much appreciated.

His mind drifted to what words were to be viewed by him alone, and he felt his pulse begin to quicken in anticipation. *No,* he chastised himself inwardly, *you must apply your rational mind to this. Do not be blinded by her charms, plentiful as they are. Desire of a woman's body is not the same as ardent love of her soul. Remember your promise to only marry for sincere and mutual affection.*

A slip of memory, tremulous and echoing, passed through his mind's eye; it was him as a young boy of fifteen, sitting at his mother's bedside during one of her bad turns. He had been at the cusp of manhood when she died; her passing had marked the end of his childhood and the beginning of a new chapter in his life. For all his appearances of a boy ready to be a man, he had wept bitter child's tears at her death. Her last request of him had been simple. *Look after your father and little Georgiana, and promise me that you will be happy.* It had sounded so easy, but in truth, what was happiness? Happiness was only an absence of sadness, and there was too much melancholy about him to feel anything else but sorrowful. He thought of his parents' blissful marriage; only a profound love would have induced him up the aisle. In marrying Elizabeth, he must have considered his promise fulfilled. Perhaps Elizabeth's diary would help him understand how he had come to that conclusion. His curiosity was piqued, he could not deny it. *As long as you can finish it before you reach old age.* Sighing a little, Darcy turned his attention to the one reliable source of happiness in the room and enjoyed a pleasant breakfast, just as Elizabeth had promised.

Elizabeth returned as Darcy was finishing his meal. She was dressed for the day now, looking so very different from last night. With a pang, Darcy realised that he missed her untamed curls. It was a privilege to see her thus, he realised a little possessively. He resolved to keep his desire at bay if he was ever to discover the truth of his accident. Collecting himself, he returned to the business at hand. Elizabeth, it seemed, had used her time to organise for their coach to be packed and had sourced someone to help Darcy with dressing. *I am hopeless with cravats* had been her excuse. They were to continue their journey to London as soon as Darcy felt ready.

"Have you eaten?"

"Only a little. It is for the best that I did not join you. I often feel unsettled on long journeys."

She does look unwell, thought Darcy. She departed not long after their conversation, leaving Darcy to the indignity of being manhandled by the equally uncomfortable Mr Mulroney.

As they made their way to London, Darcy and Elizabeth spoke of everything polite and nothing of consequence. At some point, Elizabeth fell asleep again. Darcy watched her as she slept; her lovely face was the picture of serenity. His eyes swept down the graceful curve of neck to the rise and fall of her chest as she breathed. For all her secrets, he could recall no handsomer woman of his acquaintance. He wished he could touch her as he had the night before; to feel her heart beat against his own. Instead, he reached into his pocket and touched the smooth little diary. How many days would it be before they reached London? There, he would be reunited with Georgiana, Bingley, and now Molly. He would have time enough to read it then. Squeezing his hand around the leather cover, he prayed for the answers to soothe his troubled mind.

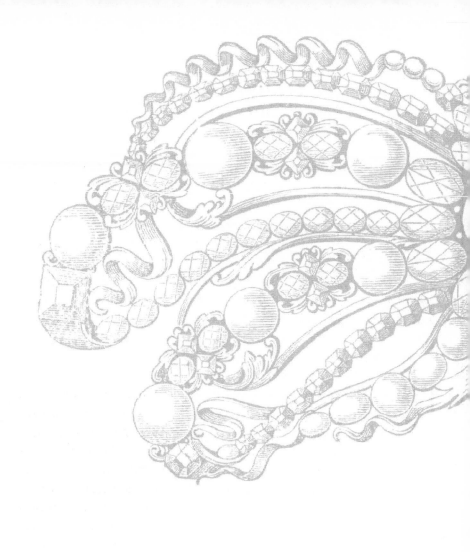

CHAPTER EIGHTEEN

I t took Darcy and Elizabeth two more days of travel to reach London. They had stopped at more distinguished establishments along the way, but if Darcy were honest with himself, nothing compared to their first night together at the modest little inn. Whenever they had stopped, Elizabeth had behaved cordially and respectfully, but there had been no suggestion that they should return to their previous arrangement. In the evenings, they would dine together in the private rooms of their accommodation, but each night she would return to her chambers after wishing him a chaste good night. He could not understand it. Had she not professed her love for him? As master of Pemberley and being in possession of the Darcy fortune, he knew his own worth as a sought-after husband. He could not countenance her behaviour. Perhaps she truly was worried that he had not yet regained his full strength. Would she always treat him thus? Part of him felt frustrated by her actions, and he found himself justly annoyed with her. But another much more profound part of him desired her company more than ever. In all honesty, he had never been more intrigued by a woman than he had by Elizabeth. Each night, her diary was by his bedside, yet he did not dare look inside. He told himself that to do so would be an act of weakness, an admission that she had caught his interest. Truth be told, this was not the entirety of the matter. To read her diary would allow Elizabeth to invade his thoughts even more deeply than she had already. He wished for his judgment to be rational; it was becoming impossible to think clearly when his mind turned to her.

Glancing out of the window, Darcy noted a change in the traffic trundling along the roads: the carriages were larger and the people within them louder; there was a greater sense of purpose in the travellers that he passed and an even greater smell; the odours of spices from every corner of the world blended with the undertones of different cultures, ideas, and colours; everything seemed newer, brighter, and altogether more cacophonous than the countryside he had just left. They were close to London.

He returned his gaze to the carriage's interior as he and Elizabeth were transported through the bustling streets. Elizabeth had not said much, he noted. She kept tapping her foot against the floor of the carriage, and she twisted the blanket in an anxious manner. Why would she be nervous? Her eyes drifted over his leg. *Is she concerned for me or because of me?* Darcy wished she would either speak her mind or stop fidgeting. It seemed most unlike Elizabeth to stay silent on a subject. She glanced at his hand. *It is because of me she is worried.* It was the only conclusion he could draw.

Darcy felt a jolt of apprehension pass through him. Aware of his altered appearance, he self-consciously shifted in his seat. He had wondered so much at the changes in others that he had not considered how he would appear to those closest to him. Georgiana must not be given cause to fret. Darcy's mouth tightened involuntarily.

And what of your daughter? The thought burned through him, causing his heart to pound. *Consider yourself lucky if she does not run away screaming,* he told himself. He glanced back at Elizabeth. Perhaps that was the cause of her nervous energy. She was anxious that he might frighten Molly. A constricting sensation gripped at Darcy. It was dread. He was dreading this. *What father dreads meeting his own child?*

A father who cannot properly care for his child. A father who cannot pick her up, cannot teach her to ride, cannot read a book to her. Yes, that sort of father has a great deal to dread.

Suddenly, he had a huge desire for air, to break the oppressive anxiety that was gnawing fervently at him. His hand shaking, he opened the window a little, the bustling streets of London providing a welcome distraction from his inner turmoil.

Elizabeth caught his gesture and smiled sympathetically. "It is not long now. Soon you will be in a more comfortable seat." Darcy gave a curt nod, relieved that he did not have to explain his sudden need for cool air.

"What should I say?" His voice came low.

Startled, Elizabeth's head turned towards him, her eyes full of surprise. "What do you mean?"

"When I meet Molly, what should I say to her?"

Elizabeth's body relaxed utterly at his words. She looked at him fondly. "You will find the words, I am sure. And if you cannot find them, I daresay she will." She turned her head back to gaze out of the window, and her face danced with pleasure. "Oh, but we are close. Do you recognise anything?"

Darcy shifted himself a little to gain a better view. "I can see the garden not far from my"—he caught himself—"not far from *our* house. I recall accompanying Georgiana there when she was a child."

Elizabeth smiled at him. "That is correct. Luxford and Georgiana have a residence not far from ours. She loves that garden too. You told me that you both used to invent names and biographies for those walking within it. I believe that the idea to name Mr and Mrs Opposite sprung from that conversation."

Quite suddenly, Darcy saw himself as an adolescent, holding an infant Georgiana's hand, pointing out which of the two elderly gentlemen on the bench was actually a knight of the realm. In that instant, he found himself lost so in the memory that he did not notice the carriage pull to a stop.

"Darcy, it is good to see you!"

Darcy watched as Bingley bounded towards them with all the grace of a wayward puppy. "When I heard of your imminent arrival, Jane and I knew we had to be here to greet you. We have all been so terribly worried!" He beckoned to Darcy with a warm smile. "Come, let me assist you."

To his intense relief, Darcy noted that dear Bingley had changed little from the jovial friend of his university days. His relief soon turned to trepidation as he witnessed Bingley nearly trip over his own feet in enthusiasm and wondered whether perhaps he should ask a footman for help instead. He steeled himself; he could bear every indignity imaginable if it meant seeing dearest Georgiana.

He glanced up. A tall man was on the steps waiting to greet them. *This must be Georgiana's husband.*

Robert Ashcombe, Viscount Luxford, was wiry and awkward, a combination of angular joints and long limbs crowned with an Adam's apple that bobbed continuously as he spoke. He was not ugly, Darcy conceded, but not at all the man he had imagined Georgiana to marry. Thankfully, Elizabeth descended first and, in a calm and efficient manner, proceeded to organise everyone to ensure maximum comfort with minimal fuss. Darcy was assisted up the steps by a sturdy-looking footman whilst using his cane to keep some semblance of pride. At the top, he found himself face-to-face with Luxford, who seemed a little dumbstruck by Darcy's altered appearance.

"Do you know, this could be the start of a joke." Elizabeth broke the silence. "What do you get when the quietest man in London meets the most reserved man in Derbyshire?"

Both looked at her in surprise.

"A supreme awkwardness, it would appear." She gave Luxford a sisterly hug, one that he was entirely unprepared for. Stepping back, she laughed at her brother-in-law's stunned expression. She squeezed his arm affectionately. "Do not leave me with a silence to fill, for you know I shall find something wicked to say." Something ahead caught her notice, and she suddenly left them both and nearly fell into the embrace of a charming young woman who was standing next to Bingley. Darcy did not recognise her, but their mode of expression was so alike that he presumed it was her sister Jane Bingley. Darcy watched them affectionately fuss about each other. Elizabeth turned to him and said gently, "You do not mind if I go ahead to see my little Molly? I cannot bear to be parted from her another instant."

Not since she had burst into his room to tell him of Georgiana's new-born son had he seen such a smile across her face. It was evident she wished for nothing more than to be reunited with their daughter, yet she was hesitant to leave him unattended. Darcy felt an unexpected pang of guilt. Perhaps he had been too quick to read her avoidance of him as a personal slight. When had he considered her feelings? She must have suffered the pain of separation acutely, yet she had not uttered one word of complaint. Inwardly chastising himself for his churlish behaviour, he said awkwardly, "Of course you should go." Then in a softer tone he added, "I imagine she will be expecting you at any moment."

Elizabeth placed a gentle hand on his arm. "I believe she will be awaiting us *both*." Darcy's stomach contracted at the thought of becoming reacquainted with his daughter. What if he should upset her? Elizabeth had such faith in his abilities as a father—what if he could not love Molly as he ought? Elizabeth thankfully read his silence correctly and squeezed his arm. "You have nothing to fear. Molly adores you."

"I shall await a footman." He carefully placed his hand over hers, admiring its softness. He was rewarded with another dazzling smile. Reaching up, she kissed his cheek, then turned to link arms with Jane as they left the men in the hall below.

Darcy stared at the ornate staircase. It was impossible for him to climb the stairs unaided, and he had no other option but to ask Luxford to arrange help. He opened his mouth to say something, but Luxford spoke first. "I must thank you for your advice, Darcy. You were entirely correct, as usual."

Darcy raised his eyebrows. He had no idea as to the meaning of Luxford's words and so replied ambiguously. "That is gratifying to know. In which area of expertise am I found to be right?"

Luxford's Adam's apple shook vigorously. "When we spoke of fatherhood."

Darcy's eyes met his, and he was struck by their earnestness. "You told me it was too miraculous to comprehend. I understand your words now." Luxford shifted his weight and smiled at Darcy. "My son is a miracle, born of love. I did not know how profound a feeling it could be. I am glad that I now share this with you."

"And I am glad for it also." Every part of Darcy hoped he could live up to the father everyone thought him to be. He glanced at Luxford again. For all his awkwardness, his new brother-in-law had every appearance of a devoted and decent man. He was beginning to see why Georgiana may have favoured this match. He wondered at the relationship he had with Luxford. They seemed to be on such friendly terms that they could freely discuss such intimate subjects.

"How fares Georgiana?"

Here, Luxford's face lit up. The love he felt for his wife was evident. Everything in his body changed as it swelled with pride. "She does admirably well. She was tired, but the doctor pronounced her as fit as a fiddle—or at least as well as can be expected in the circumstances."

"You called for a doctor?" Darcy could not keep the concern from his voice. "Was it necessary?"

Luxford stared at Darcy, his delicate features suffused with confusion. "Not necessary, merely a precaution. It was for reassurance really. I do not wish to overstep when I say you of all people would understand." Darcy did not get a chance to question his new brother-in-law further, as at that moment a footman arrived to assist him.

As he was helped up the stairs, Darcy was struck by an unpleasant thought. For the first time that he could recall, he felt nervous upon seeing Georgiana. She had long been a source of comfort to him. Dependent as she was on his care, she had been a constant in a life of tumultuousness. Georgiana alone knew how deeply he missed their parents.

Perhaps he had confided his sorrow to Elizabeth. She seemed to know a great deal about him and his childhood. It had never been a hardship to care for Georgiana; she had been a sweet-spirited and modest girl. The only pain he ever associated with her was not of her making. Listening to her broken-hearted sobbing over that wastrel Wickham was probably the last memory he had of her. The space between a fifteen-year-old girl and a twenty-one-year-old woman was sure to be far more profound than just six years. How had she changed? How would she greet him? All this and more raced through his mind as he found himself in front of an ornate door leading to a sitting room.

His heart pounding, Darcy knocked once and awaited admittance. A chorus of female voices called to him to enter, and he gingerly opened the door. The sight that greeted him would stay with him forever. Shafts of light tumbled through the lofty windows and illuminated the room with a serene glow. On the sofa by the fireplace was Georgiana, looking more radiant and lovely than he had ever seen her. In her arms was a small blanket that was moving jerkily. Elizabeth and Jane were either side of Georgiana, cooing at the baby within it.

On his entry, Elizabeth shifted her gaze to Georgiana. Her face was a picture of pride and affection. Across the room, Darcy and Georgiana locked their gazes. Years of unspoken love passed between them in that instant, and Darcy felt the sting of tears in his eyes. He opened his mouth to say something, but before he could, a flurry of ribbons and curls flung itself towards him and wrapped itself around his legs. He looked down at the little whirlwind and instantly fell in love.

The little girl clinging to him was Elizabeth in miniature. She had her mother's dark curls, an identical rose-bud mouth, and the same dark, long lashes. The only difference was her eyes. They were the darkest blue, just like her aunt Georgiana's. *A gift from your grandmother*, he thought to himself. Her smile, too, he had seen before. It was identical to his father's knowing grin whenever he had brought home an unexpected gift for his children. It was as though everyone that Darcy had ever loved was mirrored back to him in one angelic face. *Un coup de foudre*, as the French would say. The lightning bolt. Instant and irrevocable love at first sight. He was rendered speechless by it. Luckily for him, Molly was not so afflicted.

"Papa, my papa! Where did you go?" Her question brought Darcy to his senses.

"I have been ill, but I feel much better now, my darling." His eyes caught Elizabeth's as he spoke. Her eyes were glassy, and she looked at him with such earnest affection. "Although I must take a little care with my hand and leg."

His beloved daughter let out a gasp and released her grip. So awe-struck was he by Molly, Darcy had not even noticed the pain. "Do not be sorry. I feel altogether much better for seeing you."

Molly reached for Darcy's hand and recoiled a little. "Oh Papa, your fingers!" Darcy paused, searching for a way to explain. Before he could answer, Molly brought his hand to her lips and kissed each of his fingers in turn. "I kiss them better?" Little pearls of white teeth beamed up at him, and he was utterly charmed. Darcy found himself led by the hand to Georgiana.

His sister was exactly how he remembered yet also nothing like the painfully shy girl of his fractured memory. Cradling her precious baby, the Georgiana before him was nothing short of radiant. She was confident felicity personified. He bent down and kissed her on the cheek. As he did so, the little blanket moved, and Darcy could see a tiny baby. Smiling, he leant down and kissed the infant on the forehead. Neither could speak for a moment, so lost were they in their reunion.

Elizabeth appeared to sense that they might wish a more private moment and stood to leave. Jane followed suit, and they scooped up Molly. "Take all the time you need. I shall make arrangements for our return to Darcy House." She smiled at him and he nodded, smiling in return as he pictured the comfort of his London home.

"Fitzwilliam, are you well?" Georgiana's voice was a melody, soothing and soft. "They told me of your accident, but I was not sure what to think when I had not heard from you directly."

"Forgive me, dearest. I have been unwell indeed, but I am on the path to recovery. Seeing you has boosted my spirits immensely." Darcy sat next to her carefully. "Tell me of you. Are you well? I am sorry for our delay in returning to London."

"It is no matter. I only trust that whatever business that forced you to leave so abruptly is now over."

Darcy fell quiet at her words. He privately vowed to ask Fitzwilliam whether he knew why he and Elizabeth had left London so quickly. "All that matters is that I recover my strength and that I see to your happiness."

"You no longer need to see to my happiness. I have another for that task now." Georgiana looked at her baby son and laughed. "Do you know, he looks just like you when he scowls?"

"That is exactly what Elizabeth said of Molly."

Georgiana softened. "She is so very good to me. I could not wish for a better sister. Jane, too, has been an angel. There are so many questions that only a mother can answer, and it is at times like these I wish ours was still here."

Darcy nodded gently at that.

At that moment, tiny fingers, covered in delicate, papery skin started to flail about within the lace blanket. Georgiana smiled. "I hope you do not mind if I look after my other little man now."

"Of course. We only intended this to be a short visit. Truthfully, I could not stay away another minute." Darcy rang for assistance and awaited a footman. Pressing another tender kiss upon his sister's forehead, he promised that he should call upon her tomorrow.

"Elizabeth tells me that the doctor has ordered you to rest," Georgiana admonished softly.

"I could rest here as easily as I can at Darcy House."

"Let us see what tomorrow brings. A new-born baby has taken over all my plans, and I am quite at liberty to receive you at your convenience. All I ask is that it is not too early." She grinned at him.

Darcy returned her smile. "You never were an early riser at the best of times. I imagine you are less so now." Laughing, Georgiana shook her head in mock indignation, and Darcy was struck anew by the changes he saw in her. Long ago, he would have struggled to tease her, his efforts earning only deep blushes of mortification. Her whole manner was so altered; she was a self-assured, joyful young woman. Suddenly, she reached out and tucked her hand into his just as she had done when she was a young girl. Giving it a little squeeze, she bid him an affectionate adieu.

Comfort and peace washed over him. It was so good to converse freely with someone again. He bowed his goodbye and made his way down the stairs, leaning heavily upon the poor servant. He was helped into his coat and gloves and sent word for Molly and Elizabeth. It was not long before his wife and daughter were there, dressed to leave. Luxford, Bingley, and Jane were not far behind them.

"Molly is tired and is anxious to return home." Elizabeth held her daughter's hand.

"Well that makes two of us, then." Darcy smiled down at Molly as his daughter slipped her other hand through his. All three of them said their farewells and made their way to the carriage. Molly, Darcy noted, was walking carefully to match his laboured pace, and he smiled over her head at Elizabeth. Carefully, they arranged themselves in the carriage. Molly had pleaded her case to sit next to Darcy but had eventually been persuaded into curling up on Elizabeth's lap. Darcy could not break his gaze from his daughter. Her little hands were tucked into her lap and her feet were curled up under her. Truly, she was angelic. Eventually breaking his gaze, he looked up to see Elizabeth regarding him warmly.

"She is everything you said she would be," Darcy said quietly over the sound of the carriage wheels.

"And you were everything I knew you to be," Elizabeth replied. They fell into a contented silence. Darcy felt a sense of ease pass over him as his little girl smiled at him warmly. A tenderness flowed through him, so profound in its intensity. Never could he have imagined such a feeling inspired by a little child he had met only hours ago. Quietly, he whispered a prayer for the safe return of his memories. Each one containing Molly was precious. Now that he had met her, the full weight of what he had lost was a heavy burden. Hopefully, their return to Darcy House would bring some respite from this great gaping void in his mind. Suddenly struck with an aching need for the familiarity of his home, he was thankful that he had not long to wait before reaching it.

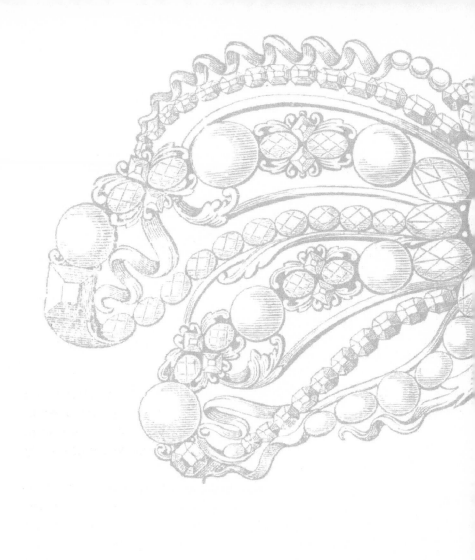

CHAPTER NINETEEN

Mrs Lister had been housekeeper at Darcy's London residence for a good number of years. She had been in service at the Darcys' house when his parents were alive, and it was pleasing to see how warmly she welcomed Molly and Elizabeth into his house. *Their house.*

His memories of his bachelor life were largely happy. Free to do what he pleased and with money enough to afford it, he had thought very little of the habits he kept. Now he shared his home with the slender slip of a woman holding his arm beside him and the little cherub holding his injured hand. What other changes would he find in this house?

The hour was later than he had anticipated. What would his usual routine be now that he was a husband and father? He knew of many men for whom having a wife and child would yield very little change in their habits. What of his marriage? Molly needed a good night kiss. That was about the extent of his understanding of his role.

A pang of hunger gripped him. When had he last eaten anything of substance? Glancing quickly at Elizabeth, he thought she looked pale again. Would she be in need of dinner? Indeed, had she even eaten today? He could not recall her nibbling more than a few bites of her meal when they had stopped to rest the horses near St Albans. Would she wish to dine with him, or was she still suffering the effects of travel?

Unbidden, his mind cast him back to their first night together at the inn. The momentous occasion of setting eyes on his daughter for the first time, as well as reuniting with Georgiana, had quite pushed lesser concerns out of his head. Her rejection of him had been clear enough, and he was unwilling to repeat the humiliation. Long accustomed to getting his own way, Darcy was unsure how to proceed. His mouth suddenly felt dry. He hoped that he would not have to repeat the rejection tonight. The arrival of a nurse-maid broke him from his thoughts.

"This is Sarah," Elizabeth gently supplied. "Molly idolises her."

On this occasion, Sarah's appearance was not welcomed by their daughter. After such a long separation, Molly did not wish to leave either parent. Her bottom lip began to tremble, and those storm-blue eyes began to fill with tears.

"I shall go," Elizabeth murmured. "You must rest after you have eaten, and I may be a while yet."

"But I want Papa," a little voice beside his knee whispered.

Looking down, Darcy could see Molly's upturned face gazing up at him. He had been fifteen when his mother died. The trauma of losing her had left a profound mark, and it had taken many years before he could bear to be parted from a loved one lest he should never see them again. When he had eventually gone back to school, he had suffered episodes of panic every night for a month.

What must it have been like for a young child like Molly? To be separated from both parents for a reason that was too difficult to comprehend, only for your father to return to you much changed. She must have been unimaginably scared. Without having any idea of what he was volunteering himself for, he said softly, "Do not worry, dearest. I am here. Tell me where I should go and I shall follow. But do not walk too fast for me, will you?" He felt a firm press of pressure. Elizabeth was resting her hand in the crook of his arm, shaking her head at him. He smiled at the expression of exasperated affection written upon her face.

"You are entirely too noble. You must take your rest."

"I shall not be long." Darcy paused. "I think." It had been a good many years since he had kissed Georgiana good night, and he anticipated that Molly should not prove markedly different. Unless there was more to it and he had unwittingly conscripted himself to something a great deal more arduous. Fortunately, Elizabeth seemed to sense his apprehension.

"We shall all go." She smiled, rescuing him from his dilemma. "Come, little one, I have missed you dreadfully as well. We shall go and get you ready, then Papa will come to kiss you good night." Addressing Darcy, she said, "Would you be so kind as to organise some supper for us? I do not need much."

"You should like to dine with me?" Darcy had not prepared himself for more of Elizabeth's company. The events at the inn had made him wary of expecting too much from her.

"Why yes, of course, if you are hungry. By the sounds escaping from your stomach, I suspect you are!" The corners of her eyes wrinkled as she attempted to conceal her giggle. "Do not worry about changing for dinner. It is late. Ask a footman to escort you to the nursery in about twenty minutes or so, and hopefully this little darling will have expended some of her energy on me." The dimple on her left cheek deepened charmingly as she spoke.

"You may depend on me to bring in the cavalry." Darcy attempted the most chivalrous bow his body would allow him. She bestowed upon him another brilliant smile and walked off holding Molly's hand. He watched them leave, a mixture of feelings churning under his breast. The prevalent one was admiration; after travelling a long way, she was clearly tired, and there were nurse-maids to do the job for her, but she had put Molly's comfort first without any hesitation. Her actions had meant the world to their daughter. Molly turned and waved at him from the stairs; her tears had disappeared the moment she knew he would wish her good night.

"Good night Papa!" Her face beamed down at him through the balustrades.

Darcy did not want to keep his daughter waiting long. After a private word with Mrs Lister, it was decided that a platter of cold meats, breads, and fruit would be sent up to his private room so he and Elizabeth could eat together. From his housekeeper's manner of speaking, Darcy inferred that sharing a meal with Elizabeth in such a fashion was not an out-of-the-ordinary occurrence. A few moments later, he had been assisted to his rooms by a young footman whose name he could not recall. In the sanctuary of his room, Robertson helped Darcy to refresh himself. Despite Elizabeth's insistence that he did not need to change for dinner, Darcy could not be easy until he looked halfway presentable. *When was the last time you cared for a woman's opinion of your appearance?* Darcy peered into the ornate gilded mirror above the fireplace. *A nonpareil veritable.* That was what Mother had called Father whenever she had coerced him into attending a formal event. It would take months of gentle coaxing and flattery before the deeply reserved George Darcy would consent to attend such a public function, only for him to spend most of the afternoon worrying about his appearance before his departure. *Whom was Father trying to impress?* Darcy smiled at his recollection. The only woman his father had eyes for was the one who had persuaded him to accept the invite in the first place. A huge feeling of loss washed over him. How long since he had thought about his parents in such a way? So much of his pain had been long buried under the responsibility of caring for Georgiana and taking charge of Pemberley. For many years he had not had the time—or the inclination—to review his memories at length. Now, it would seem, these memories—or fragments of them—were all that he had left.

Some inconsequential action of Robertson's brought him back to the present day and his promise to attend the nursery. What would Mother and Father have thought about his new family? Both would have cherished Molly, that much was certain. It was fascinating how much Molly resembled both his parents. He wondered whether she had inherited Georgiana and his mother's love of music. He made a note to ask Elizabeth.

And what would his parents have made of his wife? That answer he could not be sure of. Occasionally, his gentle mother had made mention of Lady Catherine's wish for him to marry his cousin Anne, but Darcy suspected that his mother had only entertained the notion to appease her overbearing sister. Mother had been careful never to promise anything or to commit any scheme into writing. His father had always surreptitiously rolled his eyes at Lady Catherine's mention of her matrimonial plans.

Mother would have liked Elizabeth, he decided. Her disposition was to think kindly of everyone—how else could George Wickham have been tolerated for so long? In the short time since his accident, he instinctively knew that Elizabeth's personality would have been the sort to draw his mother out of her shell. He could imagine the two sitting together in a parlour, working out the best way to lay out a treasure hunt for Molly or how best to reveal a birthday cake for maximum surprise.

His father would have been a different matter entirely. Mr Darcy senior had been fiercely protective over his family and the legacy of Pemberley. From a young age, it had been impressed upon him the very great responsibility of marrying well and preserving the Darcy name.

Of course, now that Molly was in existence, Darcy had no doubt in his mind that Father would have succumbed to her spell as easily as he himself had. No grandchild who had eyes of the same shape and colour as his beloved late wife could fail to win his heart. Darcy chided himself—that was not fair. His father had a soft spot for all small children, showing as he did infinite patience with him and Georgiana. There had never been a moment in his childhood where he had felt his father's temper, and, in the privacy of their own private rooms, the reserved, stern George Darcy loved nothing better than to make his children and wife laugh with his animated re-enactments of their favourite fairy tales. No, Father would not object to Molly, but would he have opposed Darcy's marriage in the first place?

An uncomfortable feeling took hold in the pit of Darcy's stomach. His father would have hoped for better, was the only conclusion he could draw. He would have expected someone with a title or a significant fortune, neither of which Elizabeth had. *There is no use agonising over it*, he silently told his reflection. *They are both gone, and you cannot converse with ghosts, no matter how dearly you wish it.*

The nursery was quiet when he entered. Not the sombre silence of a church, nor the deathly hush of a sickroom, but the tranquil peace one finds in a place of utter happiness. Scattered about the room were various toys. Darcy thought he recognised a doll or two from Georgiana's childhood. Along one shelf was a small collection of stories. He could not make out the titles, but he smiled when he recalled Elizabeth's description of a similar shelf at Pemberley dedicated to every book he had read with his daughter. He hoped Molly did not wish for a story tonight. A movement caught his notice, and he looked beyond the nursery to the adjoining bedchamber. Within, he saw Elizabeth pulling the coverlet over Molly.

"Now, my love, you may sleep," she spoke softly, placing a kiss on Molly's curls. *She could have been saying anything,* thought Darcy, *and the tone of her voice would soothe even the most tormented soul.*

"I want Papa." Molly's voice was tired.

"He will come soon."

Even in the soft light, Darcy saw his daughter's bottom lip tremble. His first thought was to reassure her. He took a deep breath. "Molly, your papa is here." How natural that was to say! Why had he been so worried before?

Doing his best to keep his walking cane from clattering loudly against the floor, Darcy hobbled into the room, attempting as best he could to look the picture of health. His voice startled both of them. Both looked up and Darcy was rendered mute by the identical expressions of love on their faces. Acutely self-conscious, he turned his attention to Molly.

"Thank you," Elizabeth murmured as he bent low to give Molly a good night kiss. "I know you must be fatigued after your journey."

"No more tired than you are."

"I shall be well after a good night's rest." She smiled up at him, her perfect lips parting and her face losing all signs of fatigue.

"Do you still wish to dine with me?" Darcy winced at how insecure he sounded. When had he ever been unsure of how his wishes would be received? And in his own house no less!

Elizabeth's smile widened. "Of course. You must go directly and start eating. I shall not be long here." She turned her attention back to Molly, whose long eyelashes had begun to flutter. Elizabeth gently stroked her daughter's hand as Molly's flushed cheeks relaxed into an angelic slumber. "Do you know, I think she was waiting for you to arrive before she fell asleep."

Darcy smiled. "I shall not take so long in future."

"It is no matter. You are here now, and that is all that counts. Now go, return to your room and eat, I beg you." She rose gently from Molly's bedside. "Before our presence here wakes her up."

"That would be very wise," Darcy replied. He wondered whether they did this together often. He hoped so. Watching Molly's chest rise and fall felt like both a rare privilege and also the most natural thing in the world. They both left the room as quietly as they could. Sarah, the nurse-maid, was waiting respectfully by the door. Elizabeth stopped to speak to her.

"Go and start your dinner. I shall not be long." Her eyes sparkled. "But be sure to leave some for me."

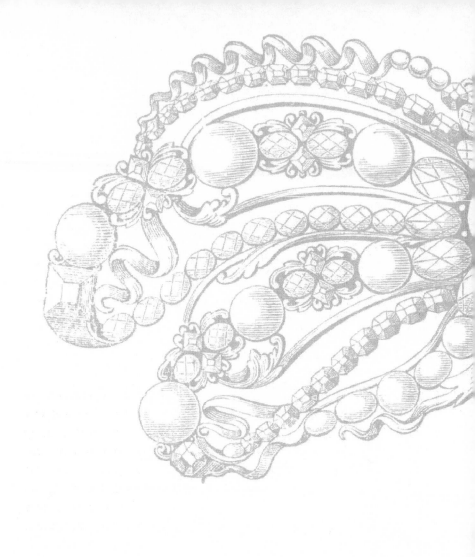

CHAPTER TWENTY

D arcy sat alone in his sitting room awaiting his wife—a most odd sensation. *Too long you have lived alone and kept your own company*, he chided himself. There was nothing more natural than dining alone with one's wife, but still he was not completely used to the intimacy of her presence. There was much he did not know about her. He thought of her back at the inn, her hair flowing loosely round her face. She had given him a glimpse of how passionate their married life had been, and now it was all he could do to keep his mind from drifting towards it. It was almost as though she had been talking of a previous lover, a man so perfect that Darcy could not live up to him. Or rather, could no longer live up to, for the man in question was him.

Raking his hands through his hair, he exhaled deeply. He was unsure how to play his hand. In truth, he was inexplicably nervous. Never before had he felt so little prepared to talk to a woman. Elizabeth knew him inside and out, whereas he knew very little of her. It was she who held all the cards in this marriage, for all his wealth and connexions.

Looking about the room, he was pleased to note the elegance of the meal placed before him. At least he could still be confident in the efficiency of his servants. Every ounce of gallantry had been required to resist taking Elizabeth's advice and helping himself to the slices of cold gammon arranged on the platter before him. *She has not eaten so neither should you*, he reminded his stomach, trying to ignore the darts of hunger. The smell of bread rolls and chutneys laid out on the porcelain plates teased his nostrils mercilessly, and Darcy poured himself a small glass of wine to tide him over while he waited. Resisting the temptation to substitute food with alcohol, Darcy gingerly took a sip of the ruby liquid. He was glad of his foresight. Coupled with an empty stomach, one mouthful of the fruity bouquet was enough to have a powerful effect. A pleasing ease passed over his body, the tension within him disappearing with every drop taken. His shoulders relaxed, until a soft knock on the door told him of Elizabeth's presence.

"I see you have not started—foolish man! How will you recover your strength on an empty stomach?"

"I thought it only fair to wait." Darcy felt a little affronted.

She glanced at him, her lips curling in amusement. "Ah! The infamous Darcy gallantry, cleverly disguised as its counterpart, the equally renowned Darcy stubbornness."

"I do not see that I have done anything wrong."

He must have sounded quite annoyed because Elizabeth's tone softened. "Forgive me, my love. You are tired, hungry, and probably in no mood to be teased. You are right. You have done nothing wrong."

The wind quite taken out of his sails, Darcy nodded, thankful that he did not need to press his point. "Pray, let us start. You surely must be as hungry as I."

Elizabeth glanced up from her plate. "In all honesty, I have little appetite today. There has been so much to do that I long for my bed."

"Then do not let me keep you." Darcy did not mean to sound abrupt, but the combination of wine and hunger made his words blunter than he had intended.

"I could go if you would prefer?" Her eyes fixed upon him quizzically.

No, he thought. *I would much rather you stayed and spoke to me of yourself, of your life, of our life together, so I may know how the devil I should behave.* Instead, he said, "I wish for your comfort, in whatever form that may be."

"Then I shall stay a while until I know you are well fed and not half-soused from drinking on an empty stomach. My comfort will be when I am reassured you are tucked up in bed, safe and well instead of lying insensible on the floor." A flash of annoyance played about her face, and Darcy caught himself admiring the way her eyes lit up in the passion of her reply.

Curling his lips about a smile, he replied, "It would appear that the Darcy stubbornness is not acquired only through bloodline but by marriage also." Rather than taking umbrage at his remark, Darcy had the very great pleasure of eliciting a genuine peal of laughter from her. She smiled at him disarmingly, and he feasted himself on the sight of her merriment.

Picking up her cutlery, she replied airily, "Well, husband dearest, I consider myself reprimanded." She smiled at him. "Come, we are both too hungry to converse sensibly. Let us stop this silliness and eat."

They passed several moments in companionable silence. Darcy could not refrain from glancing at her slyly across the table. She had changed her clothes. Her appearance was still refined and understated, but she was now wearing a dress of a deep blue. Her hair too had been pinned up into a tight chignon, with the rebellious curls on either side of her head plaited into submission. About her neck was a simple crucifix that caught the light and drew his attention to her slender neck and shoulders. When she moved her head, he noted that she had put on a pair of gold pendant earrings. So fine and delicate, they were almost invisible until she gracefully tipped her head and they flickered in the candlelight. He could not help but be fascinated by the interplay of light and reflection against the dark colours of her hair. They suited her perfectly.

"Do you plan to stare at me all night?" Elizabeth looked up from her food.

Caught off guard, Darcy faltered. "Forgive me, your earrings distracted me. I should not have stared, it was certainly impolite."

To his absolute wonder, her face broke into a broad grin and she raised her eyebrows at him. "To think that I should receive an apology from *you* of all people for staring at my person. Why, for the first part of our acquaintance all you did was sit and glower at me."

"I…glowered?" Darcy paused, unsure what to say next.

"Repeatedly. It was rather alarming."

"Forgive me, but what reason would I have to look at you thus?"

Elizabeth's hand ran to her necklace. Her delicate fingers played about with it as she considered her words. The golden crucifix dropped to her chest. It was all Darcy could do to keep his eyes on her face. "At the time, I thought it was to find fault with my person, but I have since learnt that you were doing the very opposite."

Darcy felt himself redden. "You mean to say I was…"

"Silently appreciating my body." Now it was Elizabeth's turn to blush. Crimson stained her cheeks, infusing its way down her slender neck.

Darcy took a fortifying sip—more of a gulp in truth—of his wine. "I must ask that you forgive my impertinence unless I have apologised already?" he offered at last.

To his surprise, she laughed. "Goodness no! And do not think me missish enough to demand an apology from you for simply looking at me!" She paused, looking up at him through her lashes in a way that made his pulse race. "In fact, I rather miss it."

"You do?" Darcy's heart beat faster still.

"Once I understood its origin, I found it supremely gratifying to know the effect I had on you."

Darcy noted, with a touch of sadness, how she had posed her thoughts using the past tense. He did not know quite how to respond. An unspoken tension was now flowing between them. He was in the middle of it before he even knew it had begun. As she sat before him in the firelight, all he could do was picture her bare form, his hands running over every part of her heavenly body. There was a point where the demure bodice of her dress met the soft contours of the curves underneath, and he was overcome with the urge to run his fingers along the seam, to feel the fine, flawless porcelain of the skin below. His heart was pounding mercilessly, and he was acutely aware of blood racing through every part of his body.

Searching his mind for a coherent answer, he reached again for his wine glass, but Elizabeth stilled his hand with her own. "Now it is my turn to beg for forgiveness. I forget sometimes that you do not remember me as I do you, and my familiar tongue runs away with me. I would not have you think that I am always so bold. It is only because you and..."

She paused, searching for the right phrase. "We knew each other so intimately that I could speak my mind without fear of shocking you." The candlelight illuminated her face, casting such softness about her expression that Darcy felt himself truly enraptured. She looked every inch the woman in love. Why had she broken from his embrace? He did not understand it.

Gazing at her face, he decided that Elizabeth put him in mind of a rose. The blush-pink of her skin was the exact shade of those at Pemberley. Every line of her face had the exquisite delicacy of a flower in bloom, her lips were round and full like that of a rosebud, and she had enough wit about her to be a thorn in anyone's side. But handle a rose too roughly and the petals would drop instantly. Maybe that was what had happened. He had startled her, and she had reacted accordingly. Tonight, her playful spirit had returned, and he did not wish to spoil the light-hearted conversation that had begun to blossom between them.

"You are right, of course," he replied at last. "Not that I expect an apology for it. Rather I beg for your compassion when I am at a loss for what to say." Elizabeth's eyes softened, and when she spoke, her words were laced with sympathy.

"Never ask me for my compassion, for you will always have it." She held his gaze, and he wondered what was passing through her mind, for the look she gave him was one of utter affection. He realised that her hand was still on his. Turning his fingers, he curled them around hers gently. She returned the gesture with a soft squeeze, the pressure of which sent the most delectable sensation up his arm.

"If you do not know what to say, then pray listen while I

speak," said Elizabeth gently. "I am more than equipped to talk for the two of us."

And so, Darcy listened. The details of what she spoke about were of little consequence. Small matters regarding the management of the house were discussed—apparently Mrs Lister had struggled to find an adequate replacement for one of the footmen. There had been news of an engagement—one of Darcy's old schoolfellows had finally succumbed to the matrimonial expectations of his family, and there had been an invite to a celebration for the forthcoming nuptials. Elizabeth had thought to decline given Darcy's recovery but had waited to seek his opinion. All these small domestic details wove together to create a harmonious tapestry of married life. Darcy felt an ease pass over him, unequal to any feeling he had ever had when talking to a woman. Sometimes, she would stop and ask him a question or for advice, other times she would pause and fill in a little of the history so he could fully understand the matter. Not that it would make a difference. An hour from now, when Darcy was in his bed, he would have no recollection of any of the topics about which she spoke—so enchanted was he by her manner of conversation and the feel of her hand in his. Elizabeth knew exactly how to draw out the most reticent of characters. At last, she took a sip of wine herself. "Forgive me. I have talked myself into hoarseness."

He looked at her in concern. "Allow me to refresh your glass."

"Only a little, thank you. I must retire soon, and I shall only sleep fitfully if I have any more." Darcy glanced at her—dark circles had gathered under her eyes, and she seemed drained of energy.

"Of course. Please do not stay for my benefit alone."

"It is not purely for your benefit that I wish to stay here." She met his gaze. "I miss our conversations." Her tone of voice was so wistful that Darcy wondered whether something—besides his accident—had happened to stop them.

"Then we should eat like this again," he said. "I have enjoyed it immensely."

"Let us see what tomorrow brings," she said quietly. "Once the wine wears off and your leg becomes sore you may wish for an earlier night." Darcy did not know what to make of her words—

had she not enjoyed herself too? Or was it playing on her mind that Fitzwilliam may return at any instant with news that might unsettle the renewed bond between them? All Darcy knew was that he had not wanted this meal to end.

She did not notice his confusion as she had already made to rise. He attempted to stand up with her, but she gave him an affectionate frown.

"Be still and save your energy for Robertson." This time, the Darcy gallantry had mixed with just the right amount of Darcy stubbornness and alcohol for him to ignore her request.

"I shall see you safely to the door, madam." He leant heavily on his walking stick, ignoring the light-headed feeling that came from standing abruptly on a headful of wine.

"How fortunate that the door is only a few feet away," she said, smiling at his attempted chivalry.

"But I can only manage a few steps unassisted, so you must ignore the distance and concentrate on the effort taken." He smiled back, offering his arm as though he were walking her along a sunlit country path rather than his dimly-lit sitting room.

As she approached to take his arm, every good intention fell out of his mind. Buoyed by the wine and her equally intoxicating proximity, he reached out and touched her earring. Surprised, she turned her face to him. His injured hand was frozen near her ear, almost touching the soft skin. It would only take the slightest movement for his hand to cup her face, yet he did not dare to. Lightly brushing her earlobe, his fingers met the metal of the little pendants.

"They are beautiful," he said, never once taking his eyes off her face. He did not know whether he was still speaking about the earrings or the pair of bewitching eyes that shone before him.

Elizabeth reached out with her hand and lightly felt the earrings, her fingers meeting his as she did. "You gave them to me." She placed her hand over his and gently brought it down to his side. Her gaze fell to the floor, and Darcy felt a tear splash onto his thumb. Why did she cry so in his presence? Feeling wretched, he opened his mouth to speak, but she silenced him with a gentle finger to his lips.

"No more apologies," she whispered. "And no more talk. We both need to rest." Slowly, she reached up and pressed a gentle kiss to his cheek. Closing his eyes, Darcy was only aware of the delicate rose-infused perfume that drowned his senses. A deep pain ran through him. He would have liked to attribute it to his injured leg, but it was a great deal more than that.

"Of course," he said hollowly. "You have spoken enough for the both of us. I can only thank you for it."

But the silence between them spoke of many things still unsaid. She stepped back from him. "Good night, my love."

"Good night...Elizabeth."

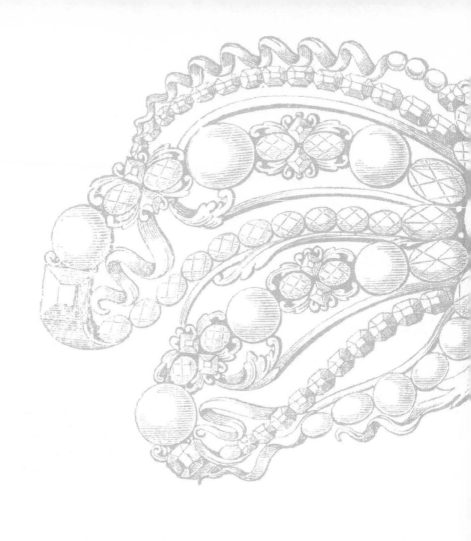

CHAPTER TWENTY-ONE

A sharp jolt shot through Darcy's leg as he eased himself into his bed. It continued for some time, preventing him from speaking. Wincing, he clenched and unclenched his hands in an attempt to regain some control over the consuming ache devouring his body. With a deep sigh, he rubbed his face and looked about his room in an effort to think of anything but his injury.

In the deepening twilight, the master's bedroom looked immaculate; Robertson had excelled himself in its preparation. At first glance, much of the room was as Darcy remembered it, but upon second perusal, Darcy began to notice signs that his wife was a frequent visitor. Upon his writing desk was a small pot full of delicate hair pins. *Do I watch as she takes down her hair?* A thrill ran through him. In the corner of the room were unfamiliar books. It took him a while to understand the titles, but Darcy was confident that the translation of Italian love poetry was not his. *Have I read them to her? Or perhaps she reads them to me.*

Darcy's eyes travelled across the room until they fell upon a small watercolour hanging upon the wall near the window. It was no masterpiece, but it was a faithful likeness to his mother's favourite view of Pemberley's lake. He knew instantly its creator.

What did it say about Elizabeth that she should spurn painting the grandeur of Pemberley for the intimate corners valued only by him? It spoke well of her, he concluded. Sinking his head into the pillow, he stretched out his weary body. A man of purpose, he had never been prone to a sedentary life. Consequently, as his body rested, his mind became alive and active, revisiting all the important moments of the day.

After a few moments of solemn contemplation about Georgiana and his new nephew, his mind turned to his wife and daughter. He wondered whether Elizabeth was lying awake in the adjoining room or if she had fallen asleep. It had been a long day for them both. He thought of her loving gaze when he had held Molly in his arms for the first time. His pulse raced a little; the mere thought of her beautiful eyes upon his person affected him deeply. Why could she not speak to him openly? A dull throb clouded Darcy's brow as he struggled to recall anything that might help him. There was no use in it.

Reaching out to the night table, his fingers curled over the smooth leather of Elizabeth's diary resting upon it. He looked upon the cover for a moment, attempting to picture himself buying it for her. It was an elegant thing, feminine and delicate, rather like its owner. Carefully, he opened the diary and took a steadying breath. Upon the first page he recognised his neat, level hand. With a great effort he read the words: *To my...to my dear-est Eliza-beth. I hope you trea-sure this as I treasure you.* He gave himself a wry smile. Apparently he was a sentimental fool.

Turning the page, he saw his own name. Tracing his fingers over Elizabeth's graceful writing, he sighed softly. He wondered where she had been sitting when she wrote in it. Did she curl up on the sofa in Pemberley's library? Or did she write it in the sanctuary of her own room? He drew a little closer to the light to gain the best advantage to read her words.

Dearest Fitzwilliam,

I am writing this to you as Molly sleeps. I should have thanked you more decidedly for your gift before you departed, but in truth I was too tired.

Reading Elizabeth's diary was not as difficult as reading the words of a lesser acquaintance; Darcy could almost hear her lovely voice speaking directly to him.

What should I have said if you were standing before me, your handsome face looking into mine? I shall give loose to my fancy and tell you that I love you. You are already aware of it, you may reply. In-in-i, here, Darcy squinted, *indulge me when you hear I only loved you as a husband and man before. Now, I love you as a father, as does darling Molly.*

Darcy smiled at the words, so lovingly scribed upon the page. He looked at the date—Molly would have been under a year, perhaps more like a new-born babe. He read on, a little falteringly.

You do not know how I miss you. When you return, I hide my sorrow from you. It is so easy to be happy when you are with me. Return soon. My head is beginning to throb, and Mrs Reynolds keeps looking at me most...

Darcy narrowed his eyes again and finally read:

Mrs Reynolds keeps looking at me most anxiously. I wish to smile at you soon. I shall save you all the love that I can spare. Be warned—I have another claim on my heart now. Fear not, with the right per-sua–

Darcy grimaced as he deciphered their meaning.

With the right per-persuasion, I could be amen-amenable to sharing my affection! And so to bed I go, to dream away this headache and to long for your return. All my love, your dearest, loveliest Elizabeth.

Darcy laid the diary on the bed. His own head was beginning to ache, and he could feel dull throbbing behind his eyes as he strained them to read. The pain did not matter. Elizabeth was right —it had been beneficial to practise. And if reading her diary gave him an insight into his wife's mind, so much the better. He smiled a little, his mind picturing the many ways in which he might have persuaded his wife to share her affection.

The next day brought more familiarity. Bingley arrived upon Darcy's doorstep unannounced. He was as energetic as ever but far earlier than Darcy could ever credit him for. Elizabeth, according to a message sent via a footman, had taken Molly to visit Jane and Georgiana. Darcy wondered whether he should feel hurt by the lack of an invitation to join them, but it did not take long for him to realise that there was another motive afoot. Apparently, Bingley had been assigned the important job of cheering Darcy up—a task somewhat hindered by Darcy's increasingly lowered tolerance for chitchat. The burning sensation that shot through his side did not help the matter either. Wincing in pain, he attempted to receive Bingley in the drawing room.

"Do not trouble yourself to stand, Darcy. I do declare you look awful."

"Are you often in the habit of inviting yourself to a friend's house with the sole intention of insult?" Darcy could not help but smile. There was nothing duplicitous about Bingley. It was refreshing.

"I must beg your pardon, but I can hardly believe it is you. Elizabeth said you had been in a riding accident, but she did not share many details. I suspect she did not want to reveal too much and cause Georgiana to worry. How does your leg? I see your cane there by the footstool. Shall I reach it for you?"

"Thank you but no—I do not wish to move about too much today."

At this, Bingley coloured, his friendly smile replaced with a sheepish look. "That is a shame. When Elizabeth mentioned you may be in need of some diversion, I made arrangements for us to visit Brooks's."

Darcy's heart sank. It was expectation rather than desire that necessitated his membership to that particular gentlemen's club. He had hoped to use his time away from Elizabeth to read her diary undisturbed. *Some parts of that diary are not to be read by anyone but you.* Her words had haunted him incessantly, arousing his curiosity and inflaming his body all at once. Bingley's offer, kindly as it was meant, entailed more endless small talk. He could hardly admit it to Bingley, but he did not want to suffer the tedium of Brooks's—the company there was stifling.

"In truth, I am not sure it would be beneficial for me to go."

Bingley looked crestfallen. "Come on, old chap. It is not too far from here, and, to own the truth, I have sent a note to other members signalling your return. You are sure you do not wish to accompany me? I know how you detest having nothing to do."

That much was true. Darcy had done enough brooding to last a lifetime. It was not his nature to sit around idly. He began to reconsider. The club was only a short carriage ride away, and he could rest there just as easily as here. Perhaps it would be better to read Elizabeth's diary tonight in the privacy of his own room. There would be no interruptions, and he would be very much at leisure to enjoy every intimate detail it revealed.

At last, he relented. "Very well, but you must answer to the doctor if my leg does not heal."

"I do not fear the doctor, but there is a coven of women who would hunt me down should any harm come to you whilst under my care." Bingley's eyes twinkled. "In truth, I have missed your company, great taciturn fellow that you are."

"Well, that is gratifying to know. I shall cripple myself more often. It is a sure way of strengthening a friendship."

Bingley laughed at Darcy's dry retort. "It is good to see you back in fine fettle. Your mood has been so changeable of late. Certainly, you seemed most out of sorts before you left for Pemberley." Darcy looked at him, puzzled. What had he done to provoke such a comment from Bingley, a man little known for his power of observation? Unaware that he was unwittingly confirming Darcy's opinion of him, Bingley did not notice Darcy's silence. "I meant to ask you whether something was amiss, but it has been difficult to leave Jane now that Charlie has become so wilful. His stubbornness is a gift from his aunt Caroline, I am sure of it!"

"Charlie?" Darcy did not understand to whom Bingley was referring.

Now it was Bingley's turn to look puzzled. "I speak of my son, little Charles. He has all the appearance of an angel but none of the virtue, the little scamp." He shook his head affectionately. "Louisa and Caroline say I spoil him, but it is every father's right to care for their child."

Grinning brightly, his blue eyes sparkled at Darcy. "I can count on your support in this matter. You are the most indulgent father I ever beheld."

Darcy hid his confusion behind a soft laugh. It was gratifying to know that Bingley thought well of him as a parent. He wondered whether little Charlie had any brothers or sisters but did not know how to ask in a way that would not arouse suspicion. He was not ready to discuss his most debilitating injury with Bingley. *Let him think it is only my leg and fingers that have been damaged.* Using a cane and Bingley's shoulder, Darcy hauled himself to his feet. The only way to do it was to ignore the tremor of pain shooting up his leg. So too did he ignore the look of doubt written upon the footman's face as he was assisted into the carriage.

"You seem better already!" exclaimed Bingley, ducking his head of curls to enter the carriage without knocking his hat askew.

"Better is a relative term, and it very much depends on the point at which one starts and ends." Darcy gritted his teeth, beginning to regret leaving the comfort of his chair.

"Stop philosophising and remember I have organised this as a means of enjoyment for you. It has been far too long since we have had the pleasure of one another's company unimpeded by wives and children."

"You operate under the illusion that I enjoy your company, Bingley." Darcy stretched out his broad shoulders, filling out more of the carriage seat.

"We shall have none of this grumpy attitude." Bingley adopted the tone of a scolding father.

Rolling his eyes, Darcy's lips curled a little in amusement. It was good to feel like himself again, for all the pain it was sure to cause. The carriage rolled away, and Darcy braced himself inwardly. Perhaps it would not be so terrible. He could use the time to learn all he could from Bingley. He smiled to himself; it would hardly be difficult to glean any information from his old friend. Such an open and honest man made for a terrible liar. *Rather like Fitzwilliam,* Darcy thought grimly.

He wondered at Fitzwilliam's errand for Elizabeth. What could have been so urgent? It seemed that something had drawn him and Elizabeth back to Pemberley even before his accident. He fell quiet. He no longer believed in coincidences, and every instinct told him the two events were connected. He would use everything in his power to discover it. Turning his thoughts back to Bingley, he sighed deeply and threw himself at the mercy of his old friend's newly-discovered powers of organisation.

CHAPTER TWENTY-TWO

Brooks's had not changed. Darcy suspected that it never would. What would it be like two hundred years from now? Would it still be imposing in its design? How would the Palladian-style columns fare against the clattering London streets? The city around the club was changing apace. Would Brooks's keep up too? Darcy surmised not and was glad of it. The exclusivity of a gentlemen's club pleased him despite the mediocrity of its members. Too often, he had found himself in the company of those not of his social sphere. People had raised their eyebrows a little at his friendship with Bingley, coming as he did from new wealth. It had taken some persuading for Bingley's membership to be accepted. Thankfully, Bingley's natural good-humour had won over anyone who might doubt his standing as a respectable man.

With Bingley's assistance, Darcy made his way through the club's imposing entrance. From where he stood in the atrium, he could see wrought-iron balustrades lining numerous flights of marble staircases. Bingley sensed his apprehension and gave his shoulder a friendly squeeze. "I have secured us a private room. It is one set of stairs, but we shall be out of the way of the usual melee." He winked. "I should be pushing my luck indeed if we ended up in the gaming hall. My wife is all that is gentle and good, but I suspect even her patience would be tested on that score."

Darcy smiled faintly back. Gambling would require a head for figures, and he was not sure he was up to the task. It was hard enough to be vulnerable around Elizabeth. To reveal his impairment to those of a lesser acquaintance was unthinkable. He was pleased at Bingley's foresight. He motioned for his friend to sign him in, not trusting himself to sign the ledger under the observation of another. Turning their backs on the principal staircase, Darcy and Bingley were shown to the smaller rooms. As they made their way down the corridor, Darcy caught sight of himself in one of the large, gilded mirrors. He did look different. The bruises and cuts to his face had all but gone, but he still looked angular somehow; perhaps it was his sharper cheekbones causing the effect. The darkness of his curls contrasted heavily with the pallor of his skin. He was so accustomed to a life of outdoor pursuits that he had forgotten how pale he could look when confined indoors. It did not help that his eyes still had prominent shadows underneath them— a sign indeed that he should really be resting.

Twisting himself from side to side, he gazed at himself at length. His body seemed leaner too. His coat and waistcoat did not fit as well as they had before. He had an altogether gaunter appearance than he had realised. He shifted about self-consciously and tucked his injured fingers under the handle of his cane.

Aware of Darcy's discomfort, Bingley gave him an encouraging smile. "Do not fear. You are still a handsome devil. Rest assured some fool out there will declare that you have set a new fashion."

Darcy's frown deepened, and Bingley continued gently, "You may as well get it over and done with. I know how you hate being the object of curiosity. Tell me when you want to leave and it will be done instantly." Darcy nodded. In a way, Bingley was right. It was better to pretend that all was well and get the probing questions over with.

Stepping into the room, Darcy was struck by its inviting elegance. A large fire crackled merrily under the carved marble mantelpiece, throwing a warm orange glow about the room. The dark green of the walls offset the deep red of the furnishings—the effect was austere but comfortable. As he moved about the room, there was a familiar faint smell of tobacco. It reminded Darcy of his father's study at Pemberley. The alcoves in the wall were lined with leather-bound books of all sizes. Small tables with decanters of red wine and cut-glass tumblers were dotted about the place, reflecting the firelight. Everything about this room was masculine and refined. He relaxed as his eyes adjusted to the comforting darkness.

"Darcy, how are you?" It was Bellington, the friend from Elizabeth's letter. Darcy was relieved to recognise him. Sitting at the card table with Bellington was Tilford. Both men had aged since Darcy's last memory of them but not so much as to make them unrecognisable. Tilford, the younger of the two gentlemen, had been a prized fighter at Cambridge. His waistline indicated that he no longer partook in regular exercise.

"What the deuce happened to you?" Tilford exclaimed, the buttons of his waistcoat straining precariously as he stood to receive Darcy.

"There was a disagreement between my horse, the ground, and me, and I fancy myself the loser of the dispute," Darcy replied drily.

"Well, you have gained yourself a pretty walking cane. Here, take a whiskey for your trouble." A glass was pressed into Darcy's uninjured hand as he sank into the Chesterfield seat near the fire.

He paused; he had not intended to drink, but what better way to ease the pain? Momentarily, Elizabeth's face flashed before him. He pushed away any sense of guilt and sipped the swirling liquid. His insides burned as he consumed his drink, leaving nothing but a warm, comforting aftertaste.

"No finer medicine than that." Bellington smiled at Darcy encouragingly.

"So says the man who spends all day at Brooks's and does not return home until the early hours." Tilford winked at Darcy. "I am sure Darcy here has a much finer tonic waiting for him at home. Surely that is the reason that you spend so much time with your lovely wife."

Darcy stared at Tilford in surprise. He did not know whether he should be insulted by Tilford's familiar tone. The man had much changed since Darcy had first known him.

Tilford paid no mind to Darcy's silence. "To be sure, it is understandable. When your marriage was announced, eyebrows were raised. You always seemed so insusceptible to feminine charms. And Miss Bennet was so unknown. We wondered whether there was a reason why it came so suddenly, if you will pardon my inference. Of course, as soon as we met her, we all understood why you married your Miss Bennet. So charming! So pretty! And her beauty has withstood the test of time. My wife has changed beyond recognition. Poor Isabelle used to be so slender and charming. My pockets have been sorely used of late, updating her wardrobe to accommodate the fluctuation of her figure. You are a fortunate man that your wife has lost none of her appeal."

"I hardly think this is something to discuss here." Darcy wondered whether he had always found Tilford so distasteful. He could not remember such vulgarity at Cambridge.

"Nonsense! Where else can we discuss this?" Tilford glanced at Bellington for support. "I cannot be alone in this matter! I shall look to Bellington, it is no use appealing to Darcy or Bingley—*your* wives have clung onto their charms and their figures. Come, Bellington, agree with me! You must admit that your wife is nothing like the beauty you married."

Shrugging his shoulders, Bellington let out a small laugh, but he did not trouble himself to contradict his friend.

Bingley, on the hand, shifted about uneasily, and Darcy felt a pang of sympathy. Bingley had gone to a good deal of trouble to organise this, and Tilford's behaviour was ungentlemanly.

Bellington sensed their unease and tactfully changed the topic. "A wife is more than a pretty face, Tilford. She must excel in household management, the efficiency of which allows for greater time spent on other pursuits such as embroidery or her musicianship—"

"Or shopping!" Tilford snorted. "Faith! I cannot be the only man whose wife spends an inordinate amount of money on clothes."

"It is better to spend money on clothes than lose it in a gaming hell," Bellington quipped lightly. "How many guineas have you lost in this week alone?"

"Better to speculate with your money than to squander it on the girls at Mrs Dodd's house in Covent Garden. Although you could argue that money spent there is never wasted." At this, Bellington coloured in annoyance. Again, Darcy observed, Bellington did not contradict Tilford's claims.

"Gentlemen! I have organised our reunion for Darcy. I am sure we can find another topic to converse on." The back of Bingley's neck was the brightest scarlet. He was clearly embarrassed by Tilford's unsavoury comments.

Suddenly, Darcy was overcome with a desire to return home. Elizabeth and Molly might have returned by now. Their conversation may be constrained by the limits of their sex and age, but at least it was palatable. Elizabeth had a wit, combined with a generous spirit, that made her an agreeable conversationalist. He wondered whether he should share Tilford's conversation with his wife. She might be scandalised by it, but Darcy suspected she would be amused. She had a great talent for enjoying the ridiculous without stooping to ridicule.

He found himself yearning to tell her a little of his day, so they could unite in laughter at their disapprobation of Tilford. *Why do you wish to share your day with a woman who does not want to share her lot with you?* That little unwelcome thought crossed his mind briefly. *You would do well to remember that she refused to tell you everything about your injury.* Some *bon mot* uttered by Bellington pulled his attention back to the room. The men had moved on to playing cards. Darcy motioned that he was in no state to play and would observe them from his chair nearby, thankful that he did not need to partake in any more of Tilford's company.

The afternoon passed more smoothly after its initial awkwardness. The comforting fire, combined with the whiskey, clouded Darcy's head with a soothing drowsiness. The sound of the other men became indistinct and muffled, and he could no longer follow the sense of their conversation. His body still ached, but any pain was deadened by the alcohol. He felt his head jerk forwards as he struggled to keep his eyelids open.

"Are you well, Darcy?" Bingley's cheeks had a faint rosy tint as he peered into Darcy's face. He had been enjoying the whiskey too, it appeared.

"I am well enough," Darcy mumbled, "but I should also like to return home. I fear the consequences to my body if I stay any longer."

"Of course. I shall ring for assistance to the carriage." Bingley disappeared to call for a footman. As he did so, Tilford quietly slipped into the seat opposite Darcy.

"Bingley has gone, so I shall be quick." He spoke so quietly that Darcy's whiskey-addled mind took a moment to understand.

"What do you wish to say?"

"Only that I asked all the pawnbrokers of my acquaintance, and nothing matching the article you described has passed through their doors."

Darcy could only nod. This was a clearly valuable piece of information, if only he understood why. "I thank you."

"No, I thank you. I was gratified indeed when you approached me with your concerns. It is not pleasant when one's servants steal from them. The gossip it can generate can linger. I promise you my discretion." Tilford's promise was as likely as the Prince Regent forsaking his claim to the throne. Instinctively, Darcy did not trust him. *I must have been in a desperate position to ask a favour of this rogue.* He could only presume that Tilford had contacts that others did not. No doubt Tilford would be well-acquainted with the pawnbrokers if his daily pursuits were gambling and visiting the bawdy houses of London.

"Please inform me directly if anything changes."

"I shall." Tilford nodded conspiratorially. "And I shall keep an eye out for that saucebox sister-in-law of yours too."

Darcy's head jerked up. "What?"

Before Tilford could elaborate, the clatter of sprightly feet signalled Bingley's return. He could see from the stricken look on Darcy's face that something was amiss. "I trust all is well, gentlemen?"

"It is very well, Bingley," Tilford responded quickly. "We were speaking of in-laws...which puts me in mind of your sister. I must wish you congratulations on her engagement. You must be glad to marry her off at long last! We should be toasting your unshackling! She has too long been sniffing around the men of our acquaintance."

Bingley's wary eyes found Darcy's, and his cheeks became rosy once more. "I am happy that finally she is content to marry." Bingley's response was polite but did not invite further comment.

Tilford took no notice and continued, "He is a great deal older than her, I recall. And immensely wealthy. Although earning one's own fortune through Blake's 'Satanic Mills' is hardly the same as cultivating generations of wealth through a noble bloodline."

"I would not know, seeing as my own fortune comes from such a mill." At last, Bingley had found his backbone as well as his limit with Tilford. A silence prevailed between the men, and Darcy was glad to leave. All four men exchanged curt bows; two of the party were as anxious to depart as the others were to remain.

Outside, the air was crisp and biting. It blew away any of the whiskey's comfort, leaving only a deadening throb at Darcy's temple and bodily awareness that his injuries were far from healed. Thankfully, they had but a short wait for Bingley's carriage.

"Forgive me. This afternoon was disastrous." Bingley scraped his hands through his hair in distress as he helped Darcy aboard. "I had intended there to be a more agreeable party. Tilford is deplorable. He has changed greatly since our student days. I have never known a more uncouth fellow."

Darcy shook his head at Bingley. "Do not apologise on his account. It was a kind thought to arrange some divertissement for me. Tilford's company notwithstanding, I have been truly distracted from my troubles." *Until the last ten minutes, when I learnt of my previous attempts to surreptitiously recover stolen jewellery,* he added privately. His interview with Tilford had been revealing. Sinking back into the carriage squabs, his body and mind ached in union.

He resolved he would say nothing about it until further enquiries could be made. He wondered whether Elizabeth would have any more information regarding this theft. A cold chill clutched at his heart. Perhaps this was the errand Fitzwilliam had been sent upon? But why with such secrecy? Fitzwilliam could handle himself well, but Darcy would never send his beloved cousin to the nefarious world of thieves and tricksters if it could be helped.

He shut his eyes, the rolling of the carriage shooting daggers of white-hot pain up his leg and into his neck. He set his teeth and stretched his shoulder muscles in an attempt to relieve the tension. Drawing a deep breath, he willed himself to think of something—anything—to escape this cage. Elizabeth's beautiful eyes came to him like a divine vision. They shone at him with love, a twinkling jewellery box of affection. Why could she not trust him? A moan stumbled from his lips.

"We should not have visited the club."

Darcy opened his eyes to see Bingley's sincerity. "Perhaps not." Upon seeing his friend's face, he hastily continued, "I should have been content enough with your company alone. You are a very good friend to have gone to such trouble."

Bingley's face relaxed into a flattered smile. "You would do the same for me, I know it," he replied.

Darcy was very much aware of Bingley's surplus of selfless modesty. He highly doubted that he could be prevailed upon to spend an afternoon in such dreary company if their positions were reversed. He smiled at Bingley. "We have only a short ride before we are home. Tell me a little of your life. I fear my powers of conversation, limited as they are, have been further restrained by my injuries. Speak freely and allow me to listen. Please do not be offended if I do not respond."

Bingley nodded in sympathy and began to regale Darcy with all manner of news, mainly in connexion with little Charlie. There was a little daughter too—a Susannah—but she was far too young to have found herself in any mischief, and consequently there was far less to say. Darcy sat in silence, trying his best to ignore the constant spasms of pain as he listened to Bingley's joyous ramblings.

"Of course, as soon as she arrived, Charlie took it upon himself to laugh at his aunt Caroline's prized feathered cap." Bingley began to laugh. "He perpetually asks her where she got her pet bird from. She says I must scold him, but in truth I cannot when we are of one mind!" Darcy managed a smile. He could well imagine it. His abiding memory of Caroline Bingley was of a woman who was guided by whatever was the latest fashion.

"How goes her engagement?" Darcy remembered Tilford's words. He did not know how recently Bingley's sister had become engaged, and he hoped his question was sufficiently vague. At his words, Bingley rolled his eyes.

"Wilson is respectable, genteel, and not as elderly as Tilford implies. He has a steady character and—importantly for Caroline— immense wealth. He worked hard to earn his fortune, eschewing love and other nonsense along the way. Now that he has reached his advancing years he is perfectly content to marry Caroline— given our background in trade and that she is still of an age to bear him an heir."

Darcy nodded. "Your good opinion of him will shape mine. I was impressed by your set-down of Tilford earlier. Never was there a sentiment more in need of being expressed."

Bingley beamed at Darcy's unsolicited praise. He continued to talk in a jovial tone. "Caroline is, of course, insufferable. No other wedding has ever had more importance, or at least you would think so from her manner of carrying on. Louisa and I have arranged a schedule to ensure that Caroline's company is shared out equally between us!" A boyish grin split his face.

"Perhaps she could stay with us if you are finding her company troublesome." Darcy wished to repay Bingley's kindness with one of his own.

Bingley let out a startled laugh. "You may wish to ask your wife first before making such an offer, generous as it may be."

Upon catching Darcy's expression, he added, "Come, it is not as though they are on friendly terms. Elizabeth looked vastly relieved to hear of Caroline's engagement. I thank you but no. I shall suffer my sister in peace."

Darcy simply nodded, wondering why Elizabeth should dislike Caroline Bingley. To be sure, she was no great wit, but he could not remember anything truly terrible about her. Before he could ask Bingley another question, the driver indicated that they had arrived. Helping Darcy from the coach, Bingley exclaimed, "Well I never! What timing! What a coincidence!"

Darcy strained his head, ignoring the constricting spasm coursing up his spine as he did so. In the space before him was the Darcy coach, with Elizabeth and Molly descending from it. Happy giggles filled the air as Molly took her mother's hand; somewhere behind them a nurse-maid was laughing too. The cheerful trio created a lovely scene. Darcy's eyes were drawn to Elizabeth as she tickled their little daughter until she squealed. Then something caught Elizabeth's notice at the top of the steps leading to the house. Pulling on her daughter's hand, Elizabeth's body tensed.

Before Darcy could say anything, he heard Bingley call from behind him, "Do you know, we were just talking about you!"

Darcy was about to contradict him when a movement caught his notice. He could see now what had caused Elizabeth to react. For there, at the top of the steps, was the woman in question, looking every inch the imperial peacock. It was Miss Caroline Bingley.

CHAPTER TWENTY-THREE

"Charles, there you are! I have been across London in search of you!" Miss Bingley did not seem to notice Elizabeth as she swept past. "Your housekeeper said you had decided to visit Darcy, but when I arrived here, nobody could tell me where you both had gone." At this point, her eyes did find Elizabeth, as though somehow she might be responsible for the Darcy servants' reluctance to reveal their whereabouts. "And dear Eliza! I understand you have come from visiting dearest Georgiana. How I long to see her new baby! Darcy, you must convey how deeply I wish to call upon them."

Her eyes did not rest long on Elizabeth as soon as she saw Darcy. "Heavens! I heard you had an accident, but I did not know you were so greatly injured. A strong horseman such as yourself, you were fortunate that it was not fatal. I am thankful for your superior skills—you are surely responsible for saving your own life." The dull ache in Darcy's leg made him doubt her belief in his horsemanship.

"If only that were true, Miss Bingley," Darcy replied. Out of the corner of his eye, he could see Elizabeth stiffen as he addressed their guest.

"You must be weary and keen to rest after your journey. Now

you are here, is there any comfort we may provide for you before you depart?" Elizabeth spoke quietly but with a clear emphasis on the final word. Her words broke Miss Bingley's curious gaze upon Darcy's injured person.

"Why, do you know, I should love to accept some refreshment. The ride down from the Hursts' was most disagreeable. So much jolting! And such uneven roads! My head quite hurts. A glass of something cool would do nicely."

Placing a hand on Darcy's arm, she continued, "As dear Eliza is so preoccupied with sweet Molly, allow me the honour of assisting you up the steps." Darcy caught Bingley rolling his eyes in amusement.

"Allow me to go home, Caroline, and inform my housekeeper of your imminent return." He turned to Darcy. "Thank you for the pleasure of your company. Next time, I shall organise something only for us two."

Elizabeth turned to Darcy in surprise. "Where have you been? Whom were you with?"

"Now Eliza, I cannot believe you know your husband so little that you should wish him confined to his bed. Such an inquisitive man would surely be driven to madness with nothing to do. You were quite correct, Charles, to take Darcy for a change of air," Miss Bingley exclaimed.

"How gratifying that you should find me right in something, Caroline. It happens so very infrequently!" Bingley gave Elizabeth a fortifying nod, to which she responded with a long-suffering smile.

"In any case, I did not confine Darcy to bed—it was the doctor." Elizabeth turned to Miss Bingley. "Such a professional is hard to contradict, no matter how accustomed one is to having their own opinions listened to."

Miss Bingley did not appear to notice Elizabeth's rather pointed remark. Instead, she addressed her brother as though she had not heard Elizabeth speak. "Charles, you must invite Darcy to your house if he is in need of some stimulating company. My betrothed —Francis Wilson of South Quarry Mills, which is, by the by, the largest cotton mill in Manchester—has bestowed upon me carte blanche, with which I have ordered a selection of Hatchard's latest publications to be delivered to your address. It was not proper to deliver it to Wilson's residence before we are married. Perhaps you should care to come and read a few of the volumes, Darcy. I know how much you enjoy stimulating your mind by extensive reading."

Fear clutched at Darcy's heart. For all the kindness of her offer, he could not accept. No one must know of his impairment. How to refuse without causing offence to Bingley's sister? She would never believe that he was busy—he was meant to be bed-bound.

"I am afraid that will not be possible, Miss Bingley. Although I am sure my husband will acutely feel the loss of your company. However, he has promised his time to me." Elizabeth slipped him a quick smile, apparently reading his panic. "And I have decided that he must rest. I would not have him injure himself further."

"I hope you do not mean to call my company injurious?" Miss Bingley forced a smile in Elizabeth's direction.

"No indeed, I am yet to find a word to best describe your company even after all these years of our acquaintance. Rest assured 'injurious' is not the word I would call upon." For all the playful tartness of her reply, Darcy meditated upon how Elizabeth would truly express her opinion of Miss Bingley. They were clearly not friends. Darcy waved his farewell to Bingley amid a promise to call again. Leaning heavily on his cane, he and Miss Bingley made their way into the entrance, Elizabeth and Molly trailing behind them. Darcy felt the awkwardness of entering the house on the arm of a woman who was not his wife.

"Papa! Wait!" Molly caught up with them breathlessly. Grateful for a reason to turn away, he stooped as best he could to allow his daughter to take his hand, ignoring the bodily pain it caused. As he glanced up, he caught a glimpse of Elizabeth's face, ashen and pale. What could have caused such sadness?

"Molly, dear child, take care not to jostle your papa!" Miss Bingley's shrill voice rang out close to his ear.

He saw Elizabeth's lips purse at Miss Bingley's command of their child. She was clearly not impressed. Sensing danger, Darcy said softly, "You need not fear hurting your papa. Your little hand in mine is just the thing I have been wanting all this afternoon." He smiled down at Molly, simultaneously casting an appeasing glance at Elizabeth. *If, one day, I must choose a career for myself, perhaps I should be a diplomat.* Elizabeth returned his smile with a grateful one of her own.

The strange atmosphere continued as Darcy and Elizabeth received their unexpected guest. To Darcy, Miss Bingley was all things polite: she complimented the elegance of the furnishings, the style of the teacups, the sweetness of the tea, even the polished silver of the ferrule atop Darcy's walking stick was singled out as evidence of his superior taste. Darcy suspected that it was Elizabeth who had selected everything that was before them but could not find a way to politely contradict Miss Bingley. It was when she began to effuse enthusiastically about the size and shape of the tablecloth that Darcy felt obliged to stop her.

"Forgive me, but I must refer you to my wife. I fear you overestimate my abilities in all things domestic." Both turned to look at Elizabeth, who had been watching their exchange in stony silence.

"Of course! Forgive me, Eliza! I should have known! You always bring such a quaint, rustic charm to all that you do."

"I thank you, Caroline. What a compliment to my taste! Indeed, I had no notion of labelling my charm in such a way. Although I suppose rustic charm is preferable to no charm at all." Elizabeth's words were spoken with a lightness that did not match the hard set of her mouth. For an instant, Darcy forgot the dull throbbing in his leg in an attempt to hide a smile. Elizabeth had a point. For all her compliments, Miss Bingley was singularly charmless. She did not utter a single opinion that was truly original or sincere. She had not half the wit or warmth of his wife. He glanced at Elizabeth again. Why was she behaving so strangely? Darcy's knowledge of Elizabeth began the moment he regained consciousness. He had no memories to rely on, but he had never seen her behave in such a prickly manner. Racking his brain, he searched for anything that might alleviate the tension. Catching a glimpse of Miss Bingley's elegant profile, a sudden glimmer—a sliver of a memory—raced through his mind's eye. It was of himself and Miss Bingley attending a performance at a theatre. Somewhere in the foreground, the actors were monotonously clomping their way through *A Midsummer Night's Dream.*

In the ebb and flow of his broken memory, Darcy could see that he and Miss Bingley were not alone but were there as part of a group. He was aware of another presence near his elbow, presumably Elizabeth. He wished he could crane his neck to see her, but the memory vanished as quickly as it had appeared.

Thankful for a means of warming the frosty atmosphere, Darcy turned to Miss Bingley—who had by now started a lengthy comparison between the Darcy silverware and her own anticipated dinner set—and said, "Tell me, Miss Bingley, have you attended any diverting plays recently? I recall we saw *A Midsummer Night's Dream* together once."

"How good of you to remember even after all this time. It was when you were a man of great leisure—forgive me, Eliza, I do not mean that Darcy is too full of responsibility that he no longer is able to have fun, but you must admit it has been an age since we saw you enjoy yourself about society."

And thus she continued, mercifully not addressing Elizabeth again, turning instead to talk of theatre performances she had attended and thought Darcy might appreciate, and those that did not meet her exacting taste. Gratified at turning the conversation away from Miss Bingley's perpetual stream of compliments, he cast his eyes towards Elizabeth, hoping for a smile of thanks. It was a relief for him that not every memory had been lost; perhaps his recollection of the theatre would bring her pleasure too.

He was shocked when he saw her face. He had misjudged her again. Not one bit of relief or happiness could be found, only a grave sadness made all the more pitiful by her attempts to bravely conceal it. He watched as she made every effort to be civil to Miss Bingley, but her lips were trembling as she fought back tears.

"Please excuse me, I find myself feeling quite unwell. It has been a long day with dear Molly. I shall go to my room directly. Tell your brother it was good of him to call, and pass on my very best wishes to your future husband. I sincerely wish to meet him." She cast sombre eyes towards Darcy, the expression of which were so unmistakably pained that it caused him to catch his breath.

"I trust you are able to see to Miss Bingley's safe departure." Her tone was quiet but firm.

He nodded, and smiled at Miss Bingley. "I must follow my wife's example. I have a very expensive doctor whose advice I am ignoring by not taking my rest."

"Oh, but of course, Mr Darcy. I can understand your frustration only too well. Why, your injury reminds me of the time my new ivory slipper caught on my new gown at Lady Everett's last Season. I was bed-ridden for a whole afternoon with a sprained ankle." And on she laboured, barely noting Elizabeth's departure or Darcy's increasing disinterest. A full eight minutes later she eventually left, leaving Darcy with a headache to accompany the throbbing spasms that were beginning to engulf his leg. He requested to be assisted to his room. Robertson helped him into more comfortable clothes, then was dismissed.

It was too early for sleep, but Darcy had no intention of spending time anywhere other than his bed. His leg had begun to swell just under the knee. Nothing would alleviate the pain except rest. Before he could ease himself onto his bed, a pitiful noise caught his notice. His eyes swept the room. It was coming from his wife's chamber. He hobbled across to the door connecting the two rooms. Pressing his ear against the smooth wooden panel, he heard it again.

It was Elizabeth, crying softly, all alone. What had caused it? He reached for the door handle and then stopped, paralysed by indecision. She clearly did not wish to be disturbed. And he was in no position to help her if she needed it. She plainly did not wish to share every burden with him, and who was he to intrude on her privacy? Yet he could not turn away from her distress. It was intolerable to think that she was upset with no one to comfort her. Any man who had the honour of calling himself a gentleman should naturally assist a woman in need. That the woman in question happened to be the most beautiful woman he had ever met was of course irrelevant to the matter, Darcy's conscience mocked him. *You allowed yourself to succumb to desire, and she turned you down. This will only end in pain for you.*

He was at the point of stepping away when somewhere, in the depths of his mind, Amstel's advice returned to him: *Mrs Darcy has a tendency to take too much upon herself.* The thought of her crying alone was too much for him. Taking a deep breath, he raised his hand and knocked softly upon his wife's door.

"Elizabeth, what is the matter? I can hear you are distressed. Please permit me to enter." He could hear Elizabeth hastily wipe the tears from her eyes as she bustled around the room.

"I am well, just dreadfully tired. I wish to rest a little."

Darcy paused at her reply, wondering what to do. "I shall not sleep unless I know the reason behind your tears. Remember your promise to me. My only desire is to help you." There was a lengthy silence. Unsure, Darcy continued in a lowered voice, "Elizabeth, I do not wish to beg."

The silence was broken by the sound of Elizabeth's door opening to him. His eyes adjusted to the soft stillness of her chamber as he looked for her. No wife opening her door to her husband could look more vulnerable than she did to him in that moment. Her eyes were red and swollen with tears. Her lips were quivering in an attempt to keep some rolling emotion at bay. Wordlessly, he limped his way towards her and clasped her delicate hand in his large masculine ones. "Good God, what is the matter? You are certainly not well. Allow me to ring for a glass of wine." Elizabeth smiled weakly and brushed his suggestion away with an unconscious flick of her other hand.

"Thank you, my love, but there is no need. I shall be well enough after a little rest. Truly, do not worry."

"You promised to tell me if you needed any assistance. What is it that has upset you so?" Darcy gazed into her downcast eyes, trying to search them for an answer to his question.

Today had been filled with half-truths interspersed with snippets of their shared past. Fatigue had begun to claim him as he said, "Why do you not wish to speak to me? Why do you not confide in me?" Elizabeth took a sharp inward breath at his words and closed her eyes in a futile attempt to contain her tears. A stab of pain filled his heart, and he continued a little more bitterly, "Why do you not trust me?"

Elizabeth bit her lip as though afraid to speak. Her voluminous eyes met his, and therein he discovered his answer. "It is *I* who have upset you." To his dismay, Elizabeth did not contradict him.

She cast her eyes down, and he watched as a solitary tear escaped down her cheek. His heart sank. Not again. He began to apologise, "I had every intention of staying at home today. I do not wish to blame Bingley, but I was under the distinct impression you had sanctioned his chaperonage of me. It was he who convinced me to attend Brooks's. I do not believe I am in the habit of drinking whiskey at midday...I made every endeavour to refuse him but he was very—"

He broke away at Elizabeth's expression. Her lips were twitching as she tried to suppress a smile. At least she had stopped crying. He offered a sheepish smile in return. "Are you always entertained by my apologies?"

"Only when you try to convince me that Charles is the more influential partner in your friendship when so often it is he who yields to you." Her words could have been offensive if they were not said with such amused affection.

Darcy felt himself redden. "I suppose you are right. If I had felt myself, then perhaps I would have had strength enough to counter Bingley's persuasive charms."

Elizabeth laughed lightly despite her tear-stained face. "You must have been feeling out of sorts to fall into Charles's plans rather than listen to your own judgment. I always thought you detested Brooks's."

Darcy cast his mind back to the events of the morning. "I can reassure you, madam, that my opinion is unchanged." He smiled quietly, gratified to see her smile gently in return.

She had never looked more irresistible to him, for all her red eyes. The tears had stuck her long eyelashes together, curling them up and around, encasing those delicate jewels of hers. Never before had she looked so innocent and young. Secrets be damned, he felt compelled to help her. Her hand was still in his as he said softly, "You have not answered me. I have noticed that you have a remarkable talent for turning the conversation away when I ask you a question that makes you uncomfortable."

"You are more astute than I would give you credit for." She laughed a little.

Darcy did not. Squeezing her hand gently, he continued, "Tell me what I have done to cause you to cry so."

Lifting her eyes to him, Elizabeth paused, searching for the words. "It was not exclusively you that made me cry. I do not wish to be unkind, but I do not like Caroline Bingley's attentions towards you. She is not a trustworthy person."

"Attentions towards me? You must be mistaken. She speaks mainly of herself!"

Elizabeth curved an eloquent eyebrow at him. "It does not matter of what she speaks. She spoke almost solely to you. Surely you felt her attention to you was a great deal more than it was to me."

Darcy considered her words. He could not deny the truth in them but could only counter, "She was undeniably attentive, but her behaviour was in no way improper. I hope I have never given you cause to doubt me. If I have, you must tell me of it."

Elizabeth held his gaze and searched his face. After a heavy pause, she said quietly, "*You* have never given me any reason to doubt your fidelity."

"Then why do you cry?"

Trembling, Elizabeth whispered, "Because you remember her but not me."

There it was. The truth, so simply put, was such a painful admission that neither could speak for an instant. They stood, hand-in-hand, in silence.

"I am sorry." Darcy was the first to find his voice. "I am sorry for all of this."

She stepped a little closer to him, breaking his hold on her hands as she raised her own to cradle his face. "You must not be sorry when the fault does not lie with you." Her touch was so soft and inviting. He sighed deeply. He could not recall ever being embraced like this, but with her it only seemed natural and familiar. She was utterly enchanting. He tentatively leant towards her, lightly resting his forehead on hers. She closed her eyes and breathed deeply. "You must not blame yourself."

Darcy revelled in her proximity when only moments ago she had seemed so distant. Carefully, she broke away from him and opened her eyes. "Oh! But your leg—you should not be standing like this, you will injure yourself further." She took him by the hand and assisted him back to his bedchamber. Perhaps he should protest, given that she had been the one crying, but Darcy found that he could not. The pain in his leg was worth Elizabeth's graceful figure bending over him seeing to his comfort. He allowed her to place a pillow behind his head. The intimacy of such an action was almost unbearable. How could he ever have thought her anything but exquisite? Her elegant neck was before him, its porcelain skin imploring to be caressed. He closed his eyes and inhaled deeply. Her scent was potent. Somewhere in him, somewhere that even his memory could not reach, his senses were stimulated by the sweet, heavy floral undertones that radiated from her body. It inflamed him, engulfing him in a desire that he had not known himself capable of. A dart of fire shot up his leg. He winced, attempting to contain his agony. A look of guilt fluttered across Elizabeth's face. Her words echoed in his mind: *I told you the truth once before, and look what good it did you.* Doubt gnawed at him. What had happened to him? His enthrallment of her was continually at war with this constricting bodily pain. It was a constant reminder to be on his guard when every one of his senses begged him to surrender to her. He opened his eyes to see her face gazing down into his, the tenderness of which forced him to catch his breath. With a whisper of a touch, Elizabeth stroked his face and placed a loving kiss to his forehead. "You must rest." He nodded, hardly trusting himself to move.

Looking up, Elizabeth's eyes caught sight of her diary resting on the cabinet beside his bed. "I see you have taken my advice. I hope that you have found its perusal useful." She attempted a gentle smile, wiping away her tears as she spoke.

"It is enlightening," Darcy replied softly. "But I must admit I have read but a little."

"That is to be expected," Elizabeth reassured him. "It is remarkable that you should read it at all, given all that your body has endured." Before Darcy could reply, she took the diary and turned it over in her hands. "You probably do not know that this little part is for any treasured keepsakes." Her delicate hands found a space between the last page and the back cover of the book. From it, she drew what appeared to be a folded theatre programme. "Perhaps this will remind you a little more of A Midsummer Night's Dream." A look of mischief swept across her face as she held his gaze.

Carefully, she placed it on top of the diary as she replaced them both on the stand next to his bed. "We have spoken too long of the past. You really ought to rest if you mean to recover." As she spoke, her eyes held his. It was a look of such infinite tenderness that, for the briefest instant, every shred of pain disappeared from his mind. He was simply a man, alone with his wife, amiably reminiscing over their life together. A nauseating wave of agony ran through him, recalling him back to his present situation. He nodded at Elizabeth through gritted teeth. She gave his hand a conciliatory squeeze. "Rest well, my love," she said softly as she noiselessly swept out of his room.

As she closed the door, the programme fluttered to the ground. Despite the excruciating throb it caused, Darcy stretched his damaged fingers out and rescued it from the cold floor. There was a sketch on the front of all the performers. Unsurprisingly, Darcy did not recognise one of them. He wondered what Elizabeth had been about, when he caught sight of his neat, level handwriting at the bottom of the page. He breathed deeply, willing himself to focus on the words which were now swimming out of focus. He was thankful for the inscription's brevity.

Dearest Elizabeth, it read. *A small keepsake of an utterly forgettable second act. I love you, FD*

Turning the paper over, he replaced it on top of the diary. What did that mean? Why give consequence to a play that was forgettable? And that final salutation—could he in all honesty say he loved Elizabeth when he did not know her? He closed his eyes. To be trapped in a life that one could barely remember. What acute agony this was! He prayed for sleep. It was the only way to abate the plague of thoughts and images that swarmed about him. Tilford's face gleaming conspiratorially, whispers of a theft, Molly's little hand clasping his, Bingley's embarrassed glance towards him at the mention of Caroline, a plea for caution against an untrustworthy acquaintance, a theatre programme with a note that did nothing but celebrate a mediocre performance, and Elizabeth—mysterious Elizabeth, a woman as beautiful as she was elusive, her eyes full of tears as she tended to him, imploring him not to blame himself—they all haunted him.

Groaning, he turned his mind back to his leg. At least there he understood why it hurt. Closing his eyes, his mind succumbed finally to exhaustion.

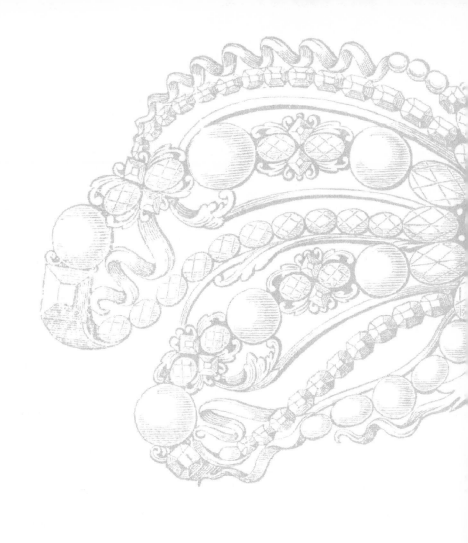

CHAPTER TWENTY-FOUR

Darcy was alone in a dark room. Behind the heavily panelled door, he heard a woman crying. He reached out and placed his hand against the mantel. It was his parents' sitting room at Pemberley. More voices could be heard behind the door. He knocked softly upon it and entered without waiting for a reply. An imposing bed dominated the room. The curtains were drawn, and the only light was from the fire and a few scattered candles.

He drew closer to the bed. Someone was at the bedside, tending to the poor soul within it. Dread filled him.

A hand slipped into the crook of his arm. He twisted his body to see who it was. Elizabeth's lovely face looked up at him. She was close to tears; tiny sparks from the fire reflected in the watery depths of her eyes. With her other hand, she softly ran her fingers through his hair, sending the most wonderful sensation down his spine.

"You will not bear this alone," she said. She guided him towards the bed. The shadowy figure was Darcy's father. Darcy's eyes trailed across his beloved father's hunched body. A tall, muscular man like himself, Darcy had never seen his father look anything but strong.

"She wants to see you," Elizabeth said softly.

"I cannot do this." The sob caught in Darcy's throat.

"I shall be with you this time." She gripped his hand tightly and pressed a gentle kiss to his cheek.

Darcy made his way to the bed and sat down on the opposite side to his father. Elizabeth sat next to him, her hand still clasping his own.

His mother's long, damp hair curled out of its plait, and her face was pale and clammy. Her breathing was shallow, and her movements were laboured. Through his child's eyes, his mother had always been the most beautiful woman. She was so gentle and patient. Even now, in her sickness, she was beautiful, an angel, ready to ascend to Heaven.

"She does not feel any pain," Elizabeth's voice murmured in his ear. *"Her suffering will soon be at an end."*

"But mine is about to begin," Darcy replied quietly.

"Your burden will always be ours to share. Never again will you struggle alone." She rested her head against his shoulder and drew their intertwined hands into her lap.

"Where is my baby boy?" his mother cried out. *"My little first-born child."*

"I am here, Mother." Darcy moved to the bedside to take his mother's hand.

His mother's watery eyes turned to his. *"I am so glad you are with me. I shall be better soon, my love, I promise. I feel so much better now that you are beside me."* She smiled a trembling smile. *"I have a gift for you."*

An ornate box appeared as if from nowhere. Inside were his mother's most treasured items: a pair of pearl earrings and a matching choker. Her favourite brooch—how many times had he helped pin it to her evening gown?—lay amongst them. Darcy ran his fingers over it. It was a sapphire, the exact shade of his mother's eyes. Around the edge were small pearls, each more delicate than the last.

"Do you want to wear your jewels, Mother?"

"You must give them to your wife," his mother said, the words expelled with great effort. *"They are yours forevermore, my dearest. Every time I wore them, I remembered your father's great love."*

His mother's voice was fading now. *"Look after your father and little Georgiana, and promise me that you will be happy."* She gripped the bedcover, her fingers contorting with the effort of speaking.

Deep breaths wracked Darcy's ribs as he fought the urge to cry. *"I promise, Mother."* He watched the tension leave his mother's body. He held tightly *to her hand as her chest swelled with her final breaths. Soon, there was only silence about the room.*

Abruptly, his father stood and removed himself to the window. Darcy watched him push away the curtains to allow in a crack of light. Fresh air and sunlight flooded the oppressive space. His father drank in the light like a man drowning in darkness. Darcy watched as his father clutched at his chest, his face absolutely grey.

This was the moment Father's heart trouble began, thought Darcy. This was the moment that broke his heart entirely.

Without warning, his father turned from the window to look upon his son, and Darcy was a young boy again, watching his hero struggle to find the words.

"Fitzwilliam, she is gone."

Nodding, Darcy's cheeks were wet with tears. When did he start crying? He ran his hand quickly over his eyes. It would not do to cry in front of Father. He turned to hide his face away. Returning his gaze to the bed, he expected to see the calm face of his beloved mother. Instead, lying there, lifeless and pale, was Elizabeth.

Gasping in horror, Darcy awoke alone in another darkened room. Cold air flooded his lungs, and he clutched at the tightness in his chest. It took him an instant to realise that he was in his bed in London. Trembling, he drew a glass of water from the jug on the side table. He contemplated ringing for Robertson but decided against it. The household would be alarmed unnecessarily. It was only a dream. Darcy pressed his eyes shut. Or was it? It felt so real. Elizabeth had not been present when his mother died; he had been a young boy. He slumped back on the pillow, his breath steadying with each gulp of air. The image of Elizabeth lying dead haunted him. He glanced about. He must have been sleeping for a while. Would Elizabeth be asleep?

Ignoring the ache in his leg that was still present when he woke, Darcy rose from the bed and made his way to the clock upon the mantelpiece. It was almost three in the morning. The house would be silent for a few more hours yet. The last time he had a dream, Elizabeth had comforted him.

You cannot seriously be contemplating waking her! Darcy chastised himself. *She is not your mother, to comfort you when you have a bad dream.*

He stretched out his broad shoulders. The image of her face, so pale as she lay on his mother's deathbed, would not leave him. The urge to look upon Elizabeth became too great. She need not be awake; he just needed to know that she was well.

The door to Elizabeth's room opened noiselessly. Darcy's body still ached, but the constricting feeling in his chest had eased. His eyes adjusted to her room. The four-poster bed was opposite the door. He could hear her breathing. Carefully, he stepped closer to where she lay sleeping. Relief flowed through him. Elizabeth's face was peaceful, her dark curls creating a halo of softness against the white pillow. Her slender neck curved elegantly, and her lashes fluttered against her ivory cheeks.

The covers moved, and Elizabeth shivered a little in her sleep. Darcy stepped back. Was it the moonlight that made her look so pale? His eyes travelled over her body. She was so soft and inviting —how often would he be a visitor to her bed? The coverlet slipped down, revealing the feminine arch of her shoulder. He sighed deeply. Watching her sleep had allayed his anxiety. He did not want to break the tranquillity of her rest; all that mattered to him was that she was safe.

"Sleep well," he allowed himself to whisper as he returned to his room. Closing his eyes, he took a deep breath and willed himself to sleep. There would be no more bad dreams of Elizabeth if he could help it.

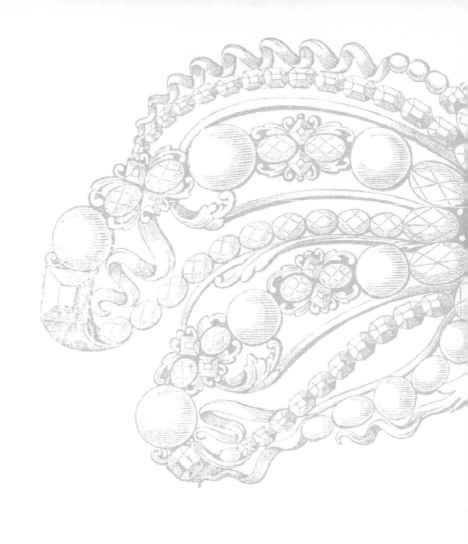

CHAPTER TWENTY-FIVE

After a few days spent convalescing, Darcy had to concede that the good Dr Amstel had been right about several things. The first was that Darcy should have rested the instant he returned to London; the second was that the company of Molly and Georgiana was a welcome tonic to the indignities of being injured; and lastly, Elizabeth's health was such that he needed to keep a close eye on her. After he had discovered her crying, he had watched her carefully. To everyone, she was all smiles, but he could not forget her tear-stained face. In quieter moments, when she thought herself absent from anyone's notice, he saw her close her eyes as if in pain. She would steady herself, just for a moment or two, then throw herself wholly into the next conversation. He noticed too that she would sometimes quietly excuse herself and disappear when she thought everyone else was occupied. Perhaps she was concealing more than just his accident from him? What if she was gravely ill? Amstel had spoken of her iron strength. Darcy had not thought much of his words at the time, but they came back to him each time he caught sight of Elizabeth rallying herself. What had the doctor known her to endure?

Another thought that plagued him was Fitzwilliam. It had been over a week since his abrupt departure. Darcy wondered that no-one mentioned it. Elizabeth took great pains to direct any conversation away from his cousin, and Georgiana seemed too enraptured with her new baby to notice Fitzwilliam's absence.

A welcome distraction had been Bingley and his wife calling upon the Darcys several times. Jane Bingley, Darcy noted, was everything and nothing like Elizabeth. Both in possession of an innate elegance, Elizabeth had all the spirit where Jane had all the gentleness. Bingley was exceedingly happy, Darcy observed. On one occasion they brought their son. Darcy soon learnt why little Charlie was best left with Mrs Turnpike, his kind—but matronly—governess. Upon arrival, young Charlie ran into a corner table in the front hall, upsetting a vase that had been in Darcy's family for as long as he could remember. Darcy found he could not be angry however, so similar was the boy to his father, their boundless enthusiasm matched by their unfailing friendliness.

Darcy soon learnt that Charlie's greatest favourite was Elizabeth. He watched Charlie attach himself to Elizabeth and bombard her with questions, the replies to which were given with unending patience. Second to Elizabeth in Charlie's affection was his little cousin Molly, whom he infinitely preferred to his *'dull baby sister Susannah'*.

Elizabeth had murmured a warning in Darcy's ear about Charlie's sway over Molly. Apparently, during one of his habitual escapes from the nursery, Charlie had overheard some colourful language from the servants' quarters which he had decided to share with his younger cousin.

Darcy was not too troubled by the notion of Charlie influencing Molly. Despite being a year his junior, Molly was more than able to keep up with him. With a touch of fatherly prejudice, Darcy reflected that it would not be long before Molly would be a match in wits for her older cousin. She resembled her mother in so many ways. He watched as they disappeared hand-in-hand in the direction of the nursery under the watchful eye of the esteemed Mrs Turnpike. Elizabeth shared a look with the older woman as the children left. Darcy wondered what unspoken agreement had taken place between them. Before he had a chance to ask her, she too had slipped out behind the little party, no doubt to keep an eye on the children. He turned his mind to their guests. Bingley and Luxford were in some deep discussion, the former having a natural ebullience making up for the reticence of the latter. Jane's attention had been called away briefly by a maid who had a question for Elizabeth. Upon seeing him alone and unable to move himself about, Georgiana moved to a sofa near his chair.

"How are you, my darling brother? I have never seen you so immobile. I wonder how you are bearing up?"

Darcy smiled ruefully at her. "I have never lied to you, as you know. I do not wish to start by telling you that all is well. Suffice it to say, I have felt better."

Georgiana lay a sympathetic hand on his arm. "I am sorry to hear it. You have suffered so much of late."

"Whatever can you mean?"

His reaction had startled her. She blushed, the shy girl of old returning for an instant. "You have endured more than enough even prior to this accident. You did not convince me when you told me that all was well. I know you too well, and for many weeks I had read the anxiety in every line of your face." She squeezed his arm gently. "Do you know, I believe that the previous weight is gone, but I cannot make out what has replaced it. You know you can always speak to me."

Georgiana lowered her voice. "I love Elizabeth dearly, and you must never make me choose between you, but you can always confide in me, even if it is something about her. I cannot promise impartiality, but you must know that I shall always have your best interests at heart."

A deep affection filled his heart. She had always been so considerate, his darling little sister. Nothing had changed in that quarter. He thought for a moment of telling her everything, of all his worries and insecurities, but he simply could not do anything to trouble the perfect serenity of her face. Never would he have conceived of a situation where he would look to Georgiana for advice. Too often she had entrusted him with her worries, and he was not yet used to this new inversion to their relationship.

"There is one matter that I wish to speak to you of. Do you

have any word of Fitzwilliam? He left soon after I regained consciousness, and he did not leave a forwarding address."

Georgiana looked at him, puzzled. "Fitzwilliam left abruptly to join you at Pemberley, just before your terrible fall. He stayed with you until you were better, sending me daily correspondence. He then returned shortly after baby Robert was born to ask after me."

"Fitzwilliam came here?"

"He had been dreadfully worried about me. You know how protective he can be. He seemed very solemn and despondent. I believe he was relieved that everything had gone well and I was in fine health."

Darcy was quiet. "It is only natural after everything that happened with our mother," he replied.

"I suppose that could have been the reason, although I should have thought that recent events may have influenced him as well. I had not considered Mother's illnesses to have been at the forefront of his mind," Georgiana said after a short pause. She did not elaborate further, and Darcy was too preoccupied with thoughts of his cousin.

"But what news of Fitzwilliam? Did he speak of anything else?" Darcy pressed. "Anything that would give an insight to his thoughts?"

"Do you have any reason to believe that we should be concerned? Our cousin's behaviour has been erratic of late. I did not consider it more than the behaviour of a bachelor soldier accustomed to keeping his own schedule. Upon reflection, he was not his talkative self. His whole manner was of introspection. What do you suspect has happened?"

"I am not sure. Perhaps I am troubling you overmuch with my thoughts. He left so suddenly and without an explanation. He did not indicate that he would come here first. I have not received word from him."

"That is strange. Elizabeth received a note from him just the other day. It was when you went to Brooks's and she and little Molly came to visit. She did not mention it, but I recognised his hand instantly. I wondered at it being delivered here and not to your home, but then it is but a short distance between the houses, and it would not take long for a servant to make the journey from one to the other."

Anger filled Darcy. His wife had concealed the truth from him yet again. "She did not mention that to me."

Georgiana caught his tone and squeezed his arm. "Do not tell me that I have unwittingly caused trouble between you both! There must be a reason why Elizabeth has not spoken to you. She has been so terribly worried for you—surely it must have escaped her mind."

Darcy thought back to the argument he had been privy to in the grounds of Pemberley and silently disagreed. He gave Georgiana a comforting smile. "Do not alarm yourself. You have not caused any trouble. You are correct in thinking that there will be a reason for Elizabeth failing to tell me of her letter from Fitzwilliam." *And I shall be certain to discover it,* he thought bleakly to himself.

Another maid entered the room, asking after Elizabeth. Darcy watched as Jane glanced over to him. The maid nodded and approached her master.

"Forgive my interruption, sir, but I was looking for Mrs Darcy. There is a question regarding Miss Darcy in the nursery, and the mistress's opinion is needed. I have looked everywhere but I cannot find her."

Darcy nodded. "Very well, I shall go." Everyone protested at this statement, but he simply waved his hand. "It does me good to move about a little. My back becomes stiff if I do not."

Jane and Georgiana would only hear of him leaving on the condition that he had a footman's assistance. Darcy was happy to acquiesce as he was unsure whether he could find his way to the nursery unaided. The footman came and helped Darcy from the drawing room. He tried not to lean too heavily on the young man as they made their way across the hall.

As they passed the top of the stairs, a movement from the lower level caught Darcy's notice. It was his wife silently shutting the front door. Her eyes and cheeks were bright from the fresh air. He wondered how long she had been outside. She quietly slipped a note to a nearby footman and softly made her way down the hall.

Another secret to be kept from him. *Or perhaps another clandestine letter from my cousin.*

Where before he had been angry, he was now struck by the clanging chill of disappointment. What was so terrible that could not be shared with him? The footman must have felt Darcy's tension as the young servant hesitated in his assistance. Turning to him, Darcy said sharply, "Mrs Darcy has returned and so shall I to the drawing room. Please inform her that she is wanted in the nursery." Nodding vigorously, the footman escorted Darcy back to the visitors.

Some emotion must have been visible on his face as he entered the room, for Georgiana instantly asked him what was the matter. "Nothing that a glass of wine and some masculine company could not resolve." Darcy did not intend to sound so terse, but he could not trust himself to be in Elizabeth's presence in his current mood.

Georgiana's eyes dropped a little but then rose to meet his again—this time with a steely defiance. "In that case, may I suggest that you and Mr Bingley confine yourselves to your study. I find myself quite willing to go home." She addressed her husband, "I hope it does not trouble you to accompany me home, Robert. I know it can be arduous to spend time in such *feminine* company."

Darcy had never been so upbraided by his sister and was at a loss for what to say. She was not the true target of his ire. Eventually, he found his voice. "My dearest Georgiana, forgive me. I am not myself of late."

At this, Georgiana's countenance visibly softened. "Of course, Fitzwilliam. I understand you are in need of rest. You must in return forgive my negligence regarding your injuries. I forget how your stoic nature often disguises the true extent of your pain." Darcy felt his cheeks redden at her astute observation. *Never show weakness.* Father's maxim echoed in his ears.

"Do not leave on account of my poor manners. Your company has brought me untold pleasure."

"You could never offend me, dear brother, but I must confess to being rather tired. I would not typically seek out company at this time, but I could not stay at home knowing you were stuck inside alone." Georgiana rang for a maid to see them out.

Rising to her feet, she gave Darcy a gentle kiss to the cheek. "Make sure you take the trouble to rest properly. Whatever is gnawing away at you is only going to impede your recovery."

Luxford stood also, his awkward limbs propelling his body towards Darcy, hand outstretched. "It is gratifying to see you looking stronger, Darcy. We shall call again soon." Darcy shook Luxford's hand and was surprised by the firmness of the other man's grip. He looked up at the younger man and saw his expression of earnest concern. Darcy had never needed a brother— Fitzwilliam and his elder brother Frederick had fulfilled that role over the years. Should such a brother ever have existed, he certainly would not have resembled shy, lanky Luxford. Yet there had been genuine affection in Luxford's face. *Georgiana is happy,* Darcy thought. And Luxford had every appearance of being a thoroughly decent man.

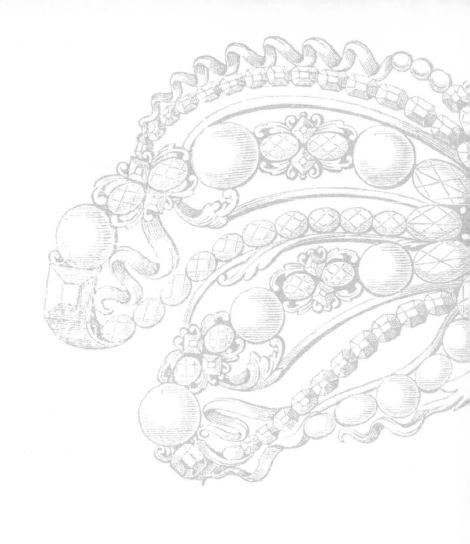

CHAPTER TWENTY-SIX

Darcy retired to his study shortly after Georgiana and Luxford's departure. Bingley accompanied him, his wife preferring to find Elizabeth. Sitting by the fire, watching Bingley, Darcy made a decision. He would confide in Charles. Disguise of any kind was abhorrent to him, and he needed answers. Before he could say anything, Bingley spoke first.

"Darcy, what troubles you? I have known you long enough to read your mood, and there is something that you have not told me. Are you worried about your injuries, or is it another matter? Is it Elizabeth? I trust she is in good health?"

"In truth, I have no idea of anything connected to Elizabeth. After my accident, I awoke to find that all my memories and thoughts from the past six years have been lost or damaged to such an extent that I cannot be certain of anything."

"What are you saying?"

Darcy ordered the things on his already-orderly desk for a moment before replying. "I have no recollection of my marriage to Elizabeth. I do not recall our courtship, our love, even the birth of our child—or indeed that of your son. I cannot remember anything of Georgiana beyond the age of fifteen."

Bingley leant back in his chair, seeming aghast. "I had no idea! Tell me how I can assist you? Is there anything you wish to know?"

Darcy took a deep breath. The great weight he had been carrying with him felt lighter with each word.

"It is torment to be surrounded by so many unfamiliar people. Everyone has a shared memory of my life that I have irrevocably lost. I implore you to help me. I remember our time together at Cambridge and countless inconsequential instances from our youth that allow me to put my trust in you. I must tell you—before I am consumed by it—that I am plagued by an unsettling suspicion that there is a truth being deliberately concealed from me. Never do I receive a straight answer to a direct question."

Bingley shifted in his chair, and his eyes took on a concerned look. "You cannot mean Elizabeth. Believe me when I say that I have never known you to be happier."

"Why should your first instinct be to talk of Elizabeth?" Darcy asked. "I did not mention her, yet you assume you must persuade me of my happiness with her."

Bingley's ears turned the deepest scarlet. "Come, man. You are being unfair. I only say her name as Elizabeth—and perhaps your sister—are the only people who would inspire such a reaction in you."

"And you are convinced that is the only reason?" Darcy looked at Bingley, searching his face for an answer.

Under Darcy's scrutiny, Bingley shifted again, then looked to the side for a moment before returning his eyes to his friend. "If you wish to learn anything about your marriage then you must talk to your wife. It is not my place to dredge up things from the past if she has not spoken to you of them."

"So you admit that Elizabeth is concealing a truth from me?"

"Heavens no! Well, not in the way you make it seem."

"How do I make it seem?"

"That Elizabeth is maliciously lying to you." Bingley paused. "I do not wish to speak any more on this subject lest I disclose something that is too painful for Elizabeth. Remember that I am married to her sister."

Darcy exhaled sharply. "Therefore you will not help me! I

thought I could depend on your friendship. Look at me as I sit beside the fire. I am not able-bodied, my memory is shattered, and still you do not wish to harm Elizabeth's sentiments. Do you not think I have asked her for the truth? She has told me that she will reveal everything when Fitzwilliam returns, but do you know what I saw as I stepped out of the door? Elizabeth, handing a note to a footman."

"There is no harm in that!"

"But why with such secrecy does she leave the room? Earlier today, I learnt that she is in receipt of a note from Fitzwilliam."

"Why would that be a cause for concern? They are good friends!"

"But why not speak of it to me when she knows of my anxiety to hear from him?"

Bingley fell silent for several long minutes. At length, he said, "You are dreaming of problems where there are none to be found. Your wife loves you. And you worship her in return. It is your accident that has made you doubt all. Once you recover—"

"I may *never* recover," Darcy cut him off. "Do you not see why it is imperative for me to learn the truth?" He sighed deeply and drummed his fingers against the side of his chair. He pictured Elizabeth's tear-stained face, so vulnerable and beautiful the night before. What was so terrible that she could not confide in him? In a low voice, he made his confession, painful as it was. "I wish very much to trust my wife. Until then, it is impossible for me to commit my heart to her."

Bingley clapped a sympathetic hand upon Darcy's shoulder. "At the risk of sounding pompous, I shall repeat my previous sentiments. Never before was there a woman more suited to you. I admit that I was very surprised when you told me of your engagement to Elizabeth, but I have never seen you laugh or smile so much in all our years together. Indeed, ever since we first met, there seemed to be a weight about your neck. After your marriage, your whole manner was so much lighter. Everyone that knew you proclaimed you to be a changed man. You even permitted me to tease you, so besotted were you by Elizabeth. If you cannot find it in yourself to trust her, then place your faith in me when I say you love her dearly. You have weathered a great deal of storms together. I urge you not to throw it away on these unfounded suspicions."

Darcy stared dully at the fire in the grate. "I have indeed weathered a storm, Charles." He raised his injured hand, revealing his scarred fingers. "I have been blessed with a constant reminder of my struggles." He closed his eyes briefly. "Sadly, my memory does not fail me in that regard." He turned his attention back to Bingley. "Forgive me, Charles. I am in poor humour and not fit for company."

"Nonsense, I understand you perfectly. I should be exactly the same in your place."

Darcy doubted that greatly but said nothing. Turning his attention back to the fire, he said, "Perhaps I have shared too much of my pain with you. I beg your pardon."

"I would much rather you shared your pain with me than sit and brood as in days of old. How many kindnesses have you shown me over the years? I would be a poor friend indeed to begrudge you any ill humour given all that you have suffered. Why, if it were not for your interference, I should not have married my beloved."

"I assisted you in your courtship?" Darcy could not keep the confusion from his voice.

"If you were not such a dear friend, I should use the word meddle." Bingley's tone was gentle, and his eyes twinkled softly. "You do not remember, I know. All that you need to know is that you had reservations about Jane's family and attempted to counsel me away from her. In a change of heart that I can only attribute to Elizabeth, you confessed the error of your ways and sought to reunite us." He smiled brightly. "My happiness paved the way for yours."

As Bingley's words sank in, Darcy was more puzzled than ever before. If he understood Bingley correctly, he had taken it upon himself to remove Bingley from Jane Bennet and her unsuitable family. Then, under the influence of Elizabeth, he had undergone a change of heart. This did not resemble the man Darcy had thought himself to be. Did he not always maintain that his good opinion, once lost, was gone forever? It would appear that Elizabeth's family had never had his estimation, so how had she convinced him to assist Bingley? It was another fragment to a story that was lost to him. Suddenly, he wished for this conversation to be at an end. The more he learnt, the less certain he became. "Pray, do not mention this to anyone."

"Upon my honour, I shall keep it between us. I am flattered by the faith you place in me." Bingley rose from his seat. "You look in need of a rest. I shall take my leave." Darcy nodded his farewell, a familiar ache beginning to take hold behind his temples.

He heard the door close behind Bingley. The fire crackled heavily. It would only be a matter of time before Elizabeth would return from the nursery. Or wherever she had deigned to go. Darcy rubbed his hand across his chin. What should his next move be? He was reluctant to confront Elizabeth. Bingley was correct—there was nothing wrong with slipping a note to a servant.

The message from Fitzwilliam was another matter. That she should knowingly conceal such a correspondence provoked a strong emotion within his breast. It was anger and disappointment, he told himself. Unbidden, Elizabeth's beautiful face shone before him, her eyes so imploring and kind. *Why can she confide in Fitzwilliam but not me?*

A new sensation clutched at him. He had never had reason to be jealous of Fitzwilliam—the cheerful second son who toiled away to earn his keep. But now his wife would correspond secretly with his cousin rather than place her trust in him. He clenched his jaw. He was not a fool, and he had the means to do his own investigation. He had promised to wait on the condition that Elizabeth spoke to him if she needed assistance. Clearly, she was withholding information from him. In the same spirit of silence, so would he conduct his own enquiries. A sound in the hall signalled Elizabeth's return. Darcy squared his shoulders as best he could from his armchair and braced himself for the coming confrontation.

The object of Darcy's ire entered the room with a soft knock. Every measured argument, every indignant phrase coursing through his mind disappeared when he saw that Elizabeth was followed by a crestfallen Molly. Whatever had summoned Elizabeth to the nursery apparently required his assistance. Little Molly's presence took some of the sting out of his ill humour.

Clearly, Elizabeth did not know that he had seen her by the front door. Her manner was open and warm. She caught his gaze, and he was struck by her beauty. When she laughed, her whole face became illuminated with a most captivating merriment. She bewitched him more than he cared to admit.

"Molly, you must explain to Papa what happened in the nursery today." Elizabeth was biting her bottom lip in an attempt to suppress a smile.

Molly cast her face down, her hands clasped together in front of her. The folds of her dress creased under her touch. "Mama, I do not want—"

"Explain in your own words or I shall have to do it for you." Elizabeth's expressive eyes sparkled as she held Darcy's gaze, drawing him into the mischief before him. His anger momentarily forgotten, Darcy looked upon his beloved daughter. She was angelic in her contrition. Glossy curls tied in ribbons bobbed as she lifted her head to meet his eyes. Curious as to what might provoke such a meeting, he attempted a severe look and waited.

"Papa, I am sorry." Molly's eyes were laced with tears, and her lashes were wet. She was truly a smaller version of Elizabeth. His resolve relented briefly.

"For what do you apologise?"

"Charlie said the scissors were enchanted."

"Which scissors?"

"In Sarah's sewing basket."

Darcy looked quizzically at Elizabeth who hastily reminded him, "Sarah is the nurse-maid, who usually keeps such objects out of the reach of children."

Darcy turned his attention back to Molly. "What else did Charlie say about the scissors?"

Lip quivering, his daughter made her confession. "He told me that if I should use them, then I would get two of anything that I cut." Darcy heard a little snort from his wife, who was suppressing her laughter in the interest of good parenting. He bit the inside of his cheek to prevent himself from joining her.

"And what did you cut?"

"I wanted two of Charlie's biscuits, so I cut one and..."

"Molly, you had two parts of the same biscuit. The enchantment did not work," Elizabeth interjected. "Besides, you have not told your papa the whole truth. You must explain what else you used the scissors for."

Molly continued in a very small voice, "I got my doll, Papa, and I cut her dress so I could get another. But it did not work so I cut some more."

"And now your doll has no dress at all. But what else did you try your magic upon?"

Molly's gaze fell to the floor as she whispered, "I wanted a little dog, just like Aunt Jane."

Elizabeth now spoke, saying, "It would appear that Charlie kidnapped poor Tiny, and he was subjected to the most undignified haircut. I have explained how disappointed I am that Molly should take scissors that do not belong to her."

Nodding his head, Darcy motioned for Molly to come closer. He placed her on his good knee, recalling his own father doing the very same. "Your mama is right. I am disappointed that you should believe your cousin when you know it is wrong to steal."

At his words, Molly buried her head in his coat and sobbed. He placed a hand on her back. She was so small and precious. Her hot, sweaty face was warm against his chest. A tenderness filled his heart. So this was fatherhood. He stroked Molly's back gently until her crying subsided.

"Keep your resolve," Elizabeth murmured to him as she disengaged Molly from his embrace. Suppressing a smile of his own, Darcy reached across and rang for a servant.

Adopting what he hoped was a stern face, he said, "You must say sorry to Sarah and to Aunt Jane." Molly nodded tearfully. "And you must not listen to your cousin when he tells you to do something that you ought not to."

"Yes Papa." Molly's bottom lip was still quivering. "I am very sorry."

Darcy nodded, his lips curling into a gentle smile. It was hard to scold her when she looked so downcast. Fortunately, the timely arrival of a maid prevented him from feeling guilty. Molly was escorted back to the nursery to make her apologies. As soon as the door shut, Elizabeth collapsed in the chair opposite and laughed heartily. Wiping tears from her eyes, she regarded Darcy.

"Never before have I seen such a sight. The poor little creature was quite bald in places. Thankfully he was not injured."

Darcy could not help joining her laughter this time. "Should I apologise to Charles and your sister?"

"Definitely not! Sarah always keeps her sewing basket on the highest shelf. The only way to reach it is to climb, and Molly would not be tall enough. Their son was as much a culprit as our daughter was."

Darcy relaxed back in his chair. "Did I acquit myself well? I did not know how strict I should be."

"You were splendid. It is hard to discipline her when she sincerely believed that they were indeed magical." Elizabeth shook her head and laughed again. "Losing your good opinion is what she fears the most."

"Charles said I was an indulgent father."

Elizabeth rolled her lovely eyes. "Charles is indulgent. *You* are tender-hearted. Therein lies the difference. He would not have chastised his son. We have spoken before about how best to teach Molly what is right and wrong. She needs to learn there are consequences for her actions."

"Of course. It would not do for Molly to learn to deceive those around her."

Elizabeth must have caught the resentment in his voice for she replied, "Of course. We must all act as examples to our children. It is an unspoken trial of parenthood. Who among us is a true paragon of virtue? Our children may perceive us as perfect. It can be a shock to learn we are mere mortals, capable of bad as well as good. And we must, of course, hope that in time they understand our intentions were noble however our actions may seem."

She glanced at Darcy and continued softly, "We can only hope that they continue to love us, flaws and all."

Darcy contemplated her words. "Some flaws may be harder to accept than others."

Elizabeth rose and placed a gentle kiss on his temple. "That is true. However, it is easy to forgive a flaw when the person who owns it is so very dear to you."

Her lovely face was suddenly serious. "I pray that you remember that." She tenderly placed his walking cane closer to his chair and promised to join him for dinner later.

The study door closed on Darcy, alone once more. Staring into the flames, he realised the futility of his anger. Confronting Elizabeth was out of the question. She had power enough to thoroughly disarm him.

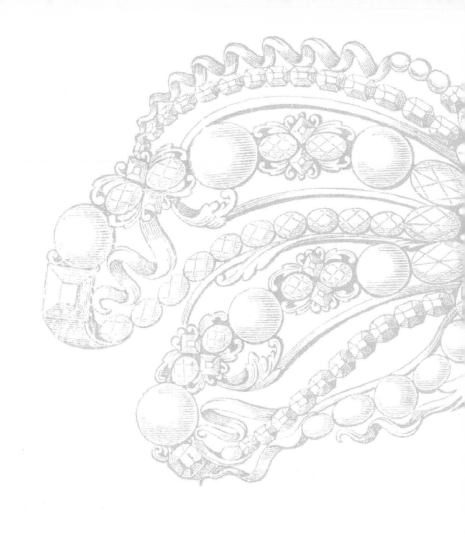

CHAPTER TWENTY-SEVEN

My dearest love,

    I am sitting in the drawing room at Rosings Park, pretending to write a letter. Thankfully, your aunt Lady Catherine has not used her powers of observation—superior as they are—to discern the truth of our secret correspondence via this little diary. And where are you now? A fine question to ask, dear husband, and worthy of an answer. You are on the sofa opposite your aunt, making every valiant attempt to pay attention to her discourse. I was so proud of my endeavours to reconcile you two, and now my reward is to be trapped in a drawing room being studiously ignored. Still, it is preferable to be overlooked by Lady Catherine than be required to join in her conversation.

    So engrossed are you in the formidable woman that I have escaped your notice. This is quite to my advantage as I may observe you at my leisure—as you once did to me, all those years ago and quite unbeknownst to me. How fine you look in your blue coat! How pleased I am that I convinced you to wear it——you may thank me later.

    But now I am distracted. Where was I? I believe I had begun my examination of you. Let me start with your face. Your countenance is severe, but that is only thanks to your present partner for conversation. I know how handsome you truly are when you smile. You keep brushing a curl from your eyes—I suspect you are making a mental note to request a trim from Robert-

213

son. Perhaps I could cut your hair for you, as we did in Italy when I tried grappa for the first time.

Oh, but what is she talking about now? Something about her expertise in chicken rearing. You deserve a prize, my love. I shall use this as an example to anyone who accuses you of possessing a discourteous disposition.

Now my eyes are travelling down your neck to your shoulders. There is something so broad and masculine about them. I can feel myself blush as I remember how they tense when you hold me in your embrace. Your shoulders are, of course, connected to your back. My neck has become quite hot at the remembrance of the musculature hidden under those impeccably tailored clothes. How was I to know the pleasure of your muscles flexing under my touch? How I long to run my fingers down the length of your body. It gives me untold gratification to see the effect I have on you. There, I have put in writing a thought that plagues me perpetually. Do you know how tiresome it is to go about my day pretending to be a respectable gentlewoman when all I wish to do is to reacquaint myself with your body over and over again?

You have stretched your legs out now. Are you getting restless? I wonder, how tall are you precisely? I know of no other man with your fine stature. Perhaps I can persuade Robertson to reveal your measurements to me. I shall say I am ordering you a surprise and watch as he tries not to blush. Am I not a wicked creature? I am sorry to say but I could never crave a short man. I love when you stand behind me and bend down to kiss me on the neck. It is an untold pleasure of being loved by a tall husband, and I could not do without it.

Half an hour has passed since Lady Catherine first demanded your attention. Perhaps I should do something to raise your spirits? What could I do to let you know that I am thinking of you continually? You are so adept at reading my body, surely you should know the reason for my flushed cheeks? What polite excuse could I give to cause us to quit the room and make our escape upstairs? Dinner is too long a wait. I have already scandalised Lady Catherine by marrying you without her express permission. I should hate to give her any reason to be proved right—her opinion of me is low enough already.

There, you have just caught my eye. I have long suspected you could read my thoughts because you are now struggling to keep your gaze from me. Do you know, every time I am congratulated for marrying such a respectable man, I must refrain from laughing. No gentleman would look at me the way you just did. I saw the flicker of your eyes over my person, scandalous man! I shall tease you mercilessly for it later. I think you must have noticed that I am not writing a letter—your lips are twisting as you hide a smile. Your cheeks dimple as you do so, and your eyes are alive with mischief. Perhaps I shall read 'my letter' to you tonight so you may know with whom I have been 'corresponding'. Or perhaps I shall keep it a secret. It would not do to encourage your proud nature. How conceited you should become if you knew the depth of my desire. I am not sure whether I could bear the smug look on your handsome face! You are, as it is, far too self-satisfied every time I find my pleasure in you. The cat who got the cream, or so the saying goes.

You are bestowing your full smile on me now over Lady Catherine's shoulder. Why must you do this to me? In her drawing room of all places! Now I can only picture that smile as we lie in our bed together later, wrapped around one another...

A noise distracted Darcy. He turned his head to look about his darkened bedroom. The only sound he could hear was the pounding of his own treacherous heart. He had been reading Elizabeth's diary again. His laborious study of it had begun anew when he had learnt of her letter from Fitzwilliam. Every time he thumbed the pages, he told himself it was purely to glean more information regarding their life together.

But to admit as such would only be a half-truth. Her words had a power over him that he could not account for. He read her words two, three times over; not just for their meaning but to bathe in their effect. In the comfort of his bed, he would dream of Elizabeth. Her words were so loving and playful, so full of admiration for his person that he could not help himself. The images she created manifested themselves into such dreams that he longed for the moment he could slumber. Never before had he been such a slave to desire. It was a cold shock each morning when he awoke to an empty bed.

Of course, it took Darcy a long time to read anything, even when it was as potent as Elizabeth's innermost thoughts. He was up for many hours in the night, straining his eyes in the candlelight. He detested his powerlessness. He could not write to any of his acquaintances and ask for their assistance. Many times over the years he had been in need of a discreet investigator. How to correspond with them without asking for assistance from another? Fitzwilliam would be his usual confidant, but now that avenue was closed.

After much deliberation, Darcy concluded that his best bet was Tilford. Distasteful as the man was, Darcy had obviously approached him before his accident. It was also entirely reasonable to go to Brooks's—he had little else to do but convalesce, and sitting in a chair was the same activity no matter in which corner of London the chair was located. Elizabeth had pursed her lips in disapproval when he told her of his plan to visit the club. Darcy had attempted nonchalance—after all, who was she to criticise how he spent his time away from home? But truthfully, he had another motive for escaping to Brooks's: the torture of being around Elizabeth and not knowing the truth had become more than he could bear.

As predicted, Tilford attended the club most days. He was, however, often surrounded by others, many of whom were unknown to Darcy. Fortunately, he was a curious man. It was not long before Tilford's interest in Darcy's solitary presence was sufficiently roused. Breaking away from the larger group, he ensconced himself next to Darcy's armchair. The buttons of Tilford's waistcoat strained as the chair groaned under his weight.

"Darcy of Pemberley graces these hallowed corridors twice in the same month." He leant rather too closely towards Darcy. "Have you finally succumbed to the fate of every gentleman in these halls whose presence denotes their quest for solitude? Or perhaps you are here for another reason entirely. One that you would not want your wife's pretty little ears to hear."

Darcy's eyes met Tilford's leery gaze. "I am here because I wish to rest," he said in an even tone. "Unless you can think of another reason that I should be here alone."

Something flickered behind Tilford's eyes. Darcy recognised it instantly. Greed. Tilford's expression was one he had witnessed many times before. He would need to be wary.

"My good man! After all these years of acquaintance, do we need a reason to converse?"

"As you say, I do not attend Brooks's often. You should tell me what has occurred in my absence. Our previous interview was interrupted if you recall." Darcy's expression was neutral, but he held Tilford's stare a fraction longer than he would have under other circumstances.

"Yes indeed. It was regarding a favour that you begged of me."

"I begged something of you? That sounds most unlike me." Darcy trained his face into a well-used mask of disdain.

"Pardon me, I spoke out of turn. You know how it can be amongst friends."

"Was there something that you wished to say?" Darcy's cold tone never failed to impress his will on those whose circumstances were decidedly beneath his own. His tactic had the desired effect on Tilford.

"Come now, old man! I see you are in no humour for conversation. I shall be brief. There is still no word from any reputable pawnbrokers about the item in question." Tilford's pudgy lips twisted into a sneer. "No sign from any disreputable pawnbrokers either."

"So you have nothing of importance to disclose?"

"Not so hasty!" Tilford's body was infused with self-importance. Finally, he had the upper-hand in the conversation, and he relished his moment. "Yesterday evening, around ten o'clock, I received a note from a contact of mine—a useful fellow by the name of Jenkins—who reported that a young woman had made enquiries at the old jeweller's on Pantheon Street. Her purpose was to secure a value for an item."

"How is that of significance?"

"The item in question matched your description."

"Did your associate reveal anything to you about the young woman?"

Tilford's eyes gleamed wickedly. "Of course, but you must understand that such information comes at a cost. You would not want an old friend such as myself to suffer a loss."

Darcy looked at Tilford without disguising his disgust. "I should pay you for this favour? I thank you for your trouble to search, but I must remind you that my friendship and influence within society also has value in itself. In demanding payment, I fear the loss would only ever be yours, as my good opinion, once lost, would be gone forever."

Tilford's face went white. "You misunderstand me."

"I am glad of it. Now, *old friend*, tell me what you know before I make my own enquiries."

"I was told—in the strictest confidence—that the young woman was about twenty or so, but she could have been a touch older. She was of a slim build with dark hair and fair skin. Very pretty. A tempting armful, according to my source."

"How close did he get? Did he get a good look at her face?"

"Sadly, no."

Darcy bristled. "A shame. Perhaps for that information I would have found my price."

Darcy looked again at Tilford. The man was unrecognisable as the genial friend he had once known at Cambridge. When had he become so unpalatable? Perhaps he had always been so and Darcy had never noticed. It was not a surprise to him that he no longer frequented the gentlemen's club. He broke the silence by offering Tilford a drink using such an unwelcoming tone that the man took the hint and refused it, taking his leave of Darcy.

What if the woman had been Elizabeth? It would explain her mysterious absences and surreptitious notes. Darcy made a mental note of the jeweller's. It was pointless writing it down. What jewellery could Tilford be referring to? The servants at Pemberley had limited access to the family jewels, but that was before he was married. How would he know what changes had been made? Elizabeth could claim to have sold something with his permission, and he would never know the truth. It was nonsensical. Elizabeth would have no need of money. He clutched the arm of the chair in anguish. Never before had he so wished for Fitzwilliam's presence. The clock chimed. Glancing up, Darcy sighed. It was time to return.

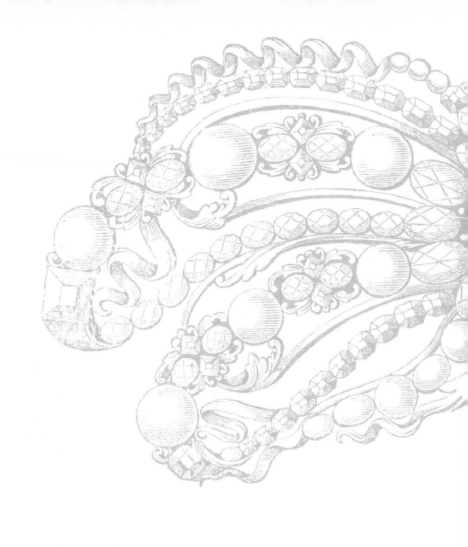

CHAPTER TWENTY-EIGHT

The Bingley carriage was waiting outside Darcy House. He wondered at its presence as his own carriage drew up next to it. He did not remember making plans with Bingley. Darcy would not have gone to Brooks's if he had known the Bingleys were to call. He fervently hoped that young Charlie and the lapdog were still at home. He did not wish to have to further reprimand Molly's behaviour.

Obtaining assistance from a footman, he made his way to the formal sitting room. The atmosphere that greeted him was strange. On the long couch in front of him sat Bingley and Jane. On the left-hand chair was Elizabeth, her face paler than he had ever seen, sitting in utter silence. Her posture was suggestive of internal tension, and Darcy was put in mind of a jack-in-the-box.

He soon discovered the reason for her mood. On the chair directly opposite, dressed in all her finery, was Caroline Bingley. "Darcy! How are you today?" Caroline drawled. "I have just heard such distressing news about your accident!"

Looking carefully at Bingley, Darcy noted the red-tips of his friend's ears and the nervous twisting of his signet ring. Something was amiss. "I do not have the pleasure of understanding you, Miss Bingley. As you can see, I am much improved."

"Physically, I can see that your strength is returning." Miss Bingley eyed Darcy's form in such a manner that he blushed. "But it is the mental anguish that concerns me the most. I have heard that your memory still suffers most persistently."

Here, Darcy glared at Bingley. "I have no idea where you got such a notion, ma'am. It distresses me to imagine such gossip is being circulated."

"Gossip? Oh dear. I know you must remember some of our acquaintance...such as our theatre trip together." Here she shot a look of triumph at the watching Elizabeth. "But you may not recall the depths of our friendship. Come, there should be no secrets among friends."

"It seems that some friends are the last people in the world to be prevailed upon to keep a secret," Darcy retorted, the whole time training his eyes on Bingley.

Under such a gaze, Bingley could only stammer, "Forgive me, Darcy, I had every intention of keeping my promise. My darling Jane knows me so well that she saw something was amiss. It was impossible to conceal my worries from her."

"Charles spoke to me in the privacy of our sitting room," Jane's soft voice interrupted. "I do not know how Caroline came to hear of it. Perhaps we had not shut the door completely."

Elizabeth snorted. "Jane, you may need thicker doors to make it impossible for people to *accidentally* overhear a conversation."

"Come now, Eliza! This attitude will not do!" Miss Bingley smirked at Elizabeth. "How will Darcy ever recall why on Earth he married you if you speak so? He will never remember how you entrapped him in the first place."

"Caroline!" Bingley hissed.

"What did you say, Miss Bingley?" Elizabeth's voice was quiet with fury. "And my name, as you seem to have forgotten, is Mrs Darcy."

Miss Bingley merely tutted with a shake of her elegant coiffure. "Pray, forgive me. It was a poor choice of words."

Darcy sat dumbfounded by Miss Bingley's insult. To speak to his wife in this manner, in his own home! He opened his mouth to say as much, but before he could do so, Elizabeth replied evenly,

"Forgive me, Miss Bingley, I must excuse myself. If you are ever married—I mean *when*, of course—you will understand the natural duties that come with becoming a wife and mother. Please stay for as long as you feel comfortable." Giving Jane a nod, Elizabeth swept out, leaving Darcy alone with the three Bingleys.

Never one for conversation at the best of times, Darcy was at a loss for what to say. Bingley kept his eyes upon the floor.

Finally, Darcy asked, "Was there a reason for your visit?"

"I wished foremost to personally apologise to you for Charlie's antics yesterday. I did not hear the full measure of it until we returned home. He is the eldest child and therefore should set an example."

"It was a relief that no one was hurt."

"Young Charlie is such a wilful child," Miss Bingley interjected again. "You really should take a firmer hand with him."

"I believe you are correct, Caroline. My husband is in great need of taking a firmer hand with his family members." All eyes turned to Jane. Quiet, gentle Jane—whose sweet softness had impressed itself upon Darcy from the very start—had reached her limit of her sister-in-law's rudeness. "Excuse me. I shall attend to my sister and assist her in any way that I am able. Perhaps you could arrange for us to return home now that everyone has said their piece. I am leaving for Longbourn with the children this afternoon and do not wish to be delayed further."

With that, she rose and departed the room without a backwards glance. Bingley looked to be on the verge of tears. Darcy almost felt sorry for his old friend. He suspected Bingley was rarely at the sharp end of his wife's displeasure.

Standing abruptly, Bingley hurried out of the room after Jane, and Darcy found himself alone with Miss Bingley. The little scene that had just played out between her and his wife had been distasteful, and he did not know what to make of it. She was staring at him, an inexplicable look of superiority writ across her features.

She rose and came to the chair nearest his; he fought against recoiling from her. Had it not been difficult for him to flee, he would have. "You may not recall, but there was a time when we were once very close." She leant towards him. Her perfume was overpowering—too musky, with nauseatingly heavy floral undertones.

Up close, he could clearly see the thick powder on her face. It seemed she was trying to look younger than she was and doing a patched-up job of it. His father used to say only the worst fields needed the best soil. He had never thought of its meaning until now. Someone who was truly lovely would not need such cosmetic help. Involuntarily, he compared her to Elizabeth. Even wearing nothing more sophisticated than a plain nightdress and a dressing gown, Elizabeth had far more natural attractiveness than Miss Bingley ever could have.

"As a friend to your brother, it is only natural we should meet often," said Darcy at last.

"Indeed, had our acquaintance been of a romantic nature, I should not have met my darling Wilson." Her voice became hard and cruel. "With his standing in society, he is set to become the most powerful industrialist in England. One day, you may come to our residence to see how a grand home should be run. If I had married you, then I should have denied myself more luxury than I could imagine. The previous established wealth of the aristocracy is under threat. The future of our great country lies with forward-thinkers such as my betrothed. I am glad to be aligned with such a man."

Her gaze was piercing. Darcy felt thoroughly upbraided. Why was she being so spiteful? He had done nothing to deserve such censure.

"Wealth is but one measure of greatness." Darcy stopped short of a direct insult.

"Wealth is the *only* measure that counts." Miss Bingley stood to take her leave. "You would do well to remember that. Perhaps it is your marriage to a penniless country chit that has so changed you."

Rendered speechless by her offensive words, Darcy did not know whether to attempt to stand with her.

"No, stay where you are, Darcy. It would do you good to look up to me for once." An ugly expression contorted her features.

Darcy readied himself for her parting shot. In that sense, Miss Bingley did not disappoint. "Keep well, Darcy. And be sure to give my love to Wickham. How does your brother-in-law fare these days?"

Upon seeing Darcy's expression, she laughed softly and showed herself out.

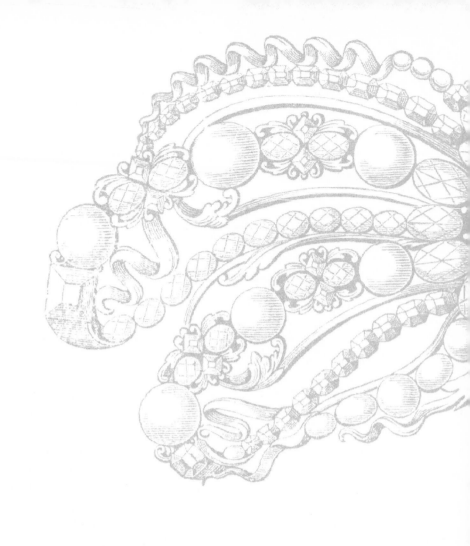

CHAPTER TWENTY-NINE

Wickham. That bounder, that seducer, that utter, utter scoundrel. George Wickham—his brother-in-law! Married to one of his wife's younger sisters he supposed. What had Fitzwilliam said of them? *Their charms diminish exponentially until you reach the youngest.* How had this deviltry come to pass? And when? Did Georgiana know of it? And what of Elizabeth? Of course, she must know. If Darcy were able to pace, he would have worn a hole in the rug. As it was, he sat perfectly still, not trusting himself to move or speak. To hear such news from Caroline Bingley! Darcy seethed. *It cannot be borne!*

Something within him broke. Grabbing the armrests, he pulled himself up and snatched his walking cane. Steeling himself against the ache and stiffness of his leg, he gritted his teeth and hobbled towards the door.

He did not have a plan. His only thought was to find out the truth. Where was Elizabeth? Where the deuce was his wife? He pulled at a door handle, bursting through the doorway to find an empty room. Nothing. He went along the corridor and tried a second. Empty again. His scowl deepened as he tried the library door. Rattling the door handle, he pushed his way through. The stillness of the room momentarily broke him from his anger.

Thinking it empty, he turned to leave when a small sigh caught his attention. He made his way towards the sound and for a moment thought he had found Elizabeth. Sitting on the chair was Molly, her glossy curls the exact shade of chocolate-brown as her mother's. She was curled up on a cushion, flicking through the pages of a fairy story. As she gave another little sigh, Darcy could see that her eyes were red and her cheeks were puffy. He instantly softened. Taking a deep breath, he said softly, "Little one, what is the matter?"

Startled, Molly looked up. "Papa! I thought you went away again!" Her face broke into an adorable smile.

"You know that I always come back."

Molly wiped a tear from her eyes. "You did not come back when you were hurt."

"That is true," Darcy conceded, "but I am here now." Very gently, he sat on the chair opposite her. "What has made you cry?"

Molly sniffed and shrugged her shoulders. "Mama is sad. I saw her crying."

"Did she say why she was crying?"

"No, she was with Aunt Jane by the stairs."

"Ah," Darcy said, surmising that Elizabeth had not known her daughter was watching. He fell silent as he pictured Jane comforting Elizabeth. Miss Bingley's words had found their mark for her too—a thought that made him angry again, although for a different reason.

Molly did not notice his silence as she asked, "When will you get better, Papa?"

"I am getting better, dearest girl. Better every day."

"You do not smile like you used to." Molly slipped off the chair and stood beside him.

"Do I not?" *Did I truly smile so much before?*

"But do not worry. I still love you." She slipped her little hand into his.

He returned her gesture with a smile. "See, my love, I can smile. I promise to do it more often."

Nodding, she gave him a tearful kiss on the cheek. "Where is Mama?" she asked.

"I do not know, but I am looking for her also." Gazing into his daughter's face, he made a silent vow never to cause her any unnecessary pain. "Perhaps we should look for her together. You may help your poor old father out of this chair." He gave her hand a squeeze, feigning an effort when he stood, causing her to giggle.

Feeling calmer, Darcy searched hand-in-hand with Molly for Elizabeth, but she was nowhere to be found. "Do you know where Mama goes when she is not with us?"

"She goes to write a letter," Molly said.

Darcy wondered to whom Elizabeth might write. Fitzwilliam presumably. Jealousy clutched at his heart. What if she was in correspondence with Wickham? It would explain why she had neglected to mention any of it. His blood boiled as he thought of the wastrel. That smug, handsome face. Wickham reminded him of a lap dog. Striking to look at, with all the appearance of a pedigree. Domesticated, docile, and over-groomed. Yet put Wickham in a corner and watch his hackles rise. *Those little yappy dogs always give the worst bites,* thought Darcy. Poor Georgiana—she barely ate for a month after Wickham's abandonment. To see her waste away had been unbearable. He had vowed never to speak the man's name again, but now here he was, related through marriage to a rake he barely considered human. A muscle in his jaw twitched. Tilford had mentioned a jeweller. How many countless items of Darcy finery had disappeared under George Wickham's light-fingered touch? And Fitzwilliam's reaction to Elizabeth in the garden. Only Wickham could provoke such an emotion.

He was in no need of help to find Elizabeth's private room, adjoined as it was to his own. He knocked on the door and, upon hearing no answer, entered regardless.

His wife's chambers were exactly like her: elegant and welcoming.

"Mama! Where are you?" Molly started to walk up and down the room, peering behind the furniture.

"Molly, I do not think your mother would be under the sofa," Darcy said gently.

She scowled at him, an expression so like his own that he

nearly laughed. "Mama hides all the time. It is our favourite game."

"Yes, I am sure your mother is fond of games of secrecy," he said wryly. Seeing Molly's nonplussed expression, he continued, "Go and look through that door and see whether Mama is in there."

Molly scampered away, leaving Darcy alone in Elizabeth's chamber. Glancing about him, he wondered what he should do. As a husband, he had every right to search her possessions. She had withheld the truth from him, and no court would hold him accountable for his actions. However, as a gentleman, his principles prevented him from acting upon his impulses. One day, he would be held accountable to a higher judgment than mortal law, and he could not rifle through her belongings in good conscience.

Undecided, he made his way to her writing table. He did not know why—it would take him a lifetime to read her correspondence. Perhaps there would be some indication of where she had gone? That was justification enough to be in her room. Drawing close to the desk, a familiar scrawl caught his eye. His heart nearly stopped. Trembling, he reached out and touched the letter, turning it over in his hands. It took him a while to read and even longer for the words to sink in. The letter was dated today.

Your presence is required at the draper's at 9 Henrietta St, Covent Garden. Ask to view the Chinese silk, from two o'clock onwards.

Come alone.

Pemberley's most trusted servant.

Dread flooded Darcy. His worst fear had been realised. Wickham had written to Elizabeth. It could be no one else. A memory flickered before him. Wickham was in Darcy's father's study, standing before the desk. Darcy was a little to the right, gazing out of the window and wishing he were elsewhere. The meeting before him was futile. His father had not heeded Darcy's warning and therefore had not confronted the scoundrel properly. Why his own father could not see the harm in Wickham had been beyond him. By offering the information as a result of an anonymous report, Darcy's father allowed Wickham to deny the charges.

"This is naught but a malicious rumour—likely a jealous classmate that wonders at my good fortune in having you as a patron. Believe me, sir, I would do nothing to harm the good reputation of this family and my home. I am Pemberley's most trusted servant."

This letter was further evidence of Wickham's duplicitous character. What business did he have with Elizabeth? Why not sign his name if he had nothing to hide?

He glanced at his watch. It was one. It was not far to Covent Garden by carriage. One way or another, he would have the truth.

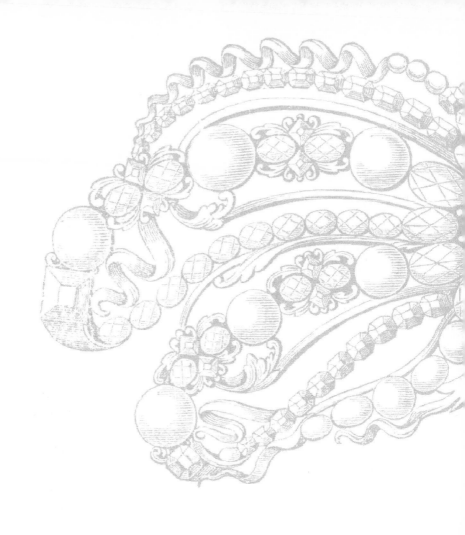

CHAPTER THIRTY

The draper's shop on Henrietta Street was almost respectable. It had a narrow little front, crooked walls, and was squashed between two much finer shops. Walk too fast and it would escape the notice of many potential customers. Alas, Darcy could not walk quickly, no matter how much he wished for it. He had asked his coachman to stop just before Henrietta Street. He did not want Wickham to know of his presence. The note had said from two o'clock. There was no guarantee that Wickham would be punctual. Indeed, there was nothing to say that Wickham would be alone.

He wondered at Elizabeth agreeing to meet him. Would she place herself in danger? No, he thought bitterly. This rendezvous would pose no threat to Elizabeth, intimate as she was with her brother-in-law. He slipped his hand inside his greatcoat, touching the cold metal of his father's old pistol within. He could not afford to take any risks. A bell rang as he entered the shop. Glancing about, he saw he was nearly the only customer. Making his way to the counter, he addressed the stooped man sitting behind it.

"I have been told your Chinese silks are of the highest quality. May I be permitted to see them?"

The man squinted at Darcy. "There is a special rate for those who wish to see them." His eyes narrowed. "A rate that is paid *upfront*."

Nodding, Darcy, took out a coin and held it before the elderly draper. The gleam of the gold reflected in the older man's eyes. "Come," he beckoned with a gnarled finger.

The draper pushed the door open to reveal a dark, panelled passage. "Make your way down there, and our store room is on the left. I shall leave you to browse the wares at your leisure." He grinned and shuffled back to the shopfront. The door shut behind the old man with a firm click. Inhaling deeply, Darcy shook away his apprehension as he approached another door at the far end of the dingy passage. Reaching out for the iron handle, it creaked quietly as he steadied his hand around it and made his way across the threshold.

The room he entered was cavernous and stale. Not a single silk could be seen. Gloomy shadows were broken only by a shaft of light from the cracked window on the far wall. Darcy heard the distant rumble of carts passing on the cobbles outside.

Could this be a trap? Did Wickham summon Elizabeth knowing Darcy would follow? *Nonsense. Elizabeth concealed this from you*, he reminded himself. *He will not expect you. And he will not expect you to be armed.* His heart pounded. What would Elizabeth's reaction be? Would she be relieved to see him? Or dismayed? Either way, he would find out. Somewhere outside the little shop, a clanging bell chimed two.

The oppressive silence was broken only by the sound of Darcy's heartbeat. He stepped a little farther into the centre of the room, the dusty floorboards straining under his weight. Why would Wickham wish to meet Elizabeth here? Was she safe?

Panic gripped him. This was a mistake. A floorboard groaned. Then he felt it. A cold, hard blade against his throat. His heart pounded. A hand gripped his wrist, clamping his arm behind him. Pain seared through his leg as he twisted about and struggled to regain balance. Kill or be killed. Plunging his free hand into his coat, he drew out the pistol, turning to get a better aim. The knife pressed more tightly against his neck.

Darcy slammed the end of the pistol against his assailant's leg.

He wound his body towards his attacker, almost grateful for a reason to finally put an end to the damned scoundrel. They grappled with each other, struggling into the light. Darcy's eyes widened. The man holding a knife to his throat was not Wickham. His heart skipped a beat. He would know that face anywhere, dear as it was to him.

The man at the other end of the blade was Fitzwilliam.

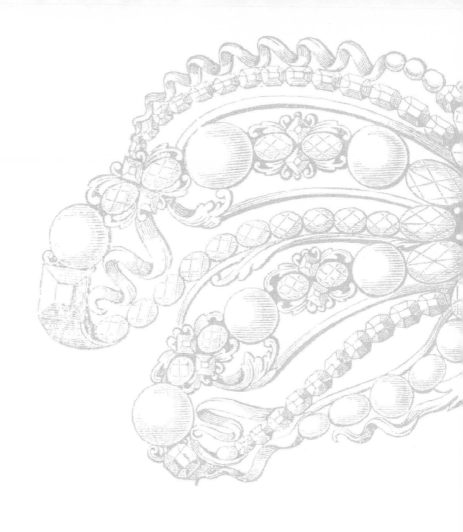

CHAPTER THIRTY-ONE

"You!" Darcy panted. Every nerve in his body was taut, readying itself for whatever came next. "Good God, what is this madness?"

"Silence, you damned fool."

"I should shoot you directly."

"You will do no such thing. You will alert Wickham to our presence. I have waited long enough to press my blade against that cur's jugular. Besides, I do not wish for a bullet to the leg. It bloody hurts."

"What in Heaven's name is happening?"

"There is much you do not know. I shall explain after I have throttled my answers from that mangy dog's mouth."

A noise drew their attention to a newcomer in the passage leading to the store room. Fitzwilliam hauled Darcy into the shadows. Finally succumbing to the mounting pain coursing through his body, he slumped against the cold stone wall. He did not know what to do next. All his energy had been used to defend himself. Reaching his hand inside his pocket, he tightened his grip on the gun. One bullet would be enough as long as he had a clear shot.

He strained his eyes in the darkness. Fitzwilliam had moved behind the door. His cousin's military training had served him

ALI SCOTT

well; he was indistinguishable from the shadowy corners of the room. It was only the odd flash of light reflecting from the blade twisting in his hands that signalled his position to Darcy. How long had Fitzwilliam been waiting like this? Darcy steeled himself. The door creaked open, and a cloaked figure stepped inside.

Without warning, Fitzwilliam struck. In one fluid motion, he grabbed the figure by the throat, just as he had done with Darcy. Sensing his opportunity, Darcy pushed himself from the wall and shoved the door shut. He grabbed at the writhing mass in Fitzwilliam's arms. Both men pulled their quarry into the broken light. Darcy stared at the stranger. The person in front of him was no more George Wickham than his cousin had been.

He was staring into the face of a woman who could almost be Elizabeth. They shared the same dark, glossy curls and ivory skin. But where Elizabeth had a slender elegance, the woman before him had a sensual voluptuousness. Her mouth was a little too wide, and her lips were too full to be considered a classical beauty, but he could appreciate how a man might find her attractive. Her eyes were the same shape as Elizabeth's and framed with identical dark lashes, but they were wide-set and of the brightest blue. Darcy was put in mind of a garish doll that had once belonged to Georgiana. He did not know the woman, but she was clearly no stranger to Fitzwilliam.

"Unhand me or I shall scream." Her voice was shrill.

"Scream and I will silence you forever." Fitzwilliam moved closer, knife in hand. Darcy could not hide his surprise. Where had his mild-mannered cousin gone? Whatever fighting he had seen had hardened him. Fitzwilliam of old would never use such a tone. *Or perhaps there are sides to him I do not know*, a little voice inside him whispered.

"You would not dare touch a woman."

"A calculating, artful shrew like you is not worthy of the name woman."

"And what of him?" The woman snorted in Darcy's direction. "Do you think he would stand by and let you harm me? What would *dearest, loveliest* Elizabeth say when she learnt of her husband's part in my demise? You would never allow it, Darcy."

238

Darcy addressed his cousin, "Fitzwilliam, who is this baggage? What connexion is she to Elizabeth?" Drawing himself up to his full height, he towered over her. His face must have revealed his disgust, as the woman cowered before him.

Fitzwilliam raised his eyebrows. "You do not recognise her?"

Darcy shook his head.

The woman's eyes widened; all the colour drained from her face. "Come, Darcy, I cannot have changed so much since last we met." There was an edge of fear in her voice; she had clearly anticipated Darcy's compassion towards her.

A grim smile spread across Fitzwilliam's face. "Allow me to renew your acquaintance." Unceremoniously hauling the woman onto a broken chair, he did not release his grip on her. "Darcy, may I present your estranged sister-in-law, Mrs Lydia Wickham."

Darcy looked again, this time more closely, at the poor creature who would bear the scoundrel's name. He understood now the resemblance to Elizabeth. She must be a younger sister, but it was difficult to determine her age. She had a weary, hungry look, not unlike the women he saw prowling the darkened street corners of London. Dark shadows circled tired eyes, and he could see the sharp outline of her collarbone from the cut of her dress. Life had not been kind to her. And perhaps Wickham had also been cruel.

What had possessed Wickham to marry such a woman? Darcy knew that Elizabeth did not bring a fortune to their marriage, and the same must have been true of her sisters. Money was the only thing that Wickham truly cared for. Money and his own self-interest. So how had Miss Lydia Bennet secured him?

Bile rising in his throat, he recalled himself to the true purpose of this meeting. "What brings you here, *Mrs Wickham*?"

"Your wife." She set her shoulders defiantly, but Darcy heard the tremor in her voice.

"How odd that you should choose such a place to meet your sister!" Fitzwilliam said. "Or perhaps it was not your suggestion. Where is your dear husband? It was his company that I anticipated."

Lydia's eyes darted from Fitzwilliam to Darcy. "He keeps his own company."

"Then why did he ask to meet Elizabeth here?"

"It was not George—it was I. I wrote to her to draw her here. I wished to speak to her."

Darcy found his voice. "The letter was in his handwriting, and he always signs his correspondence to a Darcy in the same manner."

She stared at him, clearly calculating what reply to give. Darcy curled his lip in revulsion. Lydia Wickham was evidently a stranger to the truth. He hated deceit; anything connected to Wickham customarily reeked of it.

"After all that my cousin has done for you and your wayward family, do you not think you owe him more than a little honesty?" said Fitzwilliam hotly. "How many of Wickham's debts have you bought up, Darcy? It would be poor timing indeed if my cousin were to call in some of them. I wonder how long your scoundrel husband would last in debtors' prison. What would happen to you and all the little mouths that you need to feed? Darcy and his lovely wife would not visit you in the workhouse."

Lydia gasped. "You would not dare leave your family destitute! For shame, Darcy! Little wonder why your sister was so keen to be parted from you."

It was more than Darcy could bear. Slowly, he reached into his pocket and drew out the gun. "I brought this today with every notion of using it against your husband. A debtors' prison would be preferable to a cemetery, I can assure you. Tell us what you know before we march you to the nearest gaol."

Glancing at the gun, Lydia's shoulders slumped. Her gaze fell to the floor. "Very well. I knew that George was to meet Elizabeth. I offered to go instead. I was to deliver a message to her. That is all, I promise you. I would never harm a hair on her head. Do not harm me—Elizabeth would never forgive you, despite all your cousin says."

Darcy was quiet. The image of Elizabeth, tear-stained and alone, fluttered through his mind. He had no desire to hurt anyone, least of all her. The gun had only been intended for his own protection. A wave of exhaustion filled him. He had a sudden urge to leave this dirty back room, return to his comfortable house, and wash the entire day away.

"Tell us what you know and make it brief. I have little enough patience for this," he said finally.

"The message was for my sister."

"And I shall deliver it to her."

Lydia curved her face upwards towards the window. Darcy could see the reflection of unshed tears as the light caught her eyes. He thought she might be praying.

Turning back to him, she held his gaze. She was so like Elizabeth, so direct and fearless.

"He wanted to know her price."

"Her price for what?"

She could not keep the sting from her voice. "What price would any woman pay to protect those she loves from being hurt? Should it cost her all her fine jewels and pin money? Or perhaps it should cost her self-respect? Or maybe her virtue? Or her fidelity?" Her voice grew angrier. "Or her childhood, her dreams, her innocence. That was the price George demanded of me—"

"We do not care for your relationship with Wickham," he cut her off.

"Well you should, given that my marriage to Wickham is of your making. It was *you* who forced Wickham to wed me, *you* who paid his commission, and *you* who made sure he arrived on time to the altar. My marriage was your doing. My whole life is, and always has been, at your disposal."

"Nobody forced you to elope," Fitzwilliam interrupted.

Lydia glared at him, tears tumbling down her face. "Would I have let my heart be won if his true nature had been known?"

Suddenly, the image of a youthful Georgiana sobbing desperately in Darcy's arms returned to his fractured mind. This could have been her fate. *Never*, he told himself. *I would never have allowed it. I would have protected her whatever the cost might have been.* He wondered whether anyone had ever protected the wretched woman before him.

In a gentler voice, he addressed Lydia, "Tell me the truth, and perhaps I can assist you."

"I have had more than enough of your help."

"Tell me then how I can help Elizabeth. What harm does Wickham wish upon her? You cannot wish your sister ill?"

"Elizabeth has shown me kindness even when I have been nothing but wicked. That is the reason I came today. George did not wish me to...in fact, h-he made his displeasure known...but it would have been scandalous for them to meet in such a place. Eventually, I persuaded him to allow me to come in his stead." She unconsciously shook her head, and Darcy saw for the first time the faint trace of a bruise above her temple. "Wickham thinks he can blackmail Elizabeth."

Darcy looked at her in horror. "By what means?"

"He has something of hers. Something irreplaceable. And he means to demand money for its return."

"Nothing is irreplaceable. Besides, money is no object to me."

Lydia dropped her gaze. "It was taken from her bedroom."

Silence filled the storeroom. "What was stolen?" Darcy was almost afraid to know.

Lydia rolled her eyes, some of her previous insolence returning. "Good Lord, now this I cannot understand! I have seen Elizabeth in far finer jewellery. All this fuss for such a small sapphire! Surely the mistress of Pemberley can afford to replace one tiny brooch."

Darcy met Fitzwilliam's gaze. His mother's brooch. Given to him on her deathbed, the gift was meant for his future, then-unknown, wife as his mother drew her final breath. His father had given that brooch to his mother on the day she accepted his proposal.

"How did Wickham come to have it?"

Lydia shrugged her shoulders. Her cheeks were flushed, and she did not meet Darcy's stare.

"I do not know. One day he had gone, and the next he returned with it."

"And you did not think to ask where he got this particular brooch—the one he decided to blackmail your beloved sister with?"

"I was not aware that it was Elizabeth's. George often arrives unannounced, asking me to look after particular objects." She shivered. "I have learnt it is better not to ask too many questions."

"When did you become aware of its importance?"

"About a month or two ago." Here Lydia's face grew redder still. "George had a bad debt at a…a particular house in Covent Garden, and he needed a great deal of money to clear it. He also had an altercation with someone just outside it and was in need of a tooth-drawer."

"Some things never change."

"Pay George the money, and he will return the brooch."

Darcy valiantly refrained from rolling his eyes. "And deny himself a lifetime claim to the coffers of Pemberley? You cannot think he would truly return it." He looked at Lydia. "Do you wish to be rid of him?"

Closing her eyes, she nodded. "God forgive me but I have suffered enough by that man's hands."

Darcy replied, "This is what we shall do. You must tell your beloved husband that Elizabeth does not have access to the money he demands, and she needs to write to her accountant. I have no idea as to the amount he is asking for, but I know enough about his habits to know it will be large. Explain that this will take a few days, and he must arrange another meeting. You must make it clear that Elizabeth will only hand over the money when she is in receipt of the brooch."

Lydia's eyes widened. "Is it truly so valuable?"

"Only to anyone who loved my mother," Darcy replied curtly.

Lydia nodded silently, comprehension finally dawning upon her face.

"I will ensure your safety and comfort—and that of any children —on two conditions. The first is that the brooch is returned to its rightful place unscathed." He stepped closer and narrowed his eyes. "And, more importantly, no harm will come to Elizabeth—not to her person nor to her reputation as my wife. If anything should happen to her or the brooch, then I shall not be able to assist you. I would not be able to help anyone who had brought her any pain."

Lydia nodded again. "I understand. Th-Thank you, Darcy. I shall speak to George tonight and explain that Elizabeth needs more time. I only hope that does not make him desperate enough to do something reckless."

"Say nothing of our involvement."

"Naturally."

Fitzwilliam released his grip on Lydia. Rubbing at her forearms, she stood stiffly from her chair.

"Forgive me, Mrs Wickham. I hope I did not harm you. It has been a while since I have apprehended an adversary."

Lydia gave him a dark look. "I have received worse. I have never had an apology from a man before though, so that, at least, is something."

Turning, Lydia tipped up the hood of her cloak. "Thank you again, Darcy. I shall not forget your offer." She sighed and added in a voice so soft it was almost a whisper, "Tell Elizabeth that I love her." And with that, she slipped from the room.

The door clicked shut, and Darcy felt his legs weaken. Every reserve of strength had been used in his interrogation of Lydia. Fitzwilliam glanced at him. "Darcy, are you well? What in God's name possessed you to come? You are not fully recovered."

Grimacing, Darcy nodded. "I needed the truth, Fitzwilliam."

"And you will have it. Do not let it be at the expense of your health." Fitzwilliam motioned to the door. "Speaking of truth, do you think Mrs Wickham was being honest with us? Will she keep to her part of the bargain?"

Darcy raked a hand through his hair. "I do not know. But tell me, Fitzwilliam, what other choice do we have? It was the only way I could think of to gain a little time to form a plan."

Fitzwilliam's eyes gleamed in the darkened room. "You did not think that I should come to this meeting alone?" He grinned. "Only a lovesick fool would do such a thing!"

Darcy gave him a small smile. The brooch was taken from Elizabeth's bedchamber. Lovesick fool would not be the words he would use to describe the tumult currently churning under his breast.

"I have had the shop watched. I did not wish to come to harm and there to be no witness. I gave a description of Wickham and his wife to my man, Carruthers. He will be following Mrs Wickham, and we should begin to get an idea of the scoundrel's where-abouts. Let him think we intend to rendezvous in a few days. We shall pay him a visit tonight if possible."

"Thank you, Fitzwilliam." Darcy's voice sounded faint even to his own ears. The room was oppressive, and he had an over-whelming desire to be outside.

"Come, old man. You are in dire need of a drink. I said to Carruthers to meet me in The Old Swan on the river front near the South Bank."

"I need answers more than I need a drink."

"You will get those too. Or as many as I can provide." Fitzwilliam supported Darcy's weight. "There is an exit at the back. I doubt Wickham could afford to pay someone to watch the shop as well, but we would do well to be prudent." He eyed Darcy's pocket. "Unless you feel like shooting someone."

Darcy gave a wry smile. "In that instance, I fear I would need a drink first."

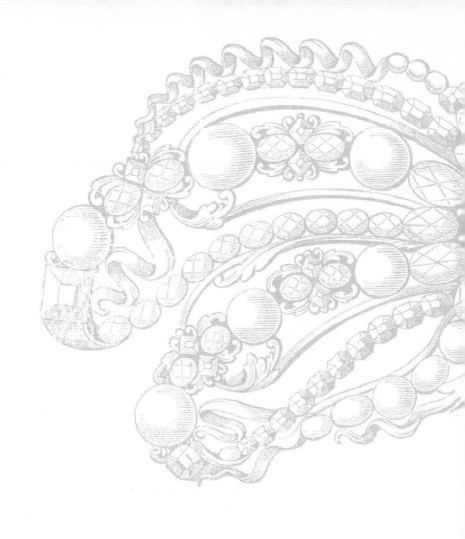

CHAPTER THIRTY-TWO

The Old Swan was a small inn that overlooked the Thames. It had the great distinction of being entirely unobservable from the road, accessible only by an unpromising-looking door that led to narrow, crooked stairs. Fitzwilliam had not asked Darcy whether he needed assistance to climb the stairs. Instead, he had wordlessly walked up beside him, which meant Darcy did not need to put all his weight on his injured leg. Darcy had been glad of the relief.

At the top of the stairs was a gloomy room, the windows of which were filthy. If he squinted, Darcy could make out the churning water of London's famous river.

"I shall not apologise for the dirt. It is a comfort to know it is as hard to look in as it is to look out."

"The dirt is the least of our concerns. How well do you know this place and its patrons? I do not wish to become a target for thieves."

"May I suggest you live in a different city? London is rife with pickpockets."

"Would that I could follow your suggestion. Unfortunately, you may remember that my home in Derbyshire has not been unaffected by thievery," Darcy replied darkly. "You promised me answers."

"I promised you a drink."

"I shall drink when Wickham is found."

"And I shall drink while we wait." Fitzwilliam found a table in a quiet corner and motioned for two glasses of ale.

It took every effort for Darcy to seat himself on the crooked little bench opposite Fitzwilliam. He drew a sharp breath of pain as he swung his legs under the table.

"Is the pain that bad?"

"It is the invisible scars that stop me from finding peace."

"You still struggle to recollect some aspects of your life?"

Darcy bristled at the understatement. "I cannot recollect a bloody thing. You must help me. What called you away so urgently from Pemberley? Why were you waiting to ambush Wickham? Where is Mother's brooch, and what in God's name has it got to do with my wife?"

Fitzwilliam was quiet for a moment and looked steadily at Darcy. "Wickham claims to have your mother's brooch. He has been attempting to extort money from Elizabeth in exchange for its safe return."

"How did he come to have it?"

"I know not." Fitzwilliam cast his eyes down. "Although, truthfully Darcy, I suspect that Elizabeth might."

"Why?"

Fitzwilliam rubbed his eyes with his hands, looking suddenly weary. "There is no specific reason that has led me to this conclusion, only that I have only ever known Elizabeth to be a merry, open sort of a person, and her behaviour of late is so uncharacteristically secretive." He glanced at Darcy. "I wondered whether she had lost the brooch when visiting her family and was too overcome with shame to tell anyone."

Darcy remained silent. Any woman who truly claimed to love him would not take such liberties with something so dear to him.

"She was devastated, you know." Fitzwilliam broke Darcy from his reverie. "I have never seen Elizabeth so unhappy."

The image of Elizabeth crumpled in Fitzwilliam's arms in the gardens at Pemberley stormed its way back to Darcy. An unwelcome pang of something not unlike jealousy tore through him. "You know her humour well?"

"As well as any cherished family member," Fitzwilliam replied. He fixed his eyes upon Darcy. "I hope I have not misunderstood you."

"Why did you leave Pemberley so abruptly?" Darcy's question caught Fitzwilliam off guard.

"Elizabeth revealed Wickham's nefarious plan to me. I wished to assist her—and by extension you—in any way possible."

"But why with nary a word to me?"

"Because you were bedridden after suffering a terrible accident. I was worried that you might try to do something foolish like procure a gun and make your way across London without a thought for your personal welfare."

Darcy ignored Fitzwilliam's pointed look. "Is that why you have been corresponding without my knowledge?"

"We were trying to spare you any undue distress. Although I am beginning to reconsider our plan to lessen the despair of a curmudgeon such as yourself."

"Lessen my despair! I have been driven out of my mind!" Darcy tightened his grip around his drink. "I used to be a logical creature who could think clearly and reasonably. My future was mapped out before me. I knew my duty to myself and to my family. Now here I am in the dingiest tavern in Christendom, grievously injured, awaiting news of a man I vowed to disown years ago. What is more, I find myself married to a woman who, from what I can ascertain, is of inferior birth and with highly questionable connexions."

He grimaced as he shifted his body weight. "A woman—I might add—who would rather involve family members than turn to me for help, who has steadfastly refused to place her trust in me, and whose family have conspired to steal from mine. From everything that I have learnt of Elizabeth there is no rational reason why I should be married to her, yet..." he swallowed, "yet...I cannot help myself. I must confess that my wife is the most bewitching woman I ever beheld. The notion she would meet Wickham, alone, was too much. I did not know what I should find, how I would be received, or even whether I would be welcomed, but my mind clouded over with such an emotion that I lost all capacity for coherent thought. I needed to know the truth. I needed to protect her, to know she was safe."

He exhaled deeply. "I wish to heal whatever has been broken between us, but I cannot if I do not know what has been lost."

Fitzwilliam's expression softened. "Any duplicity was to prevent further harm to you. I can see now that it was an error to keep information from you. It will not happen again."

"Is there anything else which I should know?"

From his inside pocket, his cousin drew out an envelope. "I received this shortly before your accident. It caused me to travel up to Pemberley the next day. I arrived just in time to rescue you. If you had stayed an hour—nay half an hour—longer at the bottom of the valley, you surely would have perished."

He slipped the small packet into Darcy's open palm. The letter was short and in Darcy's neat, level hand. His heart sank; he did not wish to reveal his impairment to Fitzwilliam. "Tell me of its contents. It hurts my head to read in this dark place," he said quietly.

"Only once before have I received a letter like this from you, and that was about Ramsgate." Darcy nodded; Ramsgate was one memory that had not been expunged. Sitting at his desk, he had poured every vitriolic thought, every vengeful wish against Wickham into that particular letter to Fitzwilliam. Anger had coloured his words, but by the end he was only able to express pain at Georgiana's heartbreak.

"In your letter, Darcy, you intimated that someone had betrayed your trust."

"You do not believe that it referred to the theft of Mother's brooch?"

"I asked Elizabeth about the letter, and she seemed genuinely unaware that you had written to me. Close as you are to one another, it puzzled me greatly. She is usually your greatest confidante."

"You think I sought your advice because the betrayal pertained to her?"

Fitzwilliam shifted uncomfortably. "I am not sure what I think. She loves you utterly, Darcy, and I daresay Elizabeth has been the very best thing to brighten up your otherwise entirely too serious life, but she has not told either of us the complete truth. I am not sure whether you are aware—whether you have been informed— but I only know of the incident regarding the brooch because I happened upon Elizabeth fainting in the garden. I was only just in time to catch her before she struck her head."

"Fainting!" Darcy's hands went cold. "No one has spoken a word of it!" Dr Amstel's warning sounded an alarm bell in his ears.

"It was only after she came round that I was able to demand the truth from her. Guilt filled me as I questioned her in such a weakened state, but she could not conceal her concerns from me. She begged me not to alarm you unduly. She seemed so desperately unhappy. Even now, I wonder whether she would have shared that particular confidence had I not found her. As for the rest, I was so angry at that abominable sister and her feckless husband that I left before I said something I might later regret. Forgive me for any distress I caused you with my abrupt departure."

"You were forgiven the instant you called Wickham a mangy dog." Tension had gathered in Darcy's shoulders, and he stared glumly into his fast-diminishing drink. "What do you think I meant by a betrayal?"

Fitzwilliam shook his head. "There could be countless reasons. Financial, personal, familial—I could not guess at it. What surprises me is that Elizabeth did not know you wrote to me."

Before Darcy had a chance to make his reply, Fitzwilliam spoke again. "Carruthers has returned. And by his sombre expression I expect he has good news."

Darcy looked up. The newcomer to the party was a short, stocky man with very little neck. Instinctively, Darcy knew Carruthers was in possession of a unique talent: his air was simultaneously innocuous and threatening. He could be mistaken for a labourer of about thirty, or a footman of over forty, a valet, or a clerk as easily as he could start a fight which—by the looks of his powerful forearms —would not be difficult at all. If Darcy had cared to wager, he should have said that Carruthers was ex-military. The curt exchange of nods between his cousin and the silent man did much to strengthen his guess. Silently, Carruthers slid onto the bench next to Darcy.

"Do you have him?" said Fitzwilliam, leaning forwards.

"He has been found. Even if we had not shadowed Mrs Wickham, he would have been easy to trace. A man such as himself indulges in certain habits and frequents particular places. There would be no end of people quite willing to point us in his direction for the correct price."

Fitzwilliam held his hand out. "Speaking of direction, do you have an address for the wastrel?"

"Unsurprisingly, he has several. But tonight, I have it on good authority that he will be at this address from eight o'clock onwards."

He passed a card to Fitzwilliam, who surveyed it. "As reliable as ever, Carruthers. I thank you."

Carruthers stood to take his leave, casting a wide shadow across the table. Darcy motioned to his pocket. Fitzwilliam stopped him with a wave of a hand. "My good man here and I have a long-standing arrangement. No payment will be needed from you."

"I must insist, Fitzwilliam."

"Wickham is as much my problem as he is yours. I shall hear no more from you." Turning to Carruthers, Fitzwilliam continued, "I shall see you at eight o'clock tonight. There is a tavern opposite the address. Find a quiet table and I shall join you."

Nodding, Carruthers stood to take his leave. Darcy noticed large rings on the fingers of his right hand. They would certainly do some damage if a punch was thrown. Fitzwilliam knew what he was about asking this man for help.

"What will we do at 8 o'clock? What address did he give you?"

"*We* will do nothing. *I* shall go and *you* will rest at home."

"I shall not leave you at Wickham's mercy."

"Do not be offended, Cousin, when I say it is not my habit to take wounded soldiers into battle. I have more than adequate armoury at my disposal." Darcy coloured at his cousin's words.

When would he be allowed to protect his family? Fitzwilliam sensed his discomfort.

"I meant you no disrespect. It is for my own benefit that I ask you to stay away. I would never hear the end of it from Elizabeth if I allowed any harm to befall you. Bloodshed, battlefields, and war are nothing in comparison to your wife's glacial stare and satirical tongue." He smiled ruefully. Darcy noted the dark shadows under Fitzwilliam's eyes; the long scar gleamed up at him from his cousin's cheek. For all his flippant tone, Fitzwilliam looked distinctly battle-weary.

"And what of you? You should rest also. Return with me to the comfort of my house."

"No, you should use your time to speak to Elizabeth. There is much to discuss." He paused. "There is something else. Pardon me if I overstep, but I advise you to ask her about the events in the month after darling Molly's birth."

"Whatever can you mean?"

"It is as I suspected. You do not know that of which I speak."

"Why can you not tell me?"

"Because it is for Elizabeth to give you the details, painful as they are. As much as I understand her reticence, you have a right to know the full truth of the matter." He sighed. "I care about you both deeply. I can understand now that keeping information from you does more harm than good. Please ask Elizabeth to forgive me. I have not betrayed her confidence in the strictest sense, but I cannot imagine she will be happy with me when you tell her it was I who brought it to your attention."

Darcy held Fitzwilliam's gaze. "I, for one, thank you most profusely for all your trouble. I apologise for any injuries I may have inflicted on you earlier."

Fitzwilliam chuckled. "You overestimate your strength, Darcy—not much has changed in that quarter!"

"Do not deflect my gratitude with quips. I pray I shall not forget your actions today—I fear my memory is not as trustworthy as it was. May I be so bold as to make a final request?"

"Naturally."

"What is the address for tonight's meeting?"

"You are forbidden from accompanying me."

"In case some harm should befall you, I wish to have all the particulars. Spare a thought for me—I shall be out of my mind with worry."

Sighing, Fitzwilliam took the note from his pocket and made a copy. He gave Darcy the original and motioned to the barman he wished to pay. "Come, Cousin. Let us return to our homes. We have a lot to do before our respective battles. I wish to eat and wash before my soiree with Wickham, and you need to scrub yourself before you speak to your wife. Quite frankly, you smell like a gutter."

Darcy twisted his lips to hide a smile. Whatever might happen next, it was good to have Fitzwilliam back.

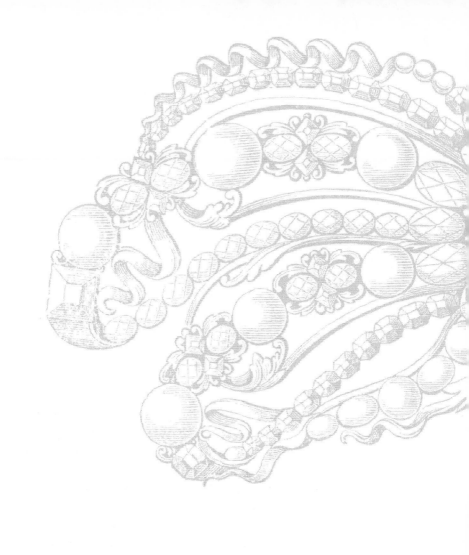

CHAPTER THIRTY-THREE

The hour had just gone five by the time Darcy returned to his residence. A handsome coach stood outside his house. For a moment, he wondered whether it was anything at all to do with Wickham, but it looked entirely too expensive for that scoundrel's pocket. Besides, even to his unreliable eye it looked rather old-fashioned. The sound of raised voices warned him of a commotion within his own home. Attempting to quell the trepidation rising in his throat, Darcy made his way into the house.

The sight that greeted him was not pleasant. Several servants stood in their positions, but, by their shocked expressions, Darcy could see that they were grievously unhappy. When they saw him, many of them averted their eyes and found something interesting on the floor to gaze upon. Somewhere on an upper level of the house, Darcy heard the sound of a door being flung open, and he heard the arguing voices now with greater clarity, his wife's comments first.

"Madam, allow me to quit your presence before I say something I may regret."

"What would you know of the word regret?"

Darcy's heart sank as he comprehended the owner of the voice.

Lady Catherine de Bourgh, his aunt. Her vitriol echoed through the halls.

"To understand such a term implies you have a heart! That you have scruples! Insolent girl! I knew my nephew would regret his marriage to you! And to think that I believed in your sincerity when you persuaded us to reconcile. Where is Darcy? No doubt he is languishing somewhere alone and injured—by your hand no doubt!"

"Darcy did not say where he went but it is likely enough that he attended his gentlemen's club."

"And no doubt you have no notion of when he might return. How convenient for you! Of course he should be absent at a time when I wish to ensure his well-being. Death by riding accident would have been most convenient—it would be hard to prove your hand, but I am sure you must have had a part in it!"

Darcy had heard enough. Ignoring the protest of the muscles in his legs, he climbed the stairs two at a time, without so much as a second glance at the servants gathering at the bottom of the staircase. Following the sound of the argument, he made his way to the library.

On one side of the library, standing behind the desk, was Elizabeth. Her eyes, which once resembled jewels, were now glittering like daggers. They reminded Darcy of a knife in the darkness, just like the one held by Fitzwilliam only hours ago. "I could hear your shouts from the street. What is the meaning of this?"

Lady Catherine turned to look at him then. "I must repeat my question. What do you mean by this intrusion?"

She smiled, although not entirely happily. "Nephew! You are well! I have just learnt of your unhappy news." She walked towards him with her hands out as though to draw him into a motherly embrace. "Quickly did I depart Rosings Park to assure myself of your well-being and to—"

"And to accuse my wife of wishing me harm," Darcy interceded. "Whatever possessed you to do such a thing?"

"I received an alarming letter," his aunt replied with no little triumph in her voice. "It does not name specifics, but it tells me to ask you a question."

Darcy rolled his eyes. "That is hardly an excuse to barge in here and—"

"Where is your mother's brooch?"

From across the room, Darcy saw the colour drain from Elizabeth's cheeks. He wondered what she might be thinking. He decided not to give his aunt the satisfaction of knowing the pain she had caused.

"That is no concern of yours," Darcy replied evenly.

"The letter says I am to tell you to ask your wife of its whereabouts." She turned to Elizabeth triumphantly. "So where is it, then? I remember the day my poor late sister received it. George Darcy was not one for large displays of affection, but he presented it to her on the day she accepted him. I think she must have cried herself to sleep with happiness. It was her absolute favourite. To think my nephew entrusted it to you! I ask again, where is it? Have you kept it safe? Precious jewels can be stolen quite easily when you welcome all-and-sundry into your chambers, as I am sure you are aware, *Miss Elizabeth*. You must be relieved your little daughter looks just like you. That way there can be no evidence of any visitors to your private rooms. For the final time, what have you done with my sister's broo—"

"You must leave." Elizabeth walked past Lady Catherine as though the older woman were no more than a forgotten hat accidently left upon a table.

Darcy stood in shock for a moment, but his anger soon held sway. "You have two minutes to remove your person from my house. Leave and do not return. You may rot at Rosings for all I care."

Lady Catherine began to speak, but Darcy walked past her just as Elizabeth had done.

He found his wife in her bedchamber; this time he did not knock but seized open the door with no other thought than to assure her well-being. She was seated at her writing desk, gazing at the scattered papers upon it. He wished that she had been standing; it would have been easier then to take her into his arms and assure her of his love. As it was, her position was defensive; her arms were crossed in front of her. Occasionally, her hand would rise to her face to smooth away an errant tear that threatened to tumble from her deep, tormented eyes.

"She has gone, never to return."

Elizabeth merely nodded wordlessly.

"Speak to me so I may understand your feelings." Darcy looked on helplessly as Elizabeth struggled to keep her emotions in check.

"Do you agree with her?" Her question threw him completely off balance.

"Of course not! She is an abomination!"

"Then why have you been rifling through my letters? My things have been moved, and the servants would not dare touch my desk without telling me." She took a rasping breath and bit her lip. Fighting back tears, she said quietly, "I asked you to trust me."

Here, Darcy faltered. "I did not know where you were... I was looking for a sign...an indication of where you might have gone."

"And did you find it?" Now, she sounded angry. Darcy took a steadying breath, reliving all that had befallen him today. She was wounded and likely still reeling from all the unpleasantness with his aunt, he could tell. But her anger towards him was not entirely fair either.

"I did as a matter of fact. Your letter from *Pemberley's most trusted servant* was truly enlightening."

Elizabeth raised her head to meet his eye. Briefly, Darcy was struck mute by her beauty. Dark curls framed her face, and every one of her delicate features was aflame with indignation. But it was not her looks that captivated him, it was her spirit. Trembling and proud, she was alive with a vibrant energy, her eyes shining with such a will that rendered her unforgettable.

"And what, may I ask, did you learn?"

"I learnt not to be shocked by my aunt's enquiry about my mother's brooch."

Elizabeth startled visibly. "You know of Wickham's involvement?"

"You do not deny that he requested a meeting with you."

"I am unable to deny it, much as I wish never to see that man again."

"When did you apply to Fitzwilliam to go in your place?"

Again, Elizabeth looked upon Darcy in shock. Her body softened a little, the fight slowly leaving it. "I only spoke to Fitzwilliam because you were so unwell. I did not want you to trouble yourself when you were still recovering. Does this mean you have spoken to him? He is unharmed?"

"Fitzwilliam is well for now. I can only guess what mischief tonight may bring."

"Whatever can you mean?" Elizabeth cried in alarm. "Tell me this instant what is to happen tonight."

"Perhaps I should prefer not to." A wall of everything that had been building within Darcy was beginning to break. He had suffered too much. His body hurt, and fatigue and hunger were taking hold. He continued, his frustration becoming harder to repress. "Maybe I should keep it a secret. Then you would know what it is like to be driven half mad from worry."

"I kept the truth from you to prevent harm. You keeping it from me will only bestow more pain."

"To whom? To you? To myself? Or to Wickham? Or perhaps to that delightful woman who came in his place—she goes by the name of Lydia Wickham."

Elizabeth gasped. "You spoke to Lydia? How did you recognise her? Did she seem well? Please tell me—has he hurt her in any way?" Distress was written plainly upon her face.

Darcy relented a little. "She had fire and spirit, although..." He paused, attempting to read Elizabeth's reaction. "...although she alluded to arousing Wickham's ire prior to our meeting, so I would not be able to entirely vouch for her well-being."

Tears had started to flow down Elizabeth's face. "It is as I feared. Lydia will bear the brunt of that brute's dissolute nature. Oh, how I wish she had never aligned herself with such a man. Such an irresponsible soul! I wish that Lydia had never...had she been shown...if I had only...if only..."

"... if only I had never forced her to marry the reprobate you mean?"

"That is not what I mean! That is not what happened at all."

"Tell me then, for once, what do you mean? Speak plainly to me. I stand before you, asking for nothing but the truth."

Elizabeth covered her face with her hands, shielding her tears from his view. Her slender shoulders shook gently. He came to the other side of the desk and silently drew up a chair next to her. Without warning, she reached out to touch his hand. Reason dictated that he should pull away from her, but he could not. Her gesture was so innocent—childlike almost in her mute request for compassion—that he blinked away tears of his own. His anger had almost fully abated; he was left only with a desire to help her. He enclosed her hand in his and gazed into her downcast face.

Finally, he spoke. "Fitzwilliam told me I should ask you of the events following Molly's birth. He asked me to beg for your forgiveness if he spoke out of turn."

Elizabeth's words came in no more than a whisper. She shook her head sorrowfully. "Forgive me, my love, I cannot. It is too painful."

Darcy spoke softer still. "Then I shall wait until you are ready." She turned her eyes to him, so large and beautiful. He saw the wonder therein as she realised the truth of his words. Silently, she lifted her face to his and met his lips with hers. Never before had he known such a sensation. It was blissful. Heavenly in all its tenderness. Her hands caressed his body; she knew every part of him so well that he could only ever surrender to her touch. It was as though he had been starving his entire life, unaware of it until now, his hunger growing ever greater now he had tasted her love, the feeling of her soul reigniting itself with his. He felt her sigh with pleasure, the sensation of which sent glorious vibrations through his body.

This was what it felt like to be a man; he knew it now. He was aware of nothing else but her. She belonged to him. Not by the decree of matrimonial law, nor by the fact she was mother to his child, but her heart was his, vulnerable and tender, she had entrusted it to his care.

Slowly, he traced his hands down her arms and rested them on her waist, pulling her womanly softness towards him and devouring each sensation as though it were the last, and not the first, that he should ever receive from her.

Elizabeth broke away from him gently. Her lips were swollen

and red, but she was smiling at him. Shallow breaths reached his ears—was it him that had been rendered breathless by their embrace or was it her? He smiled at her, unable to find the words to express fully the passionate ardour coursing through his body. She rewarded him with a laugh and a wrinkled nose. "I am sorry my love, but you smell terrible! Where on Earth have you been?"

Darcy felt a prickle of heat run up his neck. In his haste, he had forgotten to heed Fitzwilliam's advice and wash. He wondered at her kissing him at all.

"Forgive me. Lady Catherine's arrival outstripped any thought I had to refresh myself."

Elizabeth's face grew grave upon hearing his aunt's name. "Do you think there was at least one person in London who did not hear her abuse of me?"

Darcy pretended to look thoughtful. "I believe there may have been one or two up in Hackney whose ears might have been spared." His teasing was rewarded with a playful swat to his arm. Her mood did not last long. Her face grew pale and grave once more as she contemplated what had occurred.

"Loyal as they are, servants cannot help but gossip."

"Not if we discover the truth and give them our tale first," Darcy vowed grimly. He was gratified when Elizabeth gave his hand a squeeze upon hearing the word *our*.

She looked at him steadily. "And what if we should discover a truth that is ugly?" She spoke quietly, as though she was talking to herself alone. "What if the truth is more painful than any tarnished reputation?" Her eyes were gazing absently out of the window; Darcy wondered whether she might faint again, so ghostly was her countenance. Before he could speak, she turned back towards him. All her previous passion was extinguished; her face was now veiled by a heavy sadness that Darcy could not account for. It was as though the shutters had been pulled over her face, obscuring all but the pressing melancholy weighing down on her. She glanced down at their hands; their fingers now laced together. Suddenly, a glimmer of a smile tiptoed across her face, and the sadness about her lifted for an instant. "We should both wash. Dining together in a state such as this would only give the servants more to talk about."

Darcy nodded, unable to understand the changes in her manner. It was as though she had shut a great invisible door to him. *I shall wait until you are ready,* he told himself as he helped Elizabeth to her feet. He flushed at the heat of her hand in his. God help him, but he knew it would be worth it.

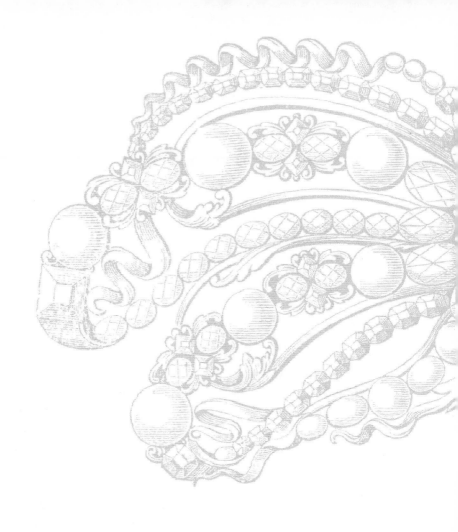

CHAPTER THIRTY-FOUR

The bell in the hall had chimed six-thirty, and Darcy was struggling to hide his restlessness. The time for Fitzwilliam's meeting with Wickham was drawing ever nearer, and every possible scenario played out in Darcy's mind. In many such visions, Wickham came to a satisfactory end. In other, more terrifying versions, it was Fitzwilliam who was hurt. It was insufferable sitting around with nothing to do. Reaching into his coat pocket, he thumbed the edges of the address given to him earlier.

Mrs Morwenna's
3, Berwick Street
Soho

He exhaled heavily, sorrow filling his chest as he thought of the shadowy marks on Lydia Wickham's face. Perhaps Fitzwilliam had been too harsh in his judgment of her. To be bound in law and body to a man such as George Wickham could not be an easy life, especially if he was a frequent visitor to a well-known bawdy house and the gaming dens.

Darcy's mind drifted back across the decades. Had Wickham ever been his friend? He had been selected, put forward, and presented as a potential playmate. At the time, there had been no other boys close to Darcy's age within twenty miles of Pemberley. Their friendship appeared to be borne of a happy, geographical necessity. Looking back, a cynical part of Darcy could not help doubting Wickham's motives even then. He remembered how much more agreeable Wickham was when any of their parents entered the room. As a young boy, Wickham knew how to make himself charming—simpering and flattering those around him. As soon as the door shut, the mask would drop. Darcy recalled Wickham helping himself to every one of his birthday gifts, as though his parents had given them to Wickham as much as to their only son. It had been hard to raise a complaint against motherless, angelic young Wickham. Indeed, any of Darcy's *soucis* against 'darling George' were dismissed as jealousy. *He has always enjoyed helping himself to whatever he wanted of mine,* thought Darcy glumly.

The notion that his mother's most precious jewellery could be within even twenty feet of that brothel set his teeth on edge. Even if Wickham were to hand it over without a fight—something that Darcy felt to be highly unlikely—who was to say that some pickpocket from that underbelly would not swipe it from Fitzwilliam soon after?

And then there was the question of how Wickham came to procure it in the first place. His aunt's words echoed around his head. She had accused Elizabeth of inviting all-and-sundry to her bedchamber. He did not believe it to be true for an instant, but how then did Wickham come to have the brooch? What he would give to extract the truth from that scoundrel! An innocent explanation. It was all he could hope for.

Another roil of nervous energy flowed through him, and he tapped the armrest of his chair impatiently. Ever since he had left Elizabeth, he had felt incomplete.

As though she could read his thoughts, his wife entered the room. Her face was serious, and she was holding a letter. She motioned that he should remain seated.

"Have you had word from Fitzwilliam?"

"No, it has nothing to do with that. It appears that your dear aunt Lady Catherine has seen fit to pay a call upon poor Georgiana.

What if she has regaled your sister with my wicked treatment of the Darcy family?"

Darcy groaned loudly. "What new depths of depravity will she stoop to?"

Elizabeth glanced at the clock. "I wish to go to the Luxfords' house. It is not far by carriage, and I shall take a footman. Hopefully it is not too late to pay a call. Molly is being attended to by her nurse-maid, and I intend to be back to wish her good night. Truthfully, I do not think I could rest until I know of Georgiana's well-being."

Darcy opened his mouth to protest, but Elizabeth bent down swiftly and silenced him with a kiss.

"Do you always do that when you wish to get your own way?"

"Not always. But it is a decidedly potent weapon to possess in my arsenal." Her eyes twinkled softly. "And I would be lying if I said you had never employed such a tactic."

Not for the first time, Darcy lamented his loss of memory. He fervently wished he could recall each and every instance that Elizabeth had yielded to his kisses. She straightened. "I do not plan to stay away for long. Just long enough to understand what fresh harm Lady Catherine has caused."

Darcy nodded. "Very well, but be careful and take a footman. I do not wish for you to travel alone in the dark."

Elizabeth smiled. "There have been many occasions when I have travelled by carriage in the dark and you have not complained, but I must concede you were accompanying me then."

"Do you wish me to accompany you now?"

"No, you have done quite enough gallivanting today," she said with a look at his leg. "Besides, Georgiana will speak more freely to me than to you."

"Because she would not wish to speak poorly of our aunt?"

"Because she knows how you will react if she tells you everything."

Darcy suppressed a grim smile. "Am I so predictable?"

"I am not sure predictable is the right term. Stubborn is far more accurate." She placed a kiss on his cheek. A shadow crossed her face; it was only a flicker, but Darcy still caught it. For all her teasing, she was still suffering from the emotional bruises bestowed by his aunt.

Darcy sat quietly for a while after she had gone. The sensation of being incomplete intensified after her departure. Who had sent Lady Catherine that note? He would bet his back teeth that Wickham was responsible. His shoulders tensed. Of course, Wickham would never be content with money—not when revenge would prove too great a temptation.

Rising slowly, he tested his leg. It was sore. He should definitely rest it. Reaching out, he found his walking cane. The pain was not so bad when he did not put his full weight down. The clock chimed seven. It was not far to Berwick Street. He could not stay here alone knowing of Fitzwilliam's danger and Elizabeth's sorrow. The wait was too agonising to contemplate. Nothing was to be done if he could not do it himself. He had to act. Wickham's mischief must be stopped.

Calling for a footman, Darcy explained briefly that he was leaving on urgent business. Mrs Darcy did not need to know where, but she must be reassured that he would be back before long. He impressed on the young servant that all should be done to alleviate any of her concerns. There would be time enough to apologise to Elizabeth later. Hopefully, he would have done enough to remove whatever made her suffer so. All he knew was that one thing was clear: Wickham had imposed on enough of Darcy's acquaintance, and the day to put an end to it all had finally come.

IF ONE WERE TO MEASURE BY DISTANCE, THEN BERWICK Street was not far from Darcy's home. If one were to measure by other units, such as wealth and respectability, then Darcy's destination was about as far away from the comforts of his life as it could possibly be. The rhythmic rattle of the curricle's wheels beat a steady tattoo against the cobbled streets. His driver clearly did not want to slow down any more than was necessary. Tensing his hand around his walking cane, Darcy began to question his judgment. He shivered and pulled his coat more tightly around himself. Through the layers of fabric, he felt the hard outline of his father's gun.

Praying he would not need to use it, he peered past the leather hood to gaze at the passing streets. Shouts echoed through the winding alleyways, and dark puddles of stagnant water oozed out of the gutters. People bustled everywhere. There were the remnants of market stalls dotted about, their respective owners packing away whatever bruised produce they had been unable to sell. Lights and raucous laughter came from various buildings; Darcy could only guess at the shades of disreputable conduct taking place within. An uneasy sense of familiarity washed over him. He had a strange sensation that he had done this before, searching for Wickham in some unsavoury part of London. Resolving to ask Elizabeth about it later, he shook the feeling away.

Eventually, the curricle stopped. Pulling his hat low over his brow, Darcy lifted the collar of his overcoat to push away the biting night air. Looking around, his eyes locked upon a tavern opposite a house which was clearly Mrs Morwenna's establishment. A tavern he could navigate, but in a house of ill-repute he was more than a little lost, especially when he had no desire to savour anything on offer. He had known friends and acquaintances that had spoken admiringly of such places, but it had only ever seemed sordid to him. To pay for a woman to pretend to love you did not appeal to him in the slightest. He recalled the sensation of Elizabeth's lips upon his. A deep thrill rushed through him as his body responded to the remembrance of her embrace. No amount of money could buy such a feeling.

It would be foolhardy to repeat the errors of this afternoon and attempt to corner Wickham single-handedly. Darcy could swallow enough of his pride to know that he would have been in serious trouble if Fitzwilliam had not recognised him when he did. He unconsciously touched his neck. Keeping his head lowered, he entered the tavern. It took a while for his eyes to adjust to the darkness. Thankfully, the establishment was cleaner and more respectable than he had expected. A fire crackled inconspicuously in one corner, and it was quiet, with only a few tables dotted here and there. On one side of the room, he could see there were two women wearing circumspect clothing attempting to draw some much older men into conversation. Darcy consciously turned to find the opposite corner of the inn.

"What in Heaven's name are you doing here?" a familiar voice hissed somewhere near his elbow.

Glancing down, Darcy was relieved to see Fitzwilliam, Carruthers, and another burly man at a small table.

"Do you really need to ask?" he replied. He remembered Elizabeth's words. "When have you known me not to be stubborn?"

He sat at the table, relieved to rest his legs. "Our aunt paid us a visit today—unannounced I may add—in order to question Elizabeth with regards to a letter she received." Darcy glanced at the other men, unwilling to reveal too much. "Needless to say, she considered herself well-informed about recent events."

Fitzwilliam scowled. "Lady Catherine considers herself to be a great many things. The accuracy of her opinions is rarely questioned."

Darcy's lips twisted. A surge of pride briefly swelled in his chest. "I believe my wife made her own opinion of Lady Catherine quite clear."

The frown lifted from Fitzwilliam's brow. "I am glad to hear it. I am only sorry I was not there to see it all."

"I was present. For all the satisfaction of seeing Lady Catherine being put in her place, it was not a pleasant scene to witness. You must understand my desire to interrogate Wickham. I can only imagine the letter was sent by him."

"Very well. But you must not exert yourself unduly," said Fitzwilliam, eyeing Darcy's cane.

Darcy nodded his reply, not trusting himself to make a promise. Elizabeth's pain was too fresh in his mind to give such an assurance. "How do you mean to enter Mrs Morwenna's house?"

Fitzwilliam laughed, sharing an amused look with the other men next to him. "By the same means as any other man wishing to enter. With a pocketful of coins."

Darcy felt the tips of his ears redden. "Of course, Fitzwilliam, I am aware how a brothel works. I meant how do you mean to enter without signalling our presence to Wickham?"

"Leave that to me," the quiet man next to Carruthers interjected. There was a tone of finality about his voice that Darcy knew was better not to question.

GAINING ENTRANCE TO MRS MORWENNA'S HAD BEEN easy. Locating Wickham proved to be much harder. There were several rooms on the ground floor, each filled with throngs of people. Naturally, he supposed, there were additional rooms on the upper floors, but Darcy decided not to contemplate the uses to be found with so many extra chambers. Indeed, at first glance, the establishment was not as bad as Darcy had feared. In fact, in some ways, it was more comfortable and refined than some of the middle-class sitting rooms he had found himself in. He could not help feeling uneasy. The habits and customs of the occupants of Mrs Morwenna's were a far cry from the conduct of the decent society which he preferred to keep.

Small tables of men, smoking over their card games, were dotted about the place. Here and there, women were perched on some of the players' knees. Snippets of conversation reached his ears. It was not completely lewd, but interspersed in the discourse was an unpalatable vulgarity that he did not care for. Darcy and the little party made their way to an empty table. The quiet man, whom Darcy had discovered was called Matthews, disappeared to make his enquiries. As soon as they sat, they were immediately approached by three women, all of differing ages, heights, and dispositions. Fitzwilliam, Darcy noted, seemed disconcertingly comfortable in their presence. *A soldier's life is indeed different to that of a gentleman*, he thought wryly. Upon a second glance about the room, he decided that given the number of well-dressed customers about the place, it would not do to pass judgment solely on the conduct of the army.

A feminine hand about his shoulders startled him. The tallest of the three women leant over him, offering to pour him wine. He tensed as he felt her body press against him. *I am here to protect Elizabeth*, he told himself, although he could not shake an enormous feeling of trepidation that his wife might not view his visit here in quite the same way.

"Would you like me to fill your glass, sir?"

"No, I thank you. I intend to drink later." Darcy hoped his glacial tone would be enough to deter her.

"Very wise, sir. Far better to have your wits about you. Many men prefer to wait to savour the tastes of our good establishment until the end of the evening." She fluttered her eyelashes at him. Darcy was entirely flummoxed. He could not help comparing this woman's flirtations to Elizabeth's diary. When *she* had spoken of desire, it had inflamed his ardour. He knew that the stranger before him would offer him any carnal sin he wished, but the only sensation he felt was revulsion. *No one but Elizabeth.* The thought brought a faint smile to his lips.

"Do you wish for anything else, or is it your intention to wait until later?" The woman interrupted his thoughts. Unable to form a coherent reply, he cast a look of panic in his cousin's direction.

Laughing, Fitzwilliam interrupted their exchange. "It is no use, madam. I have persuaded my friend to come here against his better judgment. Come and sit beside me. I am far more personable."

Darcy breathed a sigh of relief, acknowledging Fitzwilliam's wink as the woman slunk away. Casting a surreptitious look about the place, Darcy was struck by the variety of people within it. There were women to suit the tastes of any man. Many of the women were more like girls, he decided, very young indeed. He wondered what had befallen them that they should end up here. What kind of life was it, to be paid to give men attention? Who had left these women to this fate?

There was a disparity, too, amongst the gentlemen present. Many were young and looked amiable enough, but Darcy could see they would be in their cups before long. A good temper could easily change to a foul one once a drop had been taken. And then who would pay the price for it? Some of the gentlemen were older, close enough to Darcy's father in age. He thought of Tilford and pictured him as an old man, leering at girls much younger than himself. He tightened his grip on his walking cane. And what of Wickham? Where would he belong in this room? Surely not as old as the grizzled examples around him but not a young man either.

Quite unbidden, the image of Wickham appeared before Darcy. Dark hair, athletic physique, and those charming blue eyes, he had turned the head of every woman in Lambton and beyond. His manner had been so open and pleasing; he knew exactly what compliment to give and would pay it in such a way that its sincerity could never be in doubt. Men too, in a way, were charmed by him. Too often, he was given a little extra time to pay off his shop credit or permitted lenient treatment for incomplete work during his studies.

In contrast, Darcy could only ever appear to be disagreeable and sour next to him, unable as he was to stoop to behave as duplicitously as Wickham did. It had been so liberating to cut ties with him after the debacle of Father's will. For the first time, Darcy was able to form friendships without the burden of his father's late steward's son outshining him at every turn. He had finally been rid of him, until Ramsgate, until Georgiana and—he glanced around —until now.

How was it that Elizabeth's sister had married Wickham? What had been his role in this? Fitzwilliam had indicated an elopement. Hopefully Elizabeth could illuminate the matter for him later.

So lost was Darcy in his thoughts that he had not noticed that the girls had disappeared and Matthews had returned. "Wickham is here, at a card table," he said. "He is losing badly. I shall offer to pay his debts in return for a private job. We shall go to a quiet room to discuss it." He indicated which doorway. Darcy decided he did not want to know how Matthews had organised this. "I hope to bring him to you in fifteen minutes or so."

"Do you need any money to tempt him?"

Matthews smiled grimly. "It will not take much to break him away from the table. I think he would welcome the excuse." Darcy watched the smaller man disappear into the crowded room to another one beyond it.

"Come, let us ready ourselves." Fitzwilliam stood, leading the way to the room singled out by Matthews. Taking a deep breath, Darcy pushed away any thought that rushing towards a secret meeting with Wickham—in a brothel of all places—without informing anyone of his intentions might not in fact be the wisest plan.

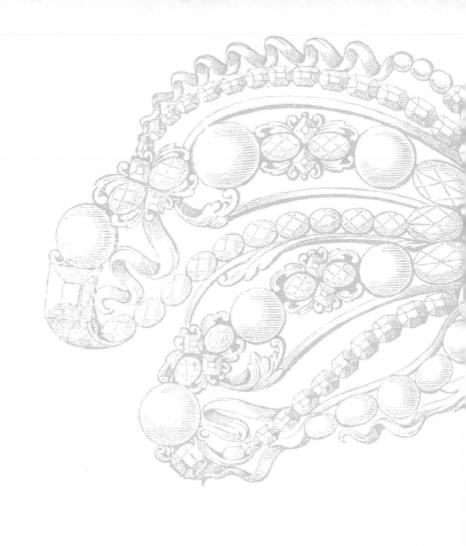

CHAPTER THIRTY-FIVE

Closing the door behind him, Darcy looked about the room. It was quiet, with elegant, if not expensive, furnishings. It was a contrast to the raucous noise and laughter elsewhere in the building. There were no obvious signs that this was a place for an intimate interlude, thought Darcy, except that the sofa was a great deal larger than was practical for the room. It seemed more like a study or private parlour.

"Stand there." Fitzwilliam motioned to a corner out of sight from the door. "Carruthers and I shall wait either side of the door and apprehend the scoundrel." Before he could protest, a sound warned them of footsteps just outside the door. Quickly assuming his position, Darcy felt his heartbeat hammering in his chest and closed his eyes for a moment. What would it be like after all this time to see that charming serpent? Darcy opened his eyes at the creak of the door. Without wasting a moment, Fitzwilliam and Carruthers were on either side of the man who had just stepped through the doorway. Matthews quickly held a sack over the captive's head to prevent him from screaming. All three men hauled the struggling figure to the sofa and pinned him down. Darcy moved to bolt the door behind them, then returned to get a better view.

"Stay still, you scoundrel, or you will find the wrong end of my blade," Carruthers hissed. The jerking motions subsided instantly. Still holding him captive from the back, Matthews reached over and pulled the bag from the man's shoulders.

A familiar voice came crying out, "What is the meaning of this? Unhand me. I am a war hero, of impeccable service, of outstanding character and I am—"

"An adept liar," Fitzwilliam replied sharply. "Who should remain quiet if he wishes to retain full use of all his fingers."

The man glared at Fitzwilliam. "Colonel Fitzwilliam. I might have known it was you. Tell me, where is the pompous ass Darcy? He is not generally far behind."

Darcy looked at the man in disbelief. He could hardly believe that this was Wickham. Beady eyes were now sunken into puffy cheeks, sallow from years of poor diet and lack of exercise. Indeed, his eyes, once considered by every young lady in East Derbyshire as so *fine*, now had a narrow appearance, not unlike a rodent. Wickham's hairline had succumbed to the same fate as his father's and had receded far too quickly for a man in his thirties. It gave greater prominence to his forehead which threw his once-handsome face out of balance. As for the man's figure, Darcy cast his eyes over Wickham's extruding paunch and could scarcely believe this podgy man in ill-fitting trousers was the same acquaintance of his youth.

"Are you sure this is Wickham? He has changed so much." Darcy attempted to keep the astonishment from his voice.

"What do you mean, much changed?" It was Wickham's voice, that much was undeniable. "I have not changed much since last we spoke."

Wickham turned towards Darcy and smiled at him, revealing yellowing teeth. There were a few gaps in his smile, his teeth presumably lost somewhere in a tavern gutter after a fight. Darcy valiantly held back a look of disgust. "Perhaps it was a little more memorable for me than it was for you?" He pointed to one of the gaps. "A little souvenir to always remember you by."

Darcy tried not to react to Wickham's goading. Satisfying as it was to think he had knocked one of the scoundrel's teeth out, he had absolutely no recollection of it. Wickham did not need to know that.

"To what do I owe the pleasure, old friend?" Wickham drawled.

"It has been a long time since I considered you a friend. In fact, I am not sure that you have ever been a friend to me. More of a nuisance that I was forced to endure."

"The price one must pay to be a Darcy of Pemberley, to consort with those so decidedly beneath you." Wickham's voice was bitter.

Elizabeth's lovely face returned to Darcy as he replied, "I no longer have any objections to consorting—as you put it—with people below me in wealth and consequence. I do, however, draw a distinction between them and you, given that I view you as no better than pond life."

Fitzwilliam began to laugh. "Well said, Cousin."

Darcy did not hear his remark, so incensed was he by Wickham's flippant tone. He continued, "Only for my father's sake did I help you. Look what good it did either of us. Have you ever known what it is like to be honourable?"

"And have you ever known what it is like to be poor?" Wickham retorted.

"You had enough of a chance to become wealthier than your father. You squandered your opportunities away. Did you honestly think that I would continue to support you, no matter what the cost to those around you? Look at this place! You truly thought you would be a good lawyer or parson? A man who gambles his earnings away in a brothel."

"I would not be the first lawyer or parson to do so."

"But you would be the first to be sponsored by a member of the Darcy family, and therefore it would have been out of the question."

"And I should content myself with whatever scraps you might provide? To aspire to be slightly wealthier than my poor servant father?"

"Your father was hardly poor."

"My father was in service. Well-dressed and well-polished, but he was a servant nonetheless. What if I wished for something more? What if I did not desire a profession at all?"

Darcy almost laughed. "You hoped to be a gentleman? You? I did not know brothels provided jokes as well as prostitutes. I can think of no one less likely to behave in a gentlemanlike manner."

"Why should I not have such an aspiration? I see no reason why you should be rich and I should not. Why is it a ludicrous notion? I had hoped to marry well. To gain enough money to do as I please, to move about as I please, and to befriend or disown whomever I please."

Fitzwilliam tightened his grip on Wickham. "You may spare us the details. We are all well-versed in your matrimonial plans."

Wickham glared at him. "Had I been permitted to marry well, I may have had my own estate by now. I could have had servants, made investments—"

"Your wife is the daughter of a gentleman, giving you more respectability than you deserve!"

"My wife is a drain on my funds, which is precisely why—" Here Wickham stopped, finally at the point of revealing too much.

"Which is precisely why you decided to blackmail her sister." Darcy filled in the gap.

Wickham's eyes grew cold and his lips fell silent.

Darcy motioned to Fitzwilliam. "The Wickham I remember would always keep anything of value in a small pouch sewn into the top-left seam of his coat."

"Let us test your memory, Cousin." With the other two men holding Wickham in place, Fitzwilliam began to cut Wickham's coat with his knife. "Stay still or I cannot be held responsible should my blade slip."

At this, Wickham stopped protesting. His shoulders slumped as he realised the futility of his actions. Eventually, Fitzwilliam's knife struck something. Twisting his fingers inside the ripped coat, he pulled out a small pouch. Wordlessly, he handed it to Darcy who carefully extracted its contents. Even Matthews and Carruthers seemed transfixed. Holding it up to the light, he revealed the inky blue of the sapphire which contrasted perfectly with the pearls. His mother's brooch. Just as beautiful and as precious as in his memories. He could not wait to return it to Elizabeth. Turning back to Wickham, he saw every emotion play out on the rogue's face.

In the end, Wickham decided to attempt a smile. "Come, Darcy! You know I would have returned it as soon as I had the money. A man such as I has many mouths to feed and—"

"—and many brothels to visit." Darcy cut him off. "No, I have had quite enough of your stories. You are as much a stranger to the truth as you are to notions of integrity and honour. There is no place for a man like you in honest society. Clearly, you have not learnt the error of your ways, as you continue to persist in destroying those closest to me. We shall take you before a judge, and you can explain how you came to steal my mother's brooch."

"But I did not steal it. It was given to me. Did your dearest Elizabeth not explain that to you? I should have known no marriage could truly be that harmonious."

Fitzwilliam glared at Wickham. "I do not know what games you are playing, but we refuse to indulge them. If you do not wish to explain yourself, then I am more than happy to introduce you to the bottom of the Thames. It would be a much quicker solution to our problem."

"You would not dare!"

Drawing nearer, Darcy leant into Wickham's face. "When it comes to protecting my family, do not underestimate what I am capable of."

"If you hand me to the magistrate, I shall tell him everything."

"Such as?"

"I shall tell them of Ramsgate. It would ruin Georgiana. Surely you would not want that?" His tone of mocking condescension galled Darcy beyond words. Glancing at both men flanking Wickham, Darcy weighed his words. Never before had he spoken of her elopement in the presence of a stranger. For too long the fear of causing her pain had prevented him from speaking the truth. The mention of her past anguish brought Georgiana to the forefront of his mind, but it was not the image of her as a young girl crying in his arms.

Instead, he saw her as she was now: blissfully content in her married life, her golden curls shimmering as she bent her head to kiss her darling son. He thought of Elizabeth too, smiling at Georgiana's side as she gazed down at her newborn nephew. His beloved little sister was safe from harm now.

Setting his teeth, he continued sharply, "In what way would she be ruined? She is happily married to a good man who loves her and the son she bore him. She has money and status to weather any storm that you may deign to bring."

Extracting himself from Wickham's presence, Darcy drew himself up to his full height. "It is time you faced the consequences of your actions. I intend to call in every debt of yours that I possess. Once I have started, I wonder how long before others join me? I know that it was the promise of money that drew you to this room. Do you even know how much money you owe?" From the look on the miscreant's face, Darcy's words had found their mark.

"You would not dare," said Wickham at last.

Fitzwilliam hauled Wickham to his feet. "We have arranged transportation, and it awaits your presence. And to think, you were just bemoaning your unfortunate circumstances. How your fortune has changed! You will be travelling by private carriage tonight."

Carruthers and Matthews seized Wickham's arms and contorted them round his back. Darcy was pleased to see the former's gold rings taking effect as they were pressed firmly into Wickham's forearms.

"Where are you taking me?" Panic began to take hold as Wickham's confident mask dropped.

"Where you can no longer be of any harm," Matthews snarled in Wickham's ear. "And no one will care if harm befalls you." The burly pair wrestled Wickham towards the door. Darcy ignored his protests. All pretence of confidence had disappeared.

"Darcy, no, I beg you!" Wickham's eyes bulged in alarm. "Think of your father! What would his wishes be?"

"I am of the opinion he wished better for you." Darcy moved forwards to assist the other men in Wickham's removal.

"And what of your wife? Do not forget her part in all this. You wish to inflict more pain on her?" At the mention of Elizabeth's name, Darcy paused mid-step. Sensing that at last he had stumbled upon a weakness to exploit, the last words he would ever utter to

Darcy were characteristically cruel. "If you wonder how I came to have your mother's damned brooch, then you only have your wife to thank."

A bitter silence filled the room after Wickham's removal. Blood coursed through Darcy's veins and he took a deep breath to quell the anger churning inside his chest. How was it that Wickham always knew his most vulnerable spot? The image of Elizabeth, so broken after the confrontation with his aunt, returned to him. Whatever had happened, he refused to believe that Elizabeth was at fault.

Beside him, Fitzwilliam cleared his throat. "It was a stroke of genius to buy up his debts, Cousin. I did not agree with you at the time, I shall admit it now. To my eyes, it allowed him too much freedom. Tell me, what is the total? I would dearly love to know the amount the blackguard has to pay back."

The thought of Wickham finally imprisoned was excessively pleasing. Perhaps it was time to own to a little falsehood of his own. Darcy gave his cousin a grim smile. "To tell you the truth, Fitzwilliam, I honestly cannot remember."

THE CURRICLE WAS LARGE ENOUGH TO ADMIT TWO, BUT Fitzwilliam had preferred to make his own arrangements. In a way, Darcy was glad of it, but he did not wish to let his cousin know. Securing a promise from Fitzwilliam that he should rest well before calling tomorrow, Darcy's guilt was eased. As obliged as he was to his cousin, he did not feel equal to his company. Today had been long and arduous.

Tempting as it was to stay up half the night drinking whiskey, Darcy's body would not let him forget Elizabeth was waiting for him at home. What would her reaction be when he showed her the recovered brooch? Would she fall into his arms, her soft hair nestled against his chest? He could only dream of such a sensation. Whatever pain she had endured would hopefully be eased by the knowledge that Wickham was apprehended. Maybe then, she would finally confide in him.

Tomorrow, Darcy would have to find a way of conveying his opinions to his aunt. A letter was out of the question. Unless it was by his own hand, she would not believe it. He did not wish to make his impairment known to her. A private interview would need to be arranged. He groaned inwardly. Lady Catherine's company was onerous at the best of times. Any meeting between them would be the last he would endure, but endure it he would for Elizabeth's sake.

No, he caught himself. All this trouble was for tomorrow. Tonight, he would have the pleasure of Elizabeth's company. He could not wait to tell her everything. Sighing, he closed his eyes. Her image danced before him. In so many ways, she was still a stranger to him, but, in every way that was important, she was more a part of him than anyone he had ever met. One look from her was enough to silence him, and when she bestowed upon him a smile, he was totally disarmed. Darcy could not contemplate what a fool he would be if she should allow him the most intimate pleasures. He groaned softly. What he would give to be totally at her mercy! A smile played about his lips. She would have the upper hand entirely. He would be a most willing pupil if she would allow him the privilege.

The curricle drew up to the house. By Darcy's watch he had been gone for just over two hours. The footman assisted him from the conveyance, and Darcy was pleased to discover that his ankle could bear a little more of his body weight. Making his way into the hall, Darcy hastened his step. As soon as he could get his coat off, he would retire upstairs to find Elizabeth. Perhaps they could check upon Molly.

Stepping through the hall, he found the stairs. "Sir, forgive me." A voice caused him to turn sharply.

"What is it?" Darcy made a point of never raising his voice to a servant, but he had never been so close as this moment. It was the genteel yet efficient Mrs Lister, who had never once in the entirety of her employment waited for him to return home. An uneasy sense of foreboding washed over him. "Is anything amiss?"

"I am not sure how to begin this, but it is Mrs Darcy, sir."

"Is she ill?" Dr Amstel's caution came flooding back in an instant. He should have known, should have stayed to comfort her after the unpleasant scene this afternoon. Please God, it was not serious, not when he was finally able to protect her from Wickham.

He heard the tremor in her voice. "She has gone."

"What do you mean, she has gone?" Darcy reached out to the bannister to steady himself. Elizabeth's face, so deathly white in his dream, drowned out all coherent thought from his mind. Had it been a premonition of what was to come? Sinking to the steps, he moaned into his hands. Unaware of his housekeeper's approach, he did not hear her reply. She called his name again, and this time he heard.

"She returned not long after her trip to Lady Luxford's residence, and, as quiet as you like, she must have slipped upstairs. When we had not heard of her plans for dinner, I decided to enquire after her myself. When I knocked upon her door there was no answer. Fearful for her well-being, I knocked again, but this time I entered when I did not hear her reply. When I entered the room it was entirely empty. There was no sign of her—only a few gowns missing and this letter addressed to you."

She slipped her hand into her pocket and passed a note to him. Ripping it open, he prayed that the many hours of labouring over Elizabeth's diary would not fail him. Still, unconsciously, he turned his shoulder to Mrs Lister. He was not ready for anyone to see him struggle. The words swam before his eyes, and even Elizabeth's familiar hand was hard to read. In the corner of his eye, Mrs Lister shifted her weight nervously.

My love,

Be not alarmed upon receiving this note. I am well, but I must leave directly. I do not wish to put anything into writing in case you need to read this note with another. When you speak to your aunt, I am sure you will understand. I shall send you a message when I know that Molly is safe—

Darcy's head jerked up. "Where is Molly? Where is our daughter?" He could hear the tension in his voice.

Shaking her head helplessly, Mrs Lister could only answer, "We do not know, only we were sure she must be with Mrs Darcy. Sarah has gone too—along with a small suitcase."

Tears were running down the old lady's face. "Forgive me, sir! I did not know what to do! Nobody knew where to find you, and I did not want to read the note as it was addressed to you. I await your instructions, and I pray that all will be well again and…"

Here the good woman broke into sobs, crying into her apron. In other circumstances, Darcy might have stopped to offer her words of comfort, but it was too much to take in. Elizabeth and Molly were gone. They had fled in the dark of night. He snatched up the note again and found his place.

…when I know that Molly is safe. Needless to say, I do not trust Lady Catherine. Please do not worry excessively. Sarah has come with us, and I have more than enough money. I have never wished to be the cause of any pain.

Forgive me for everything,

Your dearest Elizabeth

Groaning, Darcy stretched his legs out from his position on the stairs. After all the events of today, this was surely the final straw. Running his hands through his hair, he realised how much of a fool he must look, sitting on his own stairs in an empty hall. Looking up, he saw Mrs Lister anxiously awaiting his instructions. "Tell me, Mrs Lister, what happened when Mrs Darcy returned from Lady Luxford's house? How did she seem?"

"She seemed pale and quiet, but that has been her wont since you returned from Derbyshire."

"Something must have happened at my sister's house to make her leave. I must go there directly."

His housekeeper nodded. "I shall go now to arrange your departure." Turning sharply, she disappeared down the hall.

Hauling himself from the stairs, a wave of nausea passed over him. What if some evil should befall Elizabeth? *She takes too much upon herself.* Those had been the doctor's words. He understood them perfectly now. What on Earth had possessed her to flee under the cover of darkness? With their daughter and not even a footman for assistance no less. He would need to find out who had driven the carriage; perhaps they could yield some clues as to their whereabouts. Groaning, he clenched his fist. To wait for the carriage to return would be too late. It would give ample time for Elizabeth to disappear. No, whatever action was needed, it must be undertaken swiftly.

Turning the note in his hand, he traced over his aunt's name with his thumb. Anger filled him. What was happening here? Forces greater than he were at work. What could his aunt have said or done to cause Elizabeth to leave? She did not fear Lady Catherine. So what then did she fear? *Molly.* Darcy's fist was clenched so tightly that he felt his nails dig into his flesh. That could be the only reason she would embark on such a journey with their daughter. What vile threat had Lady Catherine made against their little girl?

Gripping onto his walking cane, he made his way through the hall to Mrs Lister's small office. He did not intend to startle her, but she recoiled in shock nonetheless.

"Goodness, sir! Forgive me! Is there anything else you require?"

"I hope I do not need to remind you to be discreet. My hope is to find Eliz—I mean Mrs Darcy and Miss Darcy and return them to safety."

"Safety!" Mrs Lister looked aghast. "What could be safer than here under your protection, sir?"

"My thoughts exactly. Which is why I put myself at the mercy of your discretion."

"Naturally, sir. Is there anything else?"

"Write a note to my cousin Fitzwilliam. He is staying at his parents' house in town."

"Of course, sir. You may trust me to deliver the particulars."

"Tell him if he has not heard from me again by nine o'clock tomorrow morning, then he must go to Lady Luxford's home and demand to find out what has occurred."

Mrs Lister nodded. "Sir, may I wish you Godspeed? The sooner you can return dear Mrs Darcy and little Molly to us, the sooner I shall sleep tonight. If only she had spoken to me, my poor mistress! I knew she was not quite right after the visit from that *so-called* Lady Catherine. If she had only confided in me then I would have helped her! Oh, please Lord they are safe... My prayers are with you all."

"And I thank you for them." Darcy had never seen the unflappable Mrs Lister so shaken. He added her prayers to his own. Word came for him that the curricle was ready, and he made his way to the entrance.

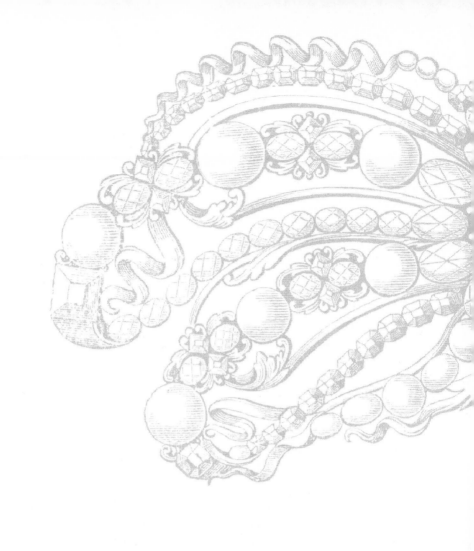

CHAPTER THIRTY-SIX

The curtains were drawn at the Luxfords'. The hour was late; it was past any respectable time to call on someone, but circumstances dictated that he could not wait. Without another thought, he descended from the carriage and unceremoniously hammered the knocker. Whoever was on night duty made their way to the door.

"I must speak to your mistress," Darcy interjected before the yawning footman could object. He pushed his way past the young lad. He could see a light coming from under the door of the sitting room. Without knocking, he stepped inside.

"Fitzwilliam!" Georgiana and her husband sat by the fire. "Heavens, what is it?"

"Have you seen Elizabeth? What happened when she came here?"

"Whatever do you mean? She is not with you?" Darcy slumped down upon a chair next to her and caught his face in his hands. He did not trust himself to speak lest he start to cry in front of Georgiana and her husband no less.

"She has gone," said Darcy flatly, no longer able to contain his misery. "Something happened here, in this house, which caused Elizabeth to leave me." He groaned, twisting the curls of his hair as he sat hunched over in his chair. "What is worse is that she has taken Molly with her, and I have no idea as to where they have gone."

He pulled himself up and looked at his sister. "What happened earlier? Elizabeth said she received a note from you, detailing a very unpleasant tête-à-tête with Aunt Catherine."

"Is that what she told you happened?" Now it was Georgiana's turn to look concerned.

"Is that not true?" Whatever Elizabeth had sought to shield him from, it could not be worse than what he was presently imagining.

Georgiana looked at Luxford. "Perhaps, my love, you would be so kind as to arrange for some tea to be brought to us directly."

Nodding discreetly, Luxford rose from his chair. "Of course. And I shall ask for something stronger should you need it, Darcy."

His words fell upon deaf ears. Darcy's eyes had not left Georgiana's face.

"Did you or did you not write her a note? I am half mad with worry for them. I must know the truth."

"I did Fitzwilliam but—"

"So what caused you to look so surprised?"

"From your description, it sounded like Lady Catherine had left us, but in truth I wrote to inform Elizabeth that Lady Catherine had arrived here unannounced and begged an audience with her."

"And you did not think it strange?"

"Why yes, under the usual circumstances, but you know what Lady Catherine is like. Her supercilious ways are so commonplace that they have almost become expected. Elizabeth and I always laugh them off after she departs." She caught herself. "I suppose I should be more kind to Mother's sister, but it is far easier to tolerate her for a small amount of time and send her on her way than to dispute some of her more ridiculous pronouncements."

"And did anything happen while they were here? Any argument or disagreement?"

"Why no, nothing," Georgiana replied blithely. "Which for those two is most unusual. Oftentimes, Lady Catherine has something ridiculous to say, and I marvel at how politely Elizabeth rebuffs it. There was not much said between them this evening."

Darcy groaned. "What if I told you that only an hour or so earlier, Lady Catherine had called upon Elizabeth unannounced and degraded her in the most humiliating way—in *our* home no less! Lady Catherine questioned everything about Elizabeth. Her morality, her fidelity...she even cast shade upon Molly's parentage."

"Why, that is dreadful!" Georgiana exclaimed incredulously. "In every way it is absurd. Elizabeth is devoted to you! She is beyond reproach. As precious to me as any sister by blood ever could be. When you were first married, I was so worried that I should feel out of place, but she was so kind and patient. Never once did I feel replaced in your affections, only cherished in hers. I love her as I do my own flesh and blood—more so when you place her next to our vile aunt."

"If it pleases you, I told Lady Catherine that she was no longer welcome in our house. After not getting her own way, it sounds as though she abused your generous nature to persuade Elizabeth to meet her again."

"I wonder why she came at all—Elizabeth that is. I should not have had the courage to accept a meeting after such an ugly scene."

"I do not know. I pray I shall have the chance to ask her." Twisting absently at his signet ring, Darcy looked at Georgiana. "Can you think of where Elizabeth might have taken Molly? I do not understand the urgency. From what you say, she and Lady Catherine barely spoke two words together the whole time she was here."

Georgiana fell quiet, looking evermore like their mother as she did so. "I was not with them the entire time. Baby Robert had started to cry, and Hannah, our nurse-maid, had come to find me. I must have left them alone for about a quarter of an hour."

"Something must have been said that caused Elizabeth to flee," he said grimly.

"And she left you no note?"

Wordlessly, he pulled out the note and handed it to his sister. She read it quickly.

"What do you think she means when she says 'in case you need to read this note with another'? It is not like her to be ambiguous. She is always so open and honest."

"I believe it refers to..." Darcy paused. "Since my accident, Georgiana, I find myself much altered. It is not just the injuries you see before you, but there are also ones you cannot see. These injuries, I fear, will never be healed. My memory has been damaged, and along with it my ability to read and write as well as I did before. I am re-learning it, but my progress has been slow. Fitzwilliam knows of my memory loss, but only Elizabeth knows of my other difficulties...as now do you. I believe she knows that I may have to show this note to another, yet does not want to reveal to them that I have struggled to read it."

Georgiana nodded. "That would be very like her. So thoughtful and clever." She placed her hand over his. "What do you mean when you speak of your memory loss? Dearest Fitzwilliam, you should have told me! I could have helped you."

"Believe me, Georgiana, how I wish that I had! My torment would have been eased, and maybe even some of this madness may have been avoided. The only excuse I can offer is that I did not wish to destroy your happiness at such a precious time—given all the worry I must have caused you when I had my accident. But we must talk no more of it, not when Elizabeth and Molly are still missing."

As he said those last words aloud, the weight of all that had befallen him took hold. An overwhelming sense of panic gripped at his chest, and he placed a hand over his heart to steady himself from the pain.

"Are you well?" She rose swiftly to call for assistance, but he stilled her with a wave of his other hand.

"There is no need. The sensation has passed." He looked earnestly into his darling sister's face. "Truly, Georgie, I am well. The pain has abated." The image of Elizabeth kissing Molly's sleeping face returned sharply; the memory of his first night in London was so vivid that he nearly lost his breath. What he would give to know that they were both safe!

"What reason did Lady Catherine have to doubt Elizabeth?"

Georgiana's voice brought him back to reality. Flexing his aching muscles as best he could, Darcy considered his words before speaking. Fragments of information were floating around in his mind, and he was struggling to piece them together.

"Lady Catherine was sent a letter which made some slanderous claims against Elizabeth. Whoever wrote the letter found a willing listener in Lady Catherine, so determined is she to find fault with my wife."

"You cannot give credence to these claims?"

"Of course not, but…"

"But what?"

"But there is more to this than meets the eye, Georgiana. I fear that there is another plot—or scheme—at work here. One that I can only glimpse. Indeed, for many days now I have felt that some of it is being actively hidden from me—for what purpose I can only guess. At some point, either before my accident or shortly after, Elizabeth was contacted by…by George Wickham."

He stopped, unsure how to continue. The last time he remembered discussing Wickham with Georgiana, his sister had wept in Darcy's arms. A girl of fifteen, she had been utterly devastated by his betrayal.

Thankfully, it was not so now. Furious red spots formed on her ivory cheeks. "What business has that damned scoundrel with Elizabeth?"

"Georgiana, your language!"

"He deserves worse."

Darcy laughed grimly. "Mother's brooch was stolen. I do not know how exactly, but it somehow ended up in Wickham's possession…I suspect through his wife, although I cannot prove it."

"She would be the most likely suspect if not for the fact that her presence has been forbidden at Pemberley for some time now."

"Forbidden? But why?"

"Oh, but of course, you do not remember. Well, after your marriage, you and Elizabeth were in agreement that although Wickham could not be allowed entrance, Lydia would still be permitted to visit—provided you and I were not there to suffer her company. However, quite suddenly, Lydia was no longer allowed admittance. You never spoke of it directly—and neither did Elizabeth—but the subject was always changed whenever her name was mentioned."

Behind Georgiana's shoulder the clock struck eleven. His heart sank. Only an hour and then it would be midnight, and he was still no closer to finding his family. Focusing his attention back to Georgiana, he clasped her hand in his.

"Think, little dove, is there anywhere she might go if she needed assistance?"

Breaking free from his hand, Georgiana stood and went to a small escritoire in the corner of the room. "Jane has taken the children to visit her parents, so it will only be Bingley at home. I shall ask Robert to call upon him directly. Let me relay the particulars to my husband, and he will ask Bingley for assistance and information."

"No, Bingley is my friend and brother-in-law. What would he think if Robert came with such news instead of me? It should be I who—"

"You must go here." She handed him a small card.

"Gracechurch Street?"

"It is the address of Mr and Mrs Gardiner, Elizabeth's uncle and aunt. They are a lovely couple whom you hold in great esteem, and they would certainly help Elizabeth in her hour of need."

Georgiana turned to the writing desk again and copied out the address for him. She wrote quickly, but Darcy noticed she had made every letter clear to read. As she handed it to him, he bent and kissed her cheek.

"God bless you. I hope to bring you glad tidings in the morning."

She nodded. "Go quickly, there is not a moment to lose." She rang for a servant, but Luxford appeared first.

"Luxford, my brother was just leaving. I shall explain everything." As the door closed, the last thing Darcy saw was his sister, a child no longer, finding strength in the warmth of her husband's embrace. He prayed to God that he could do the same for Elizabeth.

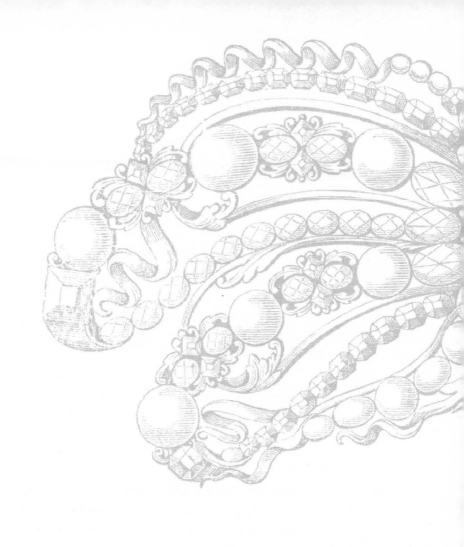

CHAPTER THIRTY-SEVEN

A man's face peered through the crack in the doorway of the Gardiner home. Darcy drew a deep breath and used his most authoritative tone. "Forgive me the late hour, but are the Gardiners in? It is a matter of great importance regarding their niece."

At the sound of his voice, the old servant stood up straight. "Mr Darcy, sir, I thought it was you! Pray come in and be seated. The master has just gone to bed. You will allow me some time to fetch him?"

Time was precisely what Darcy did not have, but it would have been useless to argue his point. He was therefore surprised when the master in question came down in his dressing gown, night cap, and slippers.

"Darcy, pardon my attire, but I knew it would only be a matter of urgency for you to call so late. What troubles you?"

The man standing in front of Darcy was about forty or so. Soft, greying whiskers framed a friendly face, and he regarded Darcy warmly, like a father would a son.

"I know the hour is late, but I come in search of Elizabeth and Molly."

Gently taking Darcy by the arm, he guided him towards an

armchair by the empty fireplace. Clearly, Darcy's injuries were known to him. He left and returned holding a lamp, the light of which cast shadows across a comfortably furnished sitting room.

"Elizabeth and Molly have gone." It was now the third time that Darcy had said this out loud to another person, and the burden of worry was beginning to take its toll. It was all he could do to prevent his voice from breaking. "In truth, I do not know where they have gone to, and I am afraid something terrible should befall them."

"How dreadfully worried you must have been. If I had known that you were unaware of their departure, then I should have written to you directly to spare you any unnecessary worry."

"Whatever do you mean?"

"Elizabeth and Molly came here this evening, just after dinner. Elizabeth said she had been called urgently to Longbourn and needed to use our carriage for the journey."

"You did not think it odd that she should not use ours?"

"She said it was her preference to leave your coach in London at your disposal. I assumed you were aware of her plans, else I should have sent a note round immediately."

Reaching forwards, Gardiner placed a fatherly hand on Darcy's shoulder. Under any other circumstances, Darcy might have recoiled at a stranger's touch, but Mr Gardiner was oddly comforting. He had no memory of this man before this very night, but everything about him felt familiar.

"Tell me how I can help," he said.

Pulling out the note, Darcy handed it to Mr Gardiner and permitted him to familiarise himself with the details.

The older man's face grew grim and pale. "What do you think this reference to your aunt means?"

"I cannot be entirely sure. But be assured that she will no longer be part of our lives from now on."

"Quite right. There is only so much poison one can withstand before it contaminates your life beyond repair. Stay here while I make enquiries."

And with that he quit the room, leaving Darcy alone with only the ticking of the carriage clock for company. A few moments later, the door opened again, but it was not Mr Gardiner who entered but rather a genteel lady who appeared only a few years older than Darcy himself. Darcy tried to stand but she waved at him to remain seated.

"Darcy, do not trouble yourself on my account. Lizzy told me about your leg." This must be Mrs Gardiner, Elizabeth's aunt. Her voice was soft, and its gentle lilt transported him immediately back to Derbyshire. Out of everything connected to Elizabeth, the woman before him had the greatest sense of familiarity—if only he could remember her name!

"Edward has gone to wake the groom and your coachman—we had said that he may stay here with your carriage and return tomorrow," she explained. "We hope that they may reveal some details to help you in your search." She wrung her hands. "Oh, poor Lizzy! What was she thinking? If only she would have confided in me, I could have offered her guidance and womanly counsel."

Darcy nodded sombrely. "Our thoughts travel along the same vein."

"Dear Lizzy has always been stubborn and wilful. I was so pleased when she married you. She would never be happy unless she wed a man whose intellect she could respect and whose opinion she valued." There was no mention of his wealth or status in her remarks. In an unguarded moment, Mrs Gardiner had revealed another puzzle piece in his life with Elizabeth. He felt his respect for Elizabeth's relations increase.

A short knock on the door told him of Mr Gardiner's return. "They have returned to Hertfordshire. That much was true. My coachman spoke to yours before he prepared our carriage. He wished to know whether Mrs Darcy had any preference over where they would stop. From their conversation, it would seem that Lizzy wanted to travel as far as she could safely, and then find somewhere to rest. Her plan was to make haste to Long-bourn as soon as it became light enough to continue their journey."

Darcy's heart leapt at the news. "I am exceedingly obliged to you, sir."

"What do you plan to do? Wait for me to be made ready, and I shall be happy enough to assist you."

"Thank you but I wish to leave directly. Please send for the coachman. I wish to take the carriage back to my house. My intention is to travel to Hertfordshire in it, but first I must leave instructions for my housekeeper should there be any developments. In my absence, all correspondence regarding this matter should be directed to my sister's home—do you have the address?" Mr Gardiner looked at his wife, who nodded.

As he made to leave, Mr Gardiner seized Darcy's hand and shook it warmly. "I bless the day you married Lizzy. Never could I have imagined a finer nephew."

Momentarily stunned by this man's praise, Darcy was further shocked when Mrs Gardiner flung her arms round him in a motherly embrace. "Our prayers are with you, Darcy. Please God, you find them safe." Tipping his hat at them, Darcy stepped out into the frosty London night. Their faith in his abilities had been moving. He could only hope he was equal to it.

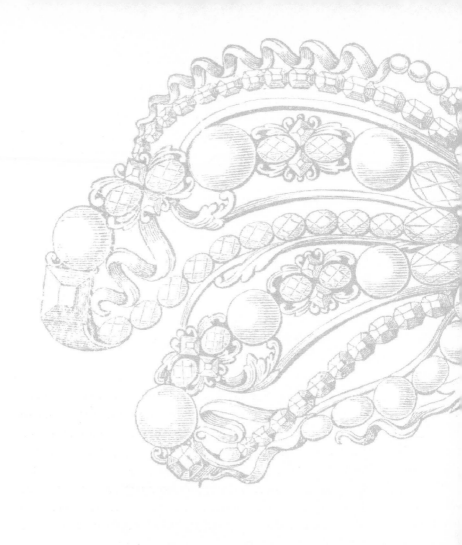

CHAPTER THIRTY-EIGHT

Darcy glanced at the clock in his study. He had not been able to sleep since returning to his London home. He had spent much of the time arguing with his coachman for an immediate departure before conceding that Mr Spiggs was entirely correct. Given the hour, it was prudent to postpone the journey until the morning. Yet to sit and wait was unbearable. Fighting the impulse to ignore his injuries and to make his own way there on horseback, Darcy had finally yielded to his coachman's advice. He now sat alone, with nothing but his own anxiety to torment him.

Carefully stretching out his legs, he stood slowly and made his way to the mirror on the far side of his study. In the dwindling lamplight, he surveyed his reflection. Dark shadows lined his eyes and his face had a ghostly pallor. Sighing deeply, he rubbed his hands over his eyes in an attempt to stay awake. The rough skin of his scarred fingers scratched across his face, reminding him of all that had happened to him since his accident. Where would Elizabeth and Molly be sleeping tonight? He said a silent prayer for their safety. A dart of pain shot through his chest. Placing his hand over his heart, he breathed deeply. The image of his father's ashen face briefly returned to haunt him. Closing his eyes, he waited for the ache to fade.

Suddenly, a knock sounded at the door. Darcy called for whomever it was to enter and was relieved to see his coachman, Spiggs, step into his study.

"Mr Darcy, sir, the carriage is ready, and I do believe we should be able to depart soon. If we leave now, then we should catch the first of the light as we leave the city."

The tension in Darcy's shoulders eased slightly as he nodded in reply. "Let us not waste another moment."

THE ROAD TO HERTFORDSHIRE WAS GOOD, AND DARCY hoped to arrive at Elizabeth's familial home at a decent hour. However, before the road to Meryton, or whatever name Mrs Lister had supplied, was a great deal of cobbled, winding London road to endure. Spiggs was pushing the horses as quickly as was safe, and Darcy was now suffering the indignity of being clattered around inside his own carriage. Suddenly, there was a change in tempo, and the cadence of hoofs smoothed to an altogether more soothing pace. Pulling back the little curtain, Darcy peered out of the window. Slivers of light had begun to dance their way across the horizon. They were crossing a bridge—he did not know which one. Even in the early morning light, he could still see the waning moon's reflection in the swirling river below. Gentle waves broke along the river bank, and there was a fresh chill in the air. Something about the scene reminded him of Elizabeth. Maybe it was her skin, so pale and delicate, that put him in mind of fading moonlight, or perhaps it was the dark swirls of water that reminded him of her unruly curls. Whatever the reason, it was her lovely face that he thought of when he finally surrendered to sleep.

SUNLIGHT CARESSED HIS FACE LIKE WAVES GENTLY BREAKING ALONG A SANDY beach. He was walking—unaided—along a forest path. Shades of green and

brown bent and quivered as the wind ran through the treetops. By his feet, there were wildflowers blooming, their heads popping up hither and thither, a brilliant patchwork quilt against the vibrant green grass. Industrious bees hovered from flower to flower, their buzzing a friendly presence along his woodland amble. The sky overhead was the most brilliant blue, deeper and richer than any he had seen before. No painting could capture it, no musical pastorale could evoke it, it was inexpressible, this sense of absolute freedom and contentment.

"My love, you must wait!" Elizabeth was calling him. He turned in the direction of her voice. She was there on the wooded path, looking every inch the forest nymph. Freckles covered her nose, and her hair was plaited loosely. Tiny daisies dotted her curls, and she was frowning so becomingly at him.

"You are too fast for me, and it is hardly fair. You have such great long legs, Fitzwilliam. I should make you take half-steps."

Darcy heard himself laugh. Pulling her close to him, he felt the softness of her body against the lean muscle of his chest.

"Do you mean like this?" He made a great pretence of taking the smallest steps he could, earning a tinkle of laughter.

"That is much better. I feel we are more evenly matched," she said, suppressing another giggle.

"When it comes to you, dearest one, then I am afraid there is no question of us being equal. You are my superior in every way."

Elizabeth grinned up at him. "How very gallant of you to say so, sir—although we both know it to be false. I am afraid this little one puts me at quite a disadvantage when it comes to our walks together." Taking his hand in hers, she placed it on her midsection.

He had seen it before but had not—perhaps wilfully—acknowledged the meaning of it, this thickening of her waist. By now, of course, it could not be denied, and he found her all the more beautiful for it. Cupping his large hand across the curve of her bump, he returned her smile.

"As if I would ever count this against you," he replied gently. "I should walk in any way you desired as long as it secured your comfort."

She raised an eyebrow at him. "Well, I shall certainly remember your promise. It would secure my comfort and my happiness if I should see the great Fitzwilliam Darcy hopscotch like a child."

Laughing, he drew her closer still and murmured, "Be merciful, dear Elizabeth, with your proclamations, because I would do them in a heartbeat if it would make you happy. You must know I am your willing slave." He felt her delicate hands run along his back and stop just under his shoulder blades.

"A willing slave?" she whispered, pulling him towards her. "I shall remind you of those words later." She raised her eyebrows, her eyes full of promise. Then she smiled, a most mischievous smile, and her eyes sparkled in the sunlight. "But for now, I must content myself with the simple request that you walk at my pace, at my side."

Tucking his arm about her waist, he pressed a kiss on her sun-kissed curls. "I shall always be at your side, Elizabeth, you may never forget it."

A LOUD THUMP ROUSED DARCY FROM HIS DREAM. IT HAD been so real, so vivid that he wondered whether it had truly happened. The thump came again, and Darcy realised it was the driver telling him that he was in need of stopping soon. Peering out of the window, he guessed the time to be about seven or so by the first signs of sunrise above the distant hills. He prayed Elizabeth had been true to her intentions and had gone to her parents' house. He had no idea what to do if she was not there. Meeting them without her would be supremely uncomfortable, and he did not want to think of their reaction when he told them she was missing. Stretching out, he extracted Elizabeth's diary from the travelling valise resting on the seat opposite. Fitzwilliam had not spoken well of the Bennets, he recalled. Longbourn. He frowned. The name was not familiar to him. Flipping through the pages, he stopped at the first Longbourn he saw. Scratching at the stubble forming on his chin, he focused on the words swimming below.

Longbourn

Dear Diary,

There is a saying about these parts that 'a bird in the hand is worth two in the bush', but if you are my papa then 'two birds in the bush are preferable to a solitary burnt one on a plate'. Or so says he in response to the crisis caused by Mrs Turner's neglect of our poor guinea fowl. It was not the good woman's fault, more Mama's for she would not leave our poor cook alone, constantly fussing and worrying that it would not rival the standard of meal her married daughters are now used to. I fear she has become worse rather than better. She is dreadfully skittish around my poor love—more so recently than ever before. I dread to tell Fitzwilliam about the dinner. He is terrible at pretending to enjoy something when he does not, and my family are well-enough acquainted with him to know when he is lying to spare our feelings. Papa looked particularly gleeful when he discovered the poor bird's fate—he has never much cared for the taste of guinea fowl, and now the opportunity to tease 'poor Mr Darcy' has been handed to him—quite literally—on a plate.

I am writing this in the drawing room at Longbourn to fill the time until we dine. Fitzwilliam has gone for a ride with Charles and Papa. Mama's histrionics have become too much for the three of them, and we ladies shall have to bear the brunt of it. In the room are Jane, Mary, and Kitty. It is so pleasant to be reunited with them, but sadness fills me that Lydia is not here. But there is no space in my heart to dwell on that unhappiness as I watch my sisters play with little Molly. Mary, in particular, is quite taken with my precious darling, and the pair of them are giggling away at the pianoforte. Mary has Molly on her lap and is placing her chubby little fingers on the keys. What a racket! But the sound of their laughter is music to my ears. I earnestly hope that Mary finds happiness of her own. She would be a marvellous mama. For too long, she has been overshadowed by all of us, and I must remember to invite her to London. Her glasses make her shy and self-conscious when she need not be. Georgiana would love to see her again—I am sure of it. There will be all sorts of concerts and recitals that they can appreciate together. I would not need to chaperon them now that darling Georgie is married. There! I have reached a capital plan, and I must endeavour to remember it when I correspond with my partner-in-crime tomorrow.

Molly has had enough of the pianoforte and has now toddled over to Aunt Kitta as she so charmingly calls Kitty. What a difference there is in Kitty since the summer! Staying with the Gardiners was just the thing for her. As I slyly peek at her, I do believe my beloved sister is attempting to write to her lovely Captain McCormack. I can tell because she pauses after each word and smiles. I wish them every joy. Perhaps I should organise a dinner party inviting the lovely captain and his mother to cajole him along into declaring himself. A winter wedding would suit me quite nicely. Or should I let love find its own path? Fate saw fit to bring my Darcy to me, and perhaps it is not for me to interfere in Kitty's destiny. But a dinner party would do no harm, and I might prevail upon my husband to get the measure of the captain and his intentions towards my sister. It would not do to have two wayward soldiers in the family! At least Kitty is not in danger of following poor Lydia's example. The sad state of my baby sister's life is a warning for any young girl who pins their hopes on a scoundrel. I shall say a prayer for her in church next Sunday.

Mama has just burst into the room with all the elegance of a wounded chicken. I am studiously avoiding her persistent flapping. No wonder Fitzwilliam calls her Mother Hen! It is my fault, naturally, that she is in such a state. If I had not fallen violently in love with the richest man in Derbyshire, then she would be able to serve quasi-burnt poultry to her guests with a clear conscience. I should remind Mama that my only other offer was from Mr Collins, and that will soon silence her. Poor Charlotte! To be shackled to such a man. What she tolerates to bear the honour of being his wife. I did not think he could become more odious or more ridiculous, but sadly I have been proved wrong on both accounts...

I have picked up my pen only to finish this entry. My time was wisely spent reassuring Mama of my darling husband's secret preference for a hearty game pie, so she may discard any singed guinea fowl and there is time enough to start again. Fitzwilliam is not half as fastidious as she believes him to be. As long as he is able to eat peacefully without suffering any ridiculous conversation, he will be happy enough with a simple shortcrust. I shall naturally thank him for all his civilities towards my family later. Reticent creature that he is, I must ensure he is adequately praised for all his efforts at sociability. Footsteps on the path and the gentlemen have returned. I must scoop up Molly for a kiss with her papa and grandpapa...

A rattle of the carriage indicated that the driver and horses had rested enough. Darcy had no idea of how much time had passed, so engrossed was he in Elizabeth's diary. It was such a loving portrait; Darcy wondered what his relationship with Elizabeth's family was like. Meryton was not so far away. He closed his eyes and prayed he would be able to ask her soon himself.

DARCY'S CARRIAGE ROLLED UP A TREE-LINED AVENUE towards a modest country house. It was not grand nor impressive, but he could understand why Elizabeth might cherish it. There was a stream running alongside the driveway up to the house—it was more of a brook really, its gushing eddies gurgling happily alongside the creaking of carriage wheels. In front of the house was a garden stocked full of wildflowers and hollyhocks, their petals still moist with droplets of dew. Everything was bathed in the morning light—the air was so much fresher here than in London, and he took in an invigorating lungful.

As the carriage drew closer, he saw that Longbourn was deceptively deep. Behind each window was a room of considerable size. Beyond the stone wall which separated the house from the gardens lay some outhouses, presumably a small farm and some stables. Longbourn must be a building of some consequence in the neighbourhood as he had not seen another to equal it. He wondered at the property Charles leased. Was it near here?

A nervous energy flowed through him. What if Elizabeth and Molly were not here? What if—God forbid—he was denied entrance? Who knows what bile Lady Catherine had poured into Elizabeth's ears? Thanking the driver, he managed to make his way from the carriage as best he could. A distant church clock told him it was nearly nine. He pulled at his collar and attempted to flatten his wrinkled shirt. Combing a hand through his curls, he wished he had time to change. He hated looking dishevelled; it put one at such a disadvantage. Fighting the tremor in his hand, he knocked on the door and awaited an answer from someone within. A flurry of female voices from one of the rooms on an upper floor signalled that his arrival had not, at least, awoken all of the residents. Some were already up.

A middle-aged butler greeted Darcy at the door. To his relief, the servant did not seem remotely surprised to see him. For the first time since last night, he began to hope—as he had scarce dared to hope before—that Elizabeth and Molly were well. His presence here was expected. He was told that the family were within but to allow them a few moments due to the early hour. Inwardly chafing, he accepted that anything else would be discourteous and prayed the delay would not be overlong. Eventually, he was shown to a sitting room. From behind the door, he heard voices which stopped instantly the moment he entered.

The room he stepped into was full of women, all looking at him in a disapproving fashion. He swallowed, his mouth suddenly dry. How many sisters did Elizabeth have exactly? In the corner, he espied Jane attempting to soothe a matronly woman whom he thought must be Mrs Bennet, Elizabeth's mother. Jane's eyes were red-rimmed, and she held the older lady's hand in hers. There were two girls of a similar age to one another sitting on the blue-patterned sofa. Mary and Kitty, he should imagine, from the description in Elizabeth's diary. A noise came from the armchair by the window, and he stared at its occupant. What game was she playing? He bowed stiffly to Mrs Wickham, her unmistakable silhouette dark against the light of the elegant wingback chair. Apprehension filled him.

"Forgive my intrusion at this early hour," he said. "I do not wish to alarm you, but I have had word that Elizabeth is here, with Molly, and I desperately need to speak to her."

There was a prolonged silence until the older lady sighed and said, "I daresay that him coming all this way speaks very well of his deep love for Elizabeth—"

"Or of the deep fear that comes with the possibility of scandal at the expense of the great Darcy name." Mrs Wickham's voice, so cutting, broke into the older lady's sentence.

Running his hand across his brow, Darcy said, "Mrs Wickham, you do me a disservice. My only thought is for Elizabeth, and our child, and their well-being."

Mrs Wickham scoffed. "Why then did she arrive here, before breakfast, with hardly a stitch of clothing in her possession? Unescorted, I may add, if you do not count a child and a nurse-maid if you would believe it! Hardly the actions of a wife secure in her husband's affections!"

"I did not know of her plans. She left abruptly with no indication of where she would go."

"My point exactly. Why does she not trust you, Darcy? Why did she run?"

Her words hit the mark so precisely that for a moment, Darcy could not speak. To hear his deepest fears aired openly in front of an audience was mortifying enough. That it was an audience composed of Elizabeth's family made it worse.

"I shall tell you why," Mrs Wickham continued. "How could she trust the man who forbade her from seeing her family?"

"Whatever do you mean?"

"Lydia, dear, you go too far." Mrs Bennet spoke softly but her voice quivered. Mrs Wickham silenced her with a wave of her hand.

"You sought to drive a wedge between Elizabeth and us, her family. This business with your aunt just confirms that *your kind* hold themselves to a different set of rules from the rest of us."

The deep, twisting pain constricted itself around Darcy's heart once more. He felt the colour drain from his face, pale and wan like Father's had been. This made no sense. What was she talking about? He had denied Elizabeth her family? He could not imagine why he would do so.

"Lydia, think before you address your brother thus." Mrs Bennet's voice was sharper now.

"A brother does not ban one sister from calling upon another! How grievously you hurt Elizabeth in separating her from me— from her own flesh and blood!"

Turning back to Darcy, she continued, "And to think, she bears your child too!"

Whatever Mrs Wickham said after this, Darcy did not hear, for the entire room about him spun and shifted as an immense pain wound itself round his chest, and everything went dark.

DARCY OPENED HIS EYES TO FIND THAT THE JURY OF women had gone, as had the sitting room, and he had been placed upon a sofa in a decidedly masculine study.

Elizabeth. His first thought was of her. Was she well? Would she see him? Gripping the sides of the seat, he attempted to haul himself to his feet. The ground beneath him lurched dangerously, and a wave of nausea took hold.

"Steady yourself, there's a good chap." A quiet male voice spoke from the other side of the room. Squinting, Darcy watched as an older man came into view. This, surely, was Elizabeth's father. They had the same dimpled chin, the same inquisitive expression, and although his father-in-law's eyes were green, they twinkled with the same curious intelligence as Elizabeth's.

"Where am I?" Darcy's head was still spinning. "And where is Elizabeth?"

"She is upstairs resting."

"And she is well? And Molly...and..." Here Darcy faltered. *And the baby*, he wanted to ask. How could he have been so blind to it? She had looked so unwell, and it had never crossed his mind to even ask her the cause of it. *Selfish man*, he reprimanded himself. *It is little wonder she ran away.*

"All are well." Mr Bennet's eyes never left Darcy's face. "And how are you?"

Darcy ran his fingers along his temples. "I have a new bruise to add to my collection. What happened?"

"It would appear that you fainted," Mr Bennet replied with a wry smile. "It quite silenced my wife. I shall have to remember it as a future strategy."

Darcy felt himself redden at his father-in-law's gentle teasing and could only manage half a smile in return.

"You must talk some sense into Lizzy." Mr Bennet's change of tone startled him. "She is typically a sensible woman. Not merely sensible in comparison to some of her relatives, but she possesses an intellect to rival the worthiest of scholars, although you would not know it of late. Her behaviour has been erratic, and I fear she does not think as clearly as she once did."

He paused. "Or perhaps, she is thinking with her heart, rather than her head—and therein lies the difficulty. Becoming a mother changed her, I believe. For the first time, she touched the unknowable love that a parent has for a child, and it has left its mark. She would do anything for that little girl and the life that grows inside her. Admirable as it is, she has forgotten to take into account your role as father. Why she has done so, I cannot think. You must speak to her, appeal to her rational sentiments, and all this unhappiness may be forgotten."

Darcy looked earnestly at Mr Bennet. "She is unhappy then? She does not speak to me of her true feelings. What have I done? Tell me how I can remedy it."

Mr Bennet handed Darcy a small whiskey. "I know it is early, but you look like you are in need of it."

Darcy did not accept the glass, rather he leant forwards to hear Mr Bennet's wisdom. Eyes twinkling, Mr Bennet placed a gentle hand on Darcy's shoulder, guiding him carefully to the study door. "Your engagement had been announced only a matter of hours before I saw you would be the man to secure the happiness of my beloved daughter...and you have never disappointed me in that regard. Your devotion to her and my granddaughter has been proved time and time again."

"So I may see her?"

"Of course, Darcy. But be gentle. Elizabeth is stronger than people expect but more vulnerable than they perceive." Opening the door, he indicated a small staircase. "She is up there, resting. It is the first door on the right. I shall tell the other members of the household to allow you some privacy." His eyes sparkled again.

"Good luck."

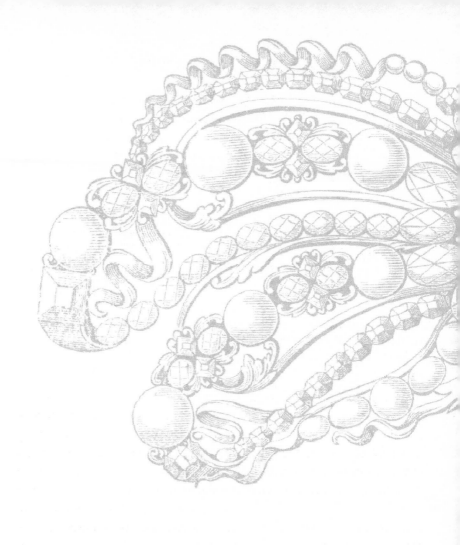

CHAPTER THIRTY-NINE

Butterflies danced in the pit of Darcy's stomach as he wrapped his hand around the door handle. Sore and tender from its collision with the floor, his body was utterly depleted of energy. He paused. A mounting sense of trepidation grew within him. Her note had indicated that she still thought well of him, but he did not think he could bear it if she pushed him away again. Was this how he had felt when he proposed to her? He had all the trepidation of a suitor, unsure of how he would be received. *She is still your wife,* he told himself, *and she called you her love in her note to you.* Steeling himself, he knocked lightly and waited. There was no answer, so he silently opened the door and went inside.

Elizabeth was lying on the sofa asleep. Her slender form curled up under a large quilted blanket, wearing what looked like an old dressing gown. Her hair was unbound, and a storm of curls framed her beautiful face. Her dark lashes fluttered with every breath, and he wondered about what she dreamt. He did not wish to disturb her, so he quietly sat on the seat opposite, thankful for a chance to rest his leg.

In doing so, he disturbed her, and for the first time in his recovered memory, Darcy had the great privilege of seeing his wife's face as she woke. Her luminous eyes widened and focused on the room around her. He did not wish for her to be alarmed, so he swiftly rose and sat on the edge of the sofa beside her, taking her hand in his.

"It is only me." He wanted desperately to reach out and caress her soft cheek, to let her know that she had nothing to fear, but instead he waited for her to become aware of him. To his dismay, her eyes brimmed with tears as her gaze met his.

"Forgive me for the pain that I have caused you."

"Any pain that I felt disappeared the moment I knew that you were safe." He turned her hand over in his. "It is I who should beg your forgiveness. I see now that I should have stayed at home to wait for your return. If I had remained at home, then I could have helped you with whatever caused you to flee." He took a deep breath. "But there is more I must say to you, and I beg of you to listen. You must allow me to say how sorry I am that you could not confide in me. I am much changed, that is true. I do not remember you as I ought, however much I try.

"I shall say only this—a mind may be a complex thing, buried with secrets and stories that may lay hidden forever, but the heart is much simpler, or at least mine is, because cut open my heart and all there is inside is you. Perhaps I cannot remember our past together, but it does not mean I do not wish a future with you. When I learnt that you and Molly had gone, it was as though my heart had been wrenched from my body."

He paused for breath, hardly daring to look into her beautiful face lest his courage should fail him. "I do not need to remember everything about you to know that I love you dearly."

Darcy watched as a tear made its way down her cheek. Trembling, she found her way into his arms, resting her head on his shoulder, running a delicate hand on the inside of his coat. Wordlessly, he held her, revelling in the feel of her slender arms snaking their way around his waist, of the blissful sensation of her heart beating next to his.

Eventually, she looked up, her cheeks wet, and quietly gave him all the hope he needed for their future. "Never doubt my love."

No more words were said as he bent down to steal the gentlest of kisses from her soft, willing lips.

After some time of heavenly silence, he pulled away gently to rest his forehead on hers. During their embrace, his hands had travelled to either side of her waist. Tracing a finger over her midriff, he felt the unmistakable firmness and the swell beneath and marvelled that it could have escaped his notice before now.

"Your family told me of your wonderful news. Are you well? Why did you not speak of it before?"

She broke away from him a little and clasped his injured hand in hers, tracing over his mangled fingers. "I did tell you before, on the day of the accident. We had an–an argument. We, who have never had a cross word between us since we married, spoke so angrily to one another, and that is when I told you about the baby."

She covered her face with both hands. "You were so upset, so stricken and afraid. I have never seen you like it. I should have broken the news to you gently, but instead I terrified you. That is why you went riding in that infernal storm, and it is the reason behind everything that has since happened to you."

Darcy considered her words for a moment. "I do not understand. A child is joyous news. Why was there anger? What did we argue about?"

"Many things." Now that Elizabeth had started, it seemed that she could not stop. "Not long after Molly was born, I became grievously ill. The doctors did not know what was wrong, but they feared an infection brought about by her birth. I deteriorated quickly and spent many days bedridden and insensible to all that was around me." The haunting image of Elizabeth's pale, lifeless face returned to Darcy. It had not all been a dream, then. No wonder why it hounded him so.

She took a deep breath. "My family were called to say goodbye, such was the fear for my life. They were all by my side. I was not conscious of it at the time. I have since learnt of many things that happened during that period."

She drew a deep breath and shuddered. "One such occurrence was that Caroline Bingley, when she heard of my illness, took it upon herself to write you a letter sending you all her condolences and reminding you that she was at hand to provide you with *every sympathy* should the time come. I was not even dead and she had already set her sights on you. That she would be step-mother to Molly! It is unthinkable!"

She shivered again. "I only learnt of the letter a few months ago. My suspicion was aroused when you attempted to cut her from a guest list, and that is when you finally confessed to me. Naturally, I did not accuse you of infidelity. I know how much you detest her, but it had hurt me greatly that you had said nothing of it. She had been a guest in my house several times since my illness, and I had had no notion of what she had done. Your actions—or lack thereof—had left me feeling humiliated and foolish. Can you imagine my pain when I discovered that you remember her and not me?"

"Why did you say nothing to me?"

"I endure her presence because to reveal the cause of my pain would cause great discomfort to Jane and dear Charles. Although after Caroline's disgusting behaviour towards me recently, I should like to think that even Jane has reached her limit. I could not contain my pain in front of her, and she invited me for a walk to discuss matters shortly after that horrible scene." Shaking her shoulders, she continued a little more firmly than before. "Although a lot of this is in the past, I am reminding you of it now as it provides a context for some of our argument." She looked at him earnestly. "You see, it took me a while to recover, and I had lost a great deal of strength. It was a long time before I realised that the brooch…"

"That the brooch was gone?" Darcy supplied. She nodded weakly.

"At first I suspected the servants, but nothing else had been taken in the months after my recovery. And then I realised the last time I had the brooch was at a private gathering just before Molly was born and I took ill, and it would have been on my dressing table…" She stopped, unable to find the words. Her cheeks were flushed with shame.

"When all your family were in attendance?" he guessed.

She nodded again, tears flowing down her cheeks. "For all your efforts, you have never held them in the highest esteem, and now there was a suspicion cast against one of them. I knew the significance of that brooch. Your hands shook so much when you pinned it to me for the first time, I was afraid I should be scratched! Giving it to me was a sign of your utter devotion, and my heart nearly broke in two when I realised what had happened. I knew how distressed you would be, and so I did all I could to conceal my suspicions. After all, I had no definite proof."

"And then what happened?"

"Eventually you learnt the truth of the matter."

"And that is when we argued?"

"No, not exactly. You were devastated, but we agreed that we could not act until we knew more. I believe you did some investigation and learnt of Wickham bragging that he had struck some deal with a pawnbroker whose speciality was jewellery...and so naturally suspicion fell on Lydia being the culprit. So incensed were you, that she was forbidden to come to any of our houses, and all lines of communication ceased. We could not accuse her directly, and my mother's powers of discretion are such that I would not have attempted it, for then everyone would have known of the theft, and there was the risk that Wickham would have disappeared and with him your mother's brooch." She sighed. "It hurt to cut off Lydia, but I too was deeply aggrieved by her actions, and I wanted nothing more to do with her...until one day, she arrived at our London residence with her youngest child. She was covered in bruises. Thankfully, you were absent, and so I took pity on her and let her in."

She looked at him earnestly. "I could not turn her away, not least when she told me of her condition."

"She is pregnant also?"

A veil of sadness crossed Elizabeth's face. "She was, very briefly, until Wickham's fist saw to it that she was not."

Darcy let her words sink in. A wave of sympathy washed over him. "She blamed me, you know. For her marriage to Wickham," he said quietly.

"It was not your fault. I love Lydia, or at least the Lydia of old. But even then, she was a thoughtless girl who was not given strong principles and was easily led by whatever scheme offered her the most fun. She knew what she was doing when she eloped with Wickham. At the time, marriage seemed like the best course, and you arranged it accordingly. You acted to save her, and in a monumental gesture of unconditional love, you did it to spare me any pain. How were we to know how low they would sink?"

She reached for his hand again and continued softly, "Unfortunately, you heard of her visit from a servant and not from me. You sat and silently brooded—I do believe that this is what you meant in your letter to Fitzwilliam. Your sense of betrayal that I had allowed Lydia back into our house and offered her food and a little of my pin money. I can only guess, for you did not share your thoughts with me. You vanished one night without any explanation to me of your intentions, which was unlike you. I presume you went in search of answers. I think you may have sought out Wickham at this point, for it was not long after Lydia's visit to our home and your subsequent disappearance that I received the first note asking for money. I can only assume that Wickham's financial straits finally caught up with him.

"Sadly, during this time you did not communicate very well with me, and I was so overcome with shame at my family's conduct that I did not know how to raise the subject. It was not my intention to conceal the truth, but I could not be sure of your reaction should you learn of the note. A letter from Patterson implied that a woman fitting Lydia's description had been seen in the village near Pemberley. We entrusted Molly to Jane and left immediately, afraid that Lydia might attempt to steal another item in her desperation. You did not speak much to me during the journey, and my mortification at Lydia's actions was so acute that I dared not risk raising the topic of Wickham's demand for money. Indeed, you spent the whole of the journey to Pemberley stirring yourself into a foul humour, and it only continued after our arrival. You confronted me in your study. I had never seen you so angry before —you called Lydia the lowest of the low and asked how I could stand having her in our house after she stole from me when I was but a moment away from death."

Here, she bit her lip. Her tears began to fall anew, and for a moment, she could not speak.

"I can see how I have hurt you." Darcy raised her hand to his lips and placed a gentle kiss upon it.

Flushing red, she shook her head. "It is not *your* words that cause my tears. I am crying as I remember what I said to you directly after."

Wiping her tears, she looked at him directly, her face hotly red. "I accused you of being a hypocrite. Caroline Bingley had imposed herself on you just as terribly as Lydia had on me, and you had hidden it to spare the feelings of your friend Bingley rather than tell me—your wife! I called you officious and...and high-handed and all sorts of things I wished I had not said. You then asked what possible inducement would I have to extend a sympathetic hand to Lydia—my own sister! I said that I could not turn away a woman in her condition and added, *'She is with child, and I cannot be but sympathetic knowing that I am in a similar condition'.*"

Darcy inhaled sharply.

"In an instant, I could see the pain that I had caused you. You never spoke about my illness, but I knew, from talking to Jane, how you had suffered. Jane said you hardly slept, hardly ate, and you would rarely leave my side. Only once before had I seen you weep, and those were tears of joy at Molly's birth. But in that moment, you turned to look out of the window, and I could see you struggle to keep the anguish from your eyes. Without another word, you walked straight past me and went out to ride in the gathering storm."

Elizabeth sighed and her voice went very quiet as she said, "Those would have been our last words to one another if Fitzwilliam had not arrived when he did and found you lying cold and bleeding at the bottom of the valley, where my thoughtlessness had sent you."

She was trembling now in his arms. Her confession, so tightly held for all this time, was released.

Silently, he put his hand in his pocket and withdrew from it his mother's brooch. When she saw it, she gasped. "Does this mean that...that Wickham is—"

"He is no longer a threat to our happiness. That was my urgent business last night, although the less said about that, the better." He paused. "This little trinket is a link to the last living memory I have of my mother. Indeed, of my mother and father together. Should you like to guess how many times I have looked at it since regaining it last night?"

"A great many times, I would say."

"The answer is never. Not once did I look at it, touch it, think of it from the moment I learnt that you and Molly were gone. I could think of nothing but your safety and your swift return to me —to our loving home. Nothing else matters but you and our daughter, my love."

Placing the brooch back inside his pocket, he turned his attention back to Elizabeth. "It was not fair of me to expect you to cut out a family member to appease my wounded pride. It was my decision to ride in the storm, and I daresay you had no more control over my anger than you did over the weather. You have borne the weight of all this alone, and I am sorry for it. Our argument is in the past, Elizabeth. I do not remember it, and even if I did, I should ask to be forgiven."

"You are too generous with me." Elizabeth wrapped her arms around his neck and buried her face in the warmth of his embrace. "I do not deserve you."

"Let us talk no more of worthiness. You are my superior in every way that matters. No woman could have acted with more integrity to herself or those she loves. God has seen fit to give us a second chance at happiness. I no longer see my accident as a curse but rather a sign that I am a man of enormous good fortune."

"How so?" She tipped her head towards him, her eyes brighter and a ghost of a smile playing about her mouth.

"How many men are permitted to fall in love with their wife twice?" he murmured, leaning forwards and capturing her lips in a loving kiss.

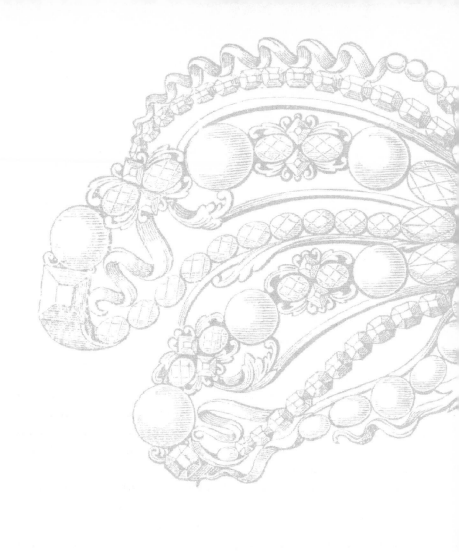

CHAPTER FORTY

After Darcy's conversation with Elizabeth, he had insisted that she continue to rest while he refreshed himself after a hard night of travelling. To his great delight, he could see that she was reluctant to be parted from him, but eventually she agreed to his plan.

It was decided that Darcy, Elizabeth, and Molly should take their breakfast alone—a scheme that pleased Darcy enormously. Molly was waiting with Elizabeth in Mr Bennet's study.

"Papa! You are here!" His precious daughter bounced into his arms and smothered his face with kisses. He pulled her close to him, breathing in her proximity. She rested her head on his shoulder, and he was reminded of Elizabeth. Capturing Molly in one arm, he reached out his other to scoop Elizabeth into his embrace.

"Watch your leg!" Elizabeth said with a laugh.

"Leg be damned," he muttered into Elizabeth's ear. "I have waited long enough for this."

They left the study, Molly between her parents, one soft hand holding on to each of theirs. She was asking Darcy a multitude of questions about his journey to Grandpapa and Grandmama's house. As much as he tried, he could only give half-answers, so lost was he in Elizabeth's eyes as she looked at him with total adoration over the head of their beloved daughter.

That morning, after breakfast, Darcy had the very great pleasure of a guided tour of Longbourn by his wife and daughter. Elizabeth, he noted, seemed so much lighter and happier since her confession that morning. He caught her gazing at Molly who was scampering around the garden trying to chase the birds. She had absently placed a hand over her stomach, and he could guess the direction of her thoughts. Standing behind her, he gently placed his hand over her own and with his other moved a wayward curl and kissed her softly on her neck. To his enormous pleasure, he heard her draw breath sharply and felt her shiver under the intimacy of his touch.

"How long before we shall be smiling at this little one?" he said, interlacing his fingers with hers as he rested them on her stomach.

She leant back into his embrace. "A few more months, at least."

He nodded. "Very good. In the meantime, you must tell me if you need anything, great or small, whatever the hour, and I shall see that it is at your disposal."

Still wrapped in his arms, she turned to face him. He could see she was laughing.

"What amuses you?"

"I cannot believe I am saying this, but I have just realised how much I have missed you ordering me about."

He laughed back. "I am not sure I believe you!"

"You only do it for the people that you care most deeply about, so I shall excuse you for it." She arched her eyebrows.

"I should think so!"

They had reached a point in their walk where there was an ornate garden bench.

"Speaking of orders, I must insist that you sit. You have been too long on your feet!" Darcy guided her towards the seat, marvelling again at the brilliance of her smile as he did.

"Are you sure it is for my legs or for yours?" she teased.

"You are my wife, and you carry my child. I must insist you rest," he replied soberly. "After all, you have just admitted how much you enjoy my commanding tone. It is the very least I could do." He broke into a smile. How good it was to tease her and see her laugh so! "It is but a happy coincidence that my legs should also benefit," he confessed.

The dimples in her cheeks deepened, and she rolled her eyes in mock exasperation. "That Darcy gallantry again!"

Curling into his arms, she rested her head upon his shoulder, and they gazed for some time at Molly who was busy searching for wildflowers and placing their petals in her pockets. Darcy traced his fingers down Elizabeth's arm until he found her hand. The last thing he wanted to do was to break the perfect tranquillity of this moment, but there was still something pressing deeply on his mind.

"Would you be so kind as to tell me what happened with my aunt? What did she say or do that caused you to flee so suddenly?"

Elizabeth sighed. "Georgiana's note said that Lady Catherine had arrived at her house and demanded my presence. I could tell from the note that no allusion had been made to our previous interlude, and, for all my actions, no impression had been made on your aunt. I did not know exactly what was said in the note your aunt received—I am presuming it was from Wickham—and I needed to know whether it had revealed anything else that might damage my family. I decided then that I should go and seek out more information. In front of Georgiana, she was all things civil, but there was a moment when darling Georgie had to step out briefly, and then your aunt played her hand."

Elizabeth's eyes flashed at the memory, and Darcy gave her hand a comforting squeeze. "She said that she finally had grounds to banish me from the family. Infidelity and theft no less! She was going to write to every gossip paper to let them know the depravity of my actions. Molly would not suffer, she said, on account of my Jezebel spirit. My daughter would be taken from my care directly and placed under the guardianship of someone who could secure the proper and moral upbringing of a child bearing the Darcy name, despite her debased parentage. I could only imagine she meant herself!"

"I would never have allowed any such thing," Darcy replied warmly.

"I knew that, but I feared you were too ill to prevent her. And at that point there was still no brooch! How could I counter her claims without accusing a loved one and potentially revealing to the world Wickham's history with the Darcy family?

"I blamed myself so dreadfully for your accident and for the loss of your brooch. How was I to tell you that I was with child? How would it look to an outsider? Would this new baby be denounced as quickly as Molly?"

"So you left," Darcy concluded.

"I left as quickly as I could. When you were not at the house I panicked. I did not know how much time I had before Lady Catherine acted. I remembered Jane had said she would be visiting Longbourn, and so I made my way to the Gardiners, to borrow their coach and make my way here to speak to my father in the hope he might have some recourse for me."

Darcy could hardly keep the anger from his voice. "My aunt is an abomination, and she is to be cut from my life. I shall not miss her. I told Georgiana of Lady Catherine's accusations towards you. Rest assured you have a staunch supporter in my sister."

Elizabeth shook her head tearfully. "I do not wish Georgiana to be estranged from her family on my account."

"Georgiana made her choice of her own volition, based upon years of tender affection and deep love for you."

Elizabeth smiled ruefully. "But what shall we do about your aunt? She might be writing to every gossip column as we speak!" Her shoulders slumped, and the pale, tired look reappeared on her face.

"I know precisely what we shall do." Upon seeing her surprised expression, he smiled and kissed her cheek. "We shall throw a party to celebrate my recovery. I shall have a new suit made—one to match whatever new dress you decide to wear. You will look beautiful and radiant, and I shall astonish everyone by dancing with you all night. Everyone will see how utterly besotted I am with my wife, and there can be no doubt of our deep and abiding love."

"What a scheme!" Elizabeth started to laugh. "But would it not seem rather convenient? As though we are putting up a lovely portrait to disguise an ugly hole in the wall?"

"Not, my love, if you are wearing this." Pulling the brooch from his pocket, he carefully drew out the pin. He gently lifted the fabric at the top of her dress, revelling in the softness of the skin beneath. With his other hand, he carefully pinned the brooch to her bodice. He could not suppress the tremor in his fingers as he traced them along the curve of her body as he moved his hand away. Elizabeth closed her eyes at his touch.

"Exquisite," he murmured as she opened her eyes and looked deeply into his. The dark murky depths of the brooch glittered in the sunlight with all the potency of an alchemist's potion. He could picture her wearing it at a ball as she entered on his arm, dressed in something ivory with the sapphire's deep-blue offsetting her creamy skin and the pearls contrasting against her dark hair.

"Once everyone sees it on your beautiful person, then the only thing they will be saying is how well it suits you. Lady Catherine is correct in one sense—the Darcy name is a great and powerful one. Woe betide any newspaper that prints anything other than a glowing report."

He stretched out his legs as best he could. "Besides, there are more than enough family secrets about Lady Catherine's late husband that she would not wish to be circulated. Out of deference to her position as matriarch of the family, I have ensured as best I could that they are not common knowledge. I feel no compunction to suppress them now." He smiled grimly.

"A party sounds wonderful...and I should like very much for us to enjoy ourselves once more. It would do us good to laugh again."

Molly had by now filled up her pinafore with so many flowers that they had begun to overflow from her pockets. Standing, Elizabeth's hand did not leave his. "Come, my love, let us return to the house and spare my father's flowerbeds."

The happy trio made their way up the path. Darcy could only walk slowly, but he found he did not mind as it gave him time to admire the colour rising in his wife's cheeks. As they approached the house, they saw Mrs Wickham—Lydia, he supposed he now should call her—walking with Mrs Bennet towards them. The small group paused awkwardly. After a short silence, Darcy said, "I fear I must clear the air between us. As you can see by the beautiful jewel that has been restored to my wife, I have no need to hold onto any resentment."

With heightened colour, Lydia replied, "Thank you. And I am sorry too for the anger with which I spoke to you." She embraced Elizabeth. "It suits you very well. Please accept my apologies that George took it from you in the first place."

"Wickham took it?" Elizabeth looked at her sister in puzzlement. "But when, Lydia? He has never been permitted entrance to Pemberley. When would he have taken it?"

Lydia shrugged, "I do not know. I thought he may know of another entrance, or maybe there might have been a previous acquaintance whose generous nature he might lean on."

"So it was not you then?" Elizabeth's voice was thick with emotion.

"How could you think so?" Lydia's face drained. "I would never do such a thing!" Addressing Darcy, she said, "Is this why I was denied admittance to your home? You believed me to be a thief?"

"It was not just my husband, but, Lydia, all the evidence pointed towards someone who was close to Wickham and who visited me when I was ill!" Elizabeth exclaimed.

"You do not believe my innocence?" Lydia's voice rose.

Elizabeth shifted uncomfortably and appeared to search the air for a suitable explanation for her doubt. She was saved from its expression by her mother.

"It was me." Mrs Bennet, her cheeks flushed red and her fingers trembling, spoke. "It was I who took your brooch, dear Lizzy, and I ask you to find it in your heart to forgive me." Darcy could feel Elizabeth's arm slacken in his grip, and for a minute, he thought she might faint. Instinctively, he put a protective arm about her waist.

"Mama, how could you do it? The brooch belonged to my poor late mother-in-law! If you were in need of money, you could have asked...but to steal from your own daughter! And at a time when I was so unwell! It is unthinkable!"

"I did not think of money when I took it! You were lying there as one dead, and I thought I should never see you again, never argue with you or worry about you, never speak to you again. And your little baby was there, crying and with no mother to care for her. I was seized by a desire for something for her to remember you by! The brooch was on your dressing table, and in a fit of madness I picked it up! I did not think of its importance! Once you began to recover, so great was my relief that I completely forgot about the brooch until a few months ago, when it fell out of a pouch with a necklace that I had not worn for years."

"How did Wickham come to have it?" Elizabeth said softly. Darcy could feel her trembling in his arms.

"I confided in him. Fool that I was, I thought he might be able to help me. If there was some way of returning it to Pemberley, of making it seem misplaced, then it could be found by a servant! It was a foolish plan. I did not know of Wickham's true nature until I realised the brooch had been stolen from me, and then what could I do?" Elizabeth looked up at Darcy.

Darcy thought of all the pain this single act of weakness had caused. By rights, he should be angry, but if all of this had taught him something, it was that the objects associated with family matter far less than the family itself. With a smile towards Mrs Bennet, he said, "If your love for Elizabeth is anything like mine, then you only have my compassion. Taking a keepsake of her is nothing in comparison to some of my foolhardy actions undertaken in the name of love for your daughter."

To his utter embarrassment, Mrs Bennet greeted his words by throwing her arms around him. "You are too good, sir! What a fine gentleman you have married, Lizzy! Thank you, sir, for your forgiveness!"

Darcy stood as still as marble, totally unprepared for such an effusive display of affection. In his panic, he caught sight of Lydia, who no longer looked affronted at being accused of theft and was doing her very best not to laugh.

Eventually, it was Elizabeth who came to his rescue. Eyes shining, she reached for Mrs Bennet and gently disengaged her from her husband. "Let us hear no more about this, for it is already forgotten."

Wrapping her arm around her mother's waist, she looked over her shoulder at Darcy and smiled. "Besides, Mama, I am in need of your advice. My husband and I are planning a party."

The End

ACKNOWLEDGMENTS

Thank you, Quills & Quartos, for giving me the opportunity to fulfil my childhood dream of becoming a published writer. I would like to express my particular thanks to Amy D'Orazio and Jo Abbott, whose invaluable insight and expertise helped to refine my story. As with many variations, *A Man of Good Fortune* began as a piece of online fan fiction, and I also wish to express my deepest appreciation to anyone that took the time to leave a positive comment–your simple act gave me the confidence to persevere with my writing.

Outside of those directly involved with publishing *A Man of Good Fortune*, I want to give a special thank you to my husband Stuart. Without his unwavering positivity and limitless encouragement, this book would not be possible. I also owe a debt of gratitude to my parents, who, throughout my life, have always supported me without hesitation.

And lastly, I would like to say thank you to Jane Austen, whose witty observations and sparkling characters have inspired me and countless others. Through her writing, I have found my own voice, and I will be forever grateful.

ABOUT THE AUTHOR

Ali Scott fell in love with reading at an early age and spent her childhood reimagining her favourite stories. A lover of languages, she studied French and film at Southampton University and is counting down the days until she can share her love of France with her two young daughters. *Pride and Prejudice* was the one of the first books that truly captured Ali's imagination and she regularly returns to it whenever she needs an escape from the modern world. During her first maternity leave, Ali fell down a rabbit hole of Austenesque variations and has been happily lost there ever since. She lives in Surrey with two beautiful girls, a wonderful husband, and an unruly allotment.

A Man of Good Fortune is Ali's first book.

Made in the USA
Monee, IL
24 June 2023

37172410R00201